A VOYAGE TO INDIA

GONÇALO M. TAVARES

A VOYAGE TO INDIA:

Contemporary Melancholy (a journey)

translated by Rhett McNeil

DALKEY ARCHIVE PRESS

Originally published in Portuguese by Editorial Caminho as Uma Viagem à Índia in 2010.

First Dalkey Archive edition, 2016

Library of Congress Cataloging-in-Publication Data
Names: Tavares, Gonðcalo M., 1970- author. | McNeil, Rhett, translator.
Title: A voyage to India : contemporary melancholy (a journey) / by Gonðcalo M. Tavares ; translated by Rhett McNeil.
Other titles: Viagem áa âIndia. English
Description: First Dalkey Archive edition. | Victoria, TX : Dalkey Archive Press, 2016. | Poem.
Identifiers: LCCN 2016031192 | ISBN 9781628971606 (pbk. : alk. paper)
Classification: LCC PQ9282.A89 V5313 2016 | DDC 869.1/42--dc23
LC record available at https://lccn.loc.gov/2016031192

Partially funded by a grant by the Illinois Arts Council, a state agency.
Funded by the General Directorate for Book and Librarires—
Direção-Geral do Livro, dos Arquivos e das Bibliotecas / Portugal.
Work published with the support of Camoes - Institute for Cooperation and Language, I.P.
Obra publicada com o apoio de Camões - Instituto da Cooperação e da Língua, I.P.

Dalkey Archive Press
Victoria, TX / McLean, IL / Dublin
www.dalkeyarchive.com

Dalkey Archive Press publications are, in part, made possible through the support of the University of Houston-Victoria and its programs in creative writing, publishing, and translation.

Printed on permanent/durable acid-free paper

This book is dedicated to Eduardo Prado Coelho

The blazing Sun had already begun to take shelter

– Luis de Camões

CANTO I

1

We shall not speak of the sacred stone
upon which the city of Jerusalem was built,
or of the most revered rock of Ancient Greece
located in Delphi, on Mount Parnassus,
that Omphalos—the navel of the world—
toward which you must direct your gaze,
sometimes your steps,
and ever your thoughts.

2

We shall not speak of Hermes Trismegistus
or of the way in which material without value
is transformed into gold
—as a result of mere patience,
belief, and false narratives.
We shall speak of Bloom
and of his voyage to India.
A man who left Lisbon.

3

We shall not speak of heroes who lost their way
in labyrinths
or of the search for the Holy Grail.
(This is not an attempt to find immortality
but to bestow some value on that which is mortal.)
No pit will be dug to find the center of the world,
nor shall we search in grottos
or forest paths
for visions worshipped by the Indians.

4
Here we are not starting a fast
atop a sacred mountain
so that weakness and the rarified air
make us quiver and fall prey to benign illness.
We are simply here to prove
how reason still allows
for a few long voyages.
We shall speak of Bloom.

5
We shall not see Vesuvius close up,
or lower animals
into its crater in order to calm the elements.
We shall not kill for the waters of eternal youth,
or curse names
by tossing tablets marked with damned letters
into the waters of Bath, in England.
We shall not speak of the great pyramids of Giza,
or of their many secret passages
which allow men to enter or escape.

6
We shall not speak of the ruins at Stonehenge
or at Avebury,
or of the exaggerated precision of the alignment of the stones
on the Isle of Lewis.
We shall not speak of these miracles scattered
here and there around the globe,
of these stone missives sent to us by the ancients.
We shall speak of one man, Bloom,
and of his voyage at the beginning of the twenty-first century.

7
We shall not speak of the terrible natural occurrences
throughout the history of the world.
Earthquakes and seaquakes, cyclones in Bangladesh
hurricanes in the Caribbean
—the world has trembled and suffered fires and floods
ever since Noah, at least.
We shall not speak of the Black Stone at Mecca
and the seven circuits around the plaza
that this stone requires of the devout.
We shall speak of Bloom and of his voyage
from Lisbon to India.

8
We shall not speak of the Incan city of Machu Picchu,
we shall not speak of the Lascaux caves,
or of their childlike,
menacing, severe drawings.
We shall not speak of Chinese horses
or of the mythological beings of the rocks
of Ontario.
We shall speak of Bloom. And of his voyage to India.

9
We shall not speak of the sudden appearance
of dwarves in certain Mexican caverns,
or of the Rockies in Colorado
where houses were built right into the stone.
We shall not speak of séance tables
and of periodic visits from the Beyond to the houses
of otherwise rational individuals.
We shall speak of a voyage to India.
And of the hero of the voyage, Bloom.

10
We shall speak of the hostility that Bloom,
our hero,
revealed in relation to the past,
when he up and left Lisbon
on a voyage to India, on which he sought wisdom
and oblivion.
And we shall speak of how with him on this voyage,
he carried a secret and then brought it back, nearly intact.

11
It is essential that terrestrial actions will be made known here,
such as the length of the world and the height of the sky,
but it is also important to speak of what is not
so long or tall.
It's clear that the Greeks tried to perfect
Truth as much as appearance,
however ideas were, by far, the things that changed the most.
It is therefore time to turn Greece
on its head
and empty its pockets, dear Bloom.

12
Beware of men who depart willingly
and happily: in the first case, if necessary,
they are capable of killing.
Beware, then, Bloom, of your will.
(But also take care, on this voyage,
of the manner in which you do things.)
However, Bloom isn't leaving Lisbon happily, so it's not all bad.

13
But let's consider this other story (a parable?).
From out of the crowd a man departs
running in the direction
of an imaginary line.
This man isn't crazy;
the crowd, however, is crazy.
The man runs until he encounters a fencer,

14
they give him a sword, he fights and wins.
He's in a hurry now, a dead man in his wake
and in his head an imaginary line
toward which he must proceed.
He knows that he must run forever, never ceasing,
but without ever reaching his objective.
That's the story—the end.

15
But nature also appears, and quite often,
on this voyage.
The wind, for example, which might appear
to be a neutral element,
which shares its mild discomforts with the rich
and the poor,
but in truth it is quite skillful:
it brings a chill to the weak and to the strong a light breeze that soothes extreme heat.

16
At palaces it blows right past the domesticated weathercock,
while on fragile houses

it beats mightily like a storm.
The wind (in certain countries)
whips against the head of the person who has just been felled and
massages the precious feet of the person on top.
The wind, my dear Bloom, is not a natural element
you can trust.

17
Besides, if a face has two halves
—one beautiful, the other fearful—,
one's enemies only see the fear
and one's lovers, the beauty.
These are, deep down, two peculiar forms
of blindness,
specializations that emerge (spontaneously)
at certain moments.

18
It's true that your ancestors
(we're talking to you, Bloom)
never built mountains,
however they killed quite a lot, and some of them told stories
that have survived to this day. Because, besides, it's well known
that when one has enough fear or courage
there are no weekends or
leisurely banquets. For certain of your valiant ancestors
nary a weekend existed.

19
We hope, then, Bloom, that you will grow and that in growing
you will head directly toward reality
and not stop. Because it isn't enough

for you to rest on mere events,
what we have in mind for you is much more profound,
it's not enough that you learn seven theories,
you will have to scale seven mountains.
And even cross the continents
as if the earth were a temporal expanse
capable of measuring your days.

20
Cross the waters as well, Bloom, dear friend,
cut the sea in two.
The sea is a mammal;
the ship, a sacrificial dagger.
Because, like all animals,
the sea is only haughty
until it finds its master.
We're speaking of the sea, but perhaps
it is the earth or the heavens that demand description.
Bloom, Bloom, Bloom.

21
You may accuse the gods of possessing
a very peculiar technique of government,
which can be summed up fundamentally by saying:
they do nothing until the very end.
You cannot, then, Bloom,
ascribe too much complexity to this lofty mode
of closing their eyes, folding their arms,
and putting up their feet. They are the gods, Bloom,
it's none of your business.

22
The gods act
as if they didn't exist and, thus,
in fact, they are extremely efficient at not existing.
It's true that among the gods
there exists a hierarchy,
just as among the brutes
in a carpenter's shop
or among the stevedores
in certain European ports.

23
And the strongest of the gods,
being right-handed, needs at least
this hand free in order to act.
Hierarchies exist, therefore, among flowers,
injurious herbs, and the divine.
You could make charts that rank abilities and give out medals
based on kindness and wickedness;
shoot more bullets at one than the other.

24
At bottom the organization of the universe
is a matter of military ribbons,
and this information frightens us (precisely)
because we don't know whether we should give out orders
or obey them.
But we shall still speak, Bloom, of irony, which
we'll apply liberally.
In what manner does catastrophe
disrupt the ancient method
of keeping a distance from the world?

25
Up above the catastrophe, from an aerial point of view,
man is capable of being ironic,
however, down below the catastrophe,
under the rubble,
irony is the last thing to appear
after the instinctive actions of defense,
of desperation—which continues to give out orders and make attempts—,
and of the final scream that signals failure.

26
Only after this final scream does irony return,
saying, if anything:
I'm dying, that's true, but even so
I maintain an elegant distance in relation
to my death.
This, Bloom, in broad strokes,
is an introduction to that old irony
which at times we utilize to avoid
laughing out loud, or crying.

27
The organ that forgets less than the head—the heart.
If you want information about the past, Bloom,
talk to the men of a city,
but if you desire to snatch up all at once
that primal wisdom
spend an afternoon beside an animal
without language.
Not all that occurs
can be written, this we already knew.

28
But Destiny has (of late) been perfected.
These days ship and airplane arrive on solid ground
by power of a mechanical compass, which normally
works, unlike Destiny
which, because it's an ancient invention,
is by now showing signs of fatigue
and even incompetence.

29
Fortunately, in addition to destiny,
we've brought adequate technology
says some captain or another, utilizing
the above-referenced contemporary irony.
It's still clear that if Destiny emerges in some obscure verse
then we're back to square one, the plane liable to take flight
or fall from the sky, for both events
will bear out the strange verse
that foretold them.

30
For this very reason—in order not to commit to anything—
the Gods, when they whisper in our ear,
avoid explicit statements and concrete promises.
And even though, shockingly, they speak
our language,
shockingly, they're not understood.
Can you perceive this, Bloom?

31
It's obvious that we can believe
that certain languages are closer to that sort of beauty

that the air has when it's empty.
However, the language of a country—
for as much as its inhabitants
jump or pray toward the heavens—
is not a mystical activity
in which human beings
are privileged participants.

32
On the contrary, language, any language,
is a domestic and economic activity;
a song invented, ultimately,
not in order to dazzle
but to sell high and buy cheap.
(ah, but what about when we start
to speak of our hero, Bloom,
and of his voyage?)

33
It is still said (and forgive this digression
—there will be many, my dear, prepare yourself),
it is still said that the universal discussions of men
are always individual discussions. Each person
is bent over, gazing at the world while
standing on a fragile parapet.
And even imbeciles lack a
collective physiognomy.
Every country is a mere detail that each inhabitant uses
as it befits him and as the law
allows.

34
However, there in the distance, a concrete nervousness
permeates behaviors and flowers,
permeates trees with big trunks
and women with skinny legs. And such disturbances
originate, at once, from both the ground and the ceiling,
thus proving that the constructions of men,
contrary to what is commonly supposed,
fall as often from top down as the other way around.

35
You could then say: a storm
is a misunderstanding between substances,
a meaningful debate, nothing more than this.
Yes, this is certain—but the opposite is also true.
The fact is that a certain storm arose,
and Bloom had his nose in his map, still planning
his voyage.
How nature gets ahead of itself!

36
But let's hear a story (another parable?):
A hard man walks along a street
that ends at a forest just as in his childhood
he had walked through a forest that ended
at a street.
He looks around in all directions but avoids looking up
for someone had told him that human beings
only participate in events that occur
below eye-level,
and this phrase—below eye level—
grows as strong as that old phrase
—below, or above, sea level.

37
And thus a reference to nature
is replaced with a reference to humanity.
Men who previously proceeded at sea level
now proceed above or below eye level.
And let's say that: above eye level proceeds
the person who hopes that divine elements,
chance and destiny, resolve that which psychology
and instruments are unable to perceive.

38
At eye level, on the contrary, proceeds the person who believes
that human actions are still, or are now,
the most powerful acceleration
that can be introduced into the world.
The person who proceeds below eye level recognizes
that progress has not been sufficient
and that only the animal part of the human,
or the part that humbles itself, can solve conflicts.
Jumping, arguing, crawling
—these are, in sum, the three human methods
of responding to a single world.
(And Bloom will employ them all.)

39
But let's return to the low, black earth,
which appreciates the progress
that a man makes between two distant worlds.
Or even the mere progress, between chest and shirt,
of respiration, which, without taking a single step,
covers a more personal, invisible distance,
which ultimately can be expressed as a decision.

Bloom, himself, in fact, shall seek the impossible:
to find wisdom while fleeing;
to flee while learning.

40
And since the arrow has already started along its path,
how do you wish to stop it? Just like death (which is a unique
thing:
if it has started you cannot interrupt it),
so, too, your will.
It's much easier to amputate a thick,
muscular arm. So take notice of the fact that thinking is a potent
act
and its effects—ideas—are hardy materials.
Go quickly to a place; so quickly you don't have time to
reconsider
—that's a word of advice, Bloom.

41
And notice that somewhere in a group of vulgar people,
a liquid passes through the mouths
of them all. A liquid that calms and unites, transforming
strong enmity into neutral approximations.
Under the effects of a mild alcoholic drink, a group thus sets
aside
violence; discreetly shaking hands,
bowing at the waist, smiling smiles.

42
There was, however, no sharing of
affection; cowardly sentiments of similar proportions merely
entered into an agreement (temporarily). But we'll get there soon.

Meanwhile, in March
someone forcefully grasps the nine lives of a cat,
killing it all at once
thus saving it from eight other
intense events.
We're in March and daily life proceeds
(as ever), but it's proceeding in the open air, which is where
it feels best.

43
And the days pass by, immobile,
and therefore foreseeable.
The wind holds a pose that starts to resemble
mere air.
Looking up at the sky it was the sky
one saw;
and Bloom's eyes and the lofty part of the world
regarded each other—like two pieces of a romantic
picture puzzle, blue and boring.

44
We shall not, then, speak of an entire people,
which is excessive and quite a task.
In this epic we shall speak of only one man: Bloom.
Bloom opened his two discordant eyes
(one wanted to see the new, the other wanted to sleep)
directing his gaze at the quiet chamber
he had just entered.
Bloom, our hero. That's what he does first: observes.

45
Here we have Bloom on the first stage of his voyage to India,
in London, alone and penniless,
not knowing a soul. Is he looking for friends
or something else?
And is it Bloom that has a strange way of seeing
or are the men who draw near to him
the strangers?
There is no way to resolve this.
Who initiates a moment: the person looking or the person
who is looked at? Can the beginning of the world be encountered
in someone who is pushed?

46
Certain men dislocated themselves, then, onto the reality
of London
as if their clumsy feet were trying
to mimic steps previously taken by dancers.
We are in the month of March
and in this month, if the world were well organized,
all facts would begin with M,
following a logic identical to that of
the crazy encyclopedia, which thus juxtaposes
irreconcilable subjects.

47
However, it is obvious that no occurrence
begins with a letter identical to any other. And if it enters
into a dictionary or encyclopedia, it is because this fact
is now a domesticated fact.
We can even say: if you amputate from these actions their energy
and forceful existence

then you will end up with a story that's
publishable. Narrative as the disloyal friend
of facts—that's one hypothesis.

48
The men approach, then, waving:
there were three of them, and Bloom, though corpulent,
was singular, just one guy.
And thus he decided to wait before acting
—he well knew that friendship and peace
are merely intermediate moments
that, deep down, augur change.

49
It isn't by chance that you're never able, try as you might,
to hit the day head-on—whatever day it may be—
the way one hits a whale with a harpoon.
Days have a thick hide,
armor made up of the hardiest material known to existence:
that which has a center that cannot be found
is safe.
Thus our days, which we really would like to obliterate
with a harpoon. An absurd, bodiless whale,
time.

50
Go then to India, dear Bloom,
leave London.
London. London and Bloom.
However, Bloom decided to have lunch with the three men,
strangers, but chatty ones.
I want to go to India, our hero thinks,
and perhaps one way to get there is through friendship.

51
Bloom told them that he'd departed from his point of departure
and that he'd yet to arrive at his point of arrival.
He was, thus, en route, in an intermediate place,
far from his armchair.
He was ultimately searching for beautiful things that would bring
him health.
He later explained, in succinct manner, that it was unacceptable
for there to be
even one ugly doctor in all existence, for curing was the process
of enchanting the patient, and an ugly physiognomy cannot
enchant.

52
Every border, as well I know, thinks Bloom,
contains a methodology
that is as impossible to be shared among two neighboring
countries
as an individual's fingerprints.
Of course there is still love,
far and away the thing most responsible for passing fingerprints
from one body
onto another. But even this effusive process
is different when we're in another country.

53
And then the three men told stories of their childhood
each of them repeating, twice, certain
trivial events, which really bored Bloom. The minutest
details of the laws of the country were described in their even
more minute
particulars

by these three men who were not only not quick in the telling,
they were decidedly slow. For this reason, in Bloom there began
to grow the rather wicked thought
of stomping his shoe three times on the ground, smashing,
with each movement, one ant: three in total.
Those men, whom he didn't know in any way,
bored him.

54
The lives of others do not move us, thinks Bloom. Your life
is an equation that I am unable to solve
because I do not love you. And also the opposite:
I cannot solve your life because
I do not hate you.
But when the air became overbearing and hot, as if someone
had left the day in the oven for too long,
that's when the men's kindness appeared.

55
They offered Bloom rest, fruit, and water.
And as if explaining everything to some imbecilic
foreigner, they said, pointing to one thing at a
time: the water is liquid, the fruit is solid, and this bed
we offer you shall be in whatever state
your dreams are in.
In principle—they continued—a good rest belongs to a volatile
state
but the quality of your sleep will be the deciding factor.
Very well, said Bloom.

56
And since the luminous day seemed to be slowly escaping
down into the fireplaces of private homes,
thus disappearing the principal public institution
of both city and countryside (the sun),
Bloom, himself escaping, and without any support in London,
a city where the ground has no ground for foreigners,
he had no alternative: he accepted the invitation,
following those three men who appeared devoid
of intelligence in a manner that Bloom
—in his ironical way—
classified as "exuberant."

57
This, then, is the reasonable way that Bloom found
to classify the conversation and reasoning
of his London hosts,
men whose paths he had crossed by chance
and who had offered him bed and table, in inverse order as well.
One of the men even offered up to Bloom
a quiet dissertation on childhood,
habits, and other particulars.
Bloom, perceiving the urgent situation,
quickly and decidedly said: this is an excellent topic
for another time,
and with a quick wave of the hand and a quicker
"goodnight!", he excused himself.

58
It's clear that a ferocious animal is ferocious still while it's sleeping,
and Bloom, ever cautious, never drank the whole glass down at once,

always allowing for the possibility of doing
something different (or even the opposite).
Mental agility is muscular
and muscular agility is mental—and Bloom knew this well.
Are you paying attention, Bloom? What do these men want?

59
Bloom didn't even go near the bed,
for before he could, the father of those three men,
who were profoundly at odds with reason, appeared;
and, looking upon the steady gaze of the old man,
he could not stop imagining an empty wardrobe
with two round, identical knobs on its doors.
From the look in his eyes, said Bloom warm-heartedly,
I soon perceived that he was family.

60
And the father of the three redundant men
—it was sufficient for just one of them to speak—
brought some presents for Bloom.
Among some trivial things and a few unnecessary ones
there were also some that were just annoying.
It's like I need to water the garden,
and they hand me a couple of matches,
thought Bloom, while aloud he said, thanking them:
it's just what I needed.

61
The presents included some beauty products
—useful but ugly—and some useful things,
which were completely useless, but beautiful.
Bloom felt like someone

who only has a right hand and is given a glove
for the left one.
Nearly a perfect fit, said Bloom,
while the coat they'd given him
ripped in two as he tried it on.

62
The fact is that during such an encounter there was mutual
embarrassment,
for the language of our hero seemed to the others
to be indiscreet stomach grumblings, which also shows,
how, ultimately, poetic verse in an unknown language can sound
just like the startling
commotion of an old sewing machine.

63
And it's clear: you can know a man by what he reads,
but that's not the only way. How he kills—what weapons he
uses—
and how he falls in love—what words he uses to
declare his love. Ah, and another detail as well: who
are you afraid of? And what does he call that mighty thing that
from the heavens never arrives because it prefers to remain just
that,
a possibility?
If you could decipher the final grunts of a dying man,
you would discover your religion, that's for sure.

64
Bloom said that he'd departed from Lisbon
and that he was on a voyage to India. On the other side of the
world

he sought a new joy
or, if possible, many new ones. Joy that combined the pleasures
of a domestic animal that is fed out of a bowl
with those of a wild, brute animal that feeds
itself from spontaneous attacks on the weakest victims
in the forest. A surprising boredom,
that's what Bloom was seeking. How to find it?

65
Every man thinks he's in possession of the precise melody,
but melody isn't the result of a problem
of quantities
but rather the result of a gnawing problem of the soul.
Each song thus responds
to the indecision that a given existence carries with it:
should I give up living or should I kill? Should I fight or just forget
about all this, which can be washed away in a flood?

66
The fact is that of the various materials in this world,
the soul is by far one of the most ancient,
however, if the brain that invents and writes verses
is merely a finely symmetrical organ,
then Bloom is through with looking up to the heavens
in hopes of human or divine events.
Nothing shall come down from the heavens save that which is natural and disposable.

67
It's said that thinking isn't as easy as it seems.
Certain men, although they remain seated,
expend so much effort trying to sketch out an idea

that they end up bathed in sweat.
And meanwhile here on the outside: nothing,
not even the carcass of the most ephemeral trace
of intelligence. Each idea seems to be trapped inside these brains
as if inside a labyrinth out of which only rarely
is one able to escape. Bloom thinks about that father and his
three sons.
What a coherent family, he mutters.

68
Being a lion among lambs is a weakness, said
a surpassingly excellent poet.
Thus, then, Bloom, opted, in front of these four imbeciles—
an entire grinning family—,
to hide his intelligence the way one hides an object.
He listened, yet didn't reply,
merely smiled; as if congeniality—like a
stupid butterfly—had landed on his lips
turning them into a useless parapet that neither kisses
nor speaks.

69
But it's clear that manners—a peaceful way
to render the phrase "don't shoot at me, for now"—
hinders men with opposing characteristics
from immediately revealing the discomfort they feel when
faced with an existence that is in opposition to theirs.
Between him and the four men,
Bloom felt that a certain watchtower had been erected.
No one shall approach me with the objective of embracing me—
at this moment, Bloom felt certain of this.
And the situation he was involved in intrigued him.

70
Bloom was searching for the uncommon, something
that was neither silent occurrence nor loud noise, something
that,
being a location, requires one to start walking toward it. If what
I'm searching for
were delivered to my armchair,
then what purpose would my shoes serve? But it's already
classic knowledge: new events
take place in new spaces, not in old ones.
Don't let your comfortable armchair damage
your curiosity.

71
Is it possible that one of these men, thought Bloom,
knows of another world, one with the same name as this one,
but happier? A second, parallel planet
where boredom, blood, and ugly women
do not exist?
It's clear that one of the advantages of the heavens is that they're
never trod upon,
but Bloom would be satisfied if someone
merely showed him a path, on earth,
that's unknown to most.

72
While a lexicon of muteness circulated
among the four men,
who, among themselves, appeared to be fine-tuning a venom
of their own making (the way an orchestra tunes
their instruments). While I'm over here
enjoying tremendous health, they're preparing a beautiful

funeral dirge for me, thought Bloom. The tension
became intolerable and Bloom thought
(or might he even have said it?):
if there were at least a flower in here
we'd be able to smell at all times.

73
It's obvious that evil likes to chomp off
mouthfuls and eat. Obvious, too, that a certain
bad mood, emanating from the back corners of the heavens,
is at the root of the foulness of certain
men. No mammal could be that cruel
unless it had some obscure support from on high.
A landscape that is above sea level
(and above your head) can either fall or fly. If it flies it will be beautiful,
and if it falls on you: it severs your neck in two. Those are two laws.

74
Certain landscapes, tall and malformed,
are identical to shelves that are poorly fastened to the wall,
laden with objects of significant weight, eager
to demonstrate the knowledge they have of certain laws
of physics, which, when they come crashing down on your head, wound you.
These laws possess the characteristic of being unable
to be turned inside out. Not even a meticulous sculptor, say,
would be able to make visible the interior
of a famous equation like E=mc2.
In sum: the lofty evil shall fall.
Better, then, to leave those things that threaten us
at ground level.

75
Bloom looks out the window.
Many armies that killed with efficient orders,
passed along this pavement
where automobiles now circulate.
Horse hooves replaced, in a mere two centuries,
with tires
(which adhere to reality better than mammals do).
Life is now inhabited by machines (without a scent)
and certain powerful industrial brands take possession, every day,
of the name that has been given up by the great conquerors.

76
Certain brands of automobiles are, today,
much more well known than the name
of Alexander the Great. ("Who?", ask the youngest among us.)
The fact is that the weather changes less over the course of a year
than a man's fame does over the same period
of time. In contemporary mythology, the factory and its machines
occupy the place of emperors
and unicorns. Thus the progress of the imagination, thinks
Bloom.

77
It's true that, despite possessing a physiognomy
in which the intelligence seems to have been ironed out
by a careless housemaid,
the old man and his three sons were still ferocious;
because to yield cruelty—one can deduce—great power of
reasoning
is unnecessary. (For the specialization
that consists of stabbing a sharp weapon many times

into a concave area of the body, what mental calculations
could be required?)

78
So spontaneous is an individual's brutality
that we shall never see academic space open up
for research in this field.
However it is clear that Bloom isn't an ethical masterpiece either.
He's neither a thief nor a treacherous bastard,
but he also isn't a saint (probably
because being such a thing hasn't yet become useful for him).
He has his own secrets, quite dark ones even,
but this isn't the time to reveal them yet.

79
Here's another historical fact: the biography of a country
is also profoundly gastronomical: what is a people
if not what it eats? For as much as we talk about language,
culture, and the loftier customs, a people,
just like the organism of an individual citizen,
is the sum total of the food ingested,
of the oxygen that the air provides,
and all the rest, water, for example.

80
But the thing that has existed in man since the Ancients
is this desire for contact;
certain pernicious interpretations direct this desire
toward the blade when it should be directed
toward the erotic movement of unbuttoning
the blouse of a beloved woman.
Mistaken routes, that's one way to put it.

81
Thus, these four strange men
(a father and three sons),
who had crossed paths with Bloom in London,
were thinking of a drawer where certain blades were kept
—immobile, yet curious—
meanwhile spitting on the ground, leaving
a stain on the floor that augured evil.

82
That wicked, strange old man thus began the plan
for the following days, demonstrating that
a premeditating and successful murderer
has a mental system similar
to that employed by a flourishing businessman:
both are meticulous inventors of the future.
They make preparations, create charts and tables,
with one eye on Bloom's suitcase
—as if they were sharpening a blade, they sharpen the following days.

83
The old man and his three children are planning unpleasant days for Bloom,
this overly curious man
who came to London to cause trouble.
If a man falls down and doesn't get back up
it's a sign that he no longer has two legs or no longer
has life. And that, thought the four wicked men,
is what we want for those who possess the riches
that we desire.
That Bloom fall and not get back up.
That only his suitcase remain intact.

84
It's clear that certain organs that are specialized in
suspicion
were present inside Bloom's body,
engaged in general activity. They often overlooked the explicit,
but when faced with minute evidence
they behaved like a sage.
Bloom was, at bottom, a poor draftsman of the present,
but extraordinary at reproducing that which does not yet exist:
the future.

85
And this was, then, the moment when, out of the realm of the invisible,
the threat became weapon, fist,
and things similar.
The four men wanted to rob Bloom
(his precious suitcase)
or even, who knows, kill him.

86
It's impossible, in fact, to distinguish the face
of someone who merely wants to steal a wallet
from the face of someone who wants to kill, behead, disembowel,
slice a person up into pieces and make a lyre out of
the innermost bones of the body.
For this reason Bloom, as a precaution, has immediately reacted
as if the old man and his three sons were already
brandishing their teeth and as if he, that poor young man,
were the cause of their appetite.

87
Bloom had beautiful movements that he had learned
from his paternal grandfather, but at that moment
he decided to use other movements, quick and useful ones he
had learned
from his other grandfather. And thus he eliminated
minute mannerisms from his hand (like that of taking hold
of a minuscule sewing thread between the thumb and the
forefinger) and pulled out of his fingers
—the way you pull something from a pocket—the brutality of
a punch,
of a precise blow.

88
And so the fight begins. The hand of
the hero
didn't fall dead when it came to a sudden stop on the right side
of the face
of one of the men and, if irony weren't ill-advised
in certain urgent instances,
we would say that the blow was so violent
that the enemy seemed, immediately,
to have only two left sides of a face,
because on the right side nothing remained intact.

89
But there were more ruins to construct, for—by the mathematical
logic that, despite everything, remains viable in these situations—
knocking down one of four
means not knocking down three.
And mathematics in fact remains viable
and walks up to Bloom.

But Bloom: boom and boom and for the third time
boom! And the four cowards flee, each of them carrying
with them an abstract,
yet painful new mark.

90
And after muscularly inverting
certain rash numerical calculations,
Bloom, keyed up, isn't satisfied
and individually pursues a plural group
that is fleeing him.
Among the cowards can be heard grumblings and
regrets, and the old man—whose shoes are making
the weakest arguments—is caught, he trips; then after
a thorough thrashing by Bloom, the sons, cowards,
just keep running, showing the world
that, ultimately, in quantity,
they were much more cowards than sons.

91
One of the cowards, in a moment of courageous relapse,
of which even the most fearful person is capable,
was able, during his flight, to pick up a potent stone,
but given his poor aim—the effect of excessive nerves
on the shoulder-blades and the elbow—
he ended up squarely hitting
the practically empty head of his old father.

92
If they were disorganized even while immobile,
peaceful, and doing nothing,
what can be expected of these men while they're fleeing?

If they were fleeing round and round a repeated circumference
it would be no different: they'd trip over each other,
grab at each other, insult one another. It was, ultimately,
as if they were at once engaged in combat amongst themselves
and fleeing;
two actions, as any grade-schooler knows,
that are difficult to reconcile.

93
And Bloom finally lost sight of them, which doesn't mean
that they had ceased to exist,
because if it were necessary to see, at every moment,
all that exists, the world would not be a world
but a concentration of all things
into the smallest possible space.
Neither the planet nor countries could exist,
just a store that contains everything.
A general store, one could well call it,
a metaphysical store.

94
Obviously the fleeing men, once they stopped running
and caught their breath, immediately started
to plot their revenge.
Thus the three surviving men decide to
call on yet another—Thom C—
and, paying him, figure out the perfect way
to cut Bloom in two.
One, two, said one of the men, counting on his fingers;
One, two, repeated another of them, carefully following
the route taken by the first hand.
That's how we want to see Bloom.

95
It is said that the raw material of an intense,
exciting event can, despite evidence to the contrary, erode down to nothing.
The material of the facts (if we look closely) is nothing at all.
The excitement that comes from a physical fight
isn't something that belongs to us forever
(like a possession that is impossible to sell).
Sensations belong to time, to the local week,
day, or time of day, and not to the individual who just happened
to cross paths with them.
Thus, Bloom—who had been wrapped up in the fight
down to his last cell—
was already strolling, carefree,
through the same city three days later.

96
Each city is different from any other in that which is superfluous to it, although
it is also different for every other reason, for nothing deep exists
in streets crammed with people, except for the sewer system
—which is closed off.
So Bloom crossed paths with Thom C,
a stranger with whom he naively
and immediately got along while still in London
—a mere through passage for someone, like him,
who wanted to forget and learn.
After speaking of the fever that had attacked their century at the neck,
Bloom asked Thom C if he knew some place
with seductive habits.
A double place, where the quotidian was metaphysical
but the cooking was also properly seasoned.

97
Thom C was able to help Bloom, for he knew of a place
where men and women were happy, even redundantly so,
a phrase that made an immediate impression on Bloom.
(In this life that we inexplicably call "real,"
the sum of two equal things normally ends up being
a subtraction.)
However, Thom C was purely planning to take Bloom
to an apartment in the suburbs of London (apartment 3D),
where three armed men were waiting
to get their revenge.

98
Thom C asserted, falsely,
that his friends were so powerful
in annulling the world of the imagination
that they had destroyed, in just a week's time,
the entire mythology of a people,
stories that, as is well known, take centuries
or millennia to appear.
And that he also had a cousin (a little crazy),
that lived, claimed Thom C, in that selfsame apartment 3D
on a street in the suburbs of London,
a cousin possessed of an aroused energy that was symmetrical
to Bloom's
—and, what's more, suggestive and ample breasts.
Bloom smiled and said: let's continue on, then,
toward this plummeting neckline.

99
Proceeding with shoes down below
and obscene cackling a meter and seventy centimeters

above sea-level,
the two of them thus left central London
toward this 3D. A little adventure, you could say.

100
It's a fact that in each cubic centimeter
of a living organism
eroticism exists and powerfully interferes with the soul
—and vice-versa, which for certain prudes constitutes
an unacceptable situation.
It's certain that Bloom's arousal was, at that moment,
much greater than his prudishness.
Maria is the most erotic of cousins, said Thom C,
and Bloom was moved by this pitch.

101
However, in the proximity of Maria E's 3D,
an obstacle of civilization was placed in the path
of an anxious Bloom and his false friend Thom C.
Along this street, progress had destroyed the sidewalks
and, despite the political sign that spoke of
"Improvements being made in this area,"
our hero cursed these interminable cities
in constant improvement,
which, at bottom, at that instant,
delayed the explicit satisfaction of his desire.
For a man aroused, the city should always be
downhill, complained Bloom.

102
Imagine a geometrical form that, on top of having perfectly
formed sides,

also gave off heat—that's Maria E, said Thom C.
Amazed at such a description of the feminine body
—geometry with a temperature—, Bloom,
while he was walking, remembered the ancient wisdom
of Plato who, at the entrance of his academy, had written:
"Let no one ignorant of geometry enter here."
Philosophy is, finally, then
capable of arousing certain organs aside from the brain,
thinks Bloom ironically; and he can't help but think
that this classical phrase would fit perfectly
if it were hung at the entrance of a brothel.

103
At last they turned onto the right street, and with a quick step
the two men arrived at the door
of an old building. This is it, said Thom C,
and with his malicious index finger he sought
the desired 3D among the doorbells.
And as if it were a goddess training her voice
for oracular proclamations, they heard, coming from a
mechanism
that would be divine itself if it didn't have dozens of wires
and electrical connections behind it, a doubly feminine voice
(like two women speaking at the same time):
Come on up, come on up!, said the twice-feminine voice.
It's her, said Thom C. I could tell, said Bloom.

104
Of course Bloom wanted to proceed like a motorcade,
however he proceeded like an animal with no paws and no north,
for in fact he wasn't proceeding, he was climbing, that's right,
three stories,

and all on foot.
And Bloom lamented while he climbed the stairs,
because, though he had certain mental mechanisms functioning
within his body,
he also still had internal organs
that were devoid of ratiocination and planning;
organs that lived only in the present.
And these were the organs that were giving orders
inside Bloom's body.

105
There are sentimental organs that have influence over a man
and these, of course, are the most sensible ones,
however the worst and most determinant are, by far,
the pornographic ones.
Why is it that life isn't just a breathing orderliness,
wherein at each moment there is just a single correct action?
Individual life as something didactic and stupid
where all that is required is the repetition of days
that others have already performed in perfect safety.

106
To abandon irony and speak seriously here:
there is a certain anguish suffered by men who have been nude
in the presence of other human beings.
And this because, at that moment, one can perceive, with a
powerful (and brutal) intensity
that a man is a distinct being from, and therefore the enemy of,
every other man. It was clothing that invented compassion
(and probably affection). Nude, men despise each other
or, at best, become aroused; fully clothed, on the other hand,
they pretend that belonging to the same species is more important

than not having the same body.
In view of all this, Bloom wants to attain India
and wisdom at the same time.
And he's still so far away from these two
destinations.

CANTO II

1
Although humanity takes time to arrive
at some place, due to shocking, unexpected events
and roadwork along the way, nature itself
is never late.
With just the right light, nature carries on.
It was already, then, late afternoon when Maria E opened the door
and said: Oh, dear Thom C, how nice to see you,
and you brought a friend?

2
In a newspaper, the news can, on rainy days,
be folded up to fit in one's pocket, remaining dry.
Whatever major news there is, a deadly earthquake
or a recently inaugurated palace, when well folded,
fits into a space of eight-by-six centimeters,
which never fails to astound. This image is even relevant
for those who wish to perceive the importance and the space
occupied by the universe or neighboring countries
in the life of a small citizen.

3
And even an individual of average stature
can forget, for months on end,
a map of the world in a back pants pocket.
This fact, seemingly parallel to our story,
doesn't fail to intersect with it, demonstrating that in the realm of ideas
the infinite is something to be left for the morning
of the following day.

4
Maria E then courteously invited Thom C
and his friend Bloom to enter, immediately offering them
comfortable armchairs, perfect whiskey, appetizers,
a dazzling view down onto the smokestacks of a factory
of great importance in the region,
and, a not-irrelevant detail, showing off still in the movements
she made,
the things that were by far the best aspects of the apartment:
joyous breasts,
legs that would make your thoughts stop, and
a pair of astonishing, vital, and robust buns.
This is the best region of London, thought Bloom,
while through the window he admired the beautiful, thick black
smoke
coming out of the factory.

5
However, Bloom didn't sit down in the armchair straightaway,
as it seemed to possess an excessive comfort.
Out of prudent curiosity he asked
if he could take a little look around such a delightful apartment,
which, despite being small, was promising,
since everyone knows
that a man can spend more time
traversing the tiny house of the woman he desires
than traveling around the world, from one side to the other,
with a backpack on his shoulders.

6
The biography of a lie
or an enormous tragedy doesn't always start off badly

or spuriously (it's said).
How often a powerful ship built
over the course of years and then inaugurated with the
expressive sounds
of joy and money and, on the very next day,
because of a captain's error or some vague problems of the sea,
sinks to the bottom,
taking less time to be swallowed whole
than it took to make the gold plaque
with its name on it.

7
Bloom found it odd that he didn't see
any photograph or personal object in the apartment. The walls
completely empty,
and the very syntax between the pieces of furniture seemed of
recent vintage,
as if the armchairs, tables, and bookshelves
were at that moment exchanging initial pleasantries
(the decoration of the house also seemed to be an invited guest).

8
Thom C, however, remained perversely friendly
and, in every glance exchanged with Bloom, displayed
the malicious smile of one who is saying:
you've got what you want here: breasts and buns, buns and
breasts
—and so on and so forth.
Maria E was, well, in sum, magnificent.

9
Almost suffocating from the presence of so many
contemporaneous things,
Bloom, controlling himself, turned his energy
to the fundamental and urgent problems of culture.
Is this a particularly industrialized area?
asked Bloom, or was it merely by the most beautiful sort of
chance
that you, Sir, bought a vacation home
three stories taller than a factory
with a specific tendency to pollute
upwards?

10
Notice that the principal difference between men
and occasional gods is obvious
and relates, in the first place, to the place
that each occupies.
Thus, men pollute upwards from down below,
just like factories,
while gods pollute downwards from on high,
like the uncouth or filthy neighbor woman who throws out
dirty water from the fifth floor down onto the sidewalk.
Beyond that there are other qualities that one or the other
possesses,
but which are, at bottom, minor details.

11
Bloom was particularly fascinated
by Maria E's small library.
However, he quickly perceived—from the titles—
that those books didn't contain, with all their strength combined,
a single idea, despite their many pages.

They were books of culinary recipes,
a completely unnecessary subject for Bloom:
we should open and shut our mouths, alternately, and that's it.
The rest of it—refined gastronomy—
was a specific perversion
played out between the mouth and the food.
And he felt excluded from that perversion.

12
"How about a quick dinner?" asked the mouth located above the breasts of Maria E,
who then went into the kitchen, saying:
"for a great guest, a small banquet."
Smiles and looks of complicity were then exchanged
between the two masculine parts of the apartment,
Thom C having said to Bloom: "Maria has taken a liking to you."
"She's the perfect woman," he said further.
"We shall see," whispered Bloom.

13
"Twofold exemplification of treason," says Thom C,
in the middle of dinner,
"first: when an airplane flies upwards,
contradicting the physics textbooks where it assures us that heavy bodies fall;
second: when, by some disaster, a fruit
falls from a tree branch and is squashed.
Treason averted:
when an airplane doesn't take off from the runway,
because of mechanical problems or out of the instinct of laziness that even exists in machines."
What sort of conversation is this? Bloom asks himself, silently.

14
Why don't you all sleep here? Maria E asks aloud,
London is a theoretical city by day
and a mammalian city by night.
We are, therefore, in the dangerous hours (and not the useless
ones).
Why don't you stay? Next door, number 3 to the left,
there's a vacant apartment with two beds,
one of them precisely your size, Bloom.
Sleep isn't just good for the aesthetic part of the face, she said,
there's a portion of slumber that increases the following day's
vocabulary.
What an absurd line of reasoning, thought Bloom.

15
The dead possess a certain tranquility, when they're well
buried, because they know that they can't be deceived
(well yes and of course).
Or, at least, we can say that a betrayal committed
against a cadaver has mild effects.
Obviously recalling a day when you were happy
won't bring you complete joy,
since memory, as is well known,
is, by definition, desynchronized
with one's present life. That's what life is:
a closed cubicle, unfortunately.

16
It takes more than just one coat of paint, life takes five or six,
if not dozens, and the trick, if one exists,
is to save the most perfect color for the end.
Here is the fact: men who wanted to take revenge on Bloom

with static weapons resting upon an almost peaceful hatred,
because in a holding position,
they were waiting in the apartment next door.
Bloom was thinking about Maria E. Four men were thinking
about Bloom.

17
True democracy is a room
that is currently occupied
—and man will have to wait.
Revenge can be exercised like any right
of the citizenry, as long as it's within the established
time period. Bloom was, at that point, already in the hallway
ready to enter the apartment where the killers
awaited him,
when something similar to a thought

18
made him deviate from the miniscule pre-established trajectory.
He therefore began to descend, one by one, the stairs
of the building's stairway, distracted by the intellectual potential
that exists in a series that reconciles
mathematics and architecture.
Thom C called out to him and Maria E said: Where are you
going, handsome Bloom?
But Bloom was borne along by his very self,
giving himself orders and obeying them.
I'm going this way, said Bloom. And he went.

19
It's said that the air isn't as transparent as you think,
and it isn't just because of airplanes; birds

and the colored balloons of children also make the air
thicker.
The air thus has pathways that produce in man
boredom or impatience, excitement or somnolence.
(Like an uncomfortable sofa or chair, you'll say.)

20
And above Bloom's individual atmosphere
was thus released an unrestrained oxygen
that oscillated between presenting the neutral smell of a machine
and the fine smell of food in front of a hungry animal.
Through the nostrils of Bloom, a traffic of contradictions:
apprehension, adverse premonitions, and curiosity.

21
There is never enough said
about the way that ambiguity is mortgaged
when one says yes or no,
and what the consequences of this mortgage are.
In what way does a decision annul
this fine form of hope
that is to be seated and say:
"for now I don't want anything"?
But Bloom can't stay in this beautiful ambiguity,
someone is demanding of him that unequivocal yes or no.

22
There is no money that can dirty one's hands,
there are only hands capable of dirtying this new Bible,
of just one page and much easier to read: the valuable note.
They reduced the essential teachings of ten thousand pages
to ten thousand dollars, which represents progress

much greater than that of getting out of an airplane and down
a stepladder
(even though they be of the most perfected sort) to the surface
of the Moon.
What, then, is the basis of the events we're relating?
Money, for some, vengeance, for others. And it's just fine
that way.

23
But let's take this opportunity, let's also speak of the Gods
and of Destiny.
It's clear that ants work more
than the Gods:
otherwise, what's the use of being a divine being?
Who would believe in miracles if a God,
even one with a low spot on the hierarchy,
worked from nine to five?
Certainly, the Gods begin life
indolent and lazy.

24
And thus (only this is of import): sometimes a man's Destiny
doesn't arrive on time;
that man already took off for some other spot
and the point of departure always influences, as is well known,
the place where one demands to arrive.
In a certain way, this was Bloom's situation.
A little confused, ultimately; he isn't where his destiny desired
him to be.

25
On that night, then, there was still time for Bloom
(coming down the stairs of the building one or two stairs at a time)
to find a policeman out on the street,
whom he asked what time it was and the right way to go
to be happy without any deceit. From the window,
those who had prepared themselves to be killers thought
that Bloom, having discovered the trap, was denouncing them,
and they began to be courageous with movements
very similar to those of an escape.

26
Thom C, if he'd had the Pacific Ocean nearby, would've dove in,
even though he didn't know how to swim.
Maria E, for her part, knowing how to swim, was trembling,
from her breasts down to her most hidden quality.
And even her buttocks seemed to lose their eroticism, little by little,
as if somewhere in the body there existed a system
through which seduction flowed,
and that in such a system there were now
a deviation of path or an uncontrollable and obvious
hole.

27
From apartment 3 on the left, the killers, seeing Bloom talk to police
from a distance, suddenly lost their method.
Emotions interfere with mechanisms
when those mechanisms are guided by human hands, and this fact

is evident in those machines of miniature engineering,
weapons. In a trembling body, a deadly weapon ends
up with the exotic and domestic violence of a dustpan.
And such a rapid transfiguration of objects isn't that
rare of an event.

28
Throughout the entire third floor permeated, then, a
three-quarters fear,
the final portion being occupied by a certain urgency
of movement that,
unaccompanied by any decision,
transformed those three men and that woman
into almost mystical animals, for although they were motionless
they nevertheless threatened to stir quite a bit.

29
Thus Bloom, astonished, saw Thom C flee
down the stairs of the fire escape, quickly followed by Maria E,
who, as a result of the fear and an optical illusion, seemed to have
innumerable buttocks,
instead of the common two. And, stupefied, Bloom further saw
three more men, running down the same stairs.
And since all five of them were fleeing, it finally became clear
that they shared the same language: now, the language of
cowardice,
moments before, the language of a trap.

30
Don't imagine that the world has a face for you,
the docile physiognomy of a waiter
or a beautiful woman;

life—the world you're grasping onto—
has, instead, a snout. And those thick lips
(which never inspire music)
from which you are born, like a judge with face
deformed, observe and judge your behavior.

31
On average: people perfect the mechanical
skills of corruption and miserly betrayals more
than the skills of hospitality. The dangers
that a body observes are incessantly fabricated
in any number of unknown, yet efficient,
factories.
There is much danger in the world
—you shall therefore have (don't get bored yet) your fine portion.

32
Do not search for a sincere multitude
because such a thing does not exist.
When numerous, men, animals,
plants, stones, and even machines
lose the hygiene of individual ratiocination;
and, if they open the window that gives out onto the garden,
it's so they can spit, never to say farewell.

33
And Bloom, like all living beings,
would prefer for life to take place on a chessboard
where all the pieces are visible, both friend
and foe. And of course Bloom, since he is not yet wise,
would prefer to have already found rather than still have to search
for.

Bloom sometimes speaks of a woman who made him
speak only in written verse, as if endowed with another voice,
a voice that was much more material than the voice of those
volatile
contemporary songs.

34
At other times he speaks of the search for an intimate joy,
a non-pornographic joy, a joy
that doesn't involve associations of crude chemical particles
or stimulations between fingers and tangible fabrics
in retreat. A mystical joy
that isn't the result of some failure. That is a choice
and not the effect of movements of jubilation
after surviving a great fall. Ultimately,
a joy that is spiritual, yet really exists.

35
It's true that in the heavens, the Gods, if they exist,
don't leap over walls, since the concept of neighbors is different.
But the most profound borders,
the most pronounced separations,
always took place at the limits of the immaterial,
like the unrealized desire
to kiss someone.
May betrayals and attempted robberies cease.
May the Gods of love come to Bloom's aid.

36
If there were a goddess of Love, would she know how to write
elegant, personal
verses? Or would she do it all industrially,

hurl sudden passions upon a whole multitude
the way you hurl water upon a populace that's unhappy
with the rising prices of bread and fabric in order to calm them?
Or, worse yet, would she hurl, through an intermediary,
pacifying arrows, the way they used to hurl hot oil
onto armies that were trying to storm the castle,
causing severe burns and immediate desistance?

37
It's evident that Nature, and its four elements,
carefully holds back its stimulating aspects:
a small fire or a fireplace,
the sea or a pot of water for washing apples,
a simple hill and the air, today filled up with fog
—if everything in the world were landscape, there wouldn't be a single
unrestrained passion (it seems to us).
But that's a sidenote.

38
But here a question remains: since the organs of joy are located in exactly
the same place as the organs of sadness, how can we conceive
of the same space being twice occupied
in a single moment? How can one be happy
and sad at the same time? Can each instant of a
living being be such a vast substance
that within it fit tightly together
two sensations of opposite expressive magnitude and
temperament?

39
A flood is inflexible indeed when it doesn't lose control
of its own organism, considering, here,
that a vast torrent of water forms, when seen from above,
a homogenous animal that obeys a single voice.
In sum, what matters is this:
will Nature want to flood Bloom or
wash Bloom?
This is something that Bloom intends to discern while there's
still time.

40
Because there are two ways for water to make contact
with living beings: flooding and drowning or washing and
making clean. And water, just like air,
fire, and earth, always has two ways of declaring
to men that they exist and are present:
by making them happy or unhappy.
And in the visible sky, which is the lowest part of Nature's elite,
there are contradictory opinions about
every man, woman, child, elder, and weed.

41
Destiny is not, therefore, the univocal decision
of a tribunal that only knows how to draw straight lines.
It's a strange sum
—of the weight of circumstances that befall
upon the head of a man—
a sum registered on a clock parallel
to the clock of time,
a clock we could call qualitative.

42

And please, Bloom, pay attention to this detail:
don't fill your house with furniture and other objects,
please, save space for beauty,
so there's room for it to fit: a chasm to the right of the person
entering the house, for example.
May beautiful things be your lookout station;
for the world, like anything else,
only becomes beautiful when the beauty is looked upon.

43

The future is coming like a shepherd who watches over
his lingering flock, which is to say: it isn't coming,
it's delayed, engendering impatience in things that exist.
Certain occurrences, it's true, can add
two or three stories to the building of one's life. But not much
more.
All substance has a future,
and even one's own memory is, in the specifics of this specific,
a substance to take into account. Memory has a future,
and that idea is not at all pessimistic.

44

But the Gods wish to protect Bloom, that much is clear.
Bloom is a human man, with an intelligence
earned through hard knocks—but his principal quality resides
in a precise, intermediate place: his heart.
Because the heart of courageous or amorous men
engenders effects
that can be seen from all angles, on the surface.
And the Gods have always enjoyed the smell that comes off of
viscera
that love or hate (or that, at least, are beating).

45
Yes, Bloom is already being entrusted with, somewhere,
a domesticated Destiny,
a watch-dog who, at the master's voice,
jumps or fetches the humiliating stick.
But the unexpected has no formula,
and even the past has things
that even tomorrow will prove surprising.

46
For Bloom, a future replete with efficient joy
is foreseen.
He shall get to know some countries and the schizophrenic taste
of certain drinks;
he shall taste foods
that look similar to a patch of untended garden,
and perceive that the gardener of these foods
is nothing more than habit.

47
Sometimes you shall receive threats, dear Bloom:
don't leave your house before nine,
don't leave after nine.
But never stay there, press on.
Don't fall asleep along the way, Bloom,
and don't let yourself become troubled. Put your ear
up to a decisive song: you'll find courage.
We would be animals if certain songs didn't exist.

48
And the importance of language. Let's talk about it.
Bloom, being intelligent,

in a country without a shared tongue
will play the role of an imbecile,
and that fact aptly demonstrates the clear disaster
that the multiplication of tongues meant
for reasoning in this world.
Among Chinese people who don't understand his language,
the European philosopher could be mistaken
for a fool or some vague animal.

49
But there are philosophers and then there are others, the encyclopedists,
who accumulate facts
in their portable storehouse, like boxes with a
more or less organized vocabulary.
For these, the confusion of tongues was most prejudicial
in terms of an international career. As for Bloom, our hero,
he is endowed with a rare mental and practical intelligence:
he can solve mathematical things and tie an efficient knot
in a rope.

50
It's said that there are problems of poetry more difficult
than the most complicated of algebra problems.
If algebra is a strict religion,
poetry would be a religion of excess, a religion somewhere between
drunkenness and a space where
the most beautiful songs rest
before they once again conquer the air.
The problems of poetry raise questions
in the most unprotected locales in the existence

of a man. But fortunately Bloom closed off
access to such dangerous places early enough.

51
Bloom's face, right now, at this moment, a man
to whom even the plants seem to bequeath a mystical oxygen
instead of the common O2,
can't be seen as one sees a photograph but rather
as a film: agitated, under constant projections,
changes in position; endless photograms,
and in the flesh.
Bloom, the hero, wants to forget the attempted assaults
and the traps;
he wants to get to India, but not just yet.

52
Only great generals, bent over the map of a potential battle,
and the tiger, a second before leaping onto its prey,
has such a face,
utterly situated and, at the same time,
in the present and the future,
like a stake planted deep and, simultaneously,
in the pliant earth and the sky.

53
Bloom, the excellent swimmer, is dreaming
of crossing the sea with admirable speed
and in novel style. Not freestyle, breast stroke, or butterfly, but
simply, and only, an intellectual style. And since it isn't easy to demonstrate oneself
to be of sound reason when swimming or running,
nor is it easy to apply the library of books read to physical proceedings

devoid of sentences,
one must, without delay,
congratulate Bloom.

54
But Bloom will make things, not just words.
Bloom will make things that belong to the world of made things
and not things that belong to the world of written things,
that is to say: not made. Because Bloom well knows that only
that
which can be placed under the leg
of a table to straighten it is material
and exists.
And a sentence, for as dense and solid as it may be,
will never balance out even the slightest divergence
between a piece of furniture and the ground.

55
Bloom has a chest so courageous that the rest of his body
seems
always to enter a room as if it were merely
the second half of that haughty prow that cuts the air in twain
and, all at once, shoves every atom
of oxygen to the side.
Even nothingness, if it existed, would be split in two
by Bloom. And, if necessary, Bloom would turn those two
halves of nothingness into food.

56
Well then, in darkest place, so dark because it's transparent,
it will have been decided that Bloom deserved to become
acquainted with at least

a part of his Destiny.
And because even heroes sleep and, sleeping, dream,
it is therefore possible for the mysterious oracle
to appear at night. Bloom is sleeping and dreaming.

57
How is such distance possible between the exterior of an organism,
with mammalian noises resounding,
and the interior of this selfsame living being,
engrossed in holy narratives?
How is it possible for such sonorous mediocrity to be the façade
of the grandeur that sometimes surfaces in dreams?
Nothing on earth is homogenous, much less
an organism, that's the conclusion.
(But Bloom, since he's asleep, concludes nothing.)

58
Clearly, the well-known "sleep-inducing wand"
could go by the domestic name of "weariness,"
eight hours per workday,
or a long walk and too many
events for a single day—as in Bloom's case.
What's certain is that Bloom fell asleep dreaming
that someone was smoothing out the days to come for him.
Tired of being poorly received and betrayed, Bloom dreamed
that being happy wasn't some superfluous good,
as are certain gems and jewelries of ephemeral beauty.

59
A luxury, happiness? A luxury, the hospitality of one's neighbors,
or of the unfamiliar inhabitants of Paris, Rome,

Vienna, Prague? Perhaps Europe is a mixture of incompatible
substances, or perhaps, thus, the whole world,
for a human never unites herself with another human
to the point of disappearing, like a liquid dissolving into another
liquid,
save for the mother who carries a child in her belly.
But wouldn't a man, once in his life, have the desire
to open his door to a stranger?
Are hatred and the survival instinct a habit
or a precise specialization that organisms universally
acquire (from the air?) as they grow?

60
Bloom, meanwhile, before these thoughts or dreams,
had entered a boardinghouse with a look of amiable hostility
about it
on the outskirts of London.
It was cold outside and the boarding house was so wretched and
full of holes that the rooms,
despite being excessively comfortable, seemed to be located
outside the boarding house
and inside the wind.
"A room that's practically in the open air in Winter,
that's what my numbered coins can afford in such an
opulent city," he muttered.
And, as was already stated, Bloom, our hero,
fell asleep, like some common mammal.

61
Rats, frogs, birds, earthworms, weasels,
the whale, goats with horns of all sorts, even arachnids,
all are animals that sleep. Presidents,

carpenters, useless saints, needful criminals,
crippled postmen, racecar drivers, paralytics,
enraged mobs, all of them, when dressed in the pajama of
weariness, fall asleep.
Even—look closely here—amorous men and women;
a fact that constitutes a conspicuous waste.

62
And Bloom dreamed. Abstract speculations and escape from the
planet
on a flying staircase, Nature being sliced
in two like a birthday cake:
half of reality like a ridiculous candle to be snuffed out
by one's breath. He dreamed still of a cloud
that was no higher than three meters above the ground:
and children on a ladder pulling it higher.
And in this place where one doesn't know where one is,
the place where dreams appear,
appeared to him further still a repulsive, dank country
full of mud and a platform, elevated on posts,
on which the inhabitants did what all inhabitants do,
but a little higher up.
And among his head's other inventions and admixtures,
Bloom also dreamed of Paris.

63
He dreamed that in the center of Paris
all angles and corners had been transformed,
by pickaxe, into rounded shapes.
Sharp substances capable of causing cranial
traumas now had the friendly structure of balloons, and an
orchestra of novices played sounds capable of mollifying

ancient institutions. Paris was a party
and, yet, people were happy.
(But all this in his dream.)

64
And even though the sun has long been part of the physiognomy of days,
like the nose on a man, the morning
—and with it the entire power station
that is progressively switched on—
continues to be a source of astonishment.
Here are the true ancient substances,
say the oldest among us,
with that instinct of the enemy of progress,
leaning on their canes.
So Bloom awoke and said at once: to Paris,
where people throw parties, yet remain happy.
To Paris, he repeated.

65
A city's style is visible in its architecture,
the clothing of its women, and the quality of its poems.
But if to know a flower, one has but to smell it,
a city, if looked upon with close attention, is merely the vestige
of a man: and that man may be a sage,
a thief, or a policeman. A single man (but where might he be?)
can epitomize the wonders of a city,
its perversions,
and the way in which liquids circulate through it.

66
Leaving the boardinghouse,
Bloom turned away from the anxious looks
directed at him, nearly shut his eyes, and
quickened his step. He was still in London,
and, like fruit at certain times of the year,
his enemies, from one day to the next,
might have ripened.
On the other hand, in Paris, in his dream,
there was only water and women. He pressed on,
therefore.

67
He was pleased with both train and boat, two nearly opposite
voyages: the train trip, a voyage in the solid world;
the boat trip, a voyage in the liquid world. But not just
two ways of traversing a distance:
they are weighty theories,
mythological ways of looking at the world.
On a plane, for example, Bloom felt nauseated,
felt the lack of air, of earth, of fire, and of water:
four relevant natural elements.
Three thousand meters above the ground,
man begins to have a poorer perception of nature,
muttered Bloom.

68
So he went by boat, London to Paris. Odd decision.
And, in a calculation of the equilibrium between two elements,
the further the boat got from land,
the more Bloom ate, in futile compensation.
At high sea, the traveler should eat, and high on

a mountaintop, should drink without end.
He believed in such fables.

69
In Paris, love is proportional to reality,
two men told him during the voyage. It's a city that
receives poets well. The women are rigid of
thigh and syntax. On the surface, there exists mental labor,
and the street sweepers employ seldom-used adjectives.
The best children's stories are told
in butcher shops. And on Sundays, in the large parks,
people do physical exercises that seem like news
recently received in a letter. In addition, there are repetitions
that are absolutely exotic.

70
I'm looking for a woman, said Bloom, or else
wisdom. If you don't find both together in Paris,
they replied, you'll at least cross paths with
one of them. And one can lead you to the other.
Of course it's less likely
that a woman will lead you to wisdom
than to her bedroom, they told Bloom,
but if by some extraordinary luck such a thing happens,
don't forget to remind her: the bedroom, first
the bedroom. And Bloom smiled.

71
Paris is voluptuous.
Publishers live in penury so that poets can have a wine-cellar
and a library.
One bottle of wine per day, two verses;

an erect foray into the best brothel in the city,
but a verse, a verse and a half, on the way back home,
leaning out the window (later)
to insult the passing bourgeois,
that's how a poet has fun. In Paris, poets
have no debts, and even the crazy ones are polite.

72
Not weeds, but flowers
rule the gardens. Courts are sensitive
to the scents wafting in through the window, and judges reduce
prison sentences by half,
for they believe that being locked up
in a city so beautiful and fragrant
is equivalent to double the sacrifice. Thus, in Paris,
crime pays. And then there are
the breakfasts, brimming with cheese
and baguette.
That's what they told Bloom about Paris.

73
And it was on a festive Easter Sunday that Bloom
arrived in Paris, a pier leading to happiness.
(You can be happy for three weeks, but leave out the fourth.)
And thus Bloom disembarks,
his ability for making friends perfected,
smiling in the syntax of a nearly perfect French,
breathing in the air and the objects.

74
In Paris, even the air is luxurious. On cold days,
the fog seems to descend down to the noses of the inhabitants,

but without ever losing a certain petulant quality that, around
these parts,
oxygen possesses.
Bloom notices that there's a woman on the pier,
with the most jumpy eyelids, who is trying to seduce him.
And that is more pleasant than an attempted robbery.

75
He can smell the metaphysics everywhere,
there's a fog and porters ready
to carry his suitcase.
And there are innumerable possibilities of employing, in these
lands,
the eroticism he learned in others.
Bloom is content.
He isn't in India, but Paris is perfect.

76
Being in complete lyric relapse, Bloom, pleased
with the hospitality, the smells, the sounds, and
the pretty girls, asked for something even more: feelings.
This theoretical elaboration didn't restrain him, however,
from reciprocating the predatory gaze of some Parisian woman
with no shame, but with a hat on her head. Outside of our own
country,
thought Bloom, women welcome us as if
they were saving a shipwrecked man.

77
Women in hats had always seemed more intelligent
to him.
The hat is, in part, an element of one's attire that is fifty percent
mental.

Certain hats in Paris are even more mental
than certain heads in other cities.
Ah, Paris! In no other city is one
closer to Paris than in Paris. Hence its grandeur.

78
Yet despite the importance given to culture
in this city, the sky remains intellectually
neutral. And sometimes it rains.
As it did here, and Bloom found himself obligated to take shelter
beneath an organized obstacle, located between him
and the Paris sky. It was the small awning of a store
that sold socks for feet,
gloves for hands, and hats for heads.

79
Likewise protecting himself from the rain, standing beside him,
a friendly man, already a little wet,
to whom Bloom, at the end of five minutes,
demonstrated his orthographically correct manner of breaking
the French silence. I have utilized twelve months of
every year of my life, said Bloom,
for I'm a balanced and
exhaustive man. Since I am now, because of meteorological
imposition, your neighbor,
allow me to introduce myself: my name is Bloom;
I'm looking for a woman or something that makes me stop
looking for one. I'm not sure if you understand me.
Wisdom, ultimately. And to make it to India.

80
It's said that each language could be defined as
a specialized manner of interrupting the silence. And though the
silence of Paris being, in a general way,
the same as the silence of London or Vienna,
the manner in which this silence is interrupted varies brutally,
even when taking into account the small
European distances. And this brutality—more or less organized
into syntax,
orthography, and chatter that interrupt, in a civilized manner,
the oxygen and the fog—we call language.
And in Paris the alphabet is French.

81
I'm not a thief, said Bloom,
and when my hand touches iron
it isn't to destroy something, but to build.
I'm not indifferent to repetitions, and I endure tedium
better than certain unnecessary adventures.
I am, thus, not obsessed with novelty.
However, I cannot tolerate, within myself,
that the lack of surprise no longer surprises me.

82
I'm not sure you understand me, but I trust you, so
I'll go on. I was poorly received in London,
they tried to rob me of the possessions that, in volume,
exceed the organism, which includes money, clothes,
the lovely suitcase, and some books.
I had to thrash them, utilizing all possible courtesy
and some punches.
I was never able to forget, even in the utmost comfort,

that I wasn't in my city,
that familiar Lisbon I left a few months back, a city
where I could fight with men in my own tongue,
which greatly facilitates one's movements.

83
I am, generally speaking,
magnificent. And, moving along to specifics,
despite being cultured, I can climb trees with the agility of a
chimpanzee. I know how to fry an egg and make a dubious
batch of rice.
And I have a strength that, when applied correctly,
transforms into congeniality. I know how to smile at two people
at once, and that isn't some lack of facial coordination,
but rather technique, training, good families, and effort.

84
And you can believe, dear Sir, that if I myself were the bearer,
at this moment, of that excellent umbrella
of which Your Excellency is the owner, you can believe, I was
saying,
that I would share it with you, the way a mother shares her bread
with her own child. Because even my most ferocious muscles
have a tendency toward sentiment, said Bloom.
And he extended his hand.

85
Pleasure to meet you, replied the friendly
Parisian named Jean M.
A foreigner is always a novelty, as much a verbal novelty
as in the number of habits he adds to the landscape.
And there is no doubt that you, Sir, are not mute,

because you speak skillfully, and he who discourses thusly
must also have patient ears,
for in conversation one must maintain equilibrium.
A man who speaks too much
is deaf, never doubt this. And that is not the case with you.

86
You can trust me, continued Jean M,
the Parisian, I will speak in French, of course,
but you may hear me in whatever language you prefer (as in
those science fiction
books where a sort of simultaneous translation occurs
on every page,
which at every instant transforms deformed sounds
into organized sounds,
and where words, each one separated from the next,
emerge as clearly as if they were drawings.).

87
That is to say: I thank you for your restrained confessions
and understand the precautions that, despite everything, you
are taking,
for it is on foreign soil that we should most remember
the lessons learned in childhood.
Look both ways before you cross the street,
or the sea, or a whole city. It's a good lesson.
Look both ways to see both sides of a person, even. This
precautionary gesture remains indispensable. Men
always have two (or more) sides, and it's advantageous not to take
one side of the cube for the whole thing.

88
My dear Bloom, I'm ready to help you.
From the start, I'll give you half of the umbrella,
assuming that that part will reach far enough to keep you out of the whole of the rain;
and tonight I will grant you, further still, half of my apartment.
And may these two mismatched halves
—half an umbrella and half an apartment—
create, as strange as it may seem, a homogenous
friendship.

89
What a beautiful scene—it's said, noted, pointed out, admired.
When men cross paths like this, in a friendly manner,
they, at last, seem to be animals
with a tendency toward even numbers
and not the selfishness of singularity,
which alone occupies the whole of a bench
or a casket.
Bloom, penniless, accepts everything—even in Paris.
My, what a beautiful scene this is.

90
Parties are a tactile affair,
joy is only sonorous on the outside,
but nothing is happy with its head outside itself.
Jubilation issues forth without a single sound accompanying it.
Sound is the false element of things.
Speaking, singing, making hideous noises,
all this is a mere annex of the body,
for you are an interior organism, dear Bloom,
just like all humans. Feeling has no sound,
this is more than clear.

91
So, we are in Paris, and two men are celebrating
—the science by which one is happy
coincides with that of the other.
Bloom opens his chest, extends an arm,
then the other one. He bids farewell to the river he can't see
from there,
almost leaps into the air with half of the umbrella in his hand
and, with the other half, Jean M almost leaps as well.
The two are talking fast and the sentences aren't spoken all the
way to the end
for the one perceives where the other wants to place
the final period.

92
But the night is so round that it
circles back on itself: thus the trees stood up
because they had become visible, and the dogs
also stood up because the sun robbed them of their anonymity.
As you can see, even complete things, like the night, have holes
where their opposites can gain strength,
mulling over an enmity that will soon become evident.
It was nighttime and it rained; now the sun is up and day is
breaking.

93
Any physicist will scoff at the numerical comparison between the
speed of light (and other things that fall from the sun)
and the speed of water.
And it's clear that in the horizontal flow of a river
water is much slower than when it falls vertically, but
even so, the rain isn't that fast

—it's an event that even allows for the reaction of distracted
children.
And sunlight comes from above just like rain does.

94
Bloom strolls through Paris and sees things that make him think
about other things.
If even luxurious fabrics and silks can be reduced to combinations
that are merely more aesthetic than our well known
filthy atoms, why marvel in the face of Paris?
And even the cathedral, the imposing cathedral, is, after all,
a stake, like all other architecture,
a religious stake, firmly planted in the right spot, respected,
requiring soft voices, but always a stake,
violently buried into Paris.

95
All architecture is therefore violence,
thinks Bloom.
Unlike swift animals, like the horse,
which do not harm the earth, but merely push off and proceed.
And then there are stones. We speak of precious stones, indeed,
so why not also speak of precious planets,
precious weeds, or a luxury chimpanzee?
What shines brightest at night? Whatever you pay attention to
shines the brightest.
It was always that way. And Bloom knows that well.

96
Oh, how elegant Bloom is! Even in his desperation.
His shoes don't get dirty, his firm gaze remains agile,
and he strides with precision along the four cardinal directions.

Look at how the Earth's orbit seems to stop
in front of Bloom. As if the Earth's orbit,
instead of continuing on its way, performed, for Bloom's delight,
a triple jump; a dangerous acrobatic feat.
Bloom is in Paris, it's true, but Paris,
in a certain way, seems to also be in Bloom.

97
Yes, Bloom is wearing French clothes and is also attempting
to dress himself in French words, accentuating his pronunciation.
Bloom is euphoric in Paris.
Ah, how terrestrial is vanity. And on Earth
it remains. What part of your jubilation reaches a bird in flight?
Vanity has one single meaning and
doesn't expire. It's a substance that one hurls into oneself,
and there it stays, swelling you up with nothing at all.

98
How happy Bloom is in Paris!
The colors here are light that has gained meaning
in the realm of beauty. And for something
that was never worth existing,
it's necessary to be even more beautiful than the others.
Paris, for example. Vain and egotistical.

99
To have an attractive door—as if every object or beast
were a building that was permanently inviting one to enter.
What beautiful light, thinks Bloom, looking around,
where do I enter?
Paris, in sum, astonishing and attracting curious Bloom.

100
The most looked-upon and admired colors are taller
—like a tower—and the irrelevant colors are lower.
And over all other phenomena in the world, and in your own
house,
you can place this grate through which to perceive the world,
which is dimension:
large and small.
Everything has, inside itself, space for being small
or large. And even swollen things have, inside themselves,
the opportunity to be minuscule.

101
Bloom and Jean M, the Parisian, took a liking to each other in
gesture
and stroll. This is synthesis.
The body creates a mass with its movements,
and this mass creates a text. That text is read
by others, and there are books that are liked
and others that aren't.
At bottom, each life, in general, is nothing more
than a literary style.

102
So it was as if Bloom were already known in Paris.
Between the two of them, a personal volume
that was much more than the simple shape of each body.
The three dimensions of Bloom in the Paris air were luminous:
he walked
as if he were in possession
of some response, or like some important person
who, all by himself, inaugurates a new season for the trees.
Spring, for instance.

103
And then Bloom thought about that public coffin:
days. In every day, more than ten thousand
people are buried. It's a public,
ordinary, grotesque, shameless day, in which
the elderly, children, women, and men—hardy, skinny, and well-fed—are anonymously buried.
Days (every day) are a mass grave,
thought Bloom. If they're not careful,
days can catch an illness. (But on Earth, thank God,
each day rapidly gives way to the next.)

104
A day that doesn't proceed forward is like stagnant water: it attracts insects, loses clarity.
And the chemical elements that, uninterrupted, circulate
invisibly in Bloom's body, are now in a state
of gratitude
for such kind, open-hearted hospitality.
Here is a mystery that no contemporary laboratory
has ever solved: happiness, sadness.
What is a day but a roll of the dice
between will and matter?

105
And Bloom said: I was met with a poor reception in London,
and welcomed by you in Paris,
and welcomed by Paris itself,
due to some secret method of air and earth.
Even the bottled water we're served
at the street café—very expensive, yes—
but even that water seems hospitable to me.

106
Yes, it's true that commerce has shoved Nature
into boxes with price tags. But that's not terrible, nor
even unpleasant. Much worse are certain children
who tear the foot off of a frog who had the misfortune
of becoming the object of the ingenuous labor of six-year-old
living beings. Between being sold whole
by usurious merchants and being torn apart by children
who don't know the value of money, Nature
will always opt for peaceful capitalism.

107
Because capitalism knows that a good
that's missing a foot is less valuable:
that's why it doesn't tear off feet or ears,
or entire heads, with its teeth. But if it made it more valuable,
it would even tear off
one of the feet of the Eiffel Tower, exclaimed Jean M.
Don't be fooled by monuments or ceremonies.
Aesthetics are over. Money remains.
Men are geniuses of virtue when it comes to gold,
geniuses of vice when it comes to the landscape.

108
But the Parisian friend wanted to know more
about Bloom's voyage.
Where had he illuminated his evenings?
And the days, how had they unfolded?
Is a day a coherent event,
with a head, body, and limbs, as the people say,
with a meaning and logic?
Is a day a date, a homogenous

event that maintains equilibrium between the light from the sun
and the actions of bodies?

109
Bloom was trying to respond simply
that his days had begun in a way that was not at all exotic:
he awoke at quarter after eight, many hours later
he fell asleep. In the interim: he looked at his watch. That's
all. Everyone always assumes
that tedium is their personal property, and the days of others
are borne atop a magnificent wagon.
As did Jean M. As did Bloom.

110
Curious, the Parisian insisted: he wanted to know the climate
in which Bloom had spent his childhood.
If it had rained upon his toys,
grass had grown up around them, or if, on the contrary,
his toys had grown warm under the sun.
And why was he traveling through Europe? From which side of
the countries
had he entered them? Better still, he noted, that the countries
are entities with volume, cobblestones
instead of those flat,
elongated things you see on maps.
How does one enter into a map, dear Bloom?

111
Tell me your story, insisted the Parisian.
I see in you a strong person who comments on life,
not a weak person who is commented on by it.
I see someone who concentrates vast energy on the details,

someone who, sitting in a place, makes it exceptional,
and who, running through a place, makes it slow down.
You, dear Bloom, seem like a man whose shoes
don't fit on a map.
Speak, insisted Jean M, I want to hear your story.

112
I don't allow myself to be fooled by the grand
ephemeral achievements, said Jean M. The sun, for example,
being persistent and never failing,
doesn't become insignificant when placed beside
an athlete, a pole-vaulter, who has just broken
some incredible world record.
Any paltry hill is more solid than
an extraordinary jumper—even at the moment of his
greatest jump. Thus the grand exultant achievements,
and thus tranquil Nature.
And what side is your life on, dear Bloom?

113
There are living beings who start traveling
to stockpile achievements for their lives, as if
thrills were enormous,
plump butterflies (so as not to escape the net).
And there are others, like Bloom, who, even before they undertake their voyage,
are already in possession of the temperature of a hot-blooded citizen:
vast passions, vengeance, struggles, venomous
and holy methods of entering the landscape.
Bloom, in fact, possessed the entire inventory of existence:
yes, in him, it made sense for man

to be endowed with this ability to hear and see backwards that is called memory.

CANTO III

1
But let's take a break.
Just like a porter laden with boxes, a writer
needs help. No one can carry a season like Autumn
to earth all alone.
The thought raises one's body temperature to that of a disastrous
auto accident, and the words, that they may be able to invent,
demand mystical support, though at the same time they must remain
on the ground, like shoes.

2
Pushed forward by certain gods of inspiration,
just as an old, broken-down truck is pushed down the road,
the writer, with his antique, primitive motor,
ultimately just wants the sentences to be made of a substance
that doesn't slowly evaporate from one day to the next;
he desires robust sentences, that forge ahead through
the centuries. Sentences that, thrown into the sea, swim,
and, thrown into the air, fly.

3
The Parisian—let's return to him—wanted Bloom
to turn on the faucet from which flows water
whose babble tells stories.
What have you done with your life, dear Bloom,
that you're now on a full-fledged voyage to India?
How and where did you do wrong? In what manner
did your shot hit the target?

4
That two hydrogen molecules and one of oxygen,
in massive, swift quantities, could sound
like a narrative was already known to be possible
from the time of the great floods
and murderous princes who washed away the blood with water.
Water retains the blood, and other filth, sure,
but stories that are told on riverbanks
dissolve completely.
However, this river is the Seine. You can tell me everything, said Jean M,
nothing will be lost.

5
If a weak sugar dissolves in water,
stories are safe-kept in the body of man
in the part of the organism that holds onto narratives
(let's imagine that this exists).
Nothing is lost, nothing is gained; it's all a tie,
like it is in boring ballgames. However, memory is not like this
—he who remembers, invents: everything begins anew.

6
I could speak of the world, said Bloom,
of the rotations of an orange around an accurate knife
and the rotations of the planet;
I could speak, further still, of enormous windows
from which sharp eyes espied
the most important things to see in all existence.
But you ask me, kind Parisian, to tell you about
my life; as if you didn't have

in front of you, this very moment, my very person—the temporary
conclusion of my adventures.

7
I come from that chunk of space called Europe,
where the pipes inside houses and the airplanes
in the skies follow each other in a mysterious symmetry
made possible by the most modern technology.
Water flows through the houses of Europe, replicating,
inside a pipe, the flight paths of sensible
airlines: this is an almost poetic fact, which I am now divulging.

8
In Europe there is wind, snow, sunlight, water, fires,
and even grammar, syntax, and vast libraries.
For parallel to Nature, language exists.
And in such an erudite continent there are more public
institutions devoted to the proper utilization of metaphors
than to hurricanes.
It is, at heart, a civilized, well-washed continent,
with hygienic habits applied to the landscape—
even down to particulars, in certain of the coldest locales,
under the magnifying glass.

9
And in Europe there are things, said Bloom,
that fritter away gestures, making the childish mistake
of dancing when they are happy.
While in other lands people meditate—as in the Orient—
in Europe, people organize dances.
In terms of fleeting joy, there's no one who can beat
Europe.

10
I like Italy, for instance, where the cats
seem to know how to ride atop motorcycles,
and where, in certain central locations, like Rome,
the past and large machines coexist
in a surprising manner,
as if they were contemporaries after all.

11
Yes, I have also taken a liking to Vienna.
A city of noble cobblestones
they call Palaces,
beautiful even when admired by
ugly people.
Vienna is interesting because it is monumental even
in its prices.

12
Greece is a whole other story. The great martial chariots
have, of course, been traded for bicycles,
however, in philosophy, the Greeks
keep themselves very up to date because they read other people.
At bottom, like someone who still hasn't woken up entirely,
the Greeks find themselves turned
toward that which millennia ago was the cutting edge of Time.

13
I also like Venice, surrounded by so much water.
The sea, in fact, is not a rare element here.
In breadth it is much larger than all the deserts,
and in depth greater than the tallest skyscrapers
of the great cities.

And if the Mediterranean were not inconsequential
to my personal life,
water would be something to keep in mind for the agenda.
But I've never lived in Venice. And it's noticeable.

14
Let me also tell you a story, said Bloom,
a parable, or whatever you want to call it. In the city, morality is taught
with the feet of the teacher and students firmly stuck
in a bog.
The rules of conduct are proffered
and exemplified by the instructor.
In a few short minutes, instructor and pupils
can no longer see their own feet
and, in a few short hours, their legs and torsos will disappear
and only the head that's teaching morality will remain above the bog

15
reiterating in tender tone
that all men are nearly brothers
and other such loveliness.
Nevertheless, from above, from the part of the city that has of yet resisted
the bog,
only a single rope will be let down, and this rope is destined for one person:
the excellent instructor.
The apprentices, therefore, become submerged
(for only buried—much too late, however—
will they manage to learn the essential lesson).

16
Of course, in days of old, Bloom continued,
following this short narrative,
a great city was the place
where an excellent philosopher lived;
now a great city is the one with a lot of citizens
of voting age and at least one building one hundred and forty
stories tall.
If there's one man among fifteen million
who thinks: that's excellent, for certain,
but it isn't indispensable.

17
In Spain, for example, they give the sort of kisses
make the most use of the lips. It's a country
where the extremities are of great importance;
and even if the tones are terrible, they dance
wonderfully.
It's a country where there's no need to go searching around for
a theory
with a flashlight; they never use formulas,
they use pickaxes: forging ever onward.

18
In Spain there are different ways for the syntax
to describe feelings and, for example, death.
The manner in which the dead are buried creates a citizenry,
and the words that are said
to a girl who has lost her parents
don't always correspond exactly on the right and left sides
of a border, as everyone knows.
A country is a thing made of exceedingly ancient agreements.

19
It's as if the concentration of oxygen
held some influence over the physiology of feelings,
over that which is called, and rightly so,
a good or bad heart.
But what matters here, my dear Parisian,
is to locate myself.
I am not the place where I stand now, that much is clear.

20
I have arrived, therefore, or my voice does so in my name,
I have arrived, I was saying, finally, at the place from which I departed:
Portugal, Lisbon, 31 Actor Isidro Street, first floor, on the right.
It's a nice neighborhood,
with a grocery store on every corner.
Even if you're in the city center, with all the noise
and car exhaust,
if you have oranges and apples on your street
you're practically in the country.

21
Absence of industry and significant factories,
that's what hygiene means in a country like ours.
And when there are no major smoke stacks,
even the smoke from a cigarette carries weight in statistical effects.
It isn't big, isn't enormous, but it's nice, this country.
Two sides facing the land, two sides facing the sea.
And so it's almost just right.

22
One day I'd like to return to Lisbon, of course,
but after I've found my joy once more
and with a woman in tow.
But what am I saying? I've gone too far ahead.
Before I recount, I should explain,
but might not these two things be one single thing?
I'll proceed ahead, then, and explain (or recount).

23
I'll speak of the person I loved
(loving a country would be a slightly perverse act.
How do you open your arms
to something that has no length, width, or height like
every other mortal thing that is held dear?)
I'll speak of the person I loved, then, and not of maps.

24
Let's let exalted patriots prepare for wars,
treaties, our tombstone and their statue,
and talk about what's important: my grandfather, John John
Bloom,
an illustrious man. We'll start with him

25
It's said that the essence of a language
is in the non-verbal sounds that women emit.
And the meticulous education of the ear
was something that John John Bloom
never neglected.
From him I received my good ear for music
and for love.

26
In eroticism, what matters is that, in the body of the beloved,
there is no way out.
A good struggle—of the amorous variety—
is thus one in which the two bodies are,
one inside the other,
as if in the middle of the famous labyrinth
from which there was no escape.

27
Women have always been more
meticulous in their vengeance, said Bloom. They leaf through it
without skipping a single page. And trim their fingernails
before grabbing the axe.
On the contrary, a man full of rage
and rancor is confused, clumsy,
unable to find the perfect pronunciation of his violence.

28
As if he were picking up absurd
tools: a plow
to pick a flower,
a hammer to see more closely.

29
Men are daring against or in favor
of grenades. And they only hit the blade of grass
if they use bombs.
And this issue of disproportionality becomes obvious
in war: they only wanted to kill one person, and in a courteous manner;
they end up eliminating thousands, in brutal form

(there are no specialized bombs,
there are no bombs that worry about the details).

30
But I was telling the story of my family,
Bloom cried out,
and without noticing it, I got sidetracked
with the presentation of a system
of the utilization of hate.
Let's return, then, to the center.

31
My grandfather John John Bloom had a son: my father,
whose name was John Bloom. When
old John John Bloom died,
new John Bloom remained, which demonstrates
that though names are not eternal
—for the associations between the letters also
wastes away—they nevertheless show considerable resistance.

32
But here's what happened: my father's brothers
didn't want to give him his due inheritance.
They became angry,
and thus, between themselves they fired bullets
of powerful legality (lawyers, that's what they're called).
This didn't go well; it could've gone worse.

33
It's true that for good lawyers, the law
is no less obscure than certain lines
of Rimbaud,

able to signify one thing or its opposite.
If a textual analyst acted as if the most convincing
interpretation of a text gained the rights
to an enormous inheritance, that would change everything.
But that's not the case, laziness is considerable, the money is
very little.

34
As for the rest, dear Jean M,
the girls are magnificent, the roses
give off their perfume,
and sometimes it snows in Winter.
Have you ever noticed?

35
And there are also faces that look like the ingenuous
drawings of children,
women who help other people, and men who are helped.
Mothers sacrifice and prefer to be sick
than have sick children. This exists, yes,
but the universe became twisted long ago.

36
Man twisted up Nature long ago.
Because man conceives of Nature as if it
were a table that can be straightened
by filing down one of its legs.
But the landscape isn't something
that can be corrected by well-equipped
citizens, the landscape is that which corrects you.
It's the Earth that eats you, and not
the other way around.

37
And cities are twisted, says someone other than Bloom,
because in men all organs are condensed into
a single function: to compete.
Machines execute the physical part
of an order previously given: dominate a day
the way a tree is dominated when the direction
of the growth of its branches has been imposed upon it.
But a day isn't a substance that can be controlled.

38
A day cannot be surrounded like an army,
as big as that army may be,
because a day is always larger than an army,
as big as that army may be.
(Time has always been a space,
just one of unbelievable dimensions.
So large that no human can
be the owner of it.
There will be a lock for each moment, it's just that you'll never
have the key.)

39
Of course cities are, after all,
a temporary organization of kindness.
Collectively, men love each other, or rather:
they negotiate. Individually, sure, the worst sort of displeasures
arise. I've seen many men in my family
humble themselves, said Bloom,
for a mere handful of dollars; reality
is something that can be bought. But it isn't cheap.

40
In centuries past, men cut off
their own noses and other parts of the face
just to better serve the power of others.
You may praise their dedication and sacrifice,
but, the most sensible thing, by far, as everyone knows and says,
is never to lose face.
Fortunately, clouds exist, of course.

41
Metropolises are, at bottom, large houses
in which the windows are there for you to insult
others—friendship is impossible
in large agglomerations.
Even among tiny animals like flies
or ants it isn't easy to detect, in a city,
behavior that bears the seal of comradeship.

42
(Ants, for example,
being deaf-mute animals,
have feet toward the front available
for dialogue, but that fact precludes them
from conversing while they're crawling
—a pleasure that is unique to the human species.)

43
There are, besides, among humans,
those who are most familiar with their pockets
and those who are most familiar with their hands.
When it comes to clothing, pockets are the parts that hold onto things

and have a memory,
and the hands, when it comes to the body, are the parts that have the greatest tendency
to turn the knobs on doors. They are, therefore, different,
but it's best not to explain it.

44
It's obvious that my father had many adversaries,
but at that time his enemies were almost artisanal;
they felt the temptation to gather together in the same place
so that the bomb that fell on them
wouldn't favor anyone in particular.

45
My father, John Bloom, was a man of faith.
And an early riser.
He said that the human organism is an unfinished work
until it finds the perfect woman to accompany it.
Up to this point, all well and good.
He also said that in the morning the body is more
unfinished than it is at night. Or rather, in the morning it had more will to forge ahead.
Look at things that are finished, he would say to me.
The next day they're still in the same place.

46
But my father also prayed.
(The abrupt acceleration of the heart,
when the result of a sacred vision,
isn't considered a cardiac disease, have you ever noticed that?)
So my father fought for his inheritance
against a complex system that combined ballistics

and religious belief.
He was a muscularly courageous man,
and he had lawyers.

47
Among the threats he made and received,
some—due to the poor workings of the transportation system
in that era—
arrived several days late
—a fact that often made
those threats out of date.
After all, they didn't want to tear off his skin,
just tear out an internal organ or two; stuff like that.

48
However, despite the weak communication system,
the hatred grew. If even in the time of the Romans
there were entire armies that couldn't get along with each other,
how much more so in recent times?
The thing is that hatred doesn't need any great technological
support:
all you need are two women for one man, or two men
for a single territory.

49
At heart, the lowest common denominator of enmity
is two living beings,
and all the rest is naïveté and useless feelings.
My father won the inheritance,
and he and his became such enemies
that they even got into physical conflict.
A conflict so bloody

that it almost seemed legal,
as my father, John Bloom, used to say.

50
An observation:
many are shocked at the occurrence of love
between living beings of very different ages,
and no one marvels at the much greater age
difference that hatred can bridge;

51
a six-year-old child can hate a plump seventy-three-year-old aunt
who, every time she comes to have tea at his parents' house,
squeezes the child as if,
instead of occupying the volume he occupies,
he occupied half of it. Hatred bridges larger generation gaps
than love does—and thus it always was.

52
Other, even more distant family members
—these ones indeed—wanted to abolish, definitively,
my illustrious father's health.
And so, like a good Bloom with a sense of self-worth,
my father dealt them such blows
that they were left stupefied, like imbeciles.
It's after a good thrashing that a citizen realizes
that he is, after all, a mammal,
and my father, in a matter of minutes, transported these men
from their wardrobes
to the corrals of animals of lesser cleanliness.

53
This nearly familial beat-down session would have gone down
in History if the country were made up of two or three rooms
in an apartment on the outskirts of town.
But no.
It was an ephemeral event with little publicity,
even though John Bloom, my father, spent three days
sitting on the couch, laughing.

54
My family, as you can see, is a hard one, said Bloom to the
Parisian,
who was still listening to him, but, aside from beating people up
with some regularity, we also
paint paintings. During those three days after the brawl, he
continued,
my father, John Bloom, painted an abstract piece
that combined flaws of consistency
with a lack of technical ability, but it's true that this canvas

55
was very successful in the city's galleries.
The important thing, at bottom, is the symbolism of things
and, of course, the money.
It's true that my father won the legal
battle—his lawyers were so perfect
that they seemed to be handmade.

56
All the lands and
buildings that had belonged to my grandparents
were thus left to my father.

It might come under criticism,
but materialism is, at heart,
what feeds us.
Without it, nothingness would occupy all space.

57
My father wouldn't rest
until he had bought buildings new and old,
land for agriculture and industry,
complex machinery, various automobiles, the yellowest of golds,
jewelry, servants that were ugly and others who were just so-so,
easy and semi-easy women,
the general respect of nearby living beings, the courtesy
and subservience of half the city. Everything was
bought, and swiftly.
(The hardest things to acquire
were, by far, the properties.)

58
The greatest part of the inheritance he'd won was
an enormous house in Lisbon.
A house that could give shelter
to the inhabitants of an entire village.
Human anatomy,
if you'll allow me to note here, dear Jean M,
is merely a suitcase

59
significant emblems are transported in.
The body is a coin that has gone out of circulation,
a coin that even myopic antiquarians wouldn't care about.
The bodies of the elderly, when they're poor,

are as important as the proper pronunciation of Latin
in the big business deals of London.

60
Lisbon, let me tell you, dear Jean M,
is a cluster of houses
with an up-to-date law of gravity,
a fact that merits our attention, given that the laws
of physics, even when they're eternal
and respected throughout space,
remain subject to periodical inspections
by Nature.
Take earthquakes, for example.

61
But I'm off-topic here. Let's get back to my father.
Well, then: avoiding at all cost meditation
and other profound forms
of practicing laziness, my father,
working arduously, and with the help of God
and others, began to acquire
properties across the entire country.

62
All rich people are at risk of becoming
even more rich (it's like an epidemic),
and this epidemic isn't a threat to the poor because
regarding the poor it isn't fitting to use the expression
"even more." And since the poor

63
are, as everyone knows,
morally much better equipped
than millionaires, they don't want to become even more rich,
they merely want to become rich, at any cost,
stepping on anyone who gets
in their way. Poor people aren't virtuous, my father used to
grumble,
it's just that they have less money for doing evil.

64
In many cities,
my father, John Bloom, made a fortune
and, at the same time, unmade marriages.
Making and unmaking: the two most perfectly parallel lines
of the human species. They never intersect.

65
The world doesn't have carpeting, don't believe that it does, my
dear friend,
not even in Paris does the real world have carpeting.
The world has wood,
and wood has obvious flaws, sharp splinters,
and whosoever walks upon it won't get off it without injury.
(which can also be said of the world).
The World wasn't made to be walked upon barefoot.

66
With just sixty banknotes, my father started
his fortune. Success progresses on the shoulders
of previous successes, it was always thus. Only those who have
already progressed

will continue to progress, which might seem unjust.
For the army as well as the businessman,
the world is something that is vulnerable to their actions:
everything
can be conquered.

67
Everything falls to the earth quite urgently, but everything
takes its time to get up or fly—the world hasn't
balanced out these two directions. As if there were
a perfect, ancient style of falling and a novel development
in movement (which doesn't work yet) in taking flight.
Even in that which doesn't move: the most ancient things
don't even make the effort to breath.

68
But let me tell you, dear Jean M,
if God exists, he has such
French, linen-napkin manners
that none of His actions
are ever visible here below
—such is His politeness.
But if someone has power,
what's the point of being polite?

69
Out in the open air it's more difficult for us to forget God,
but, actually, power and politeness
are only found together in those who have time,
in immortals.
For us, wretched humans, amid all the hurry and hopelessness
we sometimes rest—and that's it.

70
It's clear that my father, John,
also had his setbacks.
Only those who cease to fight after a victory
win every time, that's a fact. The stars,
though they seem to be constant, forge ahead.
At every moment the day is modifying the light that infiltrates
into things.

71
My father lost fortunes as he tried to gain
even more, which shows that one's will
and its practical consequences
don't also have a friendly relationship.
When our Destiny isn't working
(like a motor), it's best to invent
a new machine or a new belief.

72
Note that the most upright solid can dissolve
all at once or evaporate. Time was, only Nature
could do such a thing; now we also have technology.
It's an ancient fact—solids have always dissolved into air, as an
old man used to say—
and nowadays that occurrence has two possible origins—and
that's that.

73
No one is capable of chaining oneself to a successful day
the way you chain a dog to a post.
Days are, in general, moving,
a car that won't stop.

The most ancient, yet most perfected motor: nature.
There is evidence of beauty, for example, that should be perceived:
the beautiful woman covers up the sight of some small filthiness
that is gaining strength somewhere else. That's what good days
are.

74
But my father learned his lesson. He paid incredibly high interest
on a bad investment, but he crawled his way back
to the chair with a will to pick himself up again.
Defeats should occur
while we're young and strong, for at that point failures
give us strength, while later in life they can make us weak.
A defeat at the right time is something that
will make you victorious at the right time. And these
can be two separate times or one. It seems to me.

75
The level of intensity with which one is crushed doesn't matter,
what actually matters is the intensity that we retain
after being crushed.
Reality isn't a physical thing,
but rather a premonition that surrounds us,
nausea—or sometimes, rarely,
a certain happy surprise.

76
For example, Jean M, take note: the footsteps along a pathway
can be feminine, but the highway itself cannot.
Nature is a transversal thing, every landscape
is reproduced, day after day, without any ruckus.
If Nature has two sides, they circulate

and intermix among themselves, just as its goods do,
internally, without any show.
On the outside, Nature is homogenous.
But man is not.

77
There is a chasm between the highest part
of the head of man and the sky; and in the mines
where they search for the riches that have fallen down there,
another ancient embarrassment becomes obvious: the
disconnection
between the feet of man
and what is down there below: the center of the Earth.
Some measly thing that exists between the sky and the center
of the Earth:
thus is man.

78
But, of course, man flies and, on top of that,
has an imagination.
Man isn't contained in the space between his hat
and boots,
as old Whitman once said—you know him, Jean M?—
Man, fortunately, isn't always concrete and material.
Even the most imbecilic and uncouth person
is still a substance with promise.

79
Occurrences occur to families under the heavens
(there's no other kind). My family, the Bloom family, for example,
was always combative at the right times and mystical only
when there was time for such a thing. Taking action is a
prolonged process

that begins when we learn to walk
and only ends when we die
or when we no longer have enemies. Metaphysics, on the other hand,
can be put off until the weekend, as many
religions have already realized.

80
Sundays are also the days when Nature, as a whole,
draws near to us. Even birds seem to know
the schedule, for they sing different songs.
My father, John Bloom, among other decisions,
decided to forbid himself from having Sundays,
because he said those were the days when humans
acted the least humanly—
and, furthermore, they did very little scientific research on that day.
If progress depended on Sundays,
we'd still be riding around in horse-drawn wagons and speaking Latin.

81
For that reason, Sundays were, for him, days
on which humans took a break from their humanity,
even while remaining extremely polite.
(You tip your hat more
on Sunday than on all the other days combined.)
A Bloom was supposed to be an enemy of those
holy, stagnant days: stagnant because they were holy,
and holy because they were stagnant. Blooms are people
who blow right past tradition;
and thus, slightly diabolical.

82
The only ones who don't escape from great tragedies
are those from whom, before fleeing themselves, life has already
fled,
wrote Camões in the sixteenth century.
My father, John, further noted that
the only way a Bloom doesn't make progress is if
death first makes progress upon him.

83
It's as if the Bloom family had been pushed
to the front
and that first thrust forward hadn't yet worn off.
I'm the son of that initial thrust. And of that
I'm proud.
However, old age exists and perhaps
it's an invention of a younger generation that is not yet born.

84
Every generation is selfish,
without a doubt. Because if the days
got stuck on a specific generation
—like an ungreased cog that won't turn—
we would have before us a magnificent eternal race of people.
Which would make some very content and would be bothersome to others:
those who haven't been born yet.

85
The body of my father, John Bloom,
was, thus, conquered by an old man,
without him even noticing; a very slow conquest, day by day,

a conquest that's the opposite of the great tumultuous battles
where catapults and bombs dropped from airplanes
attempt to demolish the caste or the hidden bunker.
A slow and subtle bomb, old age,
the most primitive war that Nature
has declared on us.

86
Take note, for example, dear Jean M,
that there are no culturally-aware cells
—nature is an absolutely stupid
thing. A waterfall, for example,
or even the water that comes out of the faucet
—that useful combination of wild landscape
and comfort—both one and the other are, take note, after all,
stupid; and intellectually banal.

87
Water is common ground
for any self-respecting cultured person.
But Nature isn't our kitchen,
where we prepare feasts for illustrious
invited guests. Nature is what
is called in statistics: an independent variable.

88
But the essential thing is this:
a flower shrugs its shoulders
whether it is smelled by a pretty six-year-old
girl or by absolute ugliness.
For the beautiful flower, beauty is meaningless.

89
Man should return to the forest, dear Jean M.
Knowing the way back is knowing
what you're going to do next. And a man
shouldn't know what he's going to do next. At least not a Bloom.
Me, for example.

90
Letting the generations successively
clean the same filthy table
that one generation leaves for the next.
A Bloom, on the other hand, should eat his breakfast alone.
And a locked-up house should be, for a Bloom,
seen as an enemy. Wouldn't you say, Jean M?

91
I'm speaking of Lisbon, me, Bloom.
If you want to get a taste of a country, don't head toward
the luxurious palace
built in the middle of the city. Take
uncomfortable public transport
toward the outskirts. That's my advice. But who am I
to suggest you take public transport?

92
You can get a better smell of a country
in the toilets of run-down establishments,
where six unpleasant men piss
in parallel, vigilant manner,
than from the perfumes wafting in the city center.
But you probably already knew that; Paris is no different.
It's a city. The center is nice, the outskirts are worse;
but the center is always the place we're in.

93
May the children of others be courageous
in the face of bullets and may our children
be courageous in business strategies.
Thus is courage and its respective
Specializations.

94
At any rate, loving your own children more than those of others
isn't exactly an unusual fact,
it's the obvious nature of feelings.
What's strange is someone finding that difference in affection
to be strange.
Do I love those who are near me, or do I separate myself from
that which I hate?
—that is the question.

95
My powerful ancestors, for example,
were not loving
and vice versa (those who were loving were not powerful).
Among the various Blooms,
some have a good name in general History books,
and others have a good name among their own children.

96
Let's not speak, then, of wars
or general conflicts between these outsized landowners
we call countries. Let's speak of laws and tranquility,
and of university education
where science is a thing that students
can learn sitting down.

97
Which, it's said, might be a mistake.
Neither science nor the world
can be learned
with one's head bent
over a desk. Wouldn't you say, Jean M?
(Ah, but I'm such a fake: I like reading much more
than climbing mountains.)

98
But I'm telling you all this, dear Jean M,
because my father wanted to add culture
to my language.
Culture, which is nothing more than the way
to understand that hell
didn't exactly start today:
even in Latin they already knew about that evil dwelling place
of the devil.

99
And I remember yet another lesson from my father.
Beware the scoundrels, he used to say, and beware the men
who speak meekly; in the excess of fragility
shown, there is a plan for some evil, at least that's what I
understood.
Keep watch over men, dear Bloom, my father would say to me,
someone will lean over your tombstone
to gather roses for his own vase.

100
Nothing kills from as far away as a man does,
and you may say that this fact proves

only his superior aim or technology,
but it also proves the strategy of the species.
You cannot love from that great a distance, for instance.

101
The human condition is absurdly stingy.
Animals—a horse, for example—fail when they slip and fall
(the logic of their fast feet is a swiftness
that does not fall); for men of war, on the contrary,
failure is to fail when taking aim to shoot the enemy
(and a massacre seen from a distance merely looks like
a masterful game of chess).

102
Other women arose in the story of the Bloom family
—misfortunes seem only to grow larger
when the feminine element enters in (ever noticed?).
Before news gets back to the mothers
nothing truly historic exists.
The sadness of women seems to select
the events. (But what do I know of History
or sadness?)

103
My father was always touched
when he received a request for help from someone in the family.
Female family members would ask him for money,
and he'd give it to them, the fool.

104
When we're children, parents and close family members
tune the world the way one tunes a delicate instrument—

so that a city of excessive noise
sounds pleasant to our childish ears. But
the city is an instrument that's impossible to tune
for more than a few hours. The world exists
and it isn't filial, much less paternal.

105
Afflictions interrupt. It was always thus.
In certain eras, colossal illnesses fell
upon that species that doesn't grow taller than a meter and eighty centimeters.
However, at other times, the multiplication of misery
doesn't seem to work.
In a time of peace, for example, multitudes gather
to attend musical concerts.

106
On the back of a horse
certain men increase their stature,
while others decrease it. Ever noticed, Jean M?
When a man is atop a horse, one understands
what that man truly is.
On the ground, any old human
can feign noble deportment.

107
But what is this thing that,
penetrated by a blade, bleeds?
The body isn't just something
that captures oxygen from the air.
It isn't only that, for sure, but it also is that.
One can still be happy and have beliefs.

108
A strong economy and a weak sword.
And that much is clear: there are more enemies
in times of peace than times of war.
In times of peace, each army
takes on a familial dimension, for example,
seven elements (in the case of a couple
with five children), and all the rest are enemies.
By my account, anyway;
what can I do?—I lost my innocence long ago.

109
The good public image that the heart has is owed, in large part,
to its effective hiding place. You know this better
than me, Jean M. Other people
are merely those who look at us.
Keeping guard or seducing. All the rest is blindness.

110
The legislation of a country is a peace treaty
between its inhabitants,
but the hatred between men is much more stable
than the laws that men establish.
Because hatred is a law of nature.

111
And this is because Nature isn't sensible
in the least. Blood pooling into a "savage lake"
becomes a public liquid. And when blood
is a public liquid, it's because times are unpleasant:
in the midst of men there is fear
and the fear reproduces like rabbits.

112
Fear, in this century, is no longer an artisanal product.
Bomber planes
—or, in peacetime, unanticipated financial collapse—
impress us with their technologies put into action.
Today, people go hungry in a much more modern manner
than in the eighteenth century, for example.

113
In the current century, one goes hungry right in front
of certain expensive foods, while in centuries
past, one went hungry in the face of less sophisticated
cuisines.
At bottom, there is a group of miserable wretches
for whom the extraordinary development of cookery
hasn't had any practical effect.

114
Life is this: the moon is closer
to certain men who are training to become astronauts
than a plate of hot food is to the mouths of other men.
It's that which we could call: relative
distances. For my part, I'm not complaining.
A full stomach, good legs, a good head.

115
And of course the amount of tea depends on the teacup,
or rather, problems are appraisal
events for every human being
—nothing happens without them.
Take the transportation problem in big cities:
sometimes it seems like the Americans will get to the moon again
before we get home.

But, at heart, it's this:
each person is chosen by his or her own worries.

116
But let's get back to my family
where love stories abound.
A woman grew famous among us,
born of parents not at all respected by the more persnickety of
the Blooms
and loved very, very much by me.
Her name was Mary. She was murdered.

117
Passions, exaggerated or not, should
be protected like certain animals
on the brink of extinction. The thing is that love became lifeless
after certain peoples mistreated it, in organized fashion,
groups of people
who spoke a different language and remembered a different past.
Men are not living beings who especially
deserve love. However, love exists.

118
Mary, aside from being a tranquil person, utilized her memory,
not to remember useless facts,
but to remember me when we were apart;
Bloom, the man who loved her.
Mary was a beautiful woman, but sight deceives us,
it seems eternal, and it is not.
And maybe I'm overstating it—who knows?—
and Mary wasn't all that extraordinary.

119
But it's certain that Bloom
—allow me to speak about myself as if I were someone else—
Bloom was, in those days, unilateral, and his only side
was this one: the side turned toward Mary.

120
A man in love is an excess
of concentration
—like a ship whose cargo was
placed on one side only.
However, ships with one obsessive side are going to sink.

121
Life presupposes two feet, two legs,
two eyes, two arms, and even the brain
has two parts: a right and a left.
Only love, when it's strong, lacks
a left and a right side. It's a centralized feeling;
every quotidian, or extraordinary, occurrence
seems to occur in its environs.

122
But it's like this: allow me to tell a story.
The father, angry with his son's romantic choice
—a poor woman in the Bloom family for the first time—
decided to contract three criminals,
specialized in killing women
named Mary.

123
It appears that my father might have hesitated,
for a few seconds, but bad influences
can be decisive in actions like this one, and irreversible.
She would have begged, would have tried to arouse
feelings of mercy. But no. It was the most shameful
death ever to occur in the
many generations of Blooms.

124
And that's it, said Bloom.
You'll start to realize now the reason that I am on a voyage
and what it is I'm searching for:
I'm searching for a woman because I want to forget
a different one.
I loved a woman named Mary,
said Bloom to Jean M, the Parisian,
and my own father had her killed.
That's my story. Synthesis, synthesis. And that's it.

125
Men and their industries pollute rivers,
the sea, and the air, which already grows dark above the cities
and the earth, the mountains, and the large forest.
Of the four ancient elements—I'm not sure if you've noticed—
man is only incapable of polluting fire.
Fire must hold some mystery, undoubtedly.

126
They aren't symmetrical structures, the heart
and the brain.
The perfect control over a theorem and its consequences

is so often accompanied by cruelty that such a thing
is no longer shocking. But what is this world
if, in it, a woman who loves and is loved is not protected
by nature?

127
Perhaps lions and tigers are, ultimately,
holier than entire congregations
praying in church. In fact
the sky is incompatible with mud.
One is lofty and manifest, the other is deceitful.
The sky makes you lift your head; mud dirties your feet.
We're here below, does anyone doubt it? You, Jean M?

128
There are men who use repentance
the way you use a carpentry technique
on pieces of wood. But feelings
are useless in the world we have, where only
actions are recorded. Repentance,
when it is a slight twist of the heart, is an intimate, internal
action;
therefore, it's nothing.

129
Did my father, John Bloom, repent?
What do I know of things that can't be seen?
What's certain is that three men
killed a woman whom I felt to be
inseparable from the days.
All else is intimate and nothing.

130
A beautiful woman named Mary was killed.
All humans are incomplete,
but seeing her made them whole.
(As if having eyes were a much better thing
than had always been assumed
—that's what was said.)

131
We all espy nausea
through the crack in the open door. We know
that the sun doesn't clean a dirty table.
However, the sun does strengthen a wooden table
with nothing on it. Because the sun
likes pure objects,
and so does wind.
And even the dust first settles down
upon that which is clean.

132
Mary died and Bloom loved her,
dear Jean M.
The world is thus: we're in combat. We attack, we defend.
Millennia ago, in certain locales,
flowers were the first evidence of the factories to come.
I see this and take note: from the garden
wafts smoke that does not smell of tenderness.

133
And there is no subtle vengeance. Vengeance
is an intense thing, or else it doesn't exist.
Rancor has no middle,

if you are in it, you're always right at the edge,
at the farthest point, which forces you to disregard
all actions that are not malicious.

134
Bloom ordered the men who murdered Mary to be killed, dear Jean M.
The tradition continues: men suffer—
one after the other.
No cause becomes separated from its effect,
no effect forgets its cause.

135
The smell of a flower can be intercepted between the flower
and the sky. And that's where the smell is strongest.
Within the flower, right inside it, it is still a potential;
and in the sky, if it arrives there, it's already an abstract element.
But there are a few seconds of existence along this intermediary path.
You must, therefore, be attentive. Because it's worth it.

136
But what am I talking about? Men follow in succession, Jean M:
sons of hard men
are tender, and skinflints produce generous offspring.
Men follow in succession and procreate,
and genetics are, in part, a game
—something that can turn out well
or very badly.

137
It's true "that a base love weakens the strong"
but also that a grand love can make the grand ridiculous,
for love is, in terms of material energy in the world,
a theft—despite it being, in terms of sensations, magnificent.
Love may be internally useful,
but externally it can't haul a single brick.
I've never doubted this.

138
Life, it's clear, may not be an exceptionally propitious place for the passions.
In human countries, love is often mixed
with equivocal words.
Fire within a hearth, for example,
is a servile, cultured, well-mannered fire.
Red, yet mild,
and it obeys us.
It only becomes nature—that fire in the hearth—
when, taking its vengeance, it causes a conflagration.
And that's how love works. But the opposite is preferable.

139
It is a breakdown of strategies and plans,
a rhythm surprise, an glorified illegality that doesn't harm
the neighbors.
But pay attention here, once again: love is not beneficial for countries,
it doesn't help develop its industries or economy.
I've never doubted this. And that's why it's preferable not to.

140
Nevertheless, what country can prohibit love's
entry? It isn't a commercial good trafficked in boxes,
for boxes are objects that open in the middle
—and it's possible, with a flashlight,
to look down inside.

141
Love cannot be seen as
if it were a physical presence.
It is much too complete
to have a shape. And since they'll never
be able to collect tariffs on something
that doesn't occupy space, it's preferable not to,
it seems to me.

142
Those who make mistakes from loving overmuch should be forgiven.
Overmuch did Bloom love Mary, a beautiful woman
who was killed. But Bloom left his city
and forges ahead.

143
In part, he has forgotten; in part, he still remembers. Along the way,
he beat up men and fornicated with women. He is now in Paris,
and his fate is unknown to him:
after being robbed of the person who promised to usher in his best days,
what's there to be afraid of? Bloom is in Paris
and has nothing, save for an absence of fear,
which is a wondrous possession, indeed, but also a danger.

CANTO IV

1
But all humans belong to the Earth
the way that joy belongs to humans. A man
cannot remain in sadness
like someone buried alive. The sun exists and it isn't monstrous.
Tragic occurrences are animals that, at times,
eat half our joy,

2
but every morning a body is inaugurated;
a single period of sleep could be a century,
one night is enough for a change in habits and language,
and slumber can even be powerful enough to modify
your memory: go to sleep, then.
God is not an island. With a feminine touch, He
will mend your amorous fabric. Hold on, Bloom.
(And that's what he did, that good little Bloom.)

3
Like a wooden stake that marks
an important boundary, lucidity is a
quality that governs movement. And
Bloom is a lucid man. Coming from a turbulent
family, a mix of strong men
who make others sweat and weak men who sweat,
and intimately acquainted with noteworthy births as well as others
that gave way to rough childhoods, Bloom
likes to think, every morning, that there is another possible day
in front of him. He could climb a tree
or dig a grave.

4
And Bloom has a memory and hasn't lost it.
He had dishonest family members, old friends
whom he was now repulsed by,
enemies whom he recalls with pleasure.
He had friends and enemies. He remembers painful
affairs among perfect couples.
And he remembers Mary.

5
He remembers his father, whom he so admired,
and the way that he seemed to hold up half the world,
a father who had been so perfect in his childhood
that he remembered him in those days the way one remembers
a woman.
Further still, he remembered seeing naked men
dragged through the streets, rail-thin, abused,
much more mortal than all other men.
And he remembers Mary.

6
He remembers the History books full of Roman generals
who killed their enemies to feed them
to birds and dogs,
as if a dog were closer to a man
than a man is to his enemy.
He also remembers that the photographs of his father's
adversaries were on the same desk as the photographs
of his loved ones and remembers that the maid
cleaned the same dust from them all.

7
He remembers the hatreds that, within the family,
seemed to be the key to their collective energy.
He remembers the snouts of men and women he spied upon
in their debaucheries, and the sanctified manner in which their various fingers
greeted each other the next day
and crossed themselves in sincere public prayer.
And he still remembers Mary.

8
He remembers men possessed of knowledge
and haughty libraries,
who, in the moments following a tragedy,
became genuine—then soon after
resumed their customary manner.
He remembers seeing a large animal
have its throat slit one afternoon. And he remembers Mary.

9
He remembers illiterate farmhands
with brutish arms and misshapen paunches and male bosoms,
and he remembers at times having deluded himself
with the hope that among simple people there existed some other sort of actions;
but among these he saw only a different cuisine, rudimentary weapons,
a wooden table with more termites.
Nothing new, therefore, even among the poor.

10
And Bloom remembers the way
that poor women repeated useless maxims,
trying to pronounce the difficult words
exactly as they had heard them
on TV.
And how they failed, and how they tried again
and how they failed again.
And how, above all else, they didn't understand much of anything at all.

11
In what way, Bloom is now thinking,
looking at the ground around his feet,
does optimism make the best use of space?
As if a square meter could ultimately be,
under the feet of a hopeful animal, one hundred square
meters of possible implementation
of a second world,
one hundred square meters of some second way
for the animal to launch itself at existence.

12
Space depends on algebraic calculations, of course,
but also on the way in which one looks outside of it from the inside.
Not merely, then, quantities
—length and width—
but also the potential leap
that exists inside the motionless animal,
the optical grandeur that exists in the motionless animal
and another element besides: patience,

13
this capacity for waiting
that will make something large out of the smallest thing
because it's always been known that nothing will remain as it now is.
And that's precisely what even the shape of the terrestrial globe teaches us:
everything advances toward the other side; for only thus does a day
return again to the same place where we are now.

14
In what way does optimism make the best use
of space?—that's one question among many.
Hopelessness sees, in the square meter where it resides,
the square meter at its disposal;
those with optimistic eyes see, from the square meter where they reside,
the rest of the world, the vast
world.

15
It's because I am atop very little ground
that I can advance, thinks Bloom,
and it's because I am atop a lot of ground
that I find myself forced to defend it.
Thus is the world of the larger empires and those found wanting,
the structure of invasions,
the different ways for the human to come out of sleep
and into action;
thus, ultimately, what separates defense from attack.
As in a soccer match: the one who attacks is he who has perceived that
he, or the game that he is playing, are not immortal.

16
And contemporary men no longer want to know
about major achievements. A writer from this century
is a thousand times more preoccupied
with the search for the right adjective for a tiny sentence
than with the question of pronouncing correctly or incorrectly
the beautiful name of the king.
Ancient names are thus less important
than modern adjectives—that is History
in language.

17
The issue with days is also this: what part of the day
is the top, and what part is the bottom,
if it all looks similar and repeats?
At any rate, Bloom had always thought
that in a world where music existed
beggars should not exist.

18
But exist they do. And music carries on,
utterly calm and gorgeous.
(Wise men have forgotten everything and from the top
of a tower they just look straight ahead.)
However, Bloom has a radio, indeed, look at it: what a beauti-
ful radio!
But nothing comes out, there's no music, it doesn't work.
It was his father's radio. It never worked. And now
it's in his pocket.

19
A family's inheritance should provoke in the heir
astonishment and wonder. It's good
to be ignorant of the past with a certain amount of precision
—however, that's difficult, because to be precisely ignorant
is a combination of amnesia and perfect aim,
a combination of a rectangular garden and a catastrophe.

20
Losing a life in the army isn't a big deal
for a general sitting in his chair
in front of a map of the advances and retreats of a language
and culture.
But for the dead soldier it's the maximum
that he can receive from the World.
A general who gives orders to advance
does not know death as well
as the general who gives orders to retreat.
Isn't that right? Yes, replies Bloom.

21
Courage isn't a test
of valor. Courage
is a sudden clarity that comes from hell
or the heavens.
Courage that saves comes from that azure,
courage that kills from that very inferno.

22
Remember well, Bloom, that certain failures
were, for some of your kin,
a swift education in courage.

But for others there was always confusion
about those two asymmetrical concepts: to fail and to come to
an end.
An excellent failure produces countless ways
for a man to get back up.

23
Men gather together as if there were
an abundance of them, and together charge forward
to ratify some law in parliament
or a war between the planes
in the air and the fragile animals in a country without an air
force.
Even wars have been won by good
manners: they are voted for in meetings where someone's
lack of a necktie is an issue never to be forgotten.

24
Wars are carried out by airplanes that don't understand
the importance of knowing how to spell Pythagoras's
name.
Technology has emerged abruptly,
as if it were only the last volume
of an encyclopedia; but it isn't.
Technology is stupid; but it is a lucky charm.
(What about his dad's radio! How Bloom would love to fix it,
to bring it back to life.
I have a whole voyage for that, thinks Bloom, a voyage to India.)

25
The issue is that countries no longer
care whether or not they are creating poets.

And even the factories themselves cannot tolerate waste:
all materials must be put to use,
the way a skillful prostitute makes use of all nooks and crannies
of her body. Countries have lost their style,
and gained stockholders.

26
And it's the women who suffer.
The mothers, the sisters, the beautiful wife, now alone,
who hung her affections on the line like clothes,
hoping they would dry. Fewer women die
at war, but they suffer more.
(Death isn't an event that is proportional to sorrow,
one and the other are both independent, selfish variables.)

27
A woman is certainly an uncommon
human element: the only reason houses don't grow old is because
she exists.
The feminine touch supports the structure
(same as concrete does). The only reason houses
don't collapse is because there is some loveliness therein.
But as for war: August, for example
is a good month to start one.

28
Precisely: in Winter explosions hurt more
and have greater effect due to the temperature difference
between nature
and the ultra-heated ersatz daggers of the explosion.
The same phenomenon that takes place in the hearths of
pleasant families:
the colder it is, the more fire you need.

29
At any rate, a calamity that's mobilized in the direction
of tranquility teaches very little, no one learns anything.
Instead of that, thinks Bloom, one should favor, for example,
dangerous culture: a book read on the precipice of a great fall.
Or else, a sort of exercise: reciting a poem while
falling.
Besides, the first alternative doesn't exist: a calamity
never calms things down. Bloom knows that well.
We are born and faced with these occurrences,
without the possibility of saying anything more.

30
And how is it possible for the soldier not to be filled with the vanity
that prevents him from, at least, dying
in the middle of a war?
What happens to the man?
Who teaches him that impure math
of one being nothing more than the smallest part of a country,
when one could, after all, be the man who proceeds firmly
toward downtown?
(Ah, Jean M, excellent, those are your ethics. Bloom tips his hat to him.
Continue, please. You're making my stomach turn.)

31
Because a man isn't merely
a part of a whole.
(Yes! Bravo!)
The enormous Atlantic Ocean, indeed,
is a part of the happy fisherman

in his small boat. And that's just
one example—and Jean M, when giving an example
goes like this with his hands. Like this.

32
What is a cowardly country made of?
Bloom replies: it's made up of many courageous
men. (Sensible reply.)
That's right, my dear man, don't be fooled.
A courageous country is made up living inhabitants
that are treated well, well-fed,
capable of imagining the unusual
in the language their parents used. (Bravo!)

33
The language of a country doesn't expand
with territorial gains, as is evident.
(It's Bloom who is taking the floor now.)
If the army conquers a building and in it,
from that moment on, only speaks in the language of their
homeland,
don't imagine that the language becomes richer for it.
Language isn't a landlord that adds up the square meters
and pants in satisfaction. Language grows

34
when someone writes or says something
that carries with it a slight corruption of the norms, says Jean M.
Language grows from precise errors,
not with better outlines on a map.
Language is more enriched
in certain garrets, six square meters in size,

through fundamental toil with the words,
than on the great battlefields or in sudden,
clamorous invasions.

35
Besides, language doesn't get on well in noisy, smoke-filled environments
—as in certain dimly-lit cafés, and in war.
On the metal of a bullet we could write
a lovely poem about the happiness of a family
at the moment of the birth of their first child, because the two matters
get mixed together a lot, thus it always was.
However there are two worlds in the world:
one where people are tranquil and happy,
and another where there is collective unease
and individual unhappiness.
And these two worlds are not confusable.

36
And even the most demonstrative romantics
can't manage to believe that a bullet,
with a poem written on it,
could take flight like a bird and break into song.
Coffins exist because they are required,
and in wartime the high number of orders transforms
the earth itself into a natural coffin.
Florists would shut down their shops
if all bodies were buried beneath backyard gardens.

37
Strong men incite weak men—
it was always thus, dear Jean M;
the speed at which courage is spent
is unequal between one citizen and another
—and there's not science that explains this
phenomenon. And there's also this:
training in the unforeseen. You can't teach
something that is unpredictable, which is great.

38
Examples are given by the man who acts;
a verbalized example, even a magnificent one,
is always an act of cowardice. Strong men don't
demonstrate their strength by expounding a lengthy
theory on the blackboard. Life is noteworthy and detailed,
but it doesn't allow for explanations. (And I know this well, says Bloom.)

39
And when a life is true, only will matters.
A shove is only movement for the one doing the shoving,
not the one being shoved.
There is no one standing over the head of a
courageous man, and even if he climbed a stepladder
he couldn't get any taller. This is what it is to be courageous, said
Bloom to Jean M or Jean M to Bloom. (How could one know?)

40
What's certain is that below Bloom's exhausted eyelids,
his eyes—though they don't see—remember.
Bloom recalls old family conflicts

and tries to weigh out strange ideas:
is the number of ignorant and courageous men
more or less than the number of courageous and cultured men?

41
Does illiteracy increase bravery or not?
Might the erudite man be illiterate in terms of will?
Illiterate in the ABCs of violence?
If only this matter were that simple . . .
But no.

42
Human violence can temporarily change
the color of flowers,
giving them the reddish color that customarily announces
death, but the very next generation of vegetal elements
in the garden will have forgotten everything: and new flowers
with very feeble memories,
yet excellent colors and scents, will be born.

43
Nature not only gives the victors
the temporary joy of seeming immortal,
but also everything else: the field is left available
for building a school, a church,
a powerful factory, or even a farm
full of animals. Nature has never interfered
with the details. The First World War came and went,
then the Second, and bupkes:
nary a meaningful intervention.

44
All of the defeated detest war,
but so do the sensible victors.
There is, then, between these two groups of men,
something that, by merely existing, prevents anyone from being satisfied
and wise at the same time.
The conclusion is obvious: war was invented
by the senseless or the absentminded.

45
Either the wise and sensible don't reproduce much
or, being too pacifistic and not entering combat, they lose.
Because the world belongs to those who want to leave behind a freshly painted
body of work;
to inscribe their names on substances that are incompatible
with the vanishing nature of language. And this is an obvious error
in the handling of materials: the wise
want to write. Much more sensible are engineers.

46
The world, my dear—and let's allow the narrator to speak here—
isn't a docile blank page
that places its indolent neck
in front of Your Excellency's axe.
One example: the declarations of love
or of war carved into a tree with a pocketknife
don't make it through more than a single generation,
and for men, in comparison to trees,
generations are uncommonly swift.

47
Furthermore, a declaration of war
carved by pocketknife into a tree is ridiculous.
No one will take an army seriously
if it communicates with the enemy in this manner.
Trees are not a perfect postal system,
and their immobility should, at least,
raise doubts.
A letter and a tree are, purely in terms of function,
inimical materials.

48
Not just in Winter: the world is cold.
It's cold in every season
of the year in which men exist.
Humanity isn't a progressive drawing nearer to the gods, don't kid yourself.
Missiles and their efficient method of control
from a distance—that's one good reference.
Humanity is thus something that is perfected
through actions at a distance, from here to there,
and from there to further off still.

49
In actions of proximity, on the other hand,
progress has been practically null.
A man touches a woman with the same ineptitude
of his ancestors
from ten centuries past.
Life proceeds and is monstrous.
Bloom, or any other man,
possesses one tenth of the instinct for joy
of a well-fed cat.

50
Life is a rudimentary, primitive,
deformed object that men have never
known how to take hold of.
They still haven't even figured out which side is the top
of this strange object.
You've just feebly placed your hands on life,
and already life has forcefully laid its hands on you.

51
Dogs, cats, imbecilic chickens, all in useless
circles synchronized with marching of soldiers on holidays.
The various parts of the body that don't seem to be justified
in the organism,
a mute's throat, a pen in the hand of an illiterate
who never even learned how to draw.
The world is deformed and miserly.
It's Bloom who says this. Or else Jean M.

52
At any rate, the narrator also speaks.
(How to know who's saying what? And what does it matter?)
People take caution even in their exaggerations.
There is a precise precaution
in the relationship between one citizen and another.
The city has installed an average value between two living beings,
and the visual charts are excellent,
but life is not.
(Bloom wants to point at life, but since it's cold
he doesn't take his hands out of his pockets.)

53
Leaves fall from tall trees
more slowly than a plane falls,
from a much higher altitude, when it's crashing.
Roof tiles block out the rain and
block one's view from the inside of the house,
right in the middle of it, from going from one's shoes
up to the potent stars.
There's an enormous incompatibility
between comfort (of the domestic variety) and astronomy
—and this is man's most ancient science.

54
Ants, for example, are insignificant when it comes to any
alteration of territory.
The microscope didn't bring with it wisdom about the miniscule,
it conflates the miniscule with something that, when enlarged,
has normal dimensions;
and proceeds from there.
Life, for man, is one meter and eighty centimeters tall,
and this is his most profound
philosophy.

55
Men have been seen attempting to be courteous
with a flower in their right hand.
And other men have been seen
attempting to be courteous
with a hammer. And both methods have failed.
(Meanwhile, Bloom has a coughing fit, but it's nothing too serious.
Jean M gives him a slap on the back.)

56
Courtesy does not require exceptional
resources: the handiwork here is the hand
proper.
In less than a century no one will remember anymore
that their ancestors always exercised affection
without the aid of technology.
The world forges ahead, and metals become organized.

57
Even the tranquil night feels ambition's touch.
People are not anchors; they resist the moment
of being fixed fast to the ground. No one consents to stopping,
therefore.
At the end of one minute, the initial beauty
has lost its perfection. Men always start close to the end,
or at least very far from the beginning.
Bloom, for example, wants to go to India
and is speaking, thinking, and seeing—but in Paris.

58
Indeed, there are no fixed formulas for the mountain.
And Bloom knows man well.
For some, finding joy seems like an insult,
as if joy were nothing more than
the act of quitting. By the third step
they're asking for new shoes. Impatience
spreads quickly from infancy on.

59
Victories take place down below,
on the surface, in battle.

But, seen from above, all styles look screwy:
those beaten down seem to be in the necessary position
to be able to rise up and those who are elevated
are getting dangerously close to some boundary line in the air.
The air demarcates, parallel to the ground, an invisible line,
the infernal line; a line that cuts.
Below it, we die;
above it, we cannot pass.

60
It's obvious, says Bloom, that
many have tried what I'm now attempting:
wisdom or a woman.
However, the empire of one simple man
is no easier to control than the empire of a king.
The body has more borders
than a country. We want to find ourselves and
we get lost. And then we will have to be
found.

61
What sort of insanity is this: what is on our right side
today won't always remain on
our right side. The world is in a state of decomposition:
after a century's time, infernal noises
become children's lullabies,
and a man in love fumbles with a woman's breasts
with less dexterity than one would use to repair
a radio.
(But the radio still doesn't work. Bloom's the one grumbling here,
feeling around in his pocket.)

62
The tranquility of certain climes can become obscene;
Sicily, for instance, has a climate that forces every action
to be violent and extreme.
In Egypt, men with a thirty-nine degree fever
are called religious; the believers know nothing of medicine
and the sly sick transform their colds
and coughing fits into the effects of
mystical visions. A highly religious
and disconcerting land.

63
And no great battles have been fought
on the Red Sea. Nature already has its own
violent colors: dense green,
very popular in Spring,
and the simple blue of the sky,
very common when one raises one's head,
are not dead colors, they are active light,
matter that observes us and displays us to others.

64
The world was painted in a ferocious manner.
No one waited for the sensible
opinions of the inhabitants of a cultured city.
Nature made its presence known early on,
and intelligence and criteria regarding the utilization of colors
arrived later (like a train car itching
to get into a station that has been closed for a long time).

65
Art critics had no influence
on the color of the sky. On the ground, however,
stakes and enormous edifices are
planted. And people travel.
Members of Bloom's family had, for example, gone
to Abyssinia, fascinated with the mere name of it.
And they had died there. Dying in a place
called Abyssinia turns the life led previously
tragic.

66
And Bloom looked, in this moment, at the kind
Parisian who had been listening to him for hours on end at this point
and saw in him still, to Bloom's surprise, the eyes of someone who is listening.
I like to listen, said the Parisian. Carry on,
dear friend.
(Paris has a landscape that is favorable to memory;
each city privileges certain parts of the brain
and this Parisian, an excellent listener,
proves that Paris is a city with an inclination
toward melancholy.)

67
And so Bloom went on. It was morning, but he wasn't satisfied
with reality and continued to describe dreams and fantasies.
And since we know that dreams combine many literary styles
we can expect certain radiations, so to speak,
in the stories to come that are not very clear,
since a man asleep is closer

to astronomy than his very own
bed. For a dream, reality
is impolite intrusion.

68
Men even dream that they are fiddling with stars
and putting them in their proper places, the way one
sometimes does with a piece of furniture, when its owners are
tired of seeing it
in the same part of the house. Dreams are
to reality what an ambiguous poetic line
is to a sentence in a financial report: there is greater liberty
in the first minute of a dream than in the last
twenty years of wakefulness.

69
And the days that exist in dreams are
more liquid, fountains and seas
abound.
The state of matter is delirious, yet controlled.
There is so much water around
that the human feels nearer to fish.

70
But there are also birds
that don't need to come down to the ground
for the circulation of airplanes is so great
that these birds rest upon them
to recover their strength. In places near
airports, animals that fly
become redundant.

71
There are also old people who emerge in dreams
demonstrating a completely different sort of monotony.
Old age inspires pity the world over,
but the compassion caused in others varies
by hemisphere.
In hot climates, comforting embraces
aren't as important.

72
Other times, for example, we might think
that butterflies have been the victims of an ambush
by painters, in which each one, out of dearth of skill
or pure ill intention,
bent over a living organism arguing
over differing aesthetic concepts,
had left a splotch of their favorite color mixed together with the others.
But no. Or yes. The world is confusing,
and not only in dreams.

73
Because Bloom wanted to forget an initial tragedy
that the world had put upon him:
his own father had ordered the murder of the woman
he loved;
and, further, he wanted to forget a second tragedy
that he himself, Bloom, had put into the world
and that he only now was revealing: Bloom had murdered his own father.
Thus the urgency to leave the place
where the world had existed overmuch.
Thus: a voyage. And somewhat thus: India.

74
His father had murdered the woman that Bloom loved and
Bloom had murdered his own father.
He therefore needed to forget twice over.
And the quality of the forgetfulness needed is gargantuan
when one wants to forget the deaths of two beloved people
as well as one's own crime.

75
Nothing more difficult in the world;
for to stop feeling cold
it's not enough just to look up at the sky or a photograph
of a conflagration: Winter
keeps going and is independent of the place
toward which we direct our eyes.
Winter is cold, it has always been cold; and continues to be so now.

76
Thus is life,
but Bloom dreamed that in India
it might be different.
However, there will only be a different existence,
paradoxically,
in nonliving things, at most.
We're in the year 2003
and there's still nothing new under the sun.

77
But in Paris the fog is merely a theory
compared to the mystical life
of India. The distance between Paris and India

is that of an entire Civilization.
There's no plane that can connect these two worlds.
Bloom knew this.

78
Between Proust and the Bhagavad Gita
lies a distance that cannot be measured
in kilometers.
Though he was in Paris, Bloom dreamt of India; strange, right?
Or not so much?
Who can prevent connections in dreams?
(No one orders you around when you're unconscious,
that's great, isn't it?)

79
Between Proust and the Bhagavad Gita
there are, perhaps, more significant differences
than there are between Paris and Kolkata. Given that cities
are material, concrete things, there is less room
for inventions and lies. Literature
is at greater liberty to lie at will,
and two lies always move further away from each other
than two truths.

80
India became my obvious destination,
said Bloom to Jean M, but I immediately realized
that I couldn't just leap from one world into the other
in a matter of hours. I forced myself
to traverse a much slower path.
You should arrive exhausted at the place
where you want to grow old,

for if we arrive there in full strength still, and impatient,
we'll just take off again. And arrive at the wrong destination.

81
After the murder I committed
I was helped by two friends
who wanted to join me in my escape.
But one should always flee alone, that's
something a man who likes books
learns early on.

82
My friends helped me, continued Bloom,
first in erasing the evidence of the crime,
then in preparing for the voyage, a voyage that seemed innocent enough:
someone who departs merely in order to forget,
not to forget and also not be charged with a crime.
Thus, thanks to plenty of help,
I managed to leave Lisbon like someone who had twice suffered
and not once inflicted suffering.

83
Of course I paid for some part of the friendship received
in hard currency: the flow of capital
among men is never interrupted,
we're swindlers down to the last cent,
and from then on we're fraternal
in an almost elegant manner.
Sometimes that which is well paid almost begins
to seem instinctive.

84
Preparations were made in a fluster
devoid of the feminine element. No mother,
nor any other woman, was present for it,
I was assisted by the rougher part of humanity—the masculine
part—
which shows that such occurrences are somewhat astonishing:
you might not end up falling down if you are shoved by a person
on either side. Thus, what appears to be an act of aggression is,
ultimately,
a source of support.
However, if you're clearheaded, you'll also discern in this its
inverse:
what seems to be support is, ultimately,
two symmetrical acts of aggression.

85
It's obvious that I prepared carefully
to proceed to the other side of the world,
and even further still: to the other side of myself.
I filled my backpack with tools for light
and for thirst, maps of Europe, a bible,
a book about the soul and another about the inner workings of
cells,
as well as two books that are treasured classics; I got some money
together,
waited for the wind to die down, and took a plane to London,
my first stop.

86
But at a certain altitude it's impossible to tell precisely whether
we're

in the air between Lisbon and London
or between Lisbon and Asia. And since it would be extraordi-
narily expensive
to put up road signs thousands of meters in the air
the captain of the plane made a habit of
informing us about where we were, as if he were
a permanent autochthon whom some lost person
had asked for directions.
(Oh how I entertain myself in my head, Jean, my friend!)

87
Before my departure, however, I had prepared myself to die,
for the further away I get from the Earth,
the more I remember that I belong to it. And even with one's
shoes
tied tight, the Earth, when seen from an airplane, seems
very distant, it's almost abstract;
a theorem; a melody that ends abruptly
and disappears, a well-structured fiction.

88
But no: for men, the air is the fiction, a
temporary phenomenon—and the Earth is always the
destination.
However, even before I left, my mom appeared
on the scene, in the airport, crying.
She had lost her husband and now her son was leaving—
with a layover in London—for India,
a country that's so spiritual that women of a certain age believe
there's no ground there
(or something similar).

89
In extremely religious countries, you should watch
carefully where you put your feet,
she said to me. But not too carefully, I thought without saying,
for something coming from above
can, due to the law of gravity, lose its holiness
and acquire a malign weight.
In India, despite all that,
you still need to make an effort
to lift something heavy.

90
But let's talk seriously about maternity.
Maternity works: if we were to do an audit
of the previous century, it would be, by far, the institution
with the fewest visible defects. In times of crisis and tragedy,
it's the mothers who hand over their food
to their children.
The father, in extreme situations, eats all the family's food.
Only the mothers are, therefore, human. The other part of the city
is merely mammalian.

91
And it's only mothers who don't have general theories about the universe,
because they're always engaged in the general practice of things,
says Bloom to Jean M.
They're the only ones who place more importance on memory than the daily
newspaper. They're the only ones who are able to combine mythological tales

with refined, yet efficient, cuisine. Women are the only ones
who are able to do two important things
at the same time.
Take me, for example: I can't sing while I'm falling.

92
And men are very weak
when it comes to that aspect of human existence that is accepting one's weakness.
They only know how to be sweet, as the French poet says,
when they are sufficiently strong,
thus reducing courtesy to merely the first
part of a negotiation. And furthermore, men, even if
they never stand still, move around less than a very old woman
who can't even modify the position of her foot.
Because that woman, though still, tells stories,
and men do not. Do you understand, Jean M?

93
But I departed, says Bloom, without even raising my eyes
to meet the eyes of my mother, which were lowered,
thus showing myself to be a man until the very last moment:
I'm not even strong enough to look deeply into the weakness
of others.
Like someone who speeds up so they can't see the world,
so too did I quickly climb the stairs to board the plane,
so that I wouldn't see the person who remained below, suffering.
But I shall return, mother; and I'll return wise and clean.

94
A catastrophe can remain intact,
waiting on us: what do we know of the laboratory of the world,

if we're only the lowermost part of it?
You can't even see the future
from the top of a tower; the quality of prophesy
and the height from which one sees aren't precisely
proportional. In London, or in any other city,
you can die or fall in love.
Even the ugly cities
are unpredictable.

95
Some seek to forget, others to be remembered;
there are thousands of functions and intentions, which
rarely coincide with one another: the residents of a building
are called different names by the doorman's wife
and the poet. And the electrical structure of the doorbells
doesn't ring for them the way it customarily does for the elect:
life is vast, beautiful for some,
brutish for others, there's electricity, running water,
Autumn, and certain buildings in the city center
that are nearly perfect.

96
A rhythmic beat is unsuspicious when it occurs in the heart.
But there are other kinds.
Bloom felt, in the clothes he put on before his departure,
a movement akin to short, rhythmic starts
and realized that clothing also possesses time,
a secondary time beyond the mere material endurance
of the fabric. That clothing has a heart, and that heart can stop:
that's what Bloom realized.
(But perhaps part of the explanation was this:
his father's radio, the one that didn't work,
is right there, in his pocket.)

97
And a man doesn't know his true ambition
until he goes through a great tragedy,
a personal tragedy. You only know how to see after
you learn how to do it. And you see best in that first moment
after you wake up. To have your eyes closed is to perfect your
aim,
to prepare your black iris for the rapid
clarity that retreats from us.

98
Every generation has different curiosities,
and that's what moves them. But a generation
isn't a mineral: a particle
that foolishly waits to be observed.
It isn't composed of the same boring material
from one end to the other.
And if it possesses a single curiosity,
it also has various ways of wanting to address it.
And a man, every man, is one of these ways—
the way that fails.

99
Of course, a generation doesn't realize that its collective vanity
is evidence of great individual modesty.
A man who belongs to a generation
is someone who is insensible to the individual touch of genius.
And the genius is a stroke of luck that crosses paths with someone
at the point in their life when their head is raised the highest.
And from that point on
their good luck never leaves them. Until it does.

100
What is Bloom in search of, so far from home?
How many kilometers does a man have to traverse
before he forgets something?
Travel isn't an infallible method
for losing one's memory, it's said. Mental faculties
don't vary according to the country in which a man finds himself.
The map of the world and all its diversity
does not modify your intelligence.
You can still think in a perfect manner on the summit of a mountain.

101
And dogs have a greater aptitude for friendship
than the majority of men. It was someone in the airport
who said this—an old woman who seemed to know more
than the others. Nothing is imperceptible for someone
who has grown accustomed to listening: Bloom perceived
that that phrase promised something important:
a prophesy? A threat?

102
Dogs are too domestic,
and Bloom never had respect for an animal
that sometimes seems to adopt the behaviors
of a rose. Distancing himself from animals
who are regularly led around by the collar,
Bloom wanted to draw near to those places where discomfort
demands uncommon, yet decisive action.
Would that be India?

103
How do we perceive the elderly, if they have already lived
before we arrive? Because an old person might have started
trying to perceive thirty years before we asked our very
first question—and that's a significant amount.
Of course, there are seven-year-old children
who start to perceive before certain eighty-year-olds,
who even at eighty refuse to look straight on at what they fear.
There are cases like that, for sure. But what might that old woman want
from the still-young Bloom?

104
It's customary for old people to know how to tell stories that are old,
yet even closer to the beginnings of things
and thus more true and precise.
Indeed, a contemporary line of poetry is further away
from the first line ever written in the world
and that's the nature of distances: unequivocal and objective.
However, Bloom is in a hurry and wants to slow himself down;
he's afraid of having so much courage!
He isn't yet old enough to ignore advice,
but he no longer possesses the foolish youthfulness that obeys and trembles
before any old sensible phrase. I can only hear those who tell me "Forge ahead,"
thus is my deafness, says Bloom, our hero,
at the end of the fourth canto.

CANTO V

1
Dogs have a greater aptitude for friendship
than the majority of men—how could Bloom
forget this phrase uttered by an old woman
who, though alone, seemed so strong
that she couldn't have had any lesser company
than gods themselves? However, the plane
took off, and the high winds
interrupted her monologue and joined
together in direction and orientation that were favorable to the engine.

2
Take note that among all the heavenly bodies, only the sun
provides any indication of the season we're in:
the moon produces the same chilly feeling in living beings
and the same amount of light in Winter and Summer.
But by the light of the sun, however, one can tell that, right now, Bloom
is an inhabitant of July, and being an inhabitant
of a month, and not of a city or a country,
makes it even more obvious that we're mortal.

3
Bloom thus felt, up in the air,
as if he weren't an inhabitant of Lisbon,
but an inhabitant of that exact date: July 8th.
Because life isn't even a daily element,
it's smaller than that: it's instant after instant of survival:
one moment succeeds the next and we still haven't died,
that's all there is. Cities, in terms of temporal indications,
are absurdly inept.

4
Because not even in Paris is it always December,
nor in Brazil is the Earth's rotation always turned toward a hot month.
Proof of this: men die in all hemispheres,
and months are enigmatic things
that fall from the sky (one could say they fall at just the right time,
but it's more precise to say
that months fall from the sky, out of habit,
at just the right month).

5
It's amazing how nature, with no calendar,
always arrives right on time and is never disoriented.
Given that nature, outside of man,
still hasn't entered the age of written language,
it seems even more wondrous to us still
that it possesses an uncommonly good memory,
in which the sun is a constant and prominent figure.
But Bloom, meanwhile, through the ephemeral window held aloft in the air
by the plane, catches a glimpse of that excellent Lisbon
he's leaving behind, and as he looks he sees other regions still.
(Life only exists when it is looked at.)

6
He's going to London, Bloom is, through the air—we're returning to the beginning of the epic—
yet seen from on high, down below on earth and sea
there are no obvious changes,
neither slight nor great, in pronunciation.

There don't seem to be any linguistic differences down on either,
unless you designate as such the colors seen from above,
which depend on the concentration of brown factories,
green trees, or water.
Bloom catches sight of the sea from above and, euphoric, for a few seconds,
mistakes the sea for a washbasin for his important hands. But no.

7
The sea might look like a mere point on the horizon
upon which you lay your powerful, distant eye,
but if it's merely a point, it's an immortal one,
and your eyes, large and essential,
are ultimately just slightly less ephemeral
than the feeling of satisfaction in your gut after a meal.
And that's all. Nevertheless, Bloom continues to look out the towering
window, noticing something that's missing
from maps: the smell; indeed, the smell.

8
Of course being at high altitude in an airplane,
fortunately closed shut on every side,
it isn't easy to catch a whiff of a powerful tree
or the earth after it rains,
but seeing nature in the normal material state in which it was made
and not in some function that's been systematized by men
is to already smell it a little, even from inside an airplane,
thousands of meters in the air.
In the plane, your eyes can sense
that nature has an aroma, that's one possible observation.

9
And nothing is untouchable when
we're far enough away from it (what a paradox!).
From an airplane it seems possible for us to touch an entire
country
the way we would touch an orange. And that sensation
is superb and feeds our fingers
for months on end. An ephemeral seat
perched in the middle of sky is the invention
of a madman, and Bloom, holding fast to his seat,
thinks and repeats to himself a number of times: I am sitting
in the middle of the sky.

10
Traveling isn't only good for men,
it's also good for the routes themselves
to have men traveling along them.
A route is like a house:
it's necessary to open the window once in a while
to let the air circulate.
The route needs to be ventilated, and the men
that travel along it are the ones who carry out that function.
It is men and merchandise
that preserve the highway.

11
Even the open air needs to get some fresh air
from time to time. Circulation is a priceless
good for any form of nature.
A bicycle race that traverses a
mountain is a gift for the mountain.
Animals and everything else that moves

also moves in the name of motionless things.
Without movement around it,
a mountain would collapse like a trivial old building.

12
You should support the mountain with your joy.
But a terrestrial building in a city
needs something more: public restorations
should be added to the private loves that are gently
brought into a house.
The only reason our house doesn't collapse is because there is joy within it,
but it collapses and will continue to collapse, forever, if there is no joy.

13
There is no half portion of the world
because it is never whole: generations of animals,
men, plants, and other organized materials
succeed each other: some die, others are born:
they are never all gathered together over
a feast. The world is never complete:
it's missing the people who we've lost.

14
But look: the universe sees our impatience
in the act of surviving. Cities and their citizens
become the butt of jokes when they start building luxurious
palaces. The stars see us as
talking commercial goods that won't stop
making noise down in the basement. We're small
and incompetent: we bustle around a lot,
but we always have our own feet and death with us.

15
There are places in the world where, if you touch the waters
with a single finger, you'll become drunk. A simple
element like water varies admirably
depending on the time of the day or the fingers that touch it.
Regions have a speed that,
when seen from above, is constant,
but love interferes even in the oldest occurrences.
The planet itself, for example, is not immune to the miniscule
act of two people getting engaged.

16
The importance of the earth whereon you plant that
which will be your main source of nutriment: your house.
Where to live? That's the essential choice.
You shouldn't build a house on a plot of land
where you have never fallen down. Your tranquility will be erected
at the very center of your fall.
And in the center of your house, the stairs
that you'll climb. One, two.

17
The mythology of courage that surrounds the seafarer
is certainly warranted. The crewmember of an airplane
is a technician whether well- or ill-prepared,
while a man who boards a boat
with bare feet to go fishing isn't merely a capable man
with strong hands to support him while riding on the sea's back:
he is, in the form of man, the most courageous thing one can be
without competing with the Gods.

18
At any rate, Bloom, up in the air, thought back
on the sea.
As if the act of being in one element of nature
impelled him to pay closer attention to the
other elements. How can we look at where we are currently
from a distance? How do we observe this very instant?
I can see very well that that which, being far away, is not very
clear to me
—thus is man, his capacity for observation,
and the reason he notices nothing.

19
Bloom remembered having seen a storm out at sea
and the effects of that storm.
If the sea wasn't made to elevate us,
then fine, may it not elevate us. And Bloom then thought:
which is scarier: sea,
fire, and air, with their storms,
or the Earth and its earthquakes?
Might there exist, without us knowing it, a secret and sadistic
competition
between the elements?
Speaking for myself, said Bloom, I'm most afraid
of fire. Of fire, of fire, of fire.

20
Of fire, indeed, with fear of the sea as a close second.
And a fear of the air and the earth that sometimes trembles.
We are surrounded by elements that take no notice of us
and of which we take no notice.
Uncultured, yet powerful elements.

Uncultured, yet older than us;
uncultured, yet hardier.
You could create exhaustive taxonomies of every kingdom,
but Nature's energy cannot be filed away in an archive,
it's always just there. It has a name, yet provokes fear.

21
Even in the tallest building there is no drawer in which to file away
a thousandth part of Nature. Natural tumults start whenever they want to,
and they end when they get tired. And, despite all that,
fire is the most controllable:
there's water in great abundance to
calm it.
But how do you make an earthquake tire, how to you speed up the end
of a typhoon, how do you fetter a storm
that the air has inaugurated? Nevertheless, I'm most afraid
of fire. Of fire, of fire, of fire.

22
And the typhoon eventually stops, and so does the earthquake,
and even the storm. As do epidemics,
like the Black Death that arrives, kills, devours Europe,
then disappears. Where does Nature start to become energized?
Where does it go when it calms down? And what role do we play in the midst of it all?
There is a war to be stopped that is much stronger and on a much higher level,
but the generals have not yet noticed it.
(Bloom is bent over his father's radio, trying to repair it.

But there's nothing, nary a sound. Damn radio, he thinks.)

23
Nourished by books, philosophers
are out in the world wearing bathrobes, if they haven't yet
suffered.
Wearing bathrobes, how ridiculous! Bloom chuckles to himself.
Nobody welcomes strange visitors wearing that intermediate bathrobe,
halfway between darkened sleep and bright wakefulness.
But philosophers are, indeed, out and about in the world in
their bathrobes
if they have not yet stared squarely at nature's inexplicable
tumults
or if they haven't yet suffered for love.

24
And not even a lake, when tranquil and still,
peaceful as ever, can take us away from this ancient monologue.
Men don't speak with nature, when they speak, they speak alone,
always have. And yet there is, still, between two illiterates
from two far-off countries,
a strangeness that doesn't exist in any other animal.
It was man who invented language
and also he who invented the lack of language,
and the anguish this provokes.

25
Land!, someone just announced, and Bloom heard this.
It's something which, from the air, seems rare, he thought, yet
there is enough land
to cover up all the slain after every massacre,
as extensive as it may have been.

There are always extra square meters and grass, flowers,
and their respective scents. In terms of pure, measurable matter,
men—all of them together—aren't even as large as an island,
not even one of the smaller ones.

26
But, nevertheless, man considers himself
important—the species that has been given the position of
gardener.
However, the planet is not a garden for the creative man,
nor the essential scientist, nor the courageous general;
the human species is, indeed, one of the gardens on the planet,
the most civilized flower bed, to be sure. But little more.

27
It wasn't created for men who likes sweets:
honey was made for the bees.
And the mountain doesn't exist so that six men
can organize a climbing competition,
the mountain is a part of the earth that ascended.
And the sea doesn't have fish so that a cook can invent
some exotic new method of grilling them,
the sea has fish because nature chose a mixture
instead of rigid separation.

28
Liquids cohabitate with solids,
and solids with the air.
The sea and its fish, birds in flight,
an airplane, a man falling from a tall building
or wearing a parachute: that which is dense can, in sum,
exist in the midst of that which can never be held fast between
two hands.

The world contains so many things, and humans too, to be sure.
(Yet, meanwhile, interrupting Bloom's lengthy thoughts,
the flight attendant arrived with precious articles for sale
and a smile. Bloom stopped thinking and smiled back.)

29
I'm coming out of great tragedies, yet I'm still a consumer.
Life doesn't stop, thought Bloom,
we're still alive
if we're able to purchase things. The concept of existence
changed abruptly in the last century:
the heart beats and the brain stirs, but that
isn't sufficient to verify the existence
of man. Not consuming is a minor
stoppage of the heart, barely even felt.

30
Having little money, Bloom bought a tiny
object and asked for change.
It's interesting, he thought, that even a minor event
always carries with it the possibility of being incomplete,
of lacking something, of something left over.
Something tiny being incomplete, how strange!
It's the proof of an existence that is doubly
incomplete. It could at least be big,
grumbled Bloom.

31
It could at least be big, he insisted.
That on the enormous list of things we're lacking,
grandeur, or potent
pride, or enormous courage may not appear.

Say not: I'm big, but I'm missing half of everything.
Say, instead: I'm missing half of everything,
but I'm big.
And rearranging the position of the positive and the negative
changes a lot, as is well known.

32
Friendship could also be a machine
that always works, thought Bloom.
Beholden, as it is, to viscera that feel
or to obscure cellular strategies, friendship isn't very predictable,
it has highs and lows and depends overmuch on the general
state of the body. For many men, friendship
is a process that doesn't work;
no machine worth its salt should be sensitive
to sadness the way the organism is.

33
Bloom, still in flight, grows melancholic
down to his bones.
He spent his youth stocking up on punches
and embraces; one and the other coming to him by turns;
the act of growing up creates a connection between warlike and fraternal instincts
through the tactile element of both, he's certain of that. The face
is a manuscript for the fists of one's enemies
—and that is the first part of the very first lesson.

34
And the second part of Bloom's masculine education
was to perceive that it is after a beating that gentle
women appear, transformed into gardeners of the face.

Women should only emerge in the life of a man
after he has lost a fight, it seems to me. Before
that, it's much too early.

35
Bloom grew up intact, but his face was obviously
the last page of his diary.
A small scar below his right ear,
another across his entire forehead,
and even his eyes: they lacked even the smallest trace
of having been looked at.
And yet eyes are also created to be seen
—they aren't just made for seeing.

36
And in Bloom's eyes you could tell that few
had looked at him square on (to threaten or to seduce).
Only one woman had done so for a significant duration: Mary.
But Mary wasn't a matter of State,
she was his personal matter. And due to a politics of proper
distribution of resources
there were no collective institutions that dealt with petty
tragedies.
Ultimately, Bloom is just one human being.

37
A forest does not contaminate a factory, thinks Bloom.
However, if small animals escape from the vegetal disorganization
and enter into that geometry
governed by schedules,
specialized workers will make immediate use of
pest control products (named after saints).

The essence of the twenty-first century, as has long been known,
is that the forest cannot contaminate the factory.

38
The stairs are burnt. You
cannot go up or down: you keep quiet and wait.
Young people are not worried about syphilis—young
people are very slow to take ill—they're worried about there
being
no exit: the quantity of desires is such that it is insatiable
in a single lifetime. We have desires enough for fifty thousand
lifetimes
and yet only one brain and one heart—both mortal.

39
Meanwhile, the old man with black mouth and
yellow teeth who was sleeping next to Bloom on the plane
awoke with a start. Bloom is thinking about animals hung
by the neck on a rope dangling out the window
of some distracted family. He is thinking about children playing
in the streets
and the announcement on television of a storm
that will change the essential.
The world is violent, but only the face of the old man frightens
Bloom.

40
At any rate, nobody is that alive.
It's not inexplicable that there are often a reduced number of
passions
per day; what is, indeed, inexplicable is the reason why we don't
all toss ourselves,
one by one, at regular intervals, off a tall building.

Never are two people in the same place
at the same time: one person flees from
the others. On the bus, a person reads the paper so as not to look
at the person beside him.
The cold no longer enters through the window—it enters
through the news.
Close your newspaper; you can now raise your eyes: fortunately,
you're alone.

41
Men are lonely and insomniac.
They take pills and recite
beautiful lines of poetry, but forget to water
the plants. All living beings will die
if you spend day and night reciting lines of poetry,
correcting minor errors of recitation,
organizing, from the outside, a History of beauty.
It's ugly and remains that way: thus is Man.

42
You pay to see some ruins and say: how pretty!
From the window you see the explicit acts of animals
in rut: similarities between dogs
and our own species abound,
yet you are shocked. You almost shut the window.
They have no shame, nor cheap rooms
in sketchy boarding houses: dogs have to do it in the street,
as do all uncivilized
species. Dogs don't have
the Greeks as ancestors, and it's noticeable.

43
But everything continues to occur as if the inhabitants
of a city were, instead of degenerates,
substances somewhere between an angel and matter
that feels like velvet to the touch.
However, if you gently run your hand
along the face of someone from our species
you'll get cut. On television, young women
with marvelous voices give updates on the rise and fall of
companies
on the stock market; and tomorrow no chance of rain. And
that's great.

44
But where does this morning come from, which, despite it all,
never abandons us? We're privileged.
The sea is more catastrophic on television
and in places where we fortunately aren't located.
The earth trembles beneath the feet of others,
and the sun maintains its average, neutral immorality
as it shines down on major assassinations. Men
bury bodies on privately-owned farms where
robust plants sprout with imperceptible diseases.

45
Only machines aren't buried: such a thing
has never been seen. There's something like an incompatibility
between substances that depend on electricity,
on the one hand, and those that depend on mud: that dirty
detail on a map.
Well above the level of the trimmed grass of gardens
stand machines, the cleanest of entities.

Even relatively new buildings already have defects in the paint
job
and are covered in dust. Girls start learning everything
early on, and teenagers obscenely mock
anyone who dares to light a fire in the fireplace.

46
Well-behaved men are the food of angels
who have long since given up their fast.
Postcards with images of saints on them are stuffed
into a wallet and mixed in with a list of high-class hookers
and their respective phone numbers.
A butterfly alights on a wristwatch
forgotten on a desktop.
And a six-year-old girl shrieks, startled
because she'd never seen such a beautiful animal.

47
The world balances itself out. The poor drink
in greater quantity, but the drinks are much cheaper.
In the city, however, childhood is rectangular,
the size of the bedroom: no one under fifteen years old goes out
on the street
and no one does so unarmed.
Of course, rectangular childhoods grow, in terms of bones,
exactly like all other childhoods, but the body and existence
are vast elements, expansive surfaces.

48
Autumn looks better in photographs
than when seen out the window. Nature loses its density
when admired through double-paned glass. But
that which protects one from the bullet protects one from the
wind.

If you don't leave the house, the wind becomes just
another fiction that can make you fall ill.
If Nature didn't exist, illnesses would be
miniscule, a doctor once said.

49
Look at the way wood burns.
Men root with ravenous hands through the abundance of
trash bins.
We are all insane.
If we look hard enough, we'll even find mythologies
among all the trash.
We drew a diagonal line between beast and machine:
along it we have proceeded. The dexterous butcher,
working large cuts of meat, has trouble
lighting a match.

50
We should recognize what it means for small gestures
to be replaced
with major movements.
There are no details in the city,
check for yourself. People always cross
paths at the moment of departure or arrival.
No one stays. There are no intermediate states.
What women know of the hearts of men
are healthy electrocardiograms. And vice versa.

51
Out of ineptitude, shyness, or conflicting schedules,
ever since the last century, love
has been better expressed inside an envelope,

from a distance. Body to body, love
has been transformed into a technical skill.
Bloom, for example, is aroused—but he can't remember why.

52
And the poets have disappeared.
Indeed, what someone meant to say,
and rightly so, was that clean and beautiful poetry is unacceptable
after what men did to other men
in the 20th century. It's a fact, delicate
words are unacceptable. But don't forget the face.
Despite all this, hitting hurts worse than saying you're going to
hit someone.

53
And the city possesses a controlled fear,
which is a positive factor. Bloom counts on his fingers.
There are also tall cupolas
from which diamonds still shine,
which is a positive factor. Camera shops abound
and the naïve archives
are extremely organized: from the nineteenth century back
all the powerful have been condemned.
Again, a positive factor.

54
At least: we've become organized. But a question remains:
where are the people who live on the streets
buried? Is there some land
set aside for complicated cases?
Naïve question, almost obscene:
will those without proper identification ultimately be cremated
for the obvious reason of wanting to save land?

Plots of land in the city center deserve—
and people have always felt this way—animals with a name. And
that's quite just.

55
And the city developed a dependency: it stocks up on
men and women coming from tragic countries
and has a few charitable moments before
kicking them out. Europe is starting to tilt on its axis,
it has to stay vigilant. At night, and this is a fact, the poor scurry
under the rugs. In the Middle Ages
there was an epidemic of rats, but the situation was resolved
in time. We were born in a century in which the list
of medications is much longer, by far. Let's celebrate, then,
with just the right drink.

56
Money has become morally unimpeachable. For the poor,
laws seem quite detailed; for the rich,
they deal in generalities: we shouldn't bother the courts
with anything less than a massacre
—we'd be insulting the good name of our fellow citizens.
And we're so happy! The most perfected women
dance for a coin just like an old jukebox.
Love, for it to be of this century, is only missing a coin slot
that works with present-day pocket change.

57
We are very happy. In clinical tests, urine samples
reveal nothing, and our blood isn't drawn by force with a sword
the way it was in the battles of centuries past;
blood now comes out through a very thin needle
brought over by an obese nurse.

The State worries about your health
and—this is enormous progress—wishes you happy holidays
through your TV screen.

58
And then there are words. The relationship among men
is grammatically something else altogether. Tolerance,
respect, serene laws: the city seen from above
looks like a lake, it's so calm.
It's so perfect that it's a wonder all the animals
of the forest don't move here en masse.

59
There are children, for example, who like to hit nanny goats
and other large animals
on the back with a sharpened stick.
If it weren't for the cruelty of children, childhood
would be luminous. But, again, seen from above it remains
fantastic. They're learning English earlier and earlier.

60
But let's not be pessimistic. Even painters
say that any day now a basket full of new colors
is going to arrive.
Certain contemporary chemical treatments have been
tested in broad sunlight,
and the sunlight seems to finally have noticed our progress.
It no longer makes sense, well into the twenty-first century, for
the stars to be stubborn
and autonomous.

61
However, in spite of technology and, in painting, the new
avant-garde movements,
the color black is still scattered throughout the world.
And this color that remains on the field after a massacre
is, among men, the most ancient,
there's no doubting this.
And notice that no astronomer has ever, to this day, dared
to announce its disappearance.
Yes, vaccines have been invented, but brutality
predates them.

62
Let's move the narrative along. Bloom is a man
who, like all of us, flies above these trifles.
As long as our terrestrial blood doesn't compromise
the modern sensors of the airplane we're traveling in,
all is well. That's the way Bloom is. Sincerely, my dear.

63
The biggest scoundrels are the ones who speak gently,
don't be fooled.
Only cattle are sweet and rustic, only dullards are friendly.
Goethe said: only scoundrels are modest.
In the airplane one sings in prose at an altitude of two thousand
meters;
the song is so elevated that the prose sounds like
poetry.

64
These insects that can fit a lot of
men inside them are useful inventions,

but the stars don't envy planes
or other birds of prey; they know that gasoline
or exhaustion
will force them to descend. Bloom, our man, wants to arrive in India
older than his true age.
So he's taking his time.

65
He descended in London, then hopped over to Paris;
he wanted to get to know the mystical part of Europe.
But Europe has no mystical part: it's
all already been sold to some men from the Americas
who spoke functional English.
Of that which isn't totally comprehensible or rational,
Europe retained only the night, which is dark
and doesn't allow one to see fully what exists within it.
But a night is not enough
to illuminate a continent.

66
He tried to find wise men in the city of
London, and later on in Paris. He looked
in the phone book: he found pages of plumbers,
lawyers, restaurants, real estate firms,
plumbers, but not a single listing for a wise man.
This doesn't prove that they don't exist, just
that they don't want to be contacted, he thought.
And once again he went out on the streets.

67
Outdoors, reality has a stronger scent. At
home, the country is reduced to a letter-sized sheet of paper
—circumscribed by a window or two and a tall piece of furniture.
Someone watching a bloody revolution on the TV in their
living room
cannot believe that there is a single dead body
outside. At home
the world moves at very low speeds,
but that's just the right speed for a coward.

68
The chains that exist in each day
pull Bloom along. A day is, in its influence
on man's organism, a stronger
element than the sea.
And this chain that shackles men isn't visible,
and thus is even more dangerous: not knowing
of its existence, men do not resist it.
That which we call Destiny perfected
the sea's abilities.

69
I want to get to India on the inside first,
thought Bloom, building the forgetting
of my previous life the way one patiently builds an edifice.
Forgetfulness is a perfectible mental
faculty just like any other
(like it's inverse, for example: memory);
however, Bloom had searched for books with exercises
for forgetting and hadn't found one;
and he searched hard.

70
There are skies that are "of a quality inimical to our humanity,"
regions where it rains more often, and places where we feel
like we belong to some other species of humans. For example,
in London, Bloom had felt like he was outside
the events that occurred.
Let's think about this: a man who falls down in front of you on
the street.
How do we interpret this fact? Is it the same thing to fall down
in London
as it is in Lisbon?

71
As if occurrences could also
have their very own language. But no.
It isn't only because of the existence of foreigners
that what happens in London doesn't speak English;
the world was organized in this manner: for occurrences,
the tower of Babel was never brought down.

72
Languages separate themselves from one another, but gestures
do not.
Look at someone punching another, the act of penetration
into the vagina or into other recesses, or even look at the strong
embrace,
or a man who, at the last second,
saves someone who's about to fall from the eighth floor.
Look at all this and you'll understand all,
it isn't difficult.

73
But what matters is this: Bloom sought,
far from Lisbon, sufficient wisdom to arrive
tranquilly in the land of tranquility: India.
In the midst of the noise of contemporary animals
you have to search for something more: beasts, for example,
possess another way of existing, a different
style. They merely look and remain as they are;
not wanting to act upon what they see—
that's what Bloom wanted to learn.

74
However, you can't learn anything from the outside
that is sensible and will be retained. Perceiving something
with your eyes and hands is to perceive it incompletely.
No one recites wisdom, no one memorizes
sensible action, tranquility is so profound
and abstract that its formula isn't found in books
and there are no movements of the hand that can sketch its picture.
That which is important isn't small enough to fit
on TV.

75
Bloom spoke with men and
stared at stones at length;
he tried to think about the architecture
that exists in a potential state in every mineral.
However, a stone is not human, it's a serious substance,
a motionless element that can't deliver any news.
The thing is that if we understood stones, we'd be able to see
that they too can, for example, announce the arrival of Spring

(and changes in the weather).
Stones digest the light they receive from the sun and say:
well, it's going to rain tomorrow.

76
And Bloom understands stones better every day.
Though he remained in the same neighborhood, in this way
he was closer to India.
And since at this point in the narrative he had already left Paris
(that's another jump)
Bloom had bought a pot with a strange plant in it.
He'd arrived in Germany and asked for a characteristically
German plant
at the store. (Because, after all, nature also has maps
which don't depend so much on armies and politics,
but rather on the sun and how cold it gets, the humidity that
exists or not on the land.)

77
Bloom researched the pot and the German plant
that it contained. (But what does it mean to research something
(ask yourself)
that is apparently uncultured (and therefore imbecilic)
if not to learn how to stop thinking? To know the names of
plants
is to know nothing about plants.
—for plants are not what Man sees in them.
If you truly concentrate, you'll see that a plant is an element
with which you could even dance.)

78
Bloom was getting better every day; tranquility
was already leaving light fingerprints
on his shoulder. He now understood that days, for plants,
do not move the same way they do for Man.
A day does not have a stable,
uniform measurement for nature. Every part
of the world exists in its own unique historical period.
A man who, in 2003, looks at a plant
could be staring at a plant from last century.
And the Christian calendar is not universal.

79
A plant isn't a slow leap forward,
it isn't merely an element that ascends
gradually.
The things in this world are strongly connected, true,
but also strongly disconnected. Wise is the person
who perceives both forces; imbecilic
the one who perceives neither; so-so,
the one who just perceives one. And democracy
is based on the so-so
intellects.

80
However, a man cannot disconnect
from what happens to him. Bloom existed,
and that means being externally fragile, even
if internally one is engaged in wise learning.
Nature teaches, but we don't learn:
the domesticated dog doesn't preclude the existence of the wolf, a
magnificent climate doesn't preclude storms,
being happy doesn't prevent the following day.

81
Let's speak, then, of the following day and proceed from there:
having arrived
in Vienna the night before (yes, he's already in Vienna) Bloom
fell ill.
An unfortunate coincidence: that of being
sick in a city with an abundance of palaces.
If architecture had any influence on the state of man's
health, no one would ever be sick in Vienna.
In Vienna, one strolls through the streets as if
atop an elegant white horse.
Any given man, tourist or otherwise,
is the most powerful man in Vienna. But Bloom, Bloom
fell ill.

82
With his gums swollen, his body smelled
like certain flowers that had bloomed in the wrong Kingdom.
If he lived in another century, we would say that it was a case
of scurvy,
but even illnesses
want to be modern. Maybe it's
a bad dream, he was told by an incompetent,
but good-humored doctor. In Vienna,
those who don't dream of grandeur fall ill.

83
With doctors like that, poetry is valued,
but a lot of people die. Bloom consulted
other doctors, but no one could diagnose the illness.
They asked him ridiculous questions. He just sat there, not
answering them.

And in that thoroughly vertical city that is Vienna,
Bloom spent day after day in bed,
lying down. This is what they've taught me, he thought:
being sick is to find another body within our body.

84
But enough of that: Bloom got up.
He'd spent seven days sick; now he felt better.
Even in strange lands, my biology
remains strong, he thought. For
the cells and the organs, we're always
in the same country. We could spend months away from home:
it doesn't matter. Our feet don't send information
to the inner reaches of the organism.
On the inside, we're always stationary.

85
But Bloom wanted to leave Vienna: a given city
is as healthy as we are. Not
one day more: he hopped on a train
and the following day arrived in Prague,
where he soon was able to calm down. Newspapers
spread their horror in foreign tongue, and for that reason
seemed beautiful to him; there were birds in high places
and he saw no beggars (or trash) in low places.
He did, however, see buildings that were just the right size to be loved
and a people who used cheerful words.
If one only stops being sick when one is happy,
Bloom, then, was no longer sick.

86
We must, at this point, praise our main character,
our hero: Bloom. He had come out of a family tragedy:
Mary, his beloved, for reasons not entirely clear,
had been murdered on the orders of his father,
whom Bloom had always admired, yet quickly killed in
revenge. With no love and with paternal blood on his hands,
Bloom had decided to begin a voyage to India,
but, sensibly, understood that it was important to take
a long time to get where he wanted to get. And that much
patience,
after so much violence, can only be admired.

87
Bloom had already encountered the absolute ingredients
of action in the world, death intermingled with love
in a stupid mixture. So he still needed to get to know
what exists and does things within the body.
And the expression "does things" is beautiful, if we look at it
closely (it isn't the same thing as changing the position
or the color of elements that already exist). To do things inside
the body
is to bring something new into the world,
to make a useful piece of furniture from restless wood.
It isn't easy, and it's important.

88
He was still researching light, Bloom was,
understanding that it isn't only necessary
for illuminating pages. The light from the sun—it's good to
remember the obvious—
isn't in the world to render good service unto literature.

Light is involved in everything, in literature and in boredom
(alternating between the two),
and even makes traces of sanctity in the less elegant animals and
in men
appear and disappear.
Light is important, and Bloom wanted to understand it.

89
He also wished to understand water better. He immediately
verified that it doesn't exist solely for us to drink it,
or swim or fish in it.
If we removed these three activities from the world,
water would not disappear. What is water for, then?
Bloom didn't yet know the answer to this question,
yet he was already halfway there:
he had asked the question and proceeded from there.

90
And at this moment Bloom remembered the good Parisian
who had listened to him at length.
Bloom had previously not believed in friendship between the
deaf
and the blind.
However, he now realized that the sense of touch
tells stories
and words merely add to narratives that the skin
cannot describe in detail.
The body tells generalized stories, sure, yet they're relevant ones.
(For example, the first kiss of two adolescents
in a dark room.)

91
The fact is that nothing on our journey, nothing in the world is
done without weight;
even in the air, man knows that he'll shortly
return to that which he belongs to and, down below, calls out
to him.
Bloom looks at his shoes,
at his knees, at his chest, needs a mirror,
wants to comprehend his volume, which he sometimes forgets
while he's speaking. Through speaking (or even writing), one
can entertain,
possibly convince, seduce—but one can never solve anything.

92
Because if an agglomeration of letters
—those miniscule drawings with curved and angled
shapes—and the associations between those little drawings
were able to express Truth,
then Truth wouldn't be that important
and wouldn't be worth any effort.
Because the true Truth is unlettered (it can only be thus).
A thing that we smash; a thing that can smash us.

93
Nature would not be so ridiculous
as to be summed up by some literary or mathematical
formula.
Place the most brilliant book by Goethe
next to a stone: come back the following day,
and the day after that. And the next week.
You'll see: nothing happens to the rock,
while the book, on all sides, in every part,
has begun to lose its traits.

94
Nevertheless, language is as important an invention
as fire. Language—good language—is practically
a "fire that burns unseen." And certain lines of poetry
make us, at the same time "content and discontent,"
multiplying an ambiguity that exists in all that exists,
for nothing in this world is clear,
save, for imbeciles, the world itself.

95
Language isn't envious of reality.
But reality also isn't envious of language.
There are no hierarchies between two elements
that bid good morning from one continent to the next.
Distance has always given rise to apathy and indifference in
the world; and between "earth" the word and "earth" the element
there is a piping hot liquid that keeps them apart
and quickly dissolves an attempt bringing them closer together.

96
Language is magnificent when one has time and
nothing is urgent. It's important
during days of boredom and for following events
that don't manage to touch animals or humans.
However, the world never forgets, not even the person who wants
to forget the world.
(If writers never died;
but they die.)

97
Of course, a man of action will be more concerned
with the style of his punches

or the style of his virile penetration of other people's bodies
than with grammatical minutiae
or the pursuit of astonishing syntax and verbal
associations. The man of action starts every sentence
by rolling up his sleeves
or taking off his pants.

98
Uncultured men shake their heads at strange sentences
and point out obvious errors in the way words are joined
together; while the minimally cultured pat their bellies
as if digesting a ham hock,
satiated with the declamation of some basic poem, in which
everyone says they love their mother.

99
Power is the enemy of poetry, this is a fact.
It's like people and animals: poetry gets sick
in certain environments, it develops arthritis in unexpected
places, at first it becomes a mere sentence,
then a speech, then law by decree.
Long live language, indeed, but Bloom also has a stomach ache,
blisters on his feet when he has been walking a lot,
headaches when he's worried and when, distracted,
he runs right into a lamppost.

100
Bloom speaks, writes, listens—that's a fact—
but he also has two little eyes:
he likes to watch a woman as she undresses,
a man as he leaps, an animal as it runs in fear,
a thunderstorm and its heavy rains (when seen from inside the house),

ultimately, he likes to be alive,
as long as, of course, his own body, that idiot,
doesn't bother him.

CANTO VI

1
Bloom had received uncommon friendship
from the Parisian, and he couldn't forget it.
He had come from a country where more than half the men
spend half the day lying in bed
and mentally cultivating envy of those who get out of bed
and act; he had, therefore, come from an indispensable
(and almost beautiful) country: Portugal.
He had departed from its capital, its center: Lisbon,
and after the bad experience in London
had ended up in Paris, where the beautiful colors of butterflies
are not wasted on brutish eyes.

2
The important thing on a voyage, as is well known, is to observe
closely
what is eaten in each place, to learn the corporeal skills
and also the essential fictions of each country.
(Truth is something one gains access to via technology;
not so for fictions.
To get to know the greatest lies of a country
or a man
you must spend a long time at their feet.
No one lies from afar, yelling.)

3
But let's remember: Bloom had to leave Paris,
which was worse than finishing a book
when you want to read a thousand pages more of it. Ideal energies
had been gathered at the door of the Parisian
named Jean M,
which promised him friendship to the ends of space.

Concerning time, I can promise nothing
because I don't understand it, Jean M had said,
but concerning space, sure. Concerning space, I promise.

4

Farewell gestures, they say, have always been influenced by the
sensation of the decomposition of matter.
When two men part ways, their proximity dies,
which, though obvious, still makes evident the existence
of a corpse between the two of them—
not a material one, of course, but at least an emotional one.
They've said farewell, or rather: they have prepared themselves
to forget. That's one possible definition.

5

And there began Bloom's inner voyage
to India: the Parisian gave him the name of a friend
who knew the routes that allow one to respect
occurrences. But if you want to understand
India before you arrive there, he had said to Bloom,
you should begin by naming all of your useless movements,
and then curse every one of those names.
Neither entertainment nor waste will save you;
that which entertains you is a fortunate waste; however, waste
is waste: throw it out. First step for getting to India.

6

The outdoors are not incompatible with education,
quite the contrary. Thus Bloom was advised,
in that unhurried Indian manner of instruction,
to become enlightened naturally—to let the sun
fall down from the sun onto the things that surround it

and also let the world grow dark, generally speaking,
and that he accept this. Neither lamps
nor curtains: man should live by the light
of day, they told him, and by the night of night.
Nothing more.

7
But one doesn't learn to be wise the way you learn
to solve an equation.
Both modes of learning require total attention, to be sure,
but on the path to wisdom there are more obstacles,
as if in some other place gods with hoarse voices had assumed
the responsibility
of never allowing sensible philosophy
to reside completely in man.
And perhaps the reason is purely selfish, for if all men were wise
who would need temples?

8
However, in a lucid state,
at the moment that seems like the eve of perfection,
a rabid dog always arises, out of nowhere,
a dog that destroys, with its clamor, the calm color that had
settled into place.
There is no justice compatible with beauty;
beauty is in the trenches opposite the equal distribution of goods:
if democracy were violent and pure
it would forbid beauty, which favors obscene inequalities.
But no.

9
Bloom was thinking about the sea and of beauty.
The depths of the water are an imaginary thing,
yet you drown and die trying to understand it.
The depths of elements veiled from the eyes
of Man. The sea that was once calm,
disturbed as it napped by an adolescent dip, takes its revenge
with a death that will only be gathered up two months later
by some other people. The waters
pretend to be flowers that you can smell close up,
they attract you, you bend over, you're pulled in;
you will die.

10
The world is quite beautiful, but it is not understood. Don't
be surprised at the ignorance, not even this is cause for lamentation.
The thing is that all flesh rises up, and for the sole reason that it does not know,
like a bull or any other wounded animal that lifts itself up
once more to receive its final blade. The world
has four robust elements of which it is composed:
fire, earth, air, and water; and man is not the fifth.

11
Fire is more vast than all the
intelligence of one man. You light a tiny
match and are astonished: you don't understand.
Fire smells like some other existence:
it is proof of a life parallel to this one, a life more dense.
And in this world into which we're unable to enter,
there are many more facts, many more mysteries.

12
And even the air, which is the element of life
that gives space its name! Because every human map
illustrates nothing more than a dictionary
of warriors: multiple generations of victors
decided on the name of a piece of land.
However, land is a brownish and ancient
element: before war and disorder,
there was peace, and back then the air had already placed
the true name of each mountain
upon each true mountain.

13
Mythologies that entered into contact with
the strongest human instincts
and the earth that supports us
now enter paginated, enormously erudite
books that transform
ancient, colossal frights
into a succession of names within a simple,
yet grammatically proper narrative.
It has always been known: putting dates to events
robs them of their energy.

14
I don't remember when it happened, but
it changed my life—thus speaks one who understands
where lies the core of a myth or a story
that our grandparents have heard. And water is that mythological
element that for millennia
slowly created ships (for
it had an appetite for shipwrecks). The sea is not compatible

with teaching, with the great university;
the sea is a brute element, an element
like unto the forests where man
fears to enter.

15
And what does Bloom know of the sea? What connection
is there between machine and sea?
Among the directions provided on city
signage, indicating kilometers
to be traveled and settlements, is the sea: that
element which is the same from one side to the other,
yet which no one understands.
What connection is there between the sea and the city? How can something that appears to be homogenous be inexplicable?

16
Even the submarine, think about it,
isn't a machine that's made for
understanding the sea. It isn't an intelligent machine
that has penetrated the element that frightens,
it is simply a means of conveyance.
The scientist and the philosopher know nothing of the sea;
we find ways to traverse it,
either on it or through it. Nothing more.

17
The ship soothed us: that's what Bloom perceives.
From that point on, we considered the sea to be an element occupied
by human intelligence. But no.
On an individual level, a man can swim.

And there are buoys that can go years without
sinking. However, the sea is a
wall on its side: though you have the illusion you can, you cannot
pass through it.
If you kiss the sea or attack it with fists, you'll see:
what you have done has effect on you alone. And that is the
definition of a powerful element.

18
They advised Bloom to spend some time near
the sea the way in the village one spends time near the fireplace.
The sea isn't like fire, for which a small
portion gives one an idea of the whole: the sea does not
exist in boxes, its essence is not retained
when moved to an aquarium. The sea
is not merely salt water; its grandeur
gives it its name. The sea as a whole isn't as easily captured
in photographs as a fireplace.

19
That which can be photographed is miniscule and feeble:
see also this rule for men, animals, and the
multiple terrestrial elements: secrets strengthen
the hearts of things. Thus Bloom
submerged himself in thought,
into that sea that cannot be captured in a photograph.

20
Ah, but Bloom is not just thought
or reflection. Right now, for example, he is brushing the crust
from his eye.
Anyway, he is acting as if his index finger

were doing the correct and necessary cleaning just in the nick
of time.
What is the finger that moves toward one's own eye
to hunt the small, and apparently insignificant, useless
fragment of matter, if not a decisive action,
an action that cannot be postponed?
In truth, a man cannot always be worried
about the world.

21
Ah, but Bloom has still other tasks
before he returns to his thoughts.
For example, one of the buttons on his shirt
is unbuttoned and such a thing should have immediate solution.
And then there's his hair, which sometimes looks stable,
and other times looks autonomous and sloppy; the position of
his feet,
the private sensation of the little toe of the left foot
which is manifest at precisely this moment.

22
Bloom, in fact, wouldn't be the last to notice that
the sea is incoherent, like everything else that is worthy
of study. The coherence of a thing,
of an object or a person,
renders the intelligence of others unnecessary,
even renders research unnecessary. (Stimulation
depends more on that which is hidden
than that which is visible, everyone knows this. Or no?)

23
Classical errors in the judgment of matter: madness does not only
alter the physiognomy of men;
the sea, too, when insane, acquires a deformed face.
Below the surface of the water, another kingdom—not yet fully
formulated—seems sometimes to gain strength: the sea enters
through
the pipes of a charming home, and its inhabitants
drown because the unexpected water
kills like the worst and quickest of venoms
(this is the malediction Bloom is thinking of).

24
The thing is that from the point of view of combat, the weeds
that slowly vanquish a garden are sisters of the sharks
that rip off the slowest leg
of a man out for a swim. Besides, Nature
is more agile when on the attack than in defense:
cities are built atop forests,
but below freeways and commercial establishments
there is animal life that persists
and makes noise.

25
The distribution and variety of aromas is, below
the great surfaces of the water,
parallel to those that exist on a continent.
At the bottom of the ocean there are spaces
set apart for trash and other spaces for absolute
cleanliness. The sea smells! What an important
discovery Bloom has made
on his inner walk to India.
Yes, precisely that—and people can also walk on water.

26
The sea, maintaining its strange sameness
day after day, still also maintains
contemporary relations with ships
that are becoming more perfected with each passing century, in their motors
and in their Destiny. It's never outdated, the sea,
even at the moment of the maiden voyage
of the most modern vessel.
How can we not draw conclusions from this fact?

27
However, the sea isn't everything. Much less is individual thought everything.
Somewhere, for example, in some other spot in the world, in Lisbon,
in front of a plate of food and glass full of wine,
someone unleashes negative air in Bloom's direction.
That's how slander works: words in some perverse admixture
with aerial chemical elements. They say
of Bloom: he killed who engendered him.
He should die, they say further of Bloom; and the shadows forge ahead.

28
At this point, make note of the fact that all men know how to use a knife;
no one is so naïve that they don't know
which side of the blade should be used for killing.
It isn't a human invention, but cruelty has been particularly
perfected in the last ten centuries.
Yes, reptiles, the gluttonous

crocodile, predators of vast appetite:
half of nature's sounds come from
acts of vengeance, there's no doubt about
that. But there's still the other half.

29

The thing is that in nature as well (who could've guessed?)
there are sounds that come from acts of love.
And the greatest human arrogance and, at the same time, the
greatest human invention
isn't the powerful metallic structure
that functions properly, or the satellite, which, all by itself,
sees more than all the animal species put together
by far, the greatest of Man's invention
is the kiss.

30

Certainly any theory that wishes to put an end
to living beings killing each other
runs the risk of abolishing the perfect
and ancient equilibrium that is killing, being killed,
and awaiting the new day.
Killing is thus the right of every
species: even dogs, who feel great affection for their owners,
don't protest excessively when someone
mistreats their protectors. No one,
with the exception of mothers, mistakes their own life
for that of another. A sentimental,
stupid mistake.

31
Among the various animal kingdoms and genera,
mammals are by far the best at making friendship
work;
but even so, there are constant breakdowns
in this friendship.
Affection is indeed half divine,
but the other half is practically
commercial.
Bloom looks at how much money he has in his pocket,
how many friends in his heart. And is content.
His wallet is full.

32
The thing is that if the connection between men were perfect
it would never have been necessary to invent language.
Speaking is a civilized way of keeping
a safe distance; animals growl
at each other, men carry on at length about
the weather and quote classic authors. But both
actions have the same effect.

33
Even the wind can hurt us: take note, Bloom.
Nature doesn't support certain offenses:
men are able to conquer
seventy words of the enemy's language,
adapting them to the local pronunciation,
more easily than a single mountain. And mountains
don't change their locations, the way young couples
and certain small newsstands do.

34
Nature is simultaneous on every side,
which is sometimes irritating. A suspension of this
would be interesting: to enter a place where
nature doesn't exist, a machine
that excludes all natural materials. A
literary machine, perhaps, but one whose letters rested
upon nothing at all, for anything they might be placed on
would abound in natural particles.
The problem is still that famous Nothingness. Is Nothingness
unnatural? Doesn't seem so to us.

35
And there's also no artificial Nothingness because
there isn't, let's say, any incentive for the technological
and extremely difficult construction
of something that is Nothing—it doesn't take up space, it has no shape,
it has no function. No one invests money to invent
an empty place that doesn't exist.
Only a State governed by fools would invest in the artificial construction
of Nothingness. But, instead of this, as you can see, there are a lot of other things.

36
So let's head back to our hero.
Negative winds were then shot at Bloom
to disturb his inner voyage to India,
"repellent winds."
The Earth's bad temper,
which well-educated people call "terrible presentiments,"

this is what was forcefully shot
at Bloom's neck.
But Bloom, distracted, was thinking about an insect, twisting
his neck to espy it; something like that,
something objective.

37
Adverse events were slowly approaching Bloom,
who, though he was now stronger in philosophy,
was not stronger when it came to his body and the resistance
this offers to life's troubles.
Wise men remain vulnerable to the stupid blade,
so what then is their wisdom any good for?
At bottom, wisdom in man gradually strengthens
the details.

38
While nature is readying this tragedy,
Bloom, distracted by his thoughts
from what is happening to him, welcomes the sun the way a
garden
would welcome it: by being still and happy and getting
a little warmer. He goes to sleep and wakes up, speaks with
men, tries to understand them, reads a lot,
tests out theories for everything: for example,
he is searching for a theory that allows him
to trod upon Spring more effectively.

39
And he likes to hear stories: Bloom is a
slow listener, or rather: he is patient. That's the paradox:
a man who is capable of listening to a hundred quick stories,

one right after another, isn't a quick listener,
but is, indeed, a slow, tranquil listener.
Counterintuitively, in the act of listening, which seems passive
and calm, there is a strange active part,
which is found in the eyes. Those who listen well have attentive eyes.

40
Sometimes Blooms likes to hear
joyful stories from the old wise men. And
thus he confirms that joy also existed
in the past, and that it didn't come into existence
along with electricity, as some
maintain. Great loves and hatreds
occur with greater frequency
after midnight. And that isn't proof,
but something to consider.

41
Who is it that, in the beautiful afternoon sun,
spends his minutes cursing
the lives of others? No one wastes
such winsome, elevated energy in that manner.
If a day, like a scratched record,
never advanced past noon,
and the sun remained calm, hot, and high in the sky,
there wouldn't be a single symptom of vengeance
in the world.

42
And telling love stories to prepare soldiers
for war is the same as pointing the gun

at yourself—no general ever commits this sort of error.
Bloom, let it be said, also didn't like amorous
narratives: sitting, at this moment, beside a sensible old man,
he thus asked for a story that one could listen to
while at the same time drinking a hearty
red wine. And that's what happened.

43
To listen to a good narrative is to get nearer
to India, thought Bloom. And the old man,
a recent friend, then started
to tell a story. It was cold and windy,
recounted the old man, but an army arose
in its entirety all at once, as synchronized
as if it were only one person. And because it was cold
and windy,
and also to rectify certain details on the map,
that army declared war against another.

44
It seems that certain older women, continued the old man,
had meanwhile been accused
of exercising superior skills
on mid-level organs and distributing
these skills,
in generous manner, to sundry men
(the way a strong wind does when it blows
directly onto thousands of seeds).
Anyway, they called them competent prostitutes,
which is charming and unpleasant.

45
Sure, giving a negative name to our women
just because of some hints of obscenity
seems like an overreaction, for a hint of obscenity
is an obvious contradiction in terms,
since no one should draw conclusions
from an expression as abbreviated and clearly chaotic
as this one.
But they existed, these hints of obscenity.

46
Notice that, in nature, and not just in nature, a hint
has a tendency to be silent, while
obscenity makes a racket that carries along various surfaces and fissures.
It is also absurd to speak of a timid army.
Timidity is not a beneficial characteristic
on the battlefield—any book of strategy will tell you so.
Either you advance or beat a rapid retreat;
a prolonged hesitation customarily becomes
the final action of a soldier.

47
But let's get back to the story the old man is telling Bloom.
Insulted women are capable of causing
cracks in a country, that's a fact. Angry women
get up earlier than roosters and other birds
and prepare their vengeance, introducing it into the midday meal
of their enemies. Women
know well what is essential for a human:
eat, sleep, and see: and that is where they act.
They poison food and dreams;

and sometimes—a third alternative—they blind men
by way of seduction or use of even sharper weapons.

48
Those insulted women then asked for help
from a man who sent letters to other men,
and through this correspondence an alliance
was formed between several armies who were starting to be
invaded by boredom, which doesn't mean it wasn't an
enemy invasion. (In a quick statistical calculation, said the old
man,
half of all wars originate from a concrete invasion of
a furnished compartment of a country,
while the other half start as a result of an invasion of boredom.
And this is why peace is practically an obsolete object
in the world.)

49
Trees, for example, tolerate boredom quite well:
practically nothing happens in the plant kingdom of a forest,
and this isn't the reason that warlike exaltations
proliferate. Man,
said the old man, should learn to imitate
the sluggish impulses of the trees,
which ever ascend, without being seen and never ceasing.

50
Twelve men, continued the old man, were
contacted, by secret means, to make preparations.
Twelve women had been accused
of abusing eroticism on city streets. The twelve
gentlemen, who had a habit of making coarse

noises while someone was reading a poem, were people
of simple tastes: they valued the scent of
women, three-word sentences, the
city's great monuments. And after lunch,
they took a nap.

51
Men, you could say, who thus combine the two imbecilic moments
of an imbecilic day—eating
and sleeping—become, in a few short years,
indifferent to the most human part of humanity.
After lunch, we should go for a walk; and in the absence
of legs, one should sit and look out the window.
Never sleep. Looking and walking, yes, always.

52
And these twelve protectors of prostitutes,
violently hot-tempered because
someone had called their twelve prostitute friends
prostitutes
immediately became engrossed in long hours in front
of the mirror,
straightening their suits and ties, their hair,
trying on different outfits so that
they could choose, like any elegant assassin,
those that went the best with blood.

53
There were twelve valiant men and twelve cowards
doing this,
although only twelve men in total. And this because

each man has, in telegraphic manner, two faces:
he is afraid and makes afraid.
A unilaterally courageous man does not exist,
unless that man is unilaterally unintelligent.
The thing is that ratiocination begins with the ABCs of being
alive:
when you see the deep abyss, you should carefully back away.
That's it. Or almost it.

54
And one of the men spoke.
He said that he was so interested
in getting to know foreign countries
that, though he never traveled, for more than ten years
he had constantly forced himself to change his dietary habits,
the furniture in the kitchen,
the clothes he wore, the time he awoke and went to sleep
and other particularities—like religion,
laws, and language—in order to simulate,
without ever leaving where he was,
the many voyages he would take
if he had the patience
to put on his shoes.

55
But let's not hold back on brutality when it elucidates,
said the old man, the storyteller,
there is only one moment when your shoes are really
too tight: it's when your body
is lynched and swinging from a tree; everything else is just
a minor discomfort. Extremities
swell up, as their very name indicates, only

in extreme situations, and a tranquil,
bourgeois life does not contain, over the course of seventy years,
a single extremity: it is made up of the center and this center
is made up of nothing.

56
And this man among twelve who spoke, continued the old man,
decided to take a different path, as do
all the great saints and all
criminals. Alone, a man acquires density,
in a group, he loses it—and only gains companions.
And an apprenticeship in wisdom isn't carried out
the way one carries out an apprenticeship in a manual trade
—for wisdom is not a manual trade.

57
However, wisdom, not being a manual trade,
can be seen in the hands, and all over the body.
It isn't even necessary for that hand to touch other bodies or objects;
this is sufficient: that the right hand
—the most skillful—wait for the left hand
and respect it: this alone is a symptom of prudence
contained in the fingers. Wisdom is a complex of abilities
that are exercised in relation
to the world, in utter isolation,
and even in full flight. Knowing how to flee, that is a paragraph
of wisdom.

58
And in a man who is alone and has no
task to perform, what his hands do and how they behave

reveal his distance from that mystical India,
this was the old man telling this to Bloom.
Because there are people who feign wisdom
during public festivities, yet, when alone, are immediately conquered
by distractions of all sorts. It is, therefore, in the individual tranquility
of an individual and tranquil person
(smack dab in the middle of Lisbon, for example)
that the tranquility of Europe is set into motion. Don't you think so?
(Yes, agreed Bloom, who was enjoying listening to the old man.)

59
The continent begins on your couch, this much
you should already know. The choice of a comfortable
chair isn't a variable that is wholly independent
from a war in Europe.
Despite the abundance of warplanes, war isn't extraterrestrial,
it isn't the invention of machines flying at an altitude of
several thousand meters.
War begins at sea level
and shoe level.

60
But let's get back to the story, exclaimed the old man.
The now eleven men were
well prepared for a duel in which they
would seek revenge on the twelve men who,
one by one, had offended, one by one,
the twelve women.
women who were practically unsullied, let's say, if it weren't for

the generalized sullying that their perversions provoked
in the bodies of family men
who brought syphilis, gonorrhea, and outlandish alibis back to
their homes.

61
The only thing missing
for this duel to be well organized was a slender man, who had
decided
to take the longest path, as if he had the
time for it or were wise. Neither of these
were the case, and the slender man,
in fact, was merely late.
However, at the last moment, he appears
and, raising his head like someone picking out a dance
partner, says: who is the
man that I am supposed to hate? Where is he?

62
After they had led him to his position
—at that sort of official banquet
table symmetrical to standard banquet tables,
where the possibility of being served a tasty hunk of thigh meat
was replaced with the possibility of being served a bullet
through the forehead: with the young hero with the laggard
watch
thus relocated alongside the rest of the
most modern mechanical elements,
the perfect conditions for the start of combat
are in place. (Even hatred,
in order to achieve optimal results, needs
careful organization.)

63
And thus it begins. An excessive stroll, one might label
a duel thusly. Well-aimed bullets annihilate
the umbilical cord that connects a mature heart
to the earth and one's legs. Church bells ring
in a monotonous musical style, but the sun renders aid unto
none.
A moral (because it comes from one of our own) shot advances
from
an ally's weapon to the perverse skin of someone
we don't know. And a dead man now seems meek,
there on the ground; almost friendly.

64
Bloom is listening attentively and at this point laughs
at the old man's expression.
A dead man is always meek, that's almost a fact.
However, no one feels pleasure when they see neutral matter
that was once living intensely.
A catastrophe weighs heavily—and a dead man is a catastrophe,
albeit a private one.
Take note (thinks Bloom to himself):
it is impossible to associate levity
with great events: all change
is a sudden change in weight. And, of course, furthermore:
an inability to carry it.

65
But the duel proceeds, recounts the old man,
twelve men are shooting at twelve others.
Creative horses anticipate the chaos, kicking and
neighing as if they were doing it for the History books

—in a magnanimous and righteous tone. Horses, if you'll allow
me this aside,
are animals that end up fine in any tragedy:
their beauty contrasts in splendid
manner with the filth customarily spread by
violent deaths.

66
Elongating the narrative, continued the old man, is a method
sometimes employed in patient countries where writers
have time to delineate every contour of the letters. The elves
who protect writing thus adore details,
however, in the battle of twelve against twelve
there is only this to say:
the defenders of the women with lengthy biographies
and endless erotic resources won. Some men and
women won; others lost.

67
It was celebrated: there was a feast.
Whoever wins militarily wins morally at the same time.
And let me also talk to you about the role of Nature
in all this: the natural world isn't well-mannered,
it's a creature that is similar to nothing else,
it makes no selections: a door that has been torn down
and has left its place empty: all pass through.
It hasn't contributed a single
legal charter to balance out various forces—thus is nature.
A high-polluting factory is more civilized
than a crystal clear river.

68
If it weren't for petroleum, nature would be unnecessary,
as a whole.
Petroleum saves nature, and heroes merely save their
honor when they seems to be saving princesses or castles.
The slender man, for example, who almost didn't arrive on time
for the massacre, behaved like an unpolished line of poetry: he
arrived,
tidied up the world, and left soon after.
He was valiant: a man who kills in that manner, as if it were easy,
deserves, at the very least, to have a street named after him
in the city center.

69
And the old man, facing Bloom,
attempts to prolong the duration of the first
sentence (what is telling a story but
stretching out the distance between the first
word and the last?). Well then, Bloom exercises
patience with the retelling of the festivities and asks him to
continue:
the perfect story only ends when we die.
From time to time we interrupt it
so that our ears can have respite and the rest of our body
can be put into action, but we're born to listen to people tell
stories,
everything else is just a profession. And Bloom says: continue,
please.

70
But just then the commotion outside interrupted
the old man's sentence right in the middle, splitting it the way
supple wood

is split with the hard strike of a speedy axe.
(The sentence was broken off at an unimportant place, which immediately
became its center; the essential part of the body is
the spot where it starts to die
or wherever an illness begins to take hold.
Each death reveals which small portion of the body
is ultimately the one that you should have defended.)

71
Nature advances via phenomena
that make noise. And this is what is happening: the old man cuts off his historical
fictions, and Bloom gazes upon the liquid volume
of the sky: the sky is full and it's raining. But even a masterpiece of nature
like this one doesn't have any effect at the level of the
material progress of nations. It's a scandal,
the storm, because of the brutal energy involved and
the little use that civilization
makes of it. Not even the most perfect museum
preserves any memory of a tumult
like this one.

72
Nothing is abstract during a powerful scare, Bloom realizes.
When nature is angry, it brings men together in the same act of flight:
enemies and former lovers run down the same road
with the same face.
During an earthquake, political borders dissolve,
fissures emerge on maps. Despite being made of sturdy paper

and kept safe in secured drawers, maps become
fictional drawings—like the picture a
six-year-old child draws of the house she lives in.

73
In a storm, the motors of unimpeachable machines exhibit
obvious naivety. Every contemporary
machine suddenly seems antiquated when in the sky emerges
innovative, roaring thunder. Age-old conflicts,
commonplace in other situations, disappear in the middle of a
storm and all the intelligence of man is jeopardized.
What have we invented that is truly meaningful, if the sky is
still like this
—an element that frightens?

74
Primitive winds replace
government authority for hours on end. Animals
defend themselves like men,
philosophers stop their search for truth
and debase themselves for a meager shelter.
The earth shakes, and for half an hour
no children are born. Bloom stopped asking
questions: time had become material, demanding
actions and experience. The storm is also
a stop along the way to India.

75
Objects—the beautiful ones—are flowers without roots: they
fall over
easily. The barbarous work of art finds,
in the earthquake, its purest ideology: storms

are absolutely illegal, screams a judge, and a
strangely mild wind, in the midst of this screaming,
turns page after page in the book of laws, as if it were
consulting it.
Outdoors, the merits of the great orators
cannot be heard due to the sound the wind makes
when it knocks them to the ground and kills them.

76
The archive that six employees spent two years organizing
becomes disordered. Letters lose
the spacing between one and the next: libraries lose
their roofs and their classification by subject: seen from above,
half
the literature of the sixteenth century looks a lot like the
messy trash can outside a building in the provinces.
One can see that culture isn't a profound
human necessity: during a storm
someone asks for water and someone else, feeling cold,
asks for fire.

77
And birds, if they still exist, lost their musical spirit
long ago. No one has such a close relationship with
the sky that they dare to fly on a day like this:
bolts of lightning cut other bolts of lightning in two
when their paths cross: birds and planes do not take flight,
they hide out in the same warehouse that smells strongly of
wine because the barrels have busted open.
No one has the key when an extraordinary element enters
the day. And, during a storm, drunkards don't stand out
from anyone else.

78
No one truly comes to terms
with a part of them that has been amputated, and
nature was amputated from men;
men finally realize this when
they cannot exhaust nature in two seven-number formulas.
The energy of nature is not that which
men call the energy of nature. The brutal sound
makes a woman let out a scream that is far larger
than the man who is protecting her.

79
Trees are not bourgeois works of art,
they were already in existence before the nineteenth century;
they come
from a playful manifestation of the earth: you can climb
toward that which is important, but you will only be respected
if you climb slowly. And even trees are at this moment being
ripped out by the roots,
losing their serene music. And when they are lying flat with
roots exposed,
they're like the backs of animals that
we don't like to see; repulsive, yet inflexible,
human, mechanical animals.

80
And Bloom is scared. He had never before seen nature
violently revolt against a classroom
where English and mathematics are taught;
and now, today, he saw it. There's not even any respect for
education
in these strong winds that beat down on religious temples

and brothels with equal force, with identical moral principles,
and with the same destructive illogical rigor.
Bloom is scared and prays.

81
And praying isn't simple. Commonplace words
are brought face to face with supreme finalities.
And praying isn't easy—it's necessary to create
an organized speech
in order to converse with that which is strange.
Because that which is strange can protect or not,
but it always forces one to invent new languages.
For example, one only prays with new words that have come
from old ones;
one looks at things that only come into existence after suffering.

82
No one sweeps away that which one loves, and nature is sweeping
the city away. That which is loved is transformed into its details:
we want to look at every miniscule fragment
and perceive it completely. Yet in those moments
there isn't a single vestige of detail out on the streets
—everything becomes generalized when nature is inclined
toward
devastation. However, even there, in the midst of reality in
disarray,
if you look closely, you'll be able to distinguish between blind
men
and those that are defending themselves based on what they
can see.

83
That's what happened: in the midst of the horror, Bloom
discovered
a blind man. And at that point, within him wisdom
instinctively took novel action. He grabbed hold of the man
and guided him. I want to go to India, thought Bloom,
and here I am, who would have thought it?, in the middle
of a storm, leading a blind man.
(And what are great accomplishments, after all? Advancing along
in front
of a blind man isn't the sort of march that will certainly make
it into
History books alongside the forward advances of
an emperor. They still haven't toppled the crown
in History books—and here we are in 2003.)

84
Thus continued the high conference between absolute elements.
Nothing is abstract, as we said: it is clear that
geometry is and was invented by men
on days with good weather. A tempest makes
many theorems ridiculous all at once.
Nothing in nature has two sides of equal length;
sublime lightning bolts never form any side
of a triangle; and rain falls ceaselessly on the book
that someone, fleeing, dropped on the ground—opened
onto an important page.

85
Rainwater has already ruined the definitive
characteristics of a rectangle that someone drew
perfectly. The page becomes sodden and warped as if it were
some trivial book

and not a book of pure geometry.
And after the storm, whoever picks up the book
should preserve it as a relic,
for in it are deposited the asymmetry and disorder
that nature leaves behind when it finally sweeps clean
cities that are exclusively legalized for the human
species.

86
And it doesn't stop raining on pages eight
and nine of an important book. The rain doesn't stop,
and the lightning proliferates. However,
even in nature, there are promises and ambitions.
During the worst moments, one still prepares for
sunny days and the feeble scent of green grass.
Wait!, Bloom says to himself.
If you are sad: wait; if you're joyful: wait.
Tomorrow is not a museum.

87
And Nature is also capable of being amorphous and neutral:
that's why something, coming from some unknown somewhere,
calms
some unknown thing. Suddenly, the storm ends.
But some questions: where does tranquility come from?
Where does the absence of wind and rain come from? Where
does that
which can't be seen come from: a day stopped in its tracks,
without any storm at all? How
surprising it is, if we pay close attention,
this rational and quite serene day!

88
Somewhere behind the clouds,
still black, nothingness begins to emerge.
And nothingness is, in these circumstances,
major news. Bloom sees
the aesthetic form of the sun peeking around
a corner of the outdoors, still black and malicious. And the sun
brings with it the best of all worlds:
this great, spontaneous news
after strong fears, strong winds, and strong rains:
the sun.

89
And Bloom decides: to admire it.
He had lost track of the old man, of that magnificent storyteller,
and had left the blind man in a chair fixed to the ground,
a chair that only after the storm would recuperate
the quiet power that awaits it
(nature, we know, when it is harmful and strong
puts all of the elements of a house
in danger). But now Bloom is out of the storm,
yet he isn't in anything at all. He looks up at the sky,
and the sky doesn't look back at him.

90
For Bloom, the storm marked the end
of something old. He was ready: he would depart
for India.
The sun was poking its way in between the apple and orange trees
of small gardens. The sun was also poking its way in
at the airport, encircling airplanes that once again looked like
extremely powerful birds. So, Bloom departed.

The voyage was a long one, but the word "long" had been
one of the words whose meaning had changed the most
with technological advances. India was only hours away.
Long hours (in terms of space), but hours.

91
Bloom had been consistent.
He hadn't been in a great hurry to get to
India; technology and machines are a trick:
everything seems easy, quick, and men
rush about, forgetting the biology
they carry with them and the organic manner in which their
own sense grows.
Bloom had been sensible. In 2003 his trip to India could have
taken
less than a day; it had taken months.
(However, no one is ever old enough to go to India,
there is always, in every European,
an excess of youthfulness.)

92
And it was on a clear morning that Bloom
saw the mountains slowly become reconciled with
the great height of the plane.
But of course they (the mountains) weren't the ones growing
taller;
it was his world, rather, that now began to descend
toward a new land.
These mountains, Bloom overheard a voice say,
these mountains are in India.
And as if he were a God, Bloom,
quiet in his giant's seat, whispered:
on my right side I have India.

93
India! India! India!
On his right side a man
has India, that enormous country.
This is what Bloom had sought,
and thus it is that great things come in simple forms.
There was no celebration, no one shouted.
I made it to India, Mary.
I made it to India, Dad.
Bloom leaned over in his seat
and, thinking about his father and Mary, wept.

94
He had survived the cruelty nature
at times possesses,
and survived the cruelty that men,
out of habit, practice.
And, at that moment, in the air, several meters above India,
Bloom put his hand in his pocket;
he felt his father's radio, which had never worked,
and thought: I shouldn't return to Lisbon without music.
A strange thought at that altitude, and somewhat troubling.
However, Bloom was happy. India!

95
Dangers have never made anyone drowsy,
nor do legs tire when they are fleeing or giving chase.
Unintelligible stones only become an obstacle
for someone who, instead of living, wants to examine them.
If you fall asleep beside an incomprehensible stone and,
beside it, have nightmares, that stone
becomes one hundred percent human; flesh and blood, almost.

96
Habits satisfy those things in you that are not strong.
It was always thus, thinks Bloom.
One's matutinal gestures, if you like, are a political form
of the body starting the day. And thus an obstacle
is transformed into a beneficial,
chance intrusion.
Deep down, that obstacle is,
for Bloom, India.

97
And if you find yourself forced to stop,
don't start running in the same direction again.
You trip, get back up, close your eyes, and move forward.
In this world, suffering teaches us more
than a hundred well-intentioned professors.
Flee from suffering that impedes you from starting back up again, yes,
but not from the other forms. The various kinds of suffering
are not of the same animal species:
you come out of some perfected, thinks Bloom,
and out of others, doglike and obedient.

98
Bloom knows that the final formula for a human
agglomeration has not yet been discovered.
A utopian thinks about the unrealized
possibilities of friendship, but
automobiles honk and the smoke from factories
attacks the kingdom at its best feature:
women today are already using inelegant words
to talk about technology. What a shocking evolution, you'll say.

99
But Bloom, from the intermediate height between holiness
and a descending aircraft, thinks:
one who accumulates does not dig. The ground rises
(it never sinks) when you pile up experiences,
as if every occurrence were a dirty article
of clothing. You don't accumulate experiences like that,
he whispers. Bloom weeps and laughs, and vice versa.
He is in India, he has forgotten his previous life
and still has enough desire to brave various venoms
and many dangers.

CANTO VII

1

Riches abundant and undefiled, only in
India, where what cannot be seen is always surpassingly beautiful
and enraptures, while on the surface
live poor people whose one relationship is with
their shadow; isolated from one another,
hesitating between pressing on and stopping, rarely
bold in their actions, but sometimes, with a
magical, astonishing speech, capable
of enlightening and saving an exhausted man.
India; and Bloom.

2

Let us praise Bloom, he deserves it.
Not even for him is joy forbidden.
Uncommon circumstances sometimes
arise only to interrupt the
redundancy of days: destiny isn't
malicious: it gets bored; it wants to be creative,
it invents things. The right age for conquering
the world is today. Man lifts
the interdictions, presses on, and when he is preparing
to make the leap: falls.

3

Falls like a leaf from a tree, calmly
and slowly, and ascends like certain animals—
an eagle or a warplane.
Mobility inspires. Men, like
Bloom, quickly become intimately acquainted with
strangeness. Ten photographs of an unusual
landscape turn it into a landscape that is

known and conquered. Bloom pressed on;
he didn't stick around to rummage through his own disgrace. He didn't kill himself. He wanted to understand what it is to be alive after a tragedy. He didn't sit down in a
chair. He got up out of a chair.

4
And whole men sometimes seem
to be reduced to mere organs.
As if life came about by coincidence
inside the body.
Certain men aren't familiar with the science of personal
research; a science in which a
man experiments on himself;
a science that experiences the hell that reality
sometimes is.

5
Because it is easy to accept that you can fail
when the conditions are perfect. If you fail now,
you'll get it right later.
Real courage is to take a risk in the midst of hell,
do something (whose effects are unknown)
at the moment of panic.
There is no courage in the good times. Bloom
knows this; and also that.
He knows so many things that he's afraid.

6
However, despite the publicity, joy
hasn't entered the marketplace—much less
tranquility. There is no price list for

profound calm. Of course there are innumerable courses
that, at the end of three weeks, you'll have gained wisdom,
however, ultimately, those won't bestow more than half an hour
of wisdom on their clients. And thirty minutes
are not enough to fill up all the hours
in the future in which you still haven't died yet.

7

Theories are important, but
it is useful not to forget feelings.
It isn't because we've entered the twenty-first century
that the soul is no longer a contemporary phenomenon. It exists
and comes to the surface of a body at certain moments,
almost always tragic ones. In fact, in men, as in Bloom,
great joy can also call the soul to the surface,
but if it does so, it's at a much lower volume.

8

However, the soul hears. The soul is a noble
structure. Instinctive like any other animal,
but noble like any great
modern building, technically indestructible.
Feelings give cohesion to theory,
and theory gives it to feelings.
And Bloom, he leans over and puts on his shoes.

9

Accepting that life is a succession
of disappearances—both human and material—
is to forget that every day has resonance: things
vibrate and leave vestiges of their existence
in the air.

But these cannot be seen. Men, in fact, quickly
stop believing in apparitions,
which is a mistake, thinks Bloom.

10
It is still known that from the nineteenth century onward,
women demanded to be
beautiful, which, though it is an ideology, still
has meaning. Because in this world
everything that is vital is not accessible at first glance.
That which is vital the second time around
was incomprehensible the first. And beauty, indeed,
is evidence of this; right from the beginning.
A barrier, then, to the study of it.
If it's clear, why the need to clear things up? If it is beautiful,
why beautify it?
(Bloom is amusing himself: on his tiptoes, he is trying to look
at his own
heels.)

11
And man's loftiest endeavor is to beautify.
The world, a woman, a house, a dining room table: to make
something more
beautiful is an objective that is favored by the universe.
One who has made at least one thing in the world more beautiful
shall not go to hell.
But hell exists (and then some!), and with each passing year
it requires more territory, increasing the size of
its properties like every efficient millionaire.

12
Spirits exist. Bloom wants to prove it.
He killed, he saw his beloved killed, felt everything and its opposite.
Spirits exist and anatomy is found wanting from the
feet to the head. There are many songs and loads of varied sounds,
but a spirit is not so loud
that the century has to tell it to quiet down.

13
Sinister gold, animals whose flesh has lost
its essence, arms with idiotic and amorous
tattoos squeezing the neck of a
chicken, men who approach animals
the way ancient aristocrats approached
their slaves, women who fornicate
because they can't get ahead, the future of countries filled with concepts,
hunger, and discomfort,
men who paint the surface of their house
six times a year. The world went out for a stroll
and lost its Spirit.

14
However, Bloom has not lost his spirit. He
knows that grand gestures come about
after a prolonged effort that led to immobility and nothingness.
The right hand will make its best movement
after forty days in the desert; same
for the left hand. And Bloom knows that there is still
matter behind his eyelids that should be put to good use:

dreams contain messages that are closer
to truth than to science.

15
Bloom is in India. Let's take a look at him.
His stomach exists and is hungry. Organs for digesting food
were, from the beginning, placed
within the highborn and the commoner.
But the spirit also exists and is hungry.
For a long time now, Bloom has not possessed an appetite that
is only focused on one side;
souls, statistically, exist in all
things, but it exists more in men who bend their heads
toward the feet of
others. The soul was invented through
attention.

16
And Bloom, with his tiny shoe,
stepped upon India for the first time. How big
a country must be for someone to go there to
change their life. And how rare this is on a map.
Because there are countries where passions develop better
(products that are more adequate for the type of soil and
humidity there),
and others where you go to get rich.
Rare is the country you travel to in order to perfect
the soul.

17
India is a big country. Not because
of its dimensions, but because it is ancient. Time, in

an intelligent country, is the more significant dimension.
Thousands of square meters represent, in theory,
an important surface.
And the number of floors a building has
is a fact that is quite obvious through the window of an airplane.
However, it is the History of a country
that gives intensity to the connection between a tree and the
earth.
And each country is a tree.

18
And then there is belief, which is matter that ascends,
and by ascending, it seems, it will reach places much higher
than airplanes—which also ascend but are much heavier.
There is belief in India. And belief
in the spirit elevates an entire country,
while the common passenger plane doesn't; far from it.
(Objects without a philosophy can be useful
—a plane, for example, is extremely useful,
but there's something missing in it: even when it's right up
against the
sky, it is a petty little thing, an element that is merely trying
not to fall.)

19
In India, men shout a lot.
There is an abundant human density
in the air: the air seems less aerial,
There is a lot of shoving in the streets but few people running
into each other by chance,
and the material poverty is evident and contrasts
with the richness of the stories that old,

seated men on new street corners tell
sensible women and tourists.
An entire continent is squeezed onto a single street
so that everyone can sell what they have to sell.

20
On the streets, technology is less developed
than magic, but everything is for sale:
commerce is the prefatory experience
to every other life; the bourgeois offer lower prices
than the mystics for the same product, it's just that the mystics
claim to donate
part of their profit to the poorest among them (who are not made
aware of this fact).
Religious men can only be differentiated from merchants
when there is a fire
—the religious are the only ones who approach it.

21
In India, old men, who we listened to
for hours and deemed eternal,
suddenly stand up and start to
urinate in the middle of street, aiming at some trash
that seconds before dogs were trying to eat.
Respect and disgust are bizarrely provoked
by the same man: the world
is light at first and then dark later on; the world, every single
part of it,
is light and dark.
And when a mystic indifferently urinates right beside us
he teaches us this, and other things.

22
Bloom doesn't count on his fingers, but he knows how to make calculations.

The ratio of gods to humans is enormous
—as is, for example, the ratio of illnesses to humans—
which is perhaps not a coincidence.
Ailing people with no bread and no place to lie down
invented opulent gods who inhabit massive
palaces. Everything is large in India: the population,
the number of gods, the effects of magic, the cities—
but all of these are smaller than the patience
of the poor.

23
A tourist who promises a beggar dinner
and summarily forgets all about it will, if she returns twenty years later,
find the same beggar in the same place
awaiting that meal. And all of it would be tragic,
useless, and material, if that beggar hadn't strangely
retained the same face and the same age
from twenty years earlier.
It was into this country, which balances out the number of blind men with seers,
eyeglasses, canes, and astonishing phrases,
it was into this country that Bloom, finally, entered.

24
Bloom felt curiosity surrounding him,
for his clothes seemed to ignore the very hot climate,
and his face, the extremely ancient History of the streets
along which he was traveling. He was a foreigner.

(He carried with him a name written on a piece of paper: his Parisian friend
had referred him to his friend Anish.)
He passed through streets that look liked children's drawings:
turbulent, nary a straight line, structures being built
with deteriorating construction materials, buildings whose
structure was that of a suspended collapse—it doesn't quite instill confidence
to walk underneath a building
whose collapse is imminent. But this is India, excellent India.

25
And he then met up with the Parisian's
Indian friend. An awkward hug and some initial
incoherent noises, soon followed by them finding
a common tongue. It's too hot here,
we don't need a lot of friends,
was the Indian's first sentence. The climate
in Paris is much different, he concluded.
Bloom had made friends with the Parisian in Paris.
If it had been here, thought Bloom, we would have conducted business.

26
Bloom told him his story. The happiest people, as is well known,
have the shortest biographies; Bloom, for his part,
didn't stop speaking for three hours.
Of course part of the narrative was invented
—memory isn't a inviolable archive, that's nothing new.
Many true historical accounts lie
about everything that happened, yet are truthful
to the last drop about the date the lie occurred.

In terms of History, one must keep in mind that the sixteenth century
came about after the fifteenth, which is not
an irrelevant detail.

27
Bloom was staying at the house of Anish,
a kindly host who offered him essential
and wholly unliterary food, as was proper.
Even the food is tranquil, how do you all do
that? asked Bloom. We use a lot of spices,
yet cook slowly, replied Anish.
Meanwhile, outside, the night and the silence
came more from animals and things
than from men. There were tranquil
fires in several houses and the night
was robust. Bloom was happy and breathed deeply.

28
The voyage had changed from an inner journey to an outer one:
he was in a different continent, but he still didn't have a different
philosophy. The clouds, however, were still foreign
because they are seen in order, starting from the shoes up, and Bloom
had only recently put on the proper shoes for this land.
His feet truly became more Indian
in those shoes. Here, the clouds,
Bloom said further, circulate more slowly.
They're older, replied his friend.
And, in fact, they were.

29
Bloom wanted to know more about India. Which
way do men's necks turn most often
—toward women or things?
Why are there so many ladders scattered
throughout the streets, almost all of them lying on the ground,
as if they were an implement
that is used horizontally
and not vertically? Are people so religious
that they don't even need a ladder for minor household
repairs? joked Bloom.
Anish replied: I'll tell you about India. What you
know is nothing more than postcards.

30
But India has men and has women, said Anish.
The gold has all been taken, but sometimes it seems like they still
want to take it all again. The cities here
were initially built like poems,
but they were quickly finished up with cheap bricks
and the suffering of those who worked long hours
and earned very little. This country
is like the others: beautiful and brutal.
And if you know of a country that isn't, then
I'll tell you that you don't truly know it.
Countries were born on the wrong
side of things.

31
A country should be a space
for a people to exist, but "the people" doesn't exist, said Anish.
Ambiguous institutions delay the immediate

salvation that a meal customarily bestows
and direct beggars to
more competent departments
on the other side of the city, or the other side of the heavens,
where Gods, unskilled in urgent cookery,
have become specialists in exceedingly drawn out promises.
Thus is India: allow me to introduce this country to you.

32
From a starting point in Europe to the ends of the Earth,
the world is all the same: ambiguous like everything else
that disgusts and attracts. If you've come in search of
mystical tranquility, you need to search harder, even after
you've found it. Nothing is freely given among men,
much less between gods and men.
You should acquire knowledge of funerals
and learn technical skills for the happy delivery of newborns;
starting from two separate points at the same time,
surviving with a single center—that
is the path.

33
Because one doesn't arrive in India, my dear,
in India one walks. You will find uncomfortable
lodgings that will force you to get up
earlier. Pathways multiply
when you don't have a good bed, said Anish.
You should know this because you have come from a long
voyage. And India
is this: a country that moves because you, within it,
are moving. And even because if you stay still, the roof
will cave in on you.

The density of Gods upon each rooftop
is brutal. Gods are only lightweight when they're in
the great outdoors.

34
But in India, continued Anish, solitary animals
sometimes create movements that are holier than enormous
masses of people. Newspapers are peaceful, and the news,
despite the enormous size of the country,
is always about trivial details.
As for tragedies: it takes three thousand years
for the traces of them to disappear entirely, because for three
thousand years
people continue to weep. The Ganges is the biography,
in liquid form, of all the nearby cities,
and the fact that sadness is popular among both the rich and
the poor
serves as a justification for this natural, yet somewhat
melancholy phenomenon.

35
The Ganges River is the most important library
in the city and the most important archive.
There is no truth outside of that river, nor is there any lie of
merit,
fiction, or mythology outside of its dirty waters. But its
waters are not dirty, that expression is actually
inaccurate, says Anish, correcting himself. They are complex
waters,
which is different.
Here, water isn't an element that is just paying a visit to the
world of men,

it is the men who are paying a visit
to the water—and in India everyone knows this.

36
Water insinuates its way into houses, days, and
women. Whatsoever is not attracted to the water is
unimportant. The water is sacred. After
bathing in the river, people sing
more, there are those who come out of the water with a miraculous
voice, and there isn't a dancer out there who, on the eve
of a performance, doesn't copy certain of the river's movements.
It is the only country where the water gets you drunker than wine
and has the seductive power of young women.

37
And religion is enchanting, like everything else that doesn't have a
specific function that can be objectively alleviated.
That which is vague and abstract always gets it right
because it never defined what it means not to get it right.
Wealth never mixes with poverty,
the rain falls in the same direction as those who have been beaten down
and evaporates, some time later, in the direction of those
who haven't given up. There are certain animals who munch
on flowers, and there are others that are more civilized who invent
profoundly mystical and manual professions
—like that of the gardener. Cows on one side,
man on the other.

38
The world is round, but all its sides are of equal length.
Men have hungry bellies and adversaries,
and other men have prestige and friends, and, in this crude
division
you will find obvious similarities
with old Europe, Asia, the Americas,
Africa, and with all the continents where there are
living beings. Life is the invention of demons:
they gave it to you: you should defend yourself, you should attack
(do you understand, Bloom?). I understand, replied Bloom with
a nod.

39
Habits and customs are even more varied
than the vast population, for no individual
is ever so poor that he doesn't have a habit.
Every living being repeats
countless gestures, to be sure, but these repetitions are
what connect him to the Earth and the heavens.
But notice that even when it comes to courage, it is still
necessary for there to be
a little bit of profit in the thing.
Without a cent in the wallet, no one can change their lives;
at most, they could choose other forms of suffering.

40
But what there is most of here, as if it were
a spontaneous product of the earth, said Anish,
is a philosophy that starts
with minerals, passes through the water,
and ends up in tranquil cows that lie down in the streets
boasting with their bulk of an absolutely enviable

affection. How is it that an
animal that weighs that much managed to develop
such a peaceful system? It is by far the animal
that is closest to being able to smile naturally,
and this consideration includes men. Look
closer at the cow, Bloom: it is a detailed animal. Not at all
brutish.

41
In no other circumstances do people retreat into themselves as
intensely as when they are suffering or
when they enter the marketplace of
one of our large cities. Commerce
is carried out in an inexhaustible language:
surplus on one side, deficit on the other. Consumption,
for as much as this might be repeated, was not invented by
capitalism:
gods made men incomplete,
with stomach, chills, and vanity; how could they expect a
different result?

42
Thus spoke Anish, with the mental mobility
that the circumstances of being a recent host
always evoke. We are, he said, in the vicinity of dying people
and a recently restored palace;
we are at the very center of a diverse world,
there is no idea that doesn't exist here,
a living or sickly thing that represents it.
But let's go out, Bloom said suddenly, interrupting him.
I want to see if India exists
outside of language after all.

43
And the two of them went out—Anish and Bloom. Bloom
seemed to have dressed
as a bird, for he was whistling. And this attire,
more emotional than climate-related immediately made
him a man who stuck out as strange.
Blue, the sky; brown, the earth; whistling:
bad music. Anish, meanwhile, tried to manage expectations,
saying that, unfortunately, unicorns
were not visible at that time of day.
And Bloom, while he was appreciating Anish's
mythological humor, dexterously stepped around
the sovereign mortal remains of cows.

44
They were going to meet up with a friend of Anish. In
India, thought Bloom, given the large
population, friendships must be
magnificent in quantity. Or not.
The three of them greeted each other, and in an instant exchanged
amongst themselves
the instinctual evaluations of the deceit and kindness
that exist in everyone since the world is the world
and isn't naïve. They quickly sized each other up
and accepted, without saying so, the energy of trust.

45
And walking alongside Indians who spoke
an undetermined language, Bloom felt like the
bearer of a delicate poetry who attempts
to broach a conversation with bad prose. But
on the other hand he felt the same as ever.

Linguistic incompatibility, Bloom realized, is
less serious than moral incompatibility,
because between the ethics of a
saint and a scoundrel, there are greater differences
than where they direct their abilities.
What's that? asked Bloom.

46
So the three men were walking, with Anish
in the middle, translating from one language to the other
as if he were inhabiting a spatial middle ground and a linguistic
middle ground
all at once. The translator inhabits an intermediate country,
a
country that doesn't exist on the map, a hesitant
country, a country created from the vocal inventions
of two apparently incompatible
lovers. If there were more translators
the number of wars would decrease, does anyone
doubt this?
What's that? asked Bloom once again.

47
Because war is often nothing more than the effect
of an incorrect translation. If beauty
and the devil's appearance were more
homogenous, reflected Bloom, the living wouldn't need
so many languages. Each language invented
its own specific stories about the devil,
and each language has different places that it calls
beautiful. But, despite all this, that which disgusts,
Bloom continued in his head,

varies less throughout the universe than that which
excites. Beauty is more personal
than horror.

48
And every group of men has grown accustomed to its own gods
just as they've grown accustomed to their own foods.
One's palate for the sacred is in training
from the age of two, as is one's taste
for malagueta peppers, said Anish. Certain divinities
make too much noise and wake men up and stir
them up, while others are the silent
sort, and calm the city down. There are gods
working at cross purposes, so it shouldn't be shocking
that all occurrences obey
divine forces.

49
Of course, modern medicine has replaced
many of these effects
so that they are less harmful to one's health.
But what are the secondary effects of a strong belief?
This is the question that matters, said Anish's Indian friend.
Because in the twenty-first century there will be a war that is more significant
than all the others: between medicine and religion. Since they have
the same objectives and the same primary effects,
what ends up deciding the extent of the consumption of one
and the other of these industries will practically be a matter of minor details
(the packaging, for example, or the buzz surrounding the product).

50
Bloom listens; he pays attention to all of it. The three of them—
Bloom, Anish, and the other Indian
friend—stop in front of some local art.
This is art's shame: to be localized, like any old
wretched point on the map. No artist is
generalized throughout the entire world
from Europe to Asia, save the banker
who deals in the simplest
and most ancient work of art.
(Look at the way that all eyes shine when looking upon gold.)
Bloom is paying attention; he opens his eyes. His eyes shine.

51
The three men stop, then,
to admire the sculptures of a palace.
Palaces are beautiful on the inside,
they're beautiful on the outside. They go too far with wealth and majesty,
but somewhere in there, even if it's hidden,
there will still be trash cans ready to receive the
abundant refuse.
And thus it is that, in some tiny place within the palace,
its ruin is already foretold.

52
Bloom listens and sees. Sees and listens.
The Indian friend of his Indian friend
speaks; Anish, with a nod of his head, agrees;
Bloom: neither yes nor no; he just got here.

53
Art is beautiful, says the other friend. And sculpture,
being a matter of stones and other
dense materials, can represent
water, simulating it marvelously
—with the exception, of course, almost insignificant really,
that it cannot satiate the minor discomforts of thirst.
Despite being hard and dense, stone,
for someone with a strong belief, can even
represent gods.

54
Gods, in fact, don't do too well
resting upon soft materials.
Mud, for example, is incompatible
with mythology, especially Greek mythology. Even today,
in 2003, in the twenty-first century, it is almost
obscene for there to be mud in Greece. Politically
and historically, it is a mistake.
(It was Anish's friend who said this. Anish translated,
Bloom tried to understand. What does this guy know of Europe?)

55
Of course, art that describes the past
is outdated, continued the India.
A calendar from 1576 is historically indispensable
but quite dispensable when it comes to
punctuality. Art that duplicates the world
and reality, that copies these like a
beginner with his tongue hanging out of his mouth trying to
draw
the chair in front of him on a piece of paper,

this art is false, imbecilic, useless, decadent,
wretched, insignificant, empty, stupid,
and looks nice in catalogues.

56
Life is difficult, some of the phrases are long, but Bloom's body
can still rise up from the ground
and resist. He went on a voyage, he forgot the first
half of his life. He still hasn't entered the
second half, but believes that India
is the place where he will cross paths with what is
important. And in this moment he had so yearned for,
which happens for very few men, it is good to have
your hands free. Bloom, all alone now, raised up his neck.
He looked at the sky. I'm paying attention, he said to himself,
I am in India and I'm waiting.

57
But let's pick up the narrative again; and speed it up.
Days later, Anish finally took Bloom
to a wise man. Bloom had asked him to.
He had come to India precisely for this. And for everything else.
He is a man who is working during moments
when he seems to be resting,
Anish said of the wise man. The sounds that he
makes are of such a homogenous nature
that an unprepared person would mistake them for silence.
Can you think of a better indication that this man deserves to be investigated
and might be useful to you, Bloom?

58
The man who had never left his perspicuity
in some corner of the house, the way one sometimes leaves
behind a glass
of water, was named Shankra, and had learned
how to be old from trees. Though still, he was always
slowly ascending—like an oak that knew
its astronomy and was growing
in the direction of a particular star. Thus is Shankra.
Shankra knew that the number of stones in the universe
greatly surpassed the number of agile horses.
And for that reason, unhurriedly, he breathed, turning
the commonplace act of breathing into a ritual that everyone
respected.

59
Bloom knew that old age only exists in a body that
has gone through an illness or understood one.
There's no contradiction between the doughy stuff
that is on the table before the party and what's there afterward:
the vestiges of joy are shapeless matter,
it is the orientation of the mouth that makes one desirous
or bored. Shankra had had
incomplete masters: and this was his good fortune—there was
a path
left over for him. Complete masters
are quite dangerous: after them, there's no road left for us.

60
In front of Shankra the wise man, Bloom immediately
became more consistent, the way that, in
front of a tall mountain, there is always a desire

to climb it. The wind, for example, when it beats against a chime,
loses
its unique nature and gains a metallic sound,
as brief and minimal as it may be. And the inverse also
happens: organized metal, if it were to fall over a lake,
sinks, gets stuck in the mud, and gains unpredictability.
Bloom, in the presence of the wise man, said: I've come to learn.

61
But Bloom said further: I have brought mental
merchandise from all over Europe. I departed from Lisbon,
passed through cities that spoke languages that have been in use
for many centuries, old languages
that are perhaps closer to the heavens
than the school, closer to the muddy earth than
the formulas that describe it. I also noticed, on this voyage,
that there is no chemical formula for the element called earth.
And that is startling.

62
And that fire also lacks a formula,
no one knows the precise number of
atoms or the manner in which they are distributed in a
bonfire. Take note, master, that water has already been given
a numerical name, which might seem like a strange
expression, but that's what it is: H2O is its
numerical name or, if you'd rather, a number
that hasn't completely lost the affectivity
of a word.
Because I also learned this, dear master,
that numbers are not compatible with melancholies,
that any number, in matters of the heart, is zero.

63
But I also want to tell you this, excellent wise man:
my beloved was killed by my father,
and I killed him. I bring with me, therefore, an explicit and
localized hell. An abundance of negativity
cannot be gathered up in a garden like flowers; the logic
of misfortune is the logic of falling: negative things fall upon us,
and as for positive things: we have to carry them, pick them up,
invent them.
We are fragile in the essential things. The Earth tolerates us for
a few short moments,
and then it's had enough.

64
And Shankra listened to all of this with proper attention. Bloom
told him everything.
Without the mountain, there is no ascent,
without a good ear there are no
good words; great speeches only take place
when the crowd is excellent,
and a perfect line of poetry depends greatly
on the amount of disquietude that the piece of paper makes
available.
In sum: the world that awaits you is more intelligent
than it seems: it is a unique road
that builds an exceptional automobile, and not the other way
around.
Thus, since Shankra was a good listener, Bloom spoke well.

65
Bloom wanted to learn with Shankra how it is that
biology is counterbalanced with the infinite. The

beautiful juxtaposition of a meteor passing over a corral
had always astonished him.
Civilization and astronomy don't walk side
by side; after a great downpour, a library
building is penetrated by paltry leaks
the same way a cheap brothel
or a butcher shop is. There is no difference in the rain.

66
Shankra listened to Bloom, but requested a pause: one
doesn't teach a person that one doesn't know, and the wise man
didn't know Bloom. To know the name of your mother
and the name of the man you killed is to know
half of you; it's something, but not everything. Between
two big days there are two small days, and in these
personal, secret days resides the other half
of a living being. An exceptional life is made of
three exceptional days; but it's missing the rest.

67
Days are not separate from bodies,
a man is clothed in the days of his
past. Forgetting is a process of evaporation of
matter, matter that you could call former days,
thus spoke Shankra.
A man is the ten fundamental words he uses,
the three friends he has and the five most important
actions he has taken. However, who is Bloom?,
Shankra asked Anish, Bloom being somewhat distant.

68
Anish then told Shankra what he knew of Bloom.
He is the enemy of the ephemeral music that the rich
offer to the poor instead of blankets on cold days.
Thus an adversary of that which is abstract and accessory, such
is Bloom.
A man who hasn't given up politely tipping his hat
to women and who accepts seductions
in a natural manner. Bloom, said Anish,
is that which could be called
a European of the masculine sex, a seducer, and bearer
in full of a physical body. Bloom, Bloom.
And he has a beautiful name: Bloom.

69
But he also has mental misfortunes. Such a thing, you might say,
wouldn't be classified in the same category as miracles, but it
should be:
language can cause suffering, and Bloom
knows this strange phenomenon well. An insult
or a slight syntactical discourtesy
can ruin a
compact, biological day. The indiscreet air
that the syllables transport intermingles with facts
and, with them, forms a single landscape.
Occurrences, adjectives, and exclamation points
combine, in civilized cities, to form
a single mass, almost always bitter, rarely sensible.

70
Days, continued Anish, addressing Shankra, are to Bloom
magnificent and strange,

especially when it rains, suddenly, above
a fountain. It's that in this there is the pursuit of one fact after
another,
as if these two facts were enemies. But water
also has an effect on the quality of the air. Smoke from factories
and whatever comes out of a pig's snout when it raises
its fat, as-yet-uncooked head
are filth that is present in that space between city and sky.
That's why he likes to see it rain, said Anish of Bloom.

71
The world that is born is immediately assailable, and it's good
that way.
Bloom, said Anish to Shankra, doesn't like the events
of a week to rhyme with each other. He enjoys surprises,
especially when it comes at the very last moment.
At 11:50 at night
the day still has ten minutes to explode
indiscreetly. Nothing is firm until it is finished
And after it is finished, it is all dead. Firmness
and immortality don't exist, because they are the same thing
and neither exists.

72
And Bloom is a man with a good ear, Anish said further
to Shankra. He can easily distinguish between obese music
and the other kind, the simple kind, the kind that appears at a
certain point
and goes directly to its destination, without aural
adjectives. He who listens to good music deserves,
an optimist would say,
to be born in the next life as a flower—but Bloom would never
say that.

We should plant our stake into the blue.
That's the way he thinks. He isn't naïve:
he knows that beautiful colors want the stupid and
stagnant admiration of our eyes.
He prefers filth that might still be clean.

73
Shankra stood up. He knows that Bloom had brought with him
a small suitcase. I want to see it, he said,
calling Bloom over at the same time.
A suitcase is a tiny house and a tiny house
is an essential house. That which doesn't fit into a tiny house
isn't indispensable for joy, and whatever
isn't indispensable for joy is dispensable.
Show me what instruments this man, by the name of
Bloom, brought in order to grab the days without breaking them
and without forcing his steady hands to be overly delicate.

74
Because the defeated should temper their frailty
and the victors, their brutality, so that the world
doesn't split in two, said Shankra as he stood in front
of the sum of Bloom's days, or rather: his
suitcase. I brought a pipe, Bloom
showed him, for use after deeds are done, while,
for the deeds themselves, I brought a blade
and, within my body, a constant state of excitement, that energy
that is the basis for invasions of countries or the hearts of
women.

75
I also brought an artificial flower so that one single object
can remind me of
the wild forest and the greenhouse all at once. I brought with
me, in my memory and
whistle, a piece by the greatest orchestra.
I also brought a certainty: every invention disturbs
the existing order, but civilization is the running total
of all inventions; and, therefore, of disorder. I appreciate the fact
that a new day begins at dawn, but I don't like meteorological
forecasts. May each day invent a surprise
upon me.

76
Good weather isn't the placid sun shining on a massacre,
Bloom also said to Shankra, good weather
is weather that passes, numerical weather, that
occupies space and then leaves behind localized benefits
for living beings. "The weather is nice" isn't the observation
of a meteorologist, but of a wise man or a man in love.
It isn't the sun that makes the weather good, it is desire.

77
Days are hollow—they have more space inside them than
outside—
and they aren't influenced exclusively from the outside. Days
have within them an intimate, invisible space,
which is infiltrated by good or bad weather,
good or bad moods,
—as if, in fact, there existed a second sun capable of bringing
or not bringing
joy.

78
Thus spoke Bloom, the character, the enthusiastic hero.
But now the person who wishes to speak is the one writing.
May the nymphs and muses, and even my own
head, aid me in this writing, for writing
like this—epic poetry—demands detail
from a large animal and demands grandeur
from ferocious, yet minuscule animals. It is, therefore, always
on the other side of things.

79
And since it has been quite a while since we mentioned Bloom,
this side note can be tolerated.
Given that he was alive in October
of 2003, certain insights become apparent.
Here's one, just for a mere example:
a man's gaze is more important
to him than the things
upon which he gazes. It seems obvious, and
it is. We are selfish: we gaze and we take
our gaze with us. Even after gazing
upon the person we love. We don't want to become blind,
and that's it.

80
But it is Bloom who is speaking now. And Shankra who is listening.
It isn't just things like stones, says Bloom, trees,
families, a certain boldness in the laziest of dogs,
a glass on a table, a table, the chairs
that surround it; it isn't merely spatial things that
become more compact, isolated, and selfish.

But sensations as well. For example: childhood
went by quickly,
a climate that kindly came to rest upon us,
but life, however, isn't composed of pure kindness.
I am in the world: I know it well enough to be afraid of it.

81
And men will always bring along hell as long as
they are bringing their bodies. None of the seasons can calm down
certain disappointments. A single point
has countless sides; geometry has made a glaring
mistake: nothing is uniform or foreseeable.
And words are governed by force; we could
leaf through an entire dictionary or all the rules of syntax
and we could always find the same thing overhead, above us,
dominating: force, force, stupid force.

82
Ignorance and ingenuousness are synchronized
events.
Every happy day slowly eats away at
your joy. This is called enlightenment.
Ingenuousness with irony
is not a solution, but it's almost perfect.
Since we haven't managed to kill ourselves, we get up
in the morning; that's almost everything, says Bloom.

83
Men are what they are. Even lyric poets aren't all
that passive (even they, you see, are unable to offer up their hearts
to other people's forks).

I have met one or two saints, and I have met men
and women. I have been content and discontented.
As for the rest, the world is covered with elective affinities,
anti-democratic affinities. We like some people
a lot, others just so-so. Tears, like
all biological products, are absolutely
imperative: they are selective.

84
Individual feelings are elitist, from the feelings
of the poor man to those of the wealthiest man.
There are many animals species wherein the constituent animals
have a much greater number of differences than similarities
amongst themselves.
Madmen—an exception to this—are people who have learned
one
single song overmuch. I, on the contrary, will sing
any song you'd like.
A criminal kills,
a gardener gazes at length into the bottom of the well to
determine the quality of the water,
and beautiful children yell curse words at their
classmates who, unfortunately, have concrete physical disabilities.
Only for a few moments is the world not nocturnal, it is Bloom
who
is saying this to Shankra.

85
Armies have perfected hatred;
and progress, in almost every part of the world, means a
well-aimed
arrow. No bullet has ever gained morality

over the centuries: an explosion is a primitive moment
that is repeated. Modern airplanes leave
old death inside black plastic bags. A restless man,
full of energy, spends six months
correcting the syntax of a falsified death
certificate. A puddle of dirty water
washes the orange that a distracted dupe devours.

86
And thus the narrator goes along here,
endowed, like other people, with a personal project
that is full of perversions;
the narrator goes along here,
side by side with his hero, Bloom.
The two of them descend as low as possible and there, at the lowest point,
look for a crack, through which it might be possible to fall further.
And the only pieces of advice the narrator gives to
his character are lessons in
marksmanship: the way to make maliciousness efficient.

87
Much more important than perfecting kindness
is, ultimately, not letting that which saves us start to rust,
because that is what kills those who compete with us:
knowing martial arts, knowing how to slit a throat discreetly.
Finally, Bloom speaks to you:
the narrator of the world, the one who first began to tell stories,
knows the worst of the city perfectly
and that is where this divine narrator is taking you, not anywhere else.

Don't think, then, Bloom, that you still have time to go to some chic film premiere.

CANTO VIII

1
Just like aphorisms, personal objects condense
multiple days into a small space. (Every object
involved in a ritual or habit is, in terms of time: a lot,
even if it's only a few centimeters in size.) Bloom thus
continues to show them his suitcase and, within it, the domestic
aphorisms,
capable of being placed on a shelf, he had brought from Lisbon.
Shankra, the Indian wise man, sees this; and sometimes asks—in
the shorthand
question of a raised eyebrow; words are rare for Shankra—

2
What is the past? This: time that occupies a decreasing
amount of space, and this fact is visible in Bloom's suitcase.
The present—right now, this moment—on the other hand,
occupies all of the space that surrounds us. However, there will
be little left
of this sprawling estate that is time at this very minute:
who knows, perhaps the cleaning woman will have some ashes
to sweep up. Entire centuries are now kept in
shabby desk-drawers.

3
The marriage of History and imagination
has resulted in more children and enjoyable copulation
than the marriage of Truth and
a good memory. Howling like a wolf, thus is
the History of the world; it's hungry, it feels
isolated; History is a fluid that
flows beside men, a dense fluid
in which it is impossible to fish, swim,

or navigate; but the retelling of a country's history is as
full of lies as the story of a romance that
ended badly.

4
Shankra wanted to listen to Bloom's story.
And Bloom said, in seemingly enigmatic manner: days
split in two, as if time were
a plot of land: during the first part of the day one looks
at a tree branch in the forest in wonder,
during the second part of the day the same branch
is a nuisance: where to put it?
Thus it is to be alive: two days.

5
Since the shelves in the house are full of books, Nature
is only allowed to enter the house as an exception to the rule.
At the end of the day, the branch that was taken from the forest
is in the company of two empty wine bottles
and a wadded up piece of paper with the month's falsified
accounts on it.
Days would be perfect, said Bloom, if they didn't move.
The geometrical figure of the sphere, which
dominates the body, should have been replaced
by the cube, which is, in terms of movement, selfish:
it wants to keep all movement to itself: it doesn't move.
But the body moves; the body, indeed, and also the world,
whispered Bloom.

6
No transformation is ever premature, and Bloom
felt that talking to Shankra about his past

was preparation for a major change. Bloom
directs his momentum to the smallest facts, he wants to recount
in detail that which is already tiny. Every moment
has two sides, says Bloom. The weather of each season
has an inner scent, two sides
where all the facts occur, and a center from which the following season
will emerge.

7

When night began to fall, Bloom recalls, we didn't just turn on
the lights—prophesies were also made.
The faces of men became particularly beautiful
at the moment when they foresaw
the following week, and the young girls
took advantage of these unique moments and fell in love.
Prophets' lovers live longer,
that's a belief that the Bloom family
has never let go of.

8

Events that take place early in the morning
always seem easier to fix
than movements that come about round midnight, said Bloom.
Nocturnal strategies take centuries
to be transformed into tranquil joy,
while matutinal misfortunes have often been
resolved with just a couple of slaps to the face.

9

In the morning, Fate doesn't
yet exist; it just forges ahead—without once

looking back—to the end of the
afternoon. So, set your watches,
said Bloom, speaking, at the same time, to Shankra
and no one at all.

10
Bloom doesn't stop talking, and Shankra doesn't
stop listening. Symbols, continues Bloom,
take up two-thirds of the planet, and the other third is taken up
by the sea. Shadows are instruments of
intimacy: but we look at our own shadow and become
unsure about whether we are bipedal animals or
animals that crawl around on all fours. Where is it that we have
a greater amount of truth—in that darkened blotch that
crawls along the ground or in the upright
conversation about accounting and dictionaries?

11
Illnesses have also traced crude paths
over the fragile elements of a family. Vestiges
of sluggish misfortunes of nature are retained
in their faces like poorly safeguarded archives, open-air archives,
archives that get soaked in the rain, explained Bloom as he
bent over his suitcase, showing
and displaying what he had brought. There were photographs
in Bloom's suitcase,
many of them. Here's one: where did that black spot below the
lips of an uncle I loved
come from? Bloom doesn't know, but says:

12
Only look at the person we love
while that person is ferocious, this is advice I give to myself:
the illnesses of a beloved diminish weak love
and increase strong love, but any photograph of a dying person
is almost a crime.
Every man has a right to his own private horror,
said Bloom. At the time of the plague, he recalled,
men, in order to avoid seeing their own face,
went so far as to flee from standing water. Without proof
of the state they are in, people at death's door make plans
for the next century.

13
(In a windowless room with the doors closed
one lights matches with the same indifference
as when one flips on an electrical switch,
however, in the outdoors, fire, when it is started by
manual, ancient means, inspires controlled,
yet progressive, wonder. As the night grows darker,
the firelight presents both danger and calm.
Men gather around the fire with an animal that has been hunted down
and is now, at the central spot, a feast.

14
Enlightened people feed on fire at night, said Bloom.
The response to cold results in more movements
and mystical sensations than the response to hunger.
As a result of hunger, cities were invented,
in which men enter negotiations to avoid paying damages.
As a result of the cold, love and

prayer came into existence. Before
religions existed, there was cold. Without the cold
there would be no depth
to Man, exclaimed Bloom, raising his arm emphatically.

15
Knifes and hiding places are, as we have seen, widespread throughout
Bloom's stories. Bloom has some restless living beings as ancestors,
and he himself didn't merely move
from one place to another: he moved the location of those places. Every
individual fate can be connected to others,
he had realized this early on: life didn't disappear
when he closed his eyes,
rather, every time he opened them up again the whole thing started back up.
Filling the vessel with a new liquid.
Bloom raises his arm; then lowers it.
And he can do this thirty times over; and this is good
—and terrible.

16
Democracy, for example.
There was truly something supernatural
about a system that envisioned men
having equal rights, and Bloom, who spent so much time with
his attention turned to the sky and to this political system,
eventually tripped on the tiny,
nearby celestial bodies that geology has become familiar with
and that children make use of in neighborhood fights—stones.

But I have never tripped on a star,
said Bloom to Shankra, I'm not that idealistic.

17
Stones are trees of an even milder
intelligence, but everything is unique
and diverse in nature. No one wants
balance in the forest. Even the gesticulating
elements of the forest aren't asking for a truce:
they're fleeing, nothing more. And it's good that way.
Bloom says to Shankra: democracy isn't a spontaneous
political system, it is the invention
of a useful partnership. If it works, then it is moral—that's what matters.
And Shankra agrees, with a movement of his finger (or did he disagree?).

18
The ingredients of revenge, let's say, weren't the only things
Bloom possessed, but they were noticeable.
He had never forgiven the fact that the wealthy have their own private
judicial system. His father had ordered Mary, his beloved, to be killed,
and the law, which is implacable when it is suburban,
had once again become docile in the city center.
No one investigated the matter. A woman died, she's dead.

19
Out of tune orchestras have no significant
effect on the movement of the planets and stars,
but lack of skill always has its consequences, even

if they aren't of universal import. Songs that have become
disjointed
under the just phrases that make up a law
can completely ignore the requisite
competence. And this is what has already been understood: a law
becomes indiscreet when it is applied
to the best physiognomies of a given country.

20
Nothing new in this. Money isn't an invention
of the great outdoors: it was created in factories,
in densely packed rooms, in large buildings.
In a city, the taste of milk calls to mind a machine instead
of a cow. Evening approaches, and socks that were white
in the morning are black when they are taken off at home.
Low-lying smoke slowly eats at unwitting
ankles. The city drinks wine, and a few distracted
parents sing their children to sleep
with pornographic songs. If someone were to hear a rooster crow,
they would immediately think that some catastrophe had begun.

21
At any rate, in a city
battles are waged in a different way:
utterly civilized employees
transform into murderers
in an instant. Less than a second separates civility
from barbarity.

22
Flowers move around more in the city
than they do in the forest: the wind caused

by intense passing traffic offers them
no respite. The only thing keeping people from killing
is the chance deviation of trajectory: the desire exists,
weapons are sold at modest prices,
and two bullets connect with the body of the poor marksman.
A city is organized unhappiness.

23
Dynamite, Bloom reminded a person who already knew
everything,
was merely an invention
intended to cause the death of an individual or small
groups of people; with the robust atomic bomb
a product emerged that could be applied to an entire
population.
And of course an engaged couple, five minutes before a
wedding with two hundred invited guests, doesn't want to
hear about one hundred thousand people killed on the other side
of the world. However, if the catastrophe happens far away,
no one is going to ask the orchestra to play
softer.

24
Men and women are already humans in
an official manner. As if there were an ancient
formula that forced them to have language, good manners,
intelligence, and skills in mathematical calculations.
Gluttonous mammals, who can recite Racine,
piss out the window and onto the
street after one too many beers. The hearts of others
are not divine, dear Shankra, but mine is,
look: two atria, two ventricles. The right amount, isn't it?

25
In the cramped attics of the city, continued Bloom,
poorly paid foreigners, far from their families, upset,
slit the throat of a stolen chicken. Automobiles in line
at the automated car wash wait their turn,
and a careless driver reads a newspaper
in which two massacres are described with a certain giddiness
of detail. The hurried reader mistakes the
photographs of the corpses for pictures of disgusting culinary
festivals. The world is repulsive
and a masterpiece.

26
And look at this photograph: some idiot is extinguishing match
after match by
dunking them in the sea. He had fled from three tall, recently
painted houses, which had no compassion for him.
He smells the scent of the sea and gives a big smile. (Men
always play the role of tourists when
they're near the water, have you ever noticed this?
Madmen become more serious, and predictable men
start jumping around and pretend to have artistic
ideas. Thus is water and its effects. Foolishness, in other words.)

27
But what are the living supposed to do? Bloom doesn't know;
he had always made fun of aristocratic coteries and clubs
whose greatest adventure was to watch documentaries
about the strange beings that live on high-altitude
mountains; but what more can Bloom do?
At most, when he is sick or insane,
he can try to keep his spirit far from his body.
But not much more.

28
Hypocrisy, for example, is one of the most difficult
old habits for a man to break; it has stuck to men
like filth to a rag that is already grimy with dust.
It isn't a rare occurrence, you could say, to encounter a scoundrel:
they're usually gentle, they start off quite reserved
like a waiter at a fine dining
restaurant and end up trying to slit the throat
of someone who has just fallen asleep.

29
But let's take a break. And let's have a look at the scene:
Bloom is facing Shankra, but Shankra
is not facing Bloom. In this manner one man
dominates another, with psychological
positioning. However, Bloom carries on without
noticing it. And without noticing it he arrives at his central
point—his confession.
I abolished, Bloom says to Shankra, my entire past
all at once, at the exact moment when I killed my father.
There are certain, and rare, actions that combine a strong
memory with forgetfulness.
I remember and I forget; I forget and I remember.

30
What know we of the effects of our instinctive and
illiterate actions?
With a single hand firmly holding a dagger
one acts like a quadruped animal
connected to the ground at four points
and distanced from the heavens from these same four heavy
points. The spirit doesn't depend on quantities alone,

yet they aren't something to be
scorned.

31
Everything needs constant attention and
improvement, even the Eternal. If the Eternal
is the same today as it was in the twelfth century then
you'll notice a general disconnection between the people
and prayers made of outdated phrases.
The Eternal smells of the twelfth century, a well-informed
provocateur might shout,
but the important thing is this: even that which is immutable
will be pushed along if it doesn't change. The heavens, in my
opinion,
have become much too stagnant.

32
Matter is sounding its horn right into your ears,
into your hands—that noisy matter
that neither moves nor speaks. Matter shines, it's true,
and feels exalted when you walk by,
wants to participate in your movements,
to be included in your stroll: in fact, easy women aren't the only
things
that like to be underneath you; look at matter,
how it breathes, put your finger up its nose—
provoke things, my dear, don't let them win.

33
Places for people to kiss each other
are much fewer, in the city,
than places for people to conduct business

under proper lighting. And that's just, and that's fine, and that's
proper.
(And Bloom, at this moment, almost feels like attempting a
dance step,
however, at the last second, he decided not to.
Shankra, for his part, watches, listens, and remains vigilant.)

34
Children do not grow up in motionless
landscapes: shadows dilate with the variations
of the sun, and the sun loses importance with the
dilation of the clouds. Everything is in competition
—and even the most primitive animal understands this.
All living species cry for their dead,
but only humans get excessively overjoyed
about their own joys.

35
Seventeen black animals are circling
over the rooftop of your extraordinary joy.
Customarily, the plumbing system in homes is civilized
and respects directions and intensities,
but even an idiot knows that it is impossible
to declare the end of floods. On the eve
of heavy rainfall, the mother of the home carefully cleans up
three drops of an oily product that fell
on the floor; intolerable disorder.

36
In substances of this nature, there are no
predictable equilibriums: a single bad day
takes ten thousand days to be repaired;

how can we know precisely? A roof collapses
onto a child's feet, and bridges demonstrate
spontaneous engineering when they collapse,
drowning citizens who were formerly firm believers in the
goodwill of concrete.
(But we're ill-informed: matter
doesn't just collapse, it intentionally falls down.)

37
Matter wants to take vengeance on us.
And anger doesn't just exist in unorganized nature,
it also germinates in perfect mechanisms
that we utilize in the most superfluous
activities. May no machine replace us
at the moment when we fall in love,
this is a plea, and we do not yet know if it will be accepted.

38
Out of habit, parents meet their deaths
before their children. But if
a son kills his father, the displeasure
will be so great that if we all were to keep silent
perhaps we'd hear something. However, miracles
closed up their stables a long time ago,
leaving us the primitive brutality of the laws of physics
and survival. We've been abandoned,
and we're unable to keep silent.

39
Of course I had ancestors who were scoundrels, said
Bloom. Not even saints,
if they're honest about it,

have a spotless past. Permanent
tenderness is not a terrestrial thing; it is, rather, a lie, a falsehood:
no one believes it.
Some of my relatives were rational in their fury
(thus they made no mistakes)
and seemed to classify every quotidian action
based on an impeccable taxonomy,
as if they were living in tape delay
and not living live, on top of things.

40
These relatives, whose names I don't even
want to recall, had a respiratory system
and an amorous system, and carried out
what they had to carry out through the appropriate channels of the body:
you don't breathe and give someone a passionate kiss
through the same system
—and, despite all else, they knew this.

41
These relatives detested poetry, men, and women.
And poetry, in some
hidden place, there, where it resides, undoubtedly
detested them too. (If you look closely
you'll see that scoundrels are never contemporaries
of that which is beautiful—or that which is trying to be.
Like someone who looks in the opposite direction
when a perfect sun is setting.
Thus these relatives.)

42
It's true, continued Bloom, that in my family
there were examples of humans who spoke
a different language in their actions:
they didn't push, they touched,
they didn't ask others to repeat what they've said,
and they didn't hastily cut off chunks of meat
to eat, for they knew
that alimentation has an intimate relationship
with tranquility.

43
So they would have a calm lunch: each food
was a phrase that the tongue twirled around in search
of the nutritional position of each word.
They weren't gluttons, Bloom specified to an attentive Shankra—
rather, they were gentle people
who eat to defend themselves from the offense
that the existence of the stomach encompasses.
(Despite organic urgencies,
we are capable of being attentive to the path that the sun
traces on our fingers, and it is this that saves us
from beastliness. At least in part, of course.)

44
And at that moment, since it was getting dark,
Shankra, the Indian master who had been listening to Bloom
for hours,
asked to take a break. I'm starting to get tired,
he said. Without daylight, contrary to the normal impediment,
I can't hear as well. Because I hear by looking at the face,
said Shankra, and a lightbulb doesn't illuminate entirely,

it only helps a little.
Thus Bloom left, because for a wise man
listening under electric light was to falsify the narratives.
And Shankra was tired.

45
Bloom left; Shankra stayed behind with some companions.
And the truth is that as soon as Bloom had left,
one of the Indian wise man's friends opened an animal
as if he were opening a map
and, looking for a long time at the viscera-countries
full of bloom, said, like a prophet:

46
Master Shankra, I see that this man
is overly anxious for wisdom, instead
of calmly desiring it. He wants to get at wisdom
through movement, rather than waiting
for it. He is going to steal it from you, the way one steals a
chicken, for he is a strong and violent man:
he has seen someone die up close and killed that which was
closest to him. This man is either too
holy or too criminal. Don't trust someone who has suffered more
than you have, wise Shankra.

47
Thus it seems that a conspiracy was taking form.
What sets men at odds with other men?
What is the origin of the nausea of the man
who strolls among deserted ruins and
the envy of the man who takes his Sunday stroll
through streets full of commerce

and competent citizens? It is while they're asleep
that men become malicious, that's one possible response;
there, with eyes shut in that universal act, the bread of iniquity
bakes.

48
As if sleep provided one with knowledge
that goes from what one feels
to the handle of a weapon. For example,
the only people who commit murder are those who know the
method
of looking at others from a distance—
as if they were others, precisely.
(Bloom, we should say in relation to this, knows everything; he
has sung much worse songs.)

49
But yes: why is it that the disagreeable impression
that results from contact with another man is still around?
It's just that sometimes it seems like technological progress hasn't
even reached
the ankles of ancient envy and that
the industrial production of hatreds continues apace: in every
ego,
a productive factory. Faces,
my dear, look at the faces: there is no profound
progress that can be separated from physiognomy.
And faces haven't changed a centimeter
in two thousand years.

50
Shankra, besides, is a wise man, he knows History.
Malice comes from above and below,
and also from every other side.
Only the dead are safe from temptation.
And Shankra, he is not dead.

51
Thus Shankra was turned
against Bloom. Bloom wants to steal your wisdom,
they told him, and wants to steal your valuable
books, decapitate your library,
weaken you—he wants to turn you into a warrior instead
of a tranquil wise man. Bloom has come from Europe
to pick the best flowers here.
Don't let him, wise Shankra,
rid yourself of him.

52
And venom, as is well known, when delivered in a lovely form,
is welcomed as a peaceful condiment,
and that's what happened. The words of a friend
are always gentle and sound like poetry.
Shankra listened to them: and how could he judge the words of a friend
in a neutral manner?
For example, we're more fragile when we're dancing
and that's why we only dance around friends (we're no fools).
But that's just one example.

53
However, friends are animals like any other.
Enemies are much more inoffensive
—sensible people know this well—because they keep their
distance,
out of fear of our weapon
or preparing traps that are already waiting for us,
while friends, on the other hand, smell the same
flower we do, shoulder to shoulder with us, splitting with us,
due to the proximity, the joy that the world unleashes
upon a square meter of a garden.

54
And friends give advice, which is
highly dangerous. Enemies accumulate
threats, but threats are easily endured.
The threat of unhappiness is, after all, a nice heads-up.
An enemy's threat is, therefore, the true
advice.

55
No one can sense the ground very well when they're wearing
uncomfortable shoes, all of their attention
is directed solely toward the spot where their
foot is ailing. In the same way, no one looks
calmly at the world if they have mediocre friends
at their side, measuring diamonds in their right hand
while setting their watch with their left hand.
Either friends are perfect
or they are dangerous. Therefore, they are dangerous.

56
The truth is that Bloom had merely coveted,
in awe, a copy of the book entitled *The Mahabharata*
which seemed to be older
than many countries. (In antique copies
of books of wisdom, even the dust and the insects from Antiquity,
which jump from page to page,
have lessons to teach. Deactivated lethal bugs
transform, over time, into tame
insects and, over even more time, into
beautiful butterflies.)

57
For this reason, Bloom believed that the antique
copy of a sage book was doubly
sage. Being a bibliophile, despite the fact that he sometimes took action (and how!),
but a bibliophile from his eyes to the fingers that held the page open,
Bloom was a man who was capable of holding up an entire country
at gunpoint just to enter its private library,
and take from the third shelf from the top
a first printed edition of *The Imitation of Christ*, for example,
with its ancient, magnificent cover.

58
Bloom was a bibliophile even in unexpected places.
His mania for books went from his
fingers down to his toes, for as he read he always
accompanied the rhythm of the phrases
with a slight tapping of his toe on the ground

—as if he were listening to music. And this
madness for books of his had been notice by
Shankra and all of his friends. A man
who has loved, killed, and likes books is
an errant danger.

59
And this expression is important, let's look
at it closely: errant danger.
There are certainly precise dangers that are nothing more than those
that we encounter and have to defeat
while we are forging along the right path.
On the path that bears our name,
on days during which our ignorance meets our knowledge,
on those days, the dangers that arise are either nutritious
or mortal. If you don't die, you learn.
But in your death, others learn.

60
Errant dangers are the opposite:
dangers that arise when a man
has taken the wrong path.
They're neither nutritious nor mortal:
either they're mortal or they delay life a little, which isn't that bad.
Of course, Shankra, as has already been mentioned, listened—a lot and intensely,
for he made his ears coincide with
his attention. And he also heard these intrigues,
and digested them.

61
However, Shankra also had eyes,
and with them had seen, in Bloom's small
suitcase, two treasures,
two books that old Europe had
invented: *Epistulae Morales ad Lucilium*, by
Seneca, in such an ancient edition
and with pages in such a state of deterioration
that you could almost say that they weren't material page, but
spiritual ones; and
Shankra had also espied the complete plays
of Sophocles, also in a rare edition.

62
There was, thus, between Bloom and Shankra,
a mutual covetousness, a thing that always exists in the world.
(Unilateral covetousness is
the invention of unenlightened men
who feel that man, like the world itself,
isn't a sphere, but something else entirely.
In fact, however, within man and on the face of the Earth,
there is everything, and nothing is shocking.)

63
The planet Earth is a sphere and
it moves, has done so for a long time. However, this fact is still
presented
in certain bourgeois drawing rooms
as some enormous revelation or wretched heresy.
Some people still haven't realized
that even the right side has two sides:
and one of those sides is to the left. The wrong side,
the devil's side.

64
In fact, wretchedness also exists in saints
(and Bloom is about to realize this):
within these better organisms there is no joy
or nausea when faced with man's
mediocrity. Ethics isn't a matter of import for cells,
will is what matters to them, the unequivocal decision
to proceed down one path and not the other
And then there is always the matter of legs, which is to say: the body
can always choose to go in the opposite direction.

65
After digesting everything he'd heard and seen,
Shankra summoned Bloom to his house, days later
and brusquely said to him: you told you story,
asked to borrow books and long words
that would change you. Before, however, I teach you
I need to have proof of your suffering:
where is the weapon with which you claim to have killed
your father? And a photograph of your beloved,
where do you keep it?
We're in the twenty-first century, said Shankra,
there isn't a wise man out there who can afford the luxury
of relying on narratives
and dispensing with visible facts.

66
Stepping indecisively on a floor
that seconds before had seemed holy to him,
and now just seemed to be wood, Bloom just remained
still for a few seconds,

not knowing exactly what he was standing on.
But then he once again opened his suitcase
and, from a small hidden pocket, pulled out an even smaller dagger.

67
This is the knife, said Bloom, that cut
my life in two.
The handle is made of some anonymous material and there is no information
to relay about the blade: without any vestige, without
any promise. A simple knife, in sum,
just like many others.
Whosoever grabs the handle, dominates,
whosoever is facing the blade, loses.

68
And if you want to see a photograph of Mary,
the woman I loved, look at me,
closely, and at length:
for you will see her face. And if you don't see it,
it is because, in the end, you are merely in possession of normal vision,
and you are neither saint nor sage, but
a scoundrel who, in India, cons
Europeans who have traveled a long way, and come to
you exhausted, unable
to discern with precision.

69
And at even this point, it should be noted, nary a feature of Shankra's face

moved; nary a gesture,
nor even did the smallest of his fingers seem offended.
He was so attentive, this wise man, that it sometimes seemed
to Bloom like he was talking to a deaf man who also couldn't see.
Yet even so, Bloom continued to talk about his past.

70
I defend myself from criminals, while in the presence of professors
I become vulnerable (that's the only way I can learn).
No one is attentive in a state of complete well-being,
discomfort is necessary, a slight
insecurity. That which I already know, I have left sitting
on a couch somewhere. And I did not leave my body sitting on that couch.
That is why I decided to come to India.

71
I have come from Europe, I am European and Portuguese.
When I raise my eyes to the heavens,
I bring with me what I remember of History.
Scoundrels and saints, I carry them with me in my memory.
An old house smells worse
and collapses with greater ease—yet it has books that are more
valuable. I have come from old Europe
and I am proud of that place: it still has a future,
not everything in it is visible yet.

72
It is old, that's true, it
has selfish presuppositions, it has been invaded
by science from one side to the other, and even the most

religious people, before they kneel,
study, in detail, the anatomy
of the bones and muscles in the knee.
They don't choose their positions
according to the Gods they worship;
they obey, instead, the precise recommendations
of the family doctor, explained Bloom.

73
Be it Winter or Summer, in Europe
one suffers more in the body than in the Spirit.
And in this particular, the twenty-first century has changed
nothing.
In terms of spirit, the continent is sinking, that's true,
but it still has mountains.
It is sinking, it's true, but it still has helicopters.
It is sinking, but people can still manage to stand
on their tiptoes and there are still at least
ten living people
who deserve to be heard.
In Europe, old
Europe, there are still unpredictable brains.

74
And my life is merely a specialization
in the continent where I was a child and an adult, said Bloom.
It is the Earth that causes flowers and
trees to stoop over, not the inverse. And of course I went on
this voyage to India to become a new
tree, capable of transmitting benefits back to the old soil.
I want to return to Europe, but not with
trifles.

75
I want to take half of what you know,
which, combined with the half that I remain ignorant of,
will allow me to be curious in the right direction.
With just my ignorance, I would be curious
like a numbskull;
with a portion of your wisdom, I will be curious
like a sage.
Wanting to understand the world and our own heads
should instill in us a sense of urgency, the way someone who
is about to drown feels urgency, exclaimed Bloom.

76
Understanding is not an activity for the laggard;
it is urgent.
We are born: and we almost drown; and to understand is to attempt
to swim to dry land.
There is no dry land, you might say, Mr. Shankra,
but what do we know?
We are human: we cling to habits
that make us feel immortal. In this, we fool ourselves.
We are alive, let's lift up our heads: they cut off our heads.
That is all.

77
Shankra, meanwhile, listened
with a circumspection that is common among great conspirators
and saints. Bloom looked at him and started to waver:
what is the greatness in which this man
has specialized? However, Shankra suddenly
interrupted the silence and proposed a trade: the ancient

copy of *The Mahabharata* for the *Epistulae Morales ad Lucilium*
and the Sophocles plays that Bloom
had in his suitcase. Agreed?, asks Shankra.

78
Bloom thought: I have traveled far and long just to end up
in bibliographic negotiations. I thought (Bloom thought)
that wisdom didn't have a certain number of pages,
but I was wrong. There are books and more books—too many
books (thinks Bloom)

79
There are no longer any wise men, only readers, exclaims Bloom.
Everything is paginated:
intelligence, science, religion.
Language came into the world
via pre-battle yawps, but it improved upon itself:
it acquired details, yet not a vision of itself as a whole.
Bloom coughs, smiles, bides his time. He points to the infinite
and hits it square on.
Or else misses it entirely. What is he to do? Bloom
is confused, but wants to leave.

80
But he accepted the book trade: done deal.
Bloom was quite familiar with the damage that good
and bad European weather had done to books of wisdom;
now he could see and smell the ancient dust of India
in an old book. Intellectual merchandise:
it doesn't cease to be merchandise, but at least it provides the
illusion
of a certain grandeur.

I have always been a collector, said Bloom,
I accept the trade and shall depart. Shankra smiled.

81
Shankra coveted Bloom's two books, but
he didn't intend to trade his ancient copy of *The Mahabharata*
for them. Far from it.
Shankra knew how to declaim pretty words,
and even managed to cite, at this moment, some
apparently generous actions
(to repeat an action, it should be noted, is to quote movements;
however, a good memory isn't the same thing as sincerity, as
Bloom well knew).

82
A good memory isn't sincerity and
the biggest swindlers are those who never
forget to let maidens pass through doorways
first.
Shankra had revealed himself: one part wisdom,
three parts greed.
He asked Bloom not to leave India yet.
There's so much to see, he said.
But what he wanted was to steal Bloom's suitcase and, along
with it,
the two books.

83
The wise façade was thus revealing, little by little,
what it was hiding.
Bloom was actually in the presence of a thief.
A book thief, sure, but a thief.

Is the man who steals a book on science
a scientist?
Is the man who steals a saintly book
a saint?
What trifling questions, Bloom would say,
if he could hear me.

84
In fact, Bloom had known this for a while:
we are inseparable from our worst characteristics.
One can fake it for years,
but each person is inseparable from the evil they do.
It exists within the radiant bride
who cuts the cake with dexterous fist
and knife, and in the groom
who already has his eyes on the legs of the bride's best friend
while he's welcoming all the nuptial
congratulations. Life is disloyal to the living
because no one knows themselves entirely.

85
Evil cannot be buried, this is what Bloom is reflecting on,
it can merely be interrupted. The heart is
a miniature when placed
beside greed. No kingdom
was ever founded by pollen or
any other docile substance:
kingdoms and men
get their start through the strength they possess
and even the weakness they feign.

86
Bloom could sense what Shankra
intended to do. A man
who has seen dead people up close knows well
how to look at the living.
And a living man offers
more clues than a fowl's
viscera. All it takes is to pay close attention to
the way someone approaches
a chair and sits down, for example.
A man's ethics are brutally visible
when that man fully engages in his habits.
And Bloom, who perceives that Shankra is fully engaged in his habits,
doesn't like what he sees.

87
When we are alone with our habits
we don't protect ourselves, thinks Bloom.
In fact, there is no hiding place
for a man who is happy.
And it's easier to hunt an enamored citizen
than a rabbit in an empty field.
A touch of melancholy alone allows for the existence
of hidden places. Bloom looks around: no hiding places
or rabbits to be had. And he, indeed, is the hunted.

88
Bloom's salvation was thus owed to the
sadness he had brought from Europe—from
Lisbon, to be precise. Lacking the hobbling
naivety of the happy, his thoughts

were agile. It wasn't a "vague judgment"
that "fluctuated," it was a concrete judgment
that held steady and observed.

89
A premonition, as everyone knows, is
knowledge without content,
the wordless definition
of a concept. And when premonitions operate,
they interfere violently within the body, returning
to man that which he lost as he sat
at a desk in school. No one
is truly erudite if they do not know the historical
dates of the invisible, of these premonitions
that have revealed themselves to be powerful.

90
Because everything that happens in the world is the effect
of the actions of the body and material things,
but also the effect of incommunicable sensations:
the great general and the great poet only move forward
after they've received the message that nature gives them and immediately takes back
so that no trace of it remains.
Not even the great works of engineering look down upon
intuition.

91
He felt threatened; that was the premonition.
Bloom—and this is what's happening now, some seconds later—
found himself
surrounded by Shankra's disciples,

and understood what they wanted:
that he, generous Bloom, offer the two books
to the enormous Indian continent,
more specifically, to the one meter and sixty centimeter tall wise man
who coveted the libraries of others.
He wants to receive and, like all humans,
doesn't want to give. And he's no longer hiding that.

92
Shankra's disciples
already had their hands hidden in their pockets
—perhaps clutching a weapon (who knows?)—
but they were able, even while playing the role of bandits,
to project a mystical quality in thirty percent of their behaviors
and small gestures.
A marvel of technique and tradition.

93
Threatened by two very tangible knives,
Bloom was obliged to hand over his suitcase
to hands that vacillated between religious tremors
and that other kind of tremor originating in the nervous system,
which is commonly found in those committing a robbery.
And together with those hands, then, and his suitcase, went his two precious books
—by Sophocles and Seneca—in exceedingly rare editions, which Shankra
had effusively praised. Having been robbed up to that point in an almost polite manner,
Bloom breathed a sigh of relief, when

94
suddenly, one of the men
grabbed him by the neck, holding a dagger
that, with its blade forcefully pressed against
his neck, immediately transformed Bloom's skin
into an obsolete material (because it was threatened and fragile).
Bloom was stable at this moment:
from his feet to his head,
from the skin of his nose to the most recondite organ:
he was afraid. (How good and useful it is to be a coherent unity
in certain grievous moments.)

95
Well then: they threatened to cut his throat.
You will never be able to speak European languages
or any others again—they told him. Two agile men
threatening him with well-aimed weapons,
and this is what they want: money!
If stealing books is a cultured action,
stealing money is merely a bank transaction:
Bloom thus put all the cash he had on him into his suitcase.
In sum, they took many common banknotes
and two rare books. (But they didn't take his radio,
the one that didn't work.)

96
The mystical disciples of Shankra the mystic,
whom Bloom had come a long way to visit
in order to learn about matters of invisibility,
thus took from him, in bright and visible light,
unequivocally material things.
Religious masters, but poorly prepared ones:

unable to see a lost banknote on the ground
without blushing.

97
And money, as Bloom had known for a long time,
makes men predictable,
like a chicken who follows a straight line drawn on the ground
until the end of its days.
Money exists in the mountains, on the plains,
in city and countryside.
It destroys kings, carpenters, and saints. (And when it isn't around,
it destroys even more.)

98
The Gods gave us everything, in fact.
We just have to gather it from nature: fruits,
animals, various lettuces, water, sun, and money.
How beautiful the future is when even nature
expands with human progress (there is, right now, with the twenty-first century in full swing, a new fruit.)
This is the nonsense that Bloom is thinking about internally at the moment when,
outside his head, they declare his sudden bankruptcy.

99
Ah, money is so evil, so evil and horrible
when it doesn't belong to me, thinks Bloom,
as he directly, without any middlemen, hands
sums from ignoble Europe
over to wise, sensible, and receptive India.

CANTO IX

1

Bloom takes account of the situation.
Noisy children in shorts gather together, first,
and lost track of each other, afterward,
due to the absentmindedness of the adults. Between two rabid
dogs engaged in battle, there is no space
for a pause.
In a crowd, there is no
space for one lone man.

2

The miraculous waters of the Ganges are a religious liquid,
but, in rivers, gods dissolve more easily
than the filthy, thick substances
that are readily detected on the surface of the water by any eye
that isn't asleep. Not even the imagination is capable of banishing
the filth from the Ganges.

3

But while, in reality, Bloom is fleeing,
let us praise the imagination.
With mental solutions, for example, one doesn't need
utensils that connect material
or immaterial things: nails are replaced
(and for the better) with a rapid association of ideas.
The head still practices the ancient tradition of
mixing things up: the universe is not even divisible by two.
One; no more and no less: all is one.

4

And let's return to the narrative.
We are in India, and Shankra and his well-armed

disciples don't seem to be satisfied.
One is not happy after evil action,
yet even after acts of kindness there is still appetite
and the following day.
And Bloom, meanwhile, now standing next to Anish, is
trembling.

5
Neither infamy nor heroic acts are the end point
of anything.
If the world stopped spinning one day,
the final moment wouldn't be bombastic,
it would, instead, be discreet.
Great institutions like the universe
only ever end out of boredom; they will die
the moment they develop a habit.

6
Anish tells Bloom that the disciples of the thievish master
are not yet content, that they want to be disciples
of a murderous master.
Shankra wasn't pleased that Bloom was still alive:
the living have a tendency to recount narratives
and that fact might end up being unpleasant. So they are
coming back
to kill you, Anish advises him:
and Bloom quickly grabs his suitcase, which is much lighter now
(not because it was more mystical, but because it was more
robbed.) He is preparing to leave India.
Out of instinct, he puts his hand in his pocket, and fortunately
it's still there:
his radio.

7
However, Bloom wasn't born just
to use words at the right time.
He is a man of action: he doesn't promise
to do things, he's already done them. Thus, then, with a slight
grin, he shows his friend Anish the old
copy of the mythical book called *The Mahabharata*
which he pulls out of his shirt, then quickly
hides it again. Today, says Bloom,
recuperating his irony, today my
attire is, literarily, indispensable.

8
But there was more: Bloom shows Anish
a gold chain that he'd stolen from
Master Shankra's house. At the very moment
when they are concentrated on stealing,
thieves are more easily robbed
than a little old lady with unmoving eyes and
retrograde step. Go tell Shankra,
Bloom whispered to Anish, that I'll only return
his gold chain if he gives me back the two
books.

9
Exceedingly old editions of Seneca and Sophocles
in exchange for a gold chain: who
wouldn't agree to that? No one is so foolish
that they can't see the incomparably greater value of gold.
And the meaningful difference is this: a sentence, even one from a first edition,
can be transcribed somewhere else.

10
Bloom protected himself, in a perfect hiding spot,
from those disciples of Shankra who were after him.
And, while he waited for the negotiation with Anish
to take place, he couldn't help but recall
all that he had been through on that long voyage,
first in Europe, now in India proper.
Wanting to escape from past
sufferings, and thinking that in India he would find enlightened belief
and enlightened men that he had not found in
scientistic Europe, here is what it has come to: it is Tuesday
in a gigantic continent, and Bloom is in a dark, cramped
hole, hunched over like a fearful
wolf.

11
Hidden, like an animal who could kill or be killed,
sensing that his knees and his stomach are in proximity to his mouth,
Bloom feels, at this moment, disgusted with himself,
disgusted with his obscene temperature that was around thirty-seven degrees Celsius,
which doctors claim to be a healthy quantity
—and he also gets disgusted with himself for belonging to the human species: the most
devious animals in the universe.
I am hunched over and hidden in a hole located on a continent
where elephants have room to run for kilometers
without crossing paths with a single enemy.

12
But Anish arrived, and with him the two rare
books. Shankra preferred to get the gold back, Anish
said to Bloom. Now you have your books
and even *The Mahabharata*, about which Shankra, with his
eyes looking somewhere else, didn't even remember. But don't
waste another
minute: flee, get out of India, Bloom!
And that's what happened. With plane ticket
in hand, Bloom headed quickly
to the airport, whispering: one more day here
and I'll lose, from head to toe, all of my materiality.
And this is the Bloom who wanted to find the Spirit.
(The plane, meanwhile, is already taking off from the runway:
farewell, India.)

13
Seated beside Anish—who, at the last moment,
half out of fear and half, the smaller half, out of
friendship, decided to go with him—
Bloom was caressing the most solid and, at the same time,
most spiritual remnant of his travels in India:
the old copy of *The Mahabharata*. This is the proof
that I went to India: paltry proof, paginated proof,
but proof.

14
The word, in fact, cannot be reduced to our
will—insulting a continent from afar
isn't enough, you have to be mistreated by it first.
I am not taking immortality with me from India
(which is, without a doubt, regrettable), though I take with me

physical abuse and a definitive loss of illusion.
And I am also taking that which I brought: my father's old radio.
It didn't work then. And it still doesn't work.

15
Everywhere in the world the world is the world.
There aren't any interruptions of non-humanity form, thinks Bloom.
Even in the consistent sky,
in this extraordinary rational stroke of fortune turned bird, in this airplane,
even being infinitely far from any tavern
where infamy is merely verbal,
though still infamy,
even protected, then, in the air,
which they say is the element closest to God,
even there men don't rule out
murder, and they aren't ruled out from being the target
of a conspiracy.

16
They say that on the journey back there are no surprises
—adventures always take place on the outbound trip,
while passing through the first time. As if facts
trafficked in times that are favorable
for unease and others that are propitious for the repose
of warriors. What's certain is that Bloom and Anish, on the return trip,
like two friends who share the same origin
or food from the same plate, shared in their exhaustion;
and fell asleep.

17
Life, my dear, is illegible. It happens,
then disappears. There is no intelligence
that can decipher it: it comes about in nothing-language,
it emerges in the body the way a day emerges, and as
if a day and an individual life were parallel materials.
Life emerges neither in prose
nor in poetry—and existence doesn't speak
English, after all. The nature of occurrences
resists the material invasions of advertisements
and films. Which isn't a bad thing.

18
Wearisome episodes, once concluded,
attract a prolonged docility to the organism.
Thus, Anish and Bloom have been asleep for hours,
and men, when asleep, look more antiquated,
as if they had come from another century.
Besides, sleep is an ancient tradition:
it was given by Nature so that the gods could take a rest
from the intellectual and physical mischief of
the privileged bipeds. Humans sleep
so that the heavens may relax.

19
But the airplane also has inhabitants
the way a country does: there were one hundred and fifty of them in that
modest flying compartment.
Side by side, they were all sleeping, the way one sleeps during a presentation
at a conference: you're sleeping, but with one eye paying

attention. They were going straight to Paris, where they had a
layover of a few days. Bloom managed to inform his
Parisian friend, Jean M: I'm coming back from India,
I need rest.

20
Astronomy is a monumental science, however, it doesn't
interfere in the apparatuses that stabilize the wings
of the plane. It moves forward. And Paris, meanwhile, it should
be said, being
a city, though it is unmoving, is also moving forward.
Jean M is already putting together a welcoming party for Bloom.
In Paris, parties are, as a rule, more cultured
and have a higher occurrence of quotations; therefore, they're
less fun.
—but Jean M is preparing something different.

21
Jean M knew the tragic story that Bloom
had fled from Lisbon and he could already sense that the voyage
to India had resolved nothing.
So he prepared, in order to counterbalance this
considerable intellectual and spiritual failure, a voluminous
physiological
reward for his friend, Bloom. He bought drinks;
he selected aphrodisiacal recipes. To
easy women he added things of even greater ease.

22
If Bloom hadn't found peace
through the spirit, perhaps he would find it through
the flesh, that's what Jean M thought while

he contacted women who were sexually well
organized. Jubilation comes about through
the most varied channels; nothing is linear in
men, only the laws of physics are
predictable, thought Jean M. Invisible
songs, for example, take hold of bodies in
different ways. And since man feels sensations,
nothing can be ruled out from his future.

23
In books, virile prose might arouse
the most sensitive ears, but reality,
with its tendency to allow matter
to exist on its surface, is much
more disposed to touch and, therefore, to a
certain specialized form of joy. An imbecile
doesn't give up in imbecilic frustration
when it comes to making erect organs work properly on
organs of arrival.

24
Of course, when it comes to dense and obscene love,
it should be noted, there are departures on both sides,
and to both sides there are arrivals. And sometimes there are even
more than two sides—which may cause
a momentary disequilibrium.
Nevertheless, the matter is serious. Sometimes desire can go awry,
like a crime, and the effects are not amusing.
It's just that no scientific discovery can modify the
face of a man as powerfully
as moments of pleasure.

25
Look at the world, whispers Jean M,
the world isn't as predictable as one would think.
Hostesses at a rooftop bar
set up surreptitious lunches behind the backs of ingenuous
wives. Adulterous husbands in the turbulent city
chew up young women who just want a stable job.
That's where we are, Bloom, care to dance?

26
There are still joyful songs that are sung at
monetary ceremonies. A man marries a women,
and the two of them together create children
so that the population continues to exist. Inventions have
wreaked havoc on the present, not the other way around.
And Jean M wants to lead Bloom's future
toward the most ancient things: the body and its earliest
techniques.

27
Astrology controls and foresees great
movements in altitude, but, in suburban apartments
and basement, fragile women are
abused, and not a single insightful look up to the sky
comes in handy on the day that is existing for them.
Ancient families store books of Greek mythology
on the tallest shelves,
and buy guides
for getting rich quick.

28
Besides, as Jean M knows well, obscene men exist
in every city and all climes.
There is no element that can placate their arousal:
amorous deceit takes place near the sea
just as much as it does on the top
floors of tall buildings.
And malice does not turn black at the seaside.

29
Jean M is running around, organizing, thinking; he can see a
film in his mind.
Proverbs and important phrases accompany the wine that
precedes adultery.
In bed, perverse noises emerge from the sweat
of a soldier who conquered, in eight months,
half of a vast country. Desire
digs a grave in which to bury
ethics, and two men urinate upon that soil,
accompanied by two malevolent laughs.

30
But there is also love, of course. And Jean M is in a hurry,
walking around Paris as if Paris were all downhill.
Couples gather firewood and long stories
for Winter. Conflagrations and sudden bankruptcies
connect families to the little they have left.
A scar fuses docile hands together,
increasing their affective precision in the wake of
the slight external tragedy

31
There are songs that make you cry
and songs with other effects: if two humans
sing together, habitual hatred will never emerge
between them. But songs
that leave the heart perplexed
yield indifference in the more important organs.
Useless songs, therefore.

32
Jean M is running around, organizing, thinking; he can see a
film in his mind.
The only antiquated habit that made it
to the stupid twenty-first century intact
is the habit of love. Members of the population are exempt
from going to some delivery center
to pick up the intact amorous
instinct, for they receive this obscure thing as soon
as they are born. And they die with it. Love
as an obscure thing that refines our days.
There is Jean M, free, in a hurry, nearly on his tiptoes.

33
Days are instruments that require refinement,
and love has its own ear, capable of
recognizing the faintest variations. Only the dead
and, temporarily, those who love them are immune to death.
But without false hopes: the best side still isn't perfect
because it's a side—and one side always has the other side.

34
There is, therefore, more world:
commerce has become sensual
and the constant fluctuation of the economy has taken the place of mystery.
Fluctuations in currency rates have replaced the unprofitable fluctuations of mythological insects.
Adult men now drool over news coming
from the place where money is a fiction
that oscillates.

35
Encounters during the "nocturnal hours"
were invented by the ancients. Nothing new.
Along with philosophy and Pythagorean numerical melodies,
there also arose erotic skills, where moral perversions
were drunk down along with inebriating beverages.
In these bedrooms for virile guests,
a woman who was celebrating her immortality would soon be dead.

36
But there is more world still. Jean M looks up at windows;
he imagines scenarios.
A seducer praises the abundant breasts of the wife
of an illiterate who is not around.
Holy women manufacture diabolical experiences
with men who never tire of repeating elegant
movements in public streets. In the city,
adjectives have, for some time, been customarily employed to hide
transgressions.

37
Neckties make friends with each other
while they lower their pants in arousal
on top of a woman who doesn't have a bank account
to defend her.
Everything is desire and nothing. And nothingness always grows
tired.

38
However, Bloom is a man who deserves
not to waste time discussing eternity with a
beautiful woman. He is alive and has suffered,
and still seeks to turn his suffering into
a system for getting to know the world
and men. Because he did get to know them, men, that is.
He went to India, he was robbed. So he deserves to fall in love
one time
or fornicate a hundred times. This is what his
friend, Jean M, the Parisian, is thinking.

39
Not only is it good for your résumé, friendship also
mollifies arguments against existence
and other kinds of arguments as well, if one has any. The gentle
eroticisms
of which friendships are composed counter a
certain sort of brutality with which animals
touch each other in other situations. Jean M likes friendship,
and friendship
likes Jean M.

40
And only the heart can give touch
the insane attention that is concentrated on details.
The other way around, if touches are
only applied to large surfaces, it is because we are in the presence of
an impressive desire, which is a daily occurrence and continues to occur.
(In periods of well-paid employment, it should be noted, the Summer is
overloaded with nuptials and solemn promises.
It is vital, after all,
to have some financial resources in order
to lie.)

41
Jean M wanted to give his friend Bloom
a much-deserved reinvigoration and was planning a big party, but
carefully so—for when you're mixing disparate things, errors can
always crop up.
In Paris, women who satisfy the most particular tastes and the
most extraterrestrial desires can be found
in catalogues.
Jean M, while he awaits the arrival of Bloom and Anish's plane,
thus consults these pages, visually affirmative,
yet succinct at the level of vocabulary.
At times, his eyes bulge; at others, he closes them
and exclaims certain things.

42
Despite the useful camaraderie
of the great metropolises,
in this primitive world there are still
desires that can only be satisfied on less-than-innocent
street corners. And desire
has never been content with symbols, as Jean M knows well.
And this is why he is moving ahead, organizing, making phone calls.

43
But there is a lot of world out there. The world isn't just Bloom.
Let's take a short stroll; then we'll come right back.
Far from here, corpulent men set their wine down on the table
and leave through a door through which butterflies
had escaped earlier. A loud man
strikes a match and shows it to one of the butterflies
that didn't escape. That close to the fire, the insect
is up in flames in seconds,
and someone cynically holds out their hands
so that the beautiful colors don't fall on the ground.

44
We aren't in a painter's studio, someone whispers,
however, the butterfly has been transformed into a tiny black ball;
there are no colors in the world, and this is an indication of that fact
—the imagination invents colors to relieve boredom,
but a simple match proves that everything
is done for, everything is in its final resting place
when black emerges.

45
But let's continue our stroll.
At some other spot in the world, a Russian
grabs a plastic bag—it's six in the morning—
and places inside it a replica of an important
building in Moscow and also a replica
of his life; he puts the bag in a river, lets it float away,
and the next day the fat creature who gave birth to his children
will find him in the kitchen, hanging from the ceiling,
his neck so red that, at first glance,
it looks like a new light bulb, a strange light bulb.

46
Nearby there (or perhaps far away) is a house that is still dark:
the father hasn't come home yet. And there is world there too.
A little girl cries because her stomach hurts and there's no light
for her to see that there is nothing on the table.
The girl collapses, and her mother says that when her father gets home
he will lift her off the ground—but the father never returns.
There is a lot of world, decaying and desperate,

47
morbid, disorderly, overly mixed up, made up of promises
that aren't kept and far too many unforeseen occurrences.
Nothing ever keeps the right
time; watchmakers attempt to straighten time out,
but nothing ever comes of it: when something is fixed on one side of the world,
a new disaster is inaugurated on the other side.
Indeed, there is a lot of world, but at the main airport in Paris,
Jean M already has three women at his side; and, with them,
three significant bodies.

48
There is a lot of world, nothing is easy, but in that case
a catalogue and a quick phone call
had resolved the situation.
Jean M is at the airport and has three solutions for three problems.
In less than fifteen minutes you will
fall in love with the men who are arriving from India, said Jean M.
They deserve it, he whispered.

49
And so it was that the plane finally landed. Bloom and Anish
descend from it with diminished suitcases and overloaded memories;
brief embraces, Jean M, Bloom, and Anish greet each other.
The women are quickly introduced;
Jean M winks
at Bloom; two taxis are already waiting for them,
and the group immediately heads to the outskirts of Paris,
where a rented house will serve as the venue of the much-deserved
party. All of them—men and women—are already
aroused en route, but the women were paid handsomely beforehand
for that feeling.

50
Those women were excellent, and even professional.
They were so skilled in balancing the amounts
of modesty and seduction that the recent arrivals
—Anish and Bloom—were now only making mental calculations
about the near and tactile

future. Not for one moment did Bloom
remember that he had just returned from
a voyage to India that had spiritual objectives.

51
(The women contracted by Jean M,
though profoundly out of date
in their knowledge of the visual arts
—for them, Matisse was an opera singer
and Caravaggio an Italian general who
wore a hat—were, after all, exceedingly up-to-date
on the art of seduction in the twenty-first century, which
only goes to show how human culture isn't uniform,
but rather made up of highs and lows. We know some things,
and are ignorant of others.)

52
But the taxis stop at the entrance
to a small grove of trees, and they all get out. The house
I rented for the party is just a little
further along, said Jean M. And these six famished
elements continued on foot, passing around
a bottle full of wine that was more or less
unforeseeable. Thus joy gradually begins
to forsake the future, whereas memory
had already disappeared long before. Bloom is tired,
and the forest grove suddenly renders them all silent.
Eminent nature brought to the group a
surprising silence.

53
Because that grove is tranquil
(as if it had been organized by an
ancient Chinese poet). Brown branches
welcome the colorless wind with the joy
of a canvas welcoming the most intense pigments.
A wind so slow that it seems like a natural
proverb. Moments exist, but they seem
recoverable. Not even time is lost there,
where nary a sound from the city penetrates.

54
In the distance, a small hill. In no
other place would a simple human whistle
seem more insulting. Out in remote nature,
Sunday mornings unfold without
interruption. Only the wind seems to restrain
the spatial monotony. The sun shines through the
leaves and is the only information received from the outside
world.
Reality finally seems complete
because there isn't a single machine in the vicinity.

55
They then pass by a small lake
where the water seems to adapt itself
to angles propitious to vanity: it becomes
a mirror. The water isn't for drinking—
at that moment they all realize this
—water appeared in the world to exact
beauty. Its reflection causes
an immediate action: each one tries
to bring joy and a good name to their face.

56
Well organized fruit trees
show that human love fulfilled
the slight effort of Nature.
Orange trees laden with fruit,
which when held in the hand seem to absolve the sins of man,
show themselves in uncommon proportion to what they hide.
The trees are shy, but they instruct.
One of the women, for example, grabs an orange
and almost seems like a child.

57
Trees that are attentive (like predators) attack the early
light, slowly chewing it;
no one can see it, but they're growing. Laurels,
pines, poplars, those kinds of things. From the sky comes
the permission to grow; from the soil, the strength.
It doesn't stand out as much as it does with obsessive animals,
but the plant kingdom toils; it never stops,
never sleeps.

58
Red cherries are scattered throughout
the tree, perfect and round.
Gentle fruits possess a concentrated, ferocious
energy. With each bite, new things are
imagined: the image of a careless kiss appears on the surface
of a mulberry.
A leaf on a tree has more energy
than a running animal, and Bloom is a man
who understands this, finally.
(However, behind him, on his back, a slight itch that's
bothering him.)

59
One must never touch small fruits with the wrong hand,
because the mulberry, for example, fits in the hand like a dying
person: it gives in and waits
Besides, among the requisite preparations for the tree to grow,
we should
include the general theory of the earth, a minimum
luminosity, and the insistence that the wind come
from the proper direction.
Nothing is overly complex, nor is anything overly simple.

60
But here is an example—and it comes from below.
Flowers that deserve half the light of
a full day don't demand more
than a few glances. Vague vanities,
however, become virile in Spring.
In Spring the earth swallows parts of the sun
to nourish seeds and make them useful.

61
Innumerable are the laws
that organize the growth of living beings:
the lily, the rose, violets, each element grows
according to an intimate philosophy for one
explicit color. Flowers that almost dance—but with minutiae.
As for Bloom, he doesn't dance, but he sees.

62
The world of plants represents a country more
than its governments, that's obvious.
Trees are the oldest language.

The religious history of a given land
is ultimately in the animals
that made their houses there and in the plants appointed
by the precise dampness a country possesses
below its most recently built structures.
(But the space will only be complete with a corpse in the ground
or,
up above, a bird.)

63
A woman, meanwhile, says, oh Jean M, says, ah! And Bloom,
because he is silent, says nothing.
But deep down they are all admiring the same thing.
In fact, only due to their enviable lightness are the swans able to
glide like that across the lake, as if between
the animal element and the water there were no difference in
weight, instinct, or feeling.
The water is simple, and the swan is simple
in equal measure.

64
But as they proceed through the forest grove, the group
—which taken together is no dummy—
isn't only directing their energy
to the contemplation of the earth
and its representatives. Among the women, for example,
certain of their footsteps enlarges nature in a
conspicuous and feminine manner. Bloom, for his part, senses
music
in one of these women, in what might be her mere movement,
and that woman thus becomes essential at that moment
and in that place. She isn't perfect, but she exists
and is there.

65
It's true that the theoretical conditions for a seduction
do not include numerical equilibrium
between the two sexes, a fact that isn't
exactly an invention
of the twenty-first century. However, with the instincts
of a rural landowner, Bloom, Anish, and Jean M
decided, with three or four glances at each other,
who was going to be with whom, organizing the
spontaneous love into precise and symmetrical accounts.

66
Fastened buttons on a woman's shirt
thus quickly become redundant, and
one of them, smiling, briefly displays the
corporeal location where respiration can best be observed.
Bloom tries to think about something else.
First, he concentrates on the shape of his own
ankles, but that's not a way out.
Then he tries to imagine what a person
who is smiling the way that woman is smiling
at that moment might be thinking. And sees that there is
nothing more to see,
much less to think.

67
Never letting go of the small suitcase that seemed
to mark a border between ancient, tranquil spirit
(an area in which the valuable edition of *The Mahabharata* is
distinguished)
and external arousal, Bloom followed the woman,
who amused herself by calling him over to a small

arboreal indefiniteness;
in which place the two exchanged kisses that were short-lived,
though they possessed long-term promise. No longer troubled
by eternal thoughts, Bloom began
to prepare human instruments.

68
Anish and Jean M were mingling in there as well,
among the fine fabrics of the women's clothing and
their firm fingers, bringing into sight
elements of the body accustomed to implicit
discourse.
Certain well-trained women are capable of caressing unprepared,
ingenuous hands
with their breasts. Who is touching whom, that is the question.
Anish, for example, would have called out for help, but
it was physically impossible:
the woman was kissing him vigorously.

69
Jean M, for his part, verified, through
non-mental calculations, the physical stability of the woman
who was wearing not a skirt, but a metaphor of a skirt
—along with other indicators.
Meanwhile, other short narratives occurred in succession
until Jean M said or screamed: quick, let's go inside.
And the three women, Anish, Bloom, and Jean M
went in the house, shutting the door abruptly and forcefully
behind them.
And with that gesture they forgot about the tranquil forest grove.

70
It should be said: there is no immoral idleness. It's true that
outside of
work, men shrug off their politeness (which falls to the ground
like a weight) and, since they are lighter, are thus prepared
for iniquity or fun.
In idleness, the face frees itself from the body and, alone, acquires
a personal style; however: a dangerous one.
A solitary animal does not utilize the language
of man. And even in the company of other humans
—as in that house in the grove—it isn't easy to avoid loneliness.

71
Let's return to the house where the women are already
revealing part
of what they brought with them hidden. When there are no
liquids
like wine around, men and women behave in a
serious manner, they discuss symbols, are not abandoned
by their intelligence and the necessity to put it on display.
But there, in that house, in the middle of the woods,
in addition to the wine, there is beautiful love; and love or strong
arousal
increase the effect of the wine, just as the wine increases arousal.

72
The women quickly transform those men
into tatters. A man
—Bloom, to be precise—who has recently arrived from the
most spiritual continent—India—
carrying with him, in a small suitcase, books by Seneca
and Sophocles, as well as *The Mahabharata*, and concealing

a useless radio in a nearby and hidden place,
that man, look at him, is either hungry or thirsty.
What's true is that he is lacking something or has lost something because
in that crazy house, a prostitute is greedily pursuing him.

73
And Bloom has an aroused snout, there's no
other way to say it.
(In general, it should be noted, all movements are decent.
Even in a factory, the workers who for years and years
repeat the same tedious gesture
have a right to be praised for the quality of the movement.
Yet when men are aroused, they abandon themselves
to some other kingdom, for if all movements really
are decent, there are still some frightening faces.
In fact, beauty is superfluous when one is fornicating.)

74
The nails holding that dwelling together are shaking, and Bloom
attentively watches the women and men
who are undressing. He is once again alone in the world,
but now he is inside a dwelling,
in a forest grove, with an aroused
penis and an easy woman
who already offered—per her contract—
her mouth and heart. Bloom removes the skirt
worn by the woman who is raising her buttocks. And the thing proceeds.

75
The house has a vaulted ceiling and was free of dust.
Jean M knows that desire
is diminished in dirty places, while hell
is the perfect hiding spot for cleanliness
and pleasing scents. Anish grabs the neck
of one of the women, and the thing proceeds, even when it stops.
The potency of the man is already entering the feigned feebleness
of the woman. And vice versa and both at once, like crazy people.

76
Anish, for his part, remains delighted with this new continent.
European women bend over
with unique gestures (everything, in fact, seems extraordinary
when it begins for the first time). At any rate,
the density of that which is human in the house
diminishes: there are now certain sounds
that are added to the animal characteristics present,
moments in which men and women seem
to unburden themselves of an entire city.
Maximally aroused, those humans no longer possess homeland,
city,
friendships, and family.

77
The woman assigned to Bloom, for example, was producing wickedness
the way certain animals produce tiny points of light.
And wouldn't stop.
Bloom now grabs her forcefully;
the thing proceeds and stops
and, as sounds that enlarge the imaginations are coming from the other bedrooms,

certain gestures are, at that moment, almost autonomous.
Bloom grabs the woman by the neck,
and she bends over.

78
Bodies are still able to escape, even
in some minimal space. With
a penis disappearing inside a woman, she
still flees from him without distancing herself physically,
displaying uncommon
mastery of ancient modes of escape, down to the millimeter.
On the bed, the two of them wander through each other's
organs. For Bloom, an externally provoked joy
is approaching; but not for her.

79
A long sequence between two
bodies: the expansion and intensity
have a scent, and the scent brutally
increases what is done and the will to carry on.
Enormous movements occupy the
passive bedroom;
a crude precipitancy of Bloom's
sex, which the woman soon calms down.

80
It isn't truly repetitive
to repeat two or a thousand times
a movement that gives one pleasure.
She, for example, goes at it again,
repeating,
but now a novel manner.

81
Strength has a direct itinerary
and moves forward.
The woman still has a shoe on one foot,
but the foot is alive, turns about, wants to get out.
It could scream, but it doesn't scream.
As for the rest: the usual. Like progress:
it seems to advance and then retreat; at the end, nothing is
decided.

82
Meanwhile, the woman threatens to locally abandon
Bloom's arousal, which almost causes
an uproar.
Admirable buttocks pace
from one side to the other
as if they were mocking the virility
of the man who is restraining himself as best he can.
Bloom wants it, she retreats. She wants it, Bloom hesitates.
The two advance, and the thing happens.

83
Laughter at the aroused nudity destroys
what could still be recognized of that
man. Bodies, when engaged in reciprocal action,
reveal a mystery or two:
no one understands a man or a woman
until they see them engaged in these exertions.
What a pity, then, for Bloom that he is unable to see
himself at that moment.

84
Bloom ultimately shows what is hybrid
in a living being: there is not a single
tranquil quality right now in the man
who traveled to understand life and the living.
There is no India. Not even a desire for India.
What there is: on one side, arousal; and on the other,
whispered greed. Simple and practical things.

85
But let's get away from this confusion.
Arousal is ethically neutral.
Two minutes can be the difference
between insane physiological feats and quite lovely tenderness.
However, life is not naïve. The human species
has piled up enough perversions
to be admired, in this regard, by the other hot-blooded animals.

86
Man didn't only invent machines, secrets,
and some details of morality.
The city, and this is a fact, has legally expelled
illegal injustice and the obvious forms of torture (which, despite all else,
is progress). Collectively, the human race
has improved itself. That is a fact. (And improvement in the realm of perversion
is still progress.)

87
However, a man alone is not a collective,
and Bloom knows that well.

With a companion beside him,
Bloom becomes less than he was.
One plus one equals zero, or close to it.

88
Yet this man who has reflected upon
all things, Bloom:
this man who has loved and suffered,
who has watched someone die and who has killed;
this man who thought he could turn existence
upside down, break it in two like a shard of glass,
it is this same man who is now caressing the somewhat firm
buttocks
of a woman whose name he doesn't even know.
Who is Bloom? No one knows (especially not him: he's too close
to the thing).

89
He is an organism that possesses the potential for anything.
He could be a saint, or sell stolen angels
to the church of a priest who offers salvation.
Men grow hungry, and when
they are afraid they run away, and in this flight they step
on the ground or on other animals. Love exists,
but not within a living being that moves.
The unexpected wheedles its way into that which seems definitive,
and no one ever knows themselves before they die. Amen.

90
So two genital organs approach each other—and their
minor tasks—with solemn
speeches on

mountaintops. Insane religions banish
eternity to a single important book
that promises to save man down to his
last atom,

91
but Bloom lost this
essential book long ago;
and hardly knows the names
of the mountains.

92
An action is always incomplete,
the days that follow carry the previous day with them
—as if the calendar wasn't an idiot
or as if the numbers were aware of something.
Murderers, thieves, and other specialists
are delighted by more social sensations
than the beautiful, good, and noble layabout.
In fact, kindness isn't exclusive to good men,
which causes much confusion.

93
Bloom, for example, is good and bad.
And also (like the Chinese) is familiar with the middle ground.
Governments should surprise women who
live on the outskirts with flowers,
but that's a whole other matter.
The city does not take from one side
to give it to the other. It takes from both,
so as to be balanced.

94
Bloom is tired, he thinks about the voyage he took
and the books he read,
looks at the woman he just finished studying
(Lord be praised: in the end, she isn't beautiful)
and thinks about the people who are, perhaps,
waiting for him in Lisbon (who knows?).
Bloom, what is there to say about this man?
He went to India and came back, Bloom did, and in this
perceived that
there is no Spirit.

95
He is alive and, because of this, is less naïve,
neither saint nor wise man; he is a body and moves about,
nothing more.
Bloom again looks at the woman beside him,
but now, in his head, he can only see the city
of Lisbon. Lisbon and Lisbon.
It's time; quick, this is it!,
he buttons up his shirt, does Bloom.

CANTO X

1

But the day went on, and Bloom's shirt was
buttoned and unbuttoned countless times. Inexhaustible, the
women; exhaustible, the men.
Night approaches, and
the six human beings are happy
(the surface of the water is calm
before any strong stones rupture it).
After the transitory advance and retreat, dinner
is being prepared.

2

Professional women put just the right condiment
on the food.
Prostitutes handle napkins with techniques
that are similar to those they use
when taking off a shirt.
Bloom is observing these minor details.
Everything is so insignificant that it is almost ridiculous.
Bloom, much to everyone's astonishment, starts to laugh very
loud.

3

The three men and three women
sit facing each other, in pairs
—more amorous than the agreed-upon
price would indicate. The meal is strange, for
something is bothering Bloom.
He has taken a shower, his skin has already forgotten the
bedroom,
one smell overtakes another—an aromatic narrative.
The rice and fish are praised.

4
Wine comes to one who drinks it,
and water appears for one with thirst.
Musically restrained laughter occurs
before the wine is served. And even the neutral water
seems to want to break with a centuries-old tradition
and become a direct interference
in the enthusiasm of men.
After making love, cold water is a dreadful liquid,
said Jean M.
And he drank his transparent glass in one gulp.

5
Joys evolved.
Words lost the circumspection that exists
before a man drinks the right amount
of wine. They told stories, and
Bloom described his adventure in India.
A wise man who tried to rob him and
a ground upon which people walk barefoot,
but not as a Spiritual option.

6
With good, widespread conditions,
the various religions will disappear
in less than two centuries, said Bloom,
provocatively.
But on top of poverty
and the cold, there's also death, countered Anish.
Death, yes, the great annoyance.

7
Of course death is right beside us
or far away, or it is nothing at all
—for our death does not exist for us.
One dies outside of life,
which is absurd and also obvious.

8
Bloom couldn't know that which his
body hadn't yet done. A body makes death
when it gets old, and within Bloom
this artisanal work hadn't yet begun.
When immortality is discovered, churches will cease to exist,
thinks Bloom. Shall we make a toast, he asked?

9
One of the women had been talking, however,
with the surprising clarity that wine bestows.
One's vocabulary doesn't increase with alcohol,
but the shrill quickness with which words bind themselves together
changes abruptly.
Nothing in life is redundant, everything
is shocking. Bloom smiles.
After the ferocious obscenities,
his prostitute is gently attacked by feeling.

10
(Yes, you should give yourself over to life,
"or soon unto death," there isn't a
third option. And if you give yourself over to the fact
of being alive, you'll forge ahead. You are made

to go from one point to the next, like a line.
You obey that which you are made of
and that which you are made for. In the middle
of a path, you are neither at the beginning
nor at the end. And that is a sufficient definition.)

11
But let's return to the woman who spoke like a machine
that had acquired language.
Bloom, for his part, his stomach full and without desire,
could finally be civilized
and, thus, in an extremely polite manner, he prepares to pretend
like
the woman's statements are interesting;
and in reality, indeed, they are of interest to our hero.
Bloom abandons a certain look of mockery that was on his face
and
starts to listen.

12
She had been abused by her family, and if the portion of
nature
that shares our last name doesn't welcome us well into the world,
what are we to expect from the rest of it?
Despite having blood ties,
every man comes into this world alone
(like a machine, moreover).

13
And she was a woman, the portion that is weak of strength and
slow
of speed, and for that reason is even more alone

when born. Slow and weak, surrounded by strength and speed.
(Life is in fact dangerous for those who possess it;
it is too close to something that we cannot dominate,
a ferocious energy that has no name.)

14
And between Bloom and this energy of the great tragedies,
there isn't a single millimeter's distance.
He is resting, happy, upon something terrible.
In Autumn, gravediggers open several bank accounts
—however there are more than a thousand professions
and all of them are just because men are hungry
and vain.

15
Dogs sniff around far away from the carelessly spilt urine
of the elderly. A day, or every day, at most,
has a topmost part, but it keeps it to itself.
Nature is selfish about things that are high; for gods
with weary eyelids, monumental skyscrapers
are insignificant engineering feats.
Men are in a hurry because
they are little. When they're big, they're slow, thinks Bloom.

16
What is the difference between what I am saying
and what a singer says?, asks
the prostitute. I was abused from an early age;
how, then, could others want
to discover the truth before I do?
Ever since I was sixteen I, all by myself, have known what
the truth is: the truth is money.

17
Illness, yes, and major accidents
—those are terrible, said the woman.
But the unpredictable cannot be controlled,
unlike
money.

18
Money isn't a surprising element
that nature causes to arise in someone's life,
like a flower in a garden gone to seed.
I'm not sick, or dead, she said,
and I have one or two friends who don't always
want to fornicate for meager fees.
I don't complain, for example, about the previous centuries
I never lived in.

19
So the massacres
of a single city can't be counted on the
fingers of one hand: what does that matter to me?, she said.
I am a woman who is alive,
I have to defend myself. And whether or not others
remain alive
doesn't interfere with my own survival.
I am alone, with my sex and my
youth—the two greatest companions.

20
Everyone knows that recounting a tale of successive tragedies
diminishes the sympathy directed at the unfortunate victims,
however, the woman, distracted from this effect

by the joyous effect of the wine,
carries on with her explanations about the commerce
between her life and bad luck. Who is negotiating with Destiny
on my behalf?, she asks. Through which extremity does
bad luck enter the body?

21
Nevertheless, the table is set.
The wine bottles remain upright; the food,
cast down, as if defeated—the remains
of a fertile fish and rice that
smells divine. And in the hands of the three men
glasses raised in the air;
whereas for the three prostitutes,
their gestures are more docile and symbolic
(however their glasses are also raised).

22
An almost suitable energy organizes
the microcosm of the table;
tablecloth, silverware, leftover food, the red stain
that fell from a careless cup spreading across the white fabric;
and, still, the mouth of the woman who is repeating
a circumstantial vocabulary.
Everything is now more tranquil.
And the strange thing is this: the prostitute is becoming more restrained
as the wine flows more readily.

23
And Bloom, meanwhile, with strolling eyes,
mentally places the proper punctuation on the architecture

that surrounds him.
Commas as slight separations between two spaces,
period as a more accentuated separation,
colon as the door that opens expectations.
That house is one that is prepared for violent songs,
but also a roof capable of sheltering melancholy.
And thus Bloom, at that instant, recalls being
a child at play, and suddenly feels a nostalgic longing
(who would have thought?) for his bicycle.
How absurd, thinks Bloom.

24
We should circulate, between kindness and
cruelty, on a bicycle, thinks Bloom, facing
a woman with a vigorously low-cut blouse, which he no longer notices,
because what he sees in front of him
is his childhood.
(A bicycle is a beautiful and splendid, manual and primitive mode
of transport, but it is also technological: the
world is made up of spheres that communicate amongst themselves
in the heavens, and the two simple wheels of a bicycle
put into practice a sort of domestic
astronomy, and when one falls off it, it's not that high a fall.)

25
As a child, Bloom was pushed atop
his bicycle by the attentive hands of his father.
A tactile courage was required: the landscape
appeared and disappeared. To transverse a small space

at high speed, to rapidly open and close one's eyes:
getting to know something or not depended on the speed of the body
and the fixedness of the gaze. Those who run fast, even with
eyes wide open, see nothing.
Immobility and attentiveness are quite synonymous!
Don't run so much: you'll go blind. That's what he had learned.

26
What does external speed matter?
For example, Bloom, who is now sitting still, is rapidly looking around.
A table and a few other objects that could be broken:
a small table off to one side—a card table;
and in the middle of the room the large table (you could tell by its cut),
the table where no games are played: it's for business transactions
or lunches. Wooden chairs, a blue couch with
blue cushions, white walls,
everything clean and simple—ready, then, to become filthy.

27
And Bloom looks around and feels happy.
In a perfect brothel, can the man
who sought his Spirit in India
feel calm? The answer is yes.
The body is rarely predictable: many and varied
are the intrusions into any moral path.
But Bloom already knew this. He didn't need to have failed so badly.

28
In that house there was also a lighting system
that was like a game: the exact science
of illuminating and darkening; a metaphor
in light bulbs for another game: that of seduction.
Electricity that conceals and reveals, that's
what each woman brought into the world when she
seduced; and Bloom smiled, meanwhile, at the prostitute
who was still narrating the not at all poetic life she had led.

29
But the spirit cannot be reached from the outside
—as any anatomist
will confirm. Disconcerting errors
of ethical evaluation affect people who are trained
in creating taxonomies
based on appearance.
Eyes are machines that discern
colors and shapes, but an action isn't merely color or shape;
it is also the sensation behind it.

30
Eyes can only see the miniscule portion that,
in infinite substances, is able to be seen. (Amen.)
As has been said, bad people aren't always practicing wickedness,
nor are good people always practicing compassion.
Actions are distributed randomly
among men, and Bloom, for this reason or because of something else,
begins to cough, think, and
become nauseated in the middle of dinner.

31
So Bloom started coughing and thinking
—or else something had occupied his brain and was thinking
for him.

Books of Greek mythology
are now being attacked by the roots
of young cypress trees.
And somewhere, on a television channel,
flies are seen alighting on the wreckage
of an airplane and a man.
Turn off the television, requests Bloom. But there was
no television there.

32
Ships reach the shore
like bombs; music is being played on the pier;
a helicopter propeller smothers
a declaration of love; God's design
doesn't correspond to any day ever, these thoughts are progressing
in Bloom's head.

33
The secrets of the South are
billboards in the North.
A woman is carrying blood in her laundry basket,
and there is no night that couldn't be improved.
Bloom's head—he lets it fall
onto the low table, the card
table. If he had been conscious,
he would've rolled the dice.
I'm available to lose my head:
so roll the dice.

34
The calendar has phrases from the Bible,
and women from ancient China are undressing
at a precise rhythm. A woman is weeping.
The tradition of touch is to recommend imprudence and
manifold pleasures; it's rare for touch to be timid,
but it has its limits.

35
Tiny, malicious animals
try to chew the light, but the light survives.
The eyes of three men
see the eyes of three women,
but they seem to be organs with different functions.
And a man who was leaning against happiness with all his weight
has fallen. The others pick him up.
Bloom is the one being raised up; the others are helping him.

36
A highway is interrupted by
a perfect apple,
automobiles swerve around it;
there are a number of accidents because of a single red and
undeniable fruit.
The death of the Aztecs is still our death.
We continue to die, thinks Bloom,
unaware of the banquet around him.

37
Love spreads out until nothing is left in the center.
The intense blows of life upon the living
—and life keeps on delivering these blows, repeating them over
and over;

dogs engaged in intercourse that ears can hear;
muscles caress a beautiful yellow treasure,
gold is gorgeous, and Bloom is drunk (or something else).

38
A woman sings language,
the right names in the right chairs,
the city is whole when compared to a roasted animal;
pleasant smells and napkins;
the deaths of others are toasted.
A man peeps inside
a true song and loses his head.
Bloom agrees to something, but doesn't know what it is.

39
Maybe he had heard someone say: a toast!
Bloom stands up, doesn't hear anything, doesn't see anything
—and what he does see, nobody else can see.
A fig tree is keeping half of the sun for itself,
up above, movements in the leaves of the tree.
An important book on love begins with a page numbered zero,
but no one has ever found it.
Me!, says Bloom, raising a finger.
But no one can understand him.

40
We're starting to die, says Bloom
(did anyone hear him?).
Winter was split in two,
and Bloom grew sad.
The insane, all of them cured at once,
push against the building where all the doctors

have gathered to pray;
a box falls, it breaks. And Bloom is drunk,
or something else.

41
Three prostitutes and three men are talking amongst themselves
and gaze and keep watch and seduce.
The men look at each other,
and comprehend each other—the same exact violence and the
same will.
In the Occident, the divine has been carefully paginated;
it has an expensive binding.
In the Orient, elegant desistence is still valued,
thinks Bloom. And he suddenly gets up, but then sits back down.

42
The pork on the table—that animal
felt the hand of a woman six times.
What beautiful meat, whispers Bloom. What?,
asks Anish. There's no meat.
The landscape suffered a violent blow:
the fattest animal was plucked from the landscape
and turned into a feast.
Jean M tries to remember a wedding song;
Anish claps in applause; Bloom hears things, the women talk.

43
We are in that phase of the party in which each person
is looking out for his or her self.
Bloom is performing a balancing act.
The best words are displayed
in a crate at the market (like fruit)

and the city's inhabitants take their pick.
Bloom is performing a balancing act on a table,
and one of the prostitutes is singing or screaming.

44
Bloom almost falls, the prostitute almost shuts up.
The man is turned toward the earth; and he is going to fall.
Exactly like a coffin: religion
is the same average size as the sick.
Bloom raises his right arm,
celebrating the fact that he has found a treasure.
Anish does the same, Jean M as well.
But none of the three know what it was they found.

45
Bloom makes minor movements,
as if that which his head was seeing
had a sound.
As long as there is convergence between what our ears hear
and what our eyes see,
life moves along. However, there in that house, on that table,
the confusion is so great that if the world is moving along, it is doing zigzags, like a lunatic.

46
The universe is interrupted for someone when he
pricks his finger—this is classical egotism.
Anish cuts himself—and rails against the world.
Jean M says that he will personally have a talk
with it, with the aforementioned world. Bloom looks out the window; it seems full.

In the sky, black clouds and

birds, a smaller volume.
What was I saying?, asks Bloom.

47
Meanwhile, in the real world, at the feast,
liquor and other liquids and other smokes are being drunk—
and Anish and Jean M, with a stupid match,
melt down a substance that is simple,
yet makes one think a lot and in a strange manner.
The women devote themselves to fantastical commentaries,
and still there is, apparent and obvious, a stain on the tablecloth.

48
The collapse of buildings
—and of empires—
begins with a wine stain
on a perfect tablecloth. This is entirely accurate and well known.
Six humans seated around a lascivious table
are smoking things, drinking others
—and a prostitute is counting the number of men she has loved
on her fingers.

49
Bloom stands up and almost leaps
toward the ceiling;
he breaks a glass, his innards seesaw.
Wine encircling the heart, says Bloom,
our hero
—who is slightly ill and melancholic.
(A woman died, Bloom loved her.)

50
Bodies have arms, they feign rough gestures,
but the day escapes, you cannot lay
a single finger on the day at hand.
You are external to it, and you didn't want to be.
It took a voyage to India to verify that men
correspond,
between the Occident and the Orient,
with uninterrupted letters;
they speak the same ancient language: that of any
predator.

51
Appetite, dexterity with utensils,
fear, selfishness, greed, and arousal.
Invisible matter organized in a marketable manner:
a church has a door, a basket for money, and
charitable words. All of life is for adults.
One shouldn't enter into such a demanding world
as a child.

52
All lies have already been born
and an old man was lying down
for thirty minutes before a slower woman
went over to him and said, in a whisper:
you are dead, quite dead. Anish is the one telling this story. It
happened in India.
Old people die, teacups shatter in the kitchen,
the shards are swept up;
careful, watch out: don't cut yourself on the shards of others.

53
Step by step, rodents
in the city are taking over
the high places where
statues of angels,
two faded crosses, and an ancient
yet perfect book are kept.
A believer no longer knows how to pray,
he's hoarse
—holy words possess a unity
of a precise length. (Whispering
isn't as easy as all that.)

54
The light from the sun is too strong,
and eyelashes completely cover
that piece of man that sees.
People are dying in their own bedrooms,
and a woman ordered, recounts Jean M,
a large plastic bag
that would be able to hold one meter and eighty centimeters
of useless love.

55
Life exists, Bloom loved a woman,
and in Paris he is drinking with other women
for whom he took his shirt off.
Next to Bloom, Anish is smoking a weird cigarette
and is flicking the ashes into a crack that exists in the middle of the world.
He laughs and gives Bloom a hug.
The gravediggers are going to have a hard time

burying happy men, he mutters.

56
But the facts are more objective. Plastic bags
transport tropical fruits or bodies after accidents
(the double function of things).
It isn't proper to wash your heart
in a puddle of dirty water,
and if you wash a six-sided dice
in that same water—the numbers
won't disappear.
Don't pull a fast one in this game of chance, says Bloom.
After which he laughs a lot.

57
A primitive serpent run over
by a brand new automobile, animals
have ceremonies that machines will never know of.
On the tallest bookshelves, a book
contains a line of verse that blinds.
In taverns, people insult each other
with ill-mannered verbs and, sometimes, spit at each other.

58
And a young man who possesses intelligence
is ridiculed by a living being
who carries in his right hand a dagger
and no shame.
Bloom interrupts his visions at times and
stands up, says something, loudly, that no one understands
—but it is inside one's head that things take place.

59
Stories are told that measure time,
but every human, as is already known, has his own watch
—and never sets it.
In front of a blind man, the red color
of a painting is ridiculous,
and the thighs of the woman whom Jean M made available
are found, by Bloom, on the surface
of his body.
After all, not everything takes place inside the body.

60
The world ultimately exists and forges ahead—at least on top of the table
or just below it, at the level of her thighs
and his left hand, the least dexterous one, the one that thinks less.
But, within Bloom, inconstancy persists:
time stops or retreats
as if it had lost its north, its south, and all the rest.

61
Then he puts his hand, absent-mindedly, into his pocket and there finds
his reference point—his father's old radio,
old and antiquated and, as ever, nonfunctioning.
After Bloom had traveled so much, the object was still there,
mute and still, as if that radio had learned nothing
from the voyage.

62
But there is also the woman's beautiful thigh, and Bloom is there for that, not for other matters.

What a woman!, he exclaims or tries to think,
and in fact there is nothing better than beauty right before your eyes
to help one forget one's melancholy.
However, the woman isn't actually all that beautiful, quite the opposite
—which makes forgetting more difficult.

63
Bloom is once again listening to stories
that he is inventing in the middle of the path between the woman who is telling them
and his ear, which hears.
Seeing as he isn't in the presence of beauty,
he can close his eyes and listen.
But in the space of less than a meter, he eliminates some words
and forms others inside his head.

64
There are cigarettes and preparatory measures
a serious hand can take before it falls down upon a tiny insect.
And the tiny geography of the room acquires details:
the fingers of the woman he had touched
are now a cause of disgust.

65
Exercises in space like those of an airplane: hands
traverse the nothingness and disturb it.
An unpleasant energy presses up against the utensils
on the dinner table.
Bloom—what is Bloom thinking about?
Leftover scraps from a meal reveal the disaster:

that which remains is the adversary
of that which makes the body grow.

66
Everything is happening quickly—even the rhythm of desire.
The will to live disappears after everything is
accomplished, and intensely so: dirty plates
confirm the decadence of an entire group.
How are people still dancing?
But the prostitute is dancing.
Why in the hell is she dancing?, exclaims Bloom.

67
Shoulder blades that once aroused
are now bothersome,
osseous imperfections that make Bloom
look inside himself. How ridiculous, he thinks.
Besides, the appearance of dawn doesn't erase
the previous centuries;
the city is condemned by the iniquity
that it has allowed for two thousand years. And yesterday.
Bloom isn't iniquitous, but has the will to be.

68
Crimes revolve, like planets,
around every man,
and each crime chooses its citizen. We are born,
and the turmoil begins.
Reality accelerates. Traversed by men,
reality loses its myths and gains engineering.
Buildings now exist in greater number
than all the other animal species.

69
Metal doesn't soften at night;
it holds firm, increases the stature of reality.
Higher than fifty stories, conflicts with
the normal trajectory of heavenly bodies start to occur.
Any given action of a profane old woman
at the top of a skyscraper might be essential
to the universe. It is Jean M who says this.
You're crazy, remarks Bloom. Crazy, confirms Anish.

70
There are no symbols: everything exists and scratches. Everything
is capable of being touched. Certain animals have seven lives, but
always only one death. One, says Jean M,
his index finger raised. Bloom's woman, however,
stood up some time ago and is dancing, alone, invoking exceptional
materials that exist within the body. Bloom smiles.

71
Reveries and the abstract spirit are interrupted
by the prostitute's rump. The universe grows larger, somewhere,
when a woman dances in that manner, or more or less in that manner.
Bravo, say the men.
Bravo, say the other two women, as well.

72
Bloom's arousal, at that moment, is mixed up
with many different images. His thoughts still exist,
even while a woman with a detailed body
advances and retreats in front of him in a dangerous dance.

I need to go back to Lisbon, thinks Bloom.
And, once again, his arousal loses out to his melancholia, and
by a wide margin.

73
To return home before the disorder
caused by our absence is overtaken by a
new order that banishes us for good, this
is Bloom thinking about old matters
while he watches someone dancing in modern manner.
But the woman stops, observes;
and the feast suddenly loses, at that very moment,
its general state of joy.

74
However, Anish and Jean M applaud the dancing
—they want to keep the enthusiasm going as best they can.
Clients and prostitutes feign friendship;
temporary friendship, of course, obviously, but friendship.
The woman cuddles up to Bloom and invites him
to go out into the forest grove.
He accepts, and the two forge ahead.

75
The two of them leave the house for the forest,
and there is no full stop for surprises.
She has a beautiful décolletage, yes,
but Bloom gives the prostitute a hard slap,
and she laughs. The universe is two thousand years old,
has morality, some laws.
Bloom is nervous and annoyed; aroused and dangerous.

76
Engineers must have secretly built
that spontaneous grove.
Nature supported by posts and old machinery
—Bloom is the one saying this.
In the grove, birds mix in with Autumn,
and the woman who is accompanying Bloom
is wearing such inappropriate lipstick that it causes arousal.
Bloom gives her a kiss.

77
The woman is like this: long legs,
black hair, carefully dyed.
Mascara around her eyes, arched eyebrows,
thick, straight legs, nothing is crooked or imperfect
and every bit of her deserves to be seen.
Nevertheless, the world is vast and times change,
even within the body of one lone man.

78
Bloom looks at her, and she, at that moment,
cracks a smile that promises I don't know what
(the woman is still trying—she should receive a medal).
Bloom, for his part, has no illusions: the voyage to India
took place. The future and the past are now made of
the same substance, nothing changed.
So the trip was worth it, he thinks.
At least I realized that nothing is worth it.

79
At the end of each day, Europe washes its feet
in a bucket full of coins, and space for the Spirit

is found in cheap new
wallets—bought at a subway entrance.
The Spirit will go here,
and ID cards will go in the bottom slot.
Everything has its place,
and the twenty-first century has already realized this.
(The trip was worth it, thinks Bloom.)

80
Where do we stop? Only gravediggers know.
But it isn't necessary to die in order to stop for a moment;
trips, for instance, and that one in particular,
are a little portion of death when you arrive at a place,
and also a little portion of death when you leave somewhere.

81
The voyage to India, for someone departing from Lisbon,
was made up of long journeys and long stops.
Did Bloom learn more while he was moving
or while he was stopped? That's the main question.
It's hard to run the numbers on such matters, but what's certain is
that now, at this moment, the things of this world
are praying that Bloom moves along, leaves that place, and
returns home.

82
It might be pleasing to see the planet through a window,
blue and spherical, but there is no possible similarity
between an organism that picks out shoes
and a voluminous sphere that sails through the air.
We aren't terrestrial, we are humans
—which is different.

The woman is talking about something, and Bloom isn't listening
because he has his feet upon the earth.

83
In the perverse grove, meanwhile, the light never ceases
to be splendid in the way in which it alights
upon certain leaves in the trees.
The woman is talking, and Bloom can't hear her—this is
equilibrium.

The planet is not ethical, no heavenly body
knows what justice is. Only tiny things amuse themselves
in serious manner with courts and similar institutions.
(This isn't the case with our hero:
he doesn't worry about such things.)

84
At any rate, don't learn too much, Bloom,
and don't teach things that other people aren't yet
prepared to learn.
You already know everything, don't speak,
remain silent;
you already know everything, don't act, remain quiet.

85
It's just that the day doesn't have banks of dry land
to which we can flee.
Water, water, and water. Thus is the day,
and we don't know how to swim.
Bloom caresses the prostitute's neck,
and she is pleased with his touch.
Humans fool themselves so much!
(And why is it that Bloom can't hear the person
who is writing about him here? Is he deaf?)

86
The earth has refused to be completely
civilized: parties are thrown,
women go around succoring men
and men go around succoring women; and poems
that are read in enclosed places cause space
to explode slightly. Bloom likes words, it's true,
but he has never made ugly faces at bombs.

87
This is Bloom in the grove.
There is also a prostitute and a squirrel.
And now the rest of the group, as if they were a family.
The tactile sense can only be improved
by novel things (thinks someone).
And if all the colors have already been invented: eyes are closed.

88
Six city-dwellers now have their feet
upon stagnant nature.
One of them came from India and brought with him a friend and nary
an illusion. We are in Paris, and six humans are out for a stroll.
Bloom finds a nail on the ground in the grove.
The women laugh at the discovery,
but Anish and Jean M become apprehensive.

89
Who would go around falsifying the connections between
the elements?, they ask themselves.
It's just that finding such a thing in a forest grove is startling.
They're missing, of course, other implements:

a hammer and, above all else, a hand that
toils in order to modify. But that nail
is evidence enough.
There is a certain repressed nervousness
within the group. After all, the grove isn't as deserted as it seemed.

90
But let's return to the most important couple.
That woman, in fact, seems to be falling for Bloom,
starting with her face. The physiognomy is the first chunk
to be conquered by the heart. And once again
this is happening.
The prostitute's body had been a sort of common ground, of course,
but her face was, up to that point, intimate and hidden.
Do not save your eyes for later when you want to seduce
(someone advises), and she wasn't saving them.

91
But that song that the face sings when it falls in love,
Bloom doesn't want to hear it.
Bloom is definitively free.
He had unburdened himself of the weight that physics requires of living beings,
but not of those who have quit.
The day and Bloom are now separate materials.
And this is neither good nor bad—it's dangerous.

92
He was separated from the fact of being alive,
and that was definitive.
There was still, of course, his mother,

who was waiting for him in Lisbon,
but he had even forgotten about her.
Those who do not die during combat or who sleep for a long
time
forget that from which they have distanced themselves. Well
then, that's it—
that's the way it is; exactly like that.

93
Let's look, then, at our hero, Bloom,
with the eyes of someone who is looked upon.
We are made of the same lucidity.
All in the same boat, of course,
except for the drowned.

94
The world is made of short paragraphs,
large leaps forward, and no continuity whatsoever.
He has a rare edition of *The Mahabharata* in his suitcase;
in his head: lines of poetry and other minor bits of knowledge.
He learned at the best schools, forgot on
the best beds, and on days that were more propitious for tactile
engagements
he examined women, yet did not set reason aside.

95
He fornicated, thought, swam in the sea, fell in love,
was loved, didn't love, had a certain sense of adoration
for a certain magical melody that comes from numbers,
he sang songs, made three or four friends,
knew how to suffer without turning off his instinct for learning,
became familiar with forbidden habits and comprehended the
theory

of a thousand languages, touched more than six hundred animal
species—and now he is content or
hopeless.

96
He has possessed the speed of one who is pushed
and, later, the speed of the one doing the pushing.
He won several times and lost a sufficient amount.
He got to know the two sensations—sadness
and jubilation—and has already realized that only an instant
separates them.
(Bloom looks down, sees the grass and his shoe,
his shoe and the grass. Where to start?)

97
He has gazed long enough at the luminosity of
the stars. He has realized that eyes are redundant
during the day and insufficient at night.
He has hesitated in the right places and forged ahead with his
will, keeping rhythm
with his speed. He has been religious
and mystical in an airport, but also in damp basements
on the outskirts of second-rate cities.

98
He has been courageous and cowardly,
has fled from strangeness and approached it.
When he was strong, he realized that it was his duty
to approach it,
and when he was weak, that the better instinct
was to distance himself.
But he didn't keep strangeness company and didn't ignore it.

He realized early on that that which he didn't comprehend
was that which bit him in the backside and made him hurry
along.

99
Bloom is a man.
He has been sick, but at times has also leaped into the air
in such a manner that he had to hold himself back so as not to
break the sky to bits.
He has felt large and miniscule,
but he never mistook the size of a day
as a result of crossing paths, or not,
with events of enormous proportion.

100
He never sought after extraordinary achievements,
because he had lived enough to take note
of the many epic poems that exist
within a single Winter's day, when tedium
and the cold gently push man toward the window.
Motionlessness as a second-rate epic,
this is what he discovered after he became exhausted.

101
There isn't that much world, Bloom now thinks.
The individual organs are organized and solid:
universal earthquakes might not even interfere
with man's slightest sensation.
The universe and I
never cross paths.

102
The divine is not something that comes from the outside, the way
wind does; yet, the divine, Bloom, has set a trap for you,
the way the Devil does. Who will get to you
first? Whom will you get to first?
This is what we're going to find out next.

103
In Bloom's life, what happened on that day
was as follows: a woman in a forest grove in Paris,
after all else, asked him for a kiss,
and Bloom gave her this kiss the way someone gives an object to someone else.
Split in two, his body was no longer the place
from which he observed the world.
He wasn't participating and didn't even want to see—what to do with the body, then?

104
Having lost the heavens on his voyage to India,
he now felt like he was losing his face.
I am no longer touching the ground with the part of my body
that is commonly called feet.
I am between soil and sky, in an intermediate
place, standing on nothing, on an indecisive
path. (The worst place to be alive
is between that which the day requires of us
and that which the eternal promises us. In the middle: that's the worst spot.)

105
The inexplicable should remain intact
within the body.
Dark recesses are places that can be
illuminated. For example, Bloom made two attempts
to return to the body—just on that day and in that instant:
one when he was touched
and the other when he was touching: the two systems
in which the skin slightly overlaps with the Spirit.

106
Bloom, his two friends,
and the three women were still in the grove.
The day diffused precious lines of heat
throughout an immense number of square
meters. The land welcomes the heat and shoes.
And waits.

107
Bloom sees, pressed against his shoes, the remnants
of a country, vestiges: I've got France
on my shoes, says Bloom, and the group
smiles at this observation. But it was true.
Bending his back, Bloom carefully separates
the grove from his footwear. I've got a Parisian
grove on my shoes, insists Bloom.

108
A stone tossed in the air returns. But
there is no returning after the stone comes to a stop
on the ground. And, within a body, moral
filth is identical to a stone that has found

its resting place. Men were made
to betray. And, boy, does Bloom know this.

109
A country isn't consumed the way
other products are. It doesn't have a definitive expiration date.
However, a man can grow tired of a country
(or even an entire continent).
Enough of Paris, enough of India. Bloom wants Lisbon.

110
Bloom knows wealth, women,
and the mortality of things. And knows that even suffering
doesn't endure; everything is ephemeral. Miniscule animals draw near to each other,

but Bloom's memory
is in a place that isn't very pleasant.
Mixed in with the buttocks of the three women and with the grove,
Bloom sees images from a brief moment of joy from his childhood.

What to do?

111
But those happy facts quickly disappeared.
In life, there are three or four days,
and in all the others the Spirit's disinterest in things
is obvious.
No one is harmonious when in the company of others.
Old age frightens Bloom, and having company ages him.

112
The whole mass of men tries to blow out
the light of a single star and fails.
Words, for example, are neither practical nor useful,
they get tangled up in one's fingers, they interfere with facts.
At most, they can explain—but an explanation is not a solution.

113
The world is excited, words are panting for air,
a man repeats an ancient phrase
to a newborn, and the newborn is startled.
(And if Christ, instead of speaking, had drawn—
what would have happened?)

114
Bloom learned of the religious symbols of India,
but before that had been a drinker of Christian wine. Europe is extensive,
it contains dreadful differences: the hot nature of one side
contrasts with the great expanses of snow.
There are men from one side to the other—
how are they to understand each other?

115
There is no secret land, the accounts of voyages
cover, with detailed maps,
ninety percent of the secrets. Heroes went straight from
legend into the halls of parliaments:
they meet up to invade a sheet of paper
with very harsh words.
Bloom had gotten to know Europe, India,
all their religions, and their best singers.

116
Every religion has its own clear thoughts.
But, among the forms of ratiocination, numerical ones
are preferable, for at least they can calm a forlorn
mind—Bloom doesn't believe
in miracles. (The earth's faculties
are plainly visible: humans are not a masterpiece
created by God.)

117
An animal species headed toward perfection
or a deformed animal? At any rate,
nature is incompatible with pleasant prayers;
knees—as is well known—are a source of discomfort
when they're pressed too closely against a given country.

118
Bloom is familiar with Europe and the Americas,
went on a grand voyage to India: the words,
the ceremonies: half of the great truths
are minor lies.

119
No one should desist until the most foreign
hand tries to pull them back and fails to do so.
However, Bloom possesses the minimum fundamentals of survival,
as disorderly and inactive as they may be.
A man loses the essential when he doesn't have
a single strong desire; should he stop
or move along, what does it matter?

120
The world
is in proximity to nothingness,
disorder
is a prognostication,
and hell
becomes indispensable
during certain monotonous
weeks.

121
Bloom is vexed and distracted
at the same time.
He is in the middle of a forest,
but it seems like he is in a kitchen with his toes
stepping in something foul.
At any rate, he laughs when it's time to laugh
and gets serious when seriousness is required of him.

122
The counterpart to the soul is the fact
that man is sensitive to touch:
two complimentary forces.
The sun rises, and man wakes up and washes his face
with water the city delivers to him in a pipe.
It isn't great, but it's civilized.

123
Bloom recalls masses in which the words
were wonderfully declared over the altar,
as if they were gold or kindness.
But words are repugnant to someone who has seen and done
everything.

And there are no holy professions,
only certain holy men.

124
Not even nature has clean silverware.
Things get mixed together and cease to be things.
Ethics is a sword that separates, it has never joined anyone to anyone else.

It smell like man all around,
and sometimes having a nose is disgusting.

125
And in this impassive rhythm, love had paid a visit on
certain days like an intruder.
Bloom had had a woman named Mary and
had killed his own father for her:
and what now remained of those excesses?
Three prostitutes, two friends, and him, Bloom: six humans,
in the kingdom of leaves and weeds;
and also tedium and a book brought back from India: *The Mahabharata*.
And the radio, of course, always in his pocket: but it doesn't work.

126
Time, as is well known,
digs the graves for intensity. Look at the elderly:
they begin their grand voyage as if they had introduced dread
into the world. But happiness never remains still, and
after a certain age, man clings to the state of being alive
and counts on his fingers the principal pleasures and failures
to which the heart is subject in an industrialized
city.

127
Inside the mind, for its part, the future gains more ground
until the moment when apathetic stupidity
arrives intact inside a person.
Humans are either too young or too
old: no one is capable of being contemporary.
In China, for example, a wall, just in its measurements,
defines an architectural border that is taller than normal.

128
Disgust between living elements is moderate
and utilizes very little engineering,
and if that weren't the case between every living expanse,
sincerity would also require a
tall wall. There is no one speaking words
that are interesting to hear, and there is no material
that has enough tactile sense to be able to occupy the skin
with something that modifies it.
We are animals surrounded by a very ancient
wall.

129
Bloom is so indifferent to the bad
grammar of the prostitute who won't stop talking,
and he is feeling so little—be it the nature that surrounds him
or the citizens beside him—that he is almost,
at that moment, a Spirit.
Bloom is thus suddenly holy.
And, thinking about this, becomes happy.
To arrive at religious profundity
through tedium and abject neutrality,
this is what remains for him.

130
Every biography goes like this: someone advances
toward the place from which they departed.
Mistakes provide a short period of careless joy, at first,
but in the second part of life those mistakes
prepare us for that undiscovered country, as do well-paid
gravediggers.
Love does not exist, and one's childhood home is closed shut.

131
There is no holy part of any country.
And geography is ethically
neutral: long voyages to see just the same way with
the same eyes. Going blind is the only real voyage,
all the rest is just a stroll around the backyard.
Truths and fictions are useless,
daylight does not depend on the proper
application of an adjective to its noun,
and even when a man leaps through the air, he is ever crawling
on the ground.

132
But look, come see: theory is holding
its breath, and there's evidence of this on the ground.
A corpse was found in a lake in the park:
three children (where did they come from?) screamed loudly,
elated,
mistaking the silent corpse
for a small boat with a broken hull.

133
Bloom, Anish, and Jean M flee.
But it was Bloom, it was our hero Bloom

who killed the woman
who was already dead when she was dumped in the lake
with a pocket full of high-denomination banknotes.

134
What we do when we feel nothing at all is brutal,
and the circumstances wrest all good advice away from us.
And that was precisely what happened: the sudden physical
contact
definitively disgusted Bloom.
The woman wanted to embrace him; he picked up
a mineral element of nature
and, in a single action, took revenge for his long days
with no will to action.
The woman's head became deformed,
and the blood proved itself to be an element
that, in others, is almost imperceptible.

135
He didn't pick her up; instead he dragged her to the lake,
then tossed her into the official water of the grove.
The world exists, and liquids accept everything,
embracing and swallowing it all.
When all the resistance was drained from the woman,
that's when the gentle lake becomes lethal.
The other two women scream:
one of them immediately runs off, the other
hesitates. Grass on the ground, an almost mild wind.

136
The place was suddenly on edge:
a gigantic mechanism, previously invisible,

starts to move.
Crazy sounds; three men are running.
Within Bloom's heart, a certainty, a refrain:
I am no longer an impulsive man who kills, I am a murderer.
But when one flees, when one is afraid,
ethics are meaningless. And that which, in man, is animal feet and speed
becomes important.

137
The grove abruptly changes color
when the three children are startled by
a dead body floating in the lake. Like the surprise
arrival of Winter: the corpse casts shadows over the pure trees
and the unique shade of green is
blemished. There certainly isn't a single moment of silence
when the body of a woman has her head smashed
with a stone. The shock of it
makes noise.

138
In the sky, there are no blimps flying by
displaying advertisements, coincidences like that
do happen. In the propeller-less sky, clouds
shaped like happy heads try to compensate
for what happened on the ground. The horror, now
homogenous, is in dispute, between a drowned body and the
children who discovered it. However, reality
hasn't given up, in other places, on its Sunday stroll.

139
In men who kill, there exists a certain temporary
pride that is very close to the feeling of immortality,
which religious manuals describe in detail.
Demons, a bat that flies smack into the face of a young woman,
a man who digs through ashes for a feeble coin,
a date that should be banished from the world because that's when
someone's beloved died, a psychic gastronomy that
creates one crazy person after another, the end of boredom,
forty thousand names possess iniquity, and for half of them it is hidden
within a blade, in metal, and in stones.

140
An extraordinary flower attempts to revive a body
with its scent,
but the body is dead, and its nose has lost the whole lot
of its capacities with the loss of its heart and intelligence. One dies
in the fundamental things, but also in every single one of the details
that existed in the living body.

141
A woman's blood is already being gathered on the banks
of the lake, and all around three colors are
coming together: red, green, and black.
The frightened hands of strangers touch the
woman, whom they will still remember
many weeks hence.

142
Meanwhile, virile strength has not been attenuated:
Anish, Jean M, and Bloom: the three of them were
co-conspirators because
at the first moment they had fled in the same direction.
Frightened, they made quick plans, then said abbreviated
goodbyes. Anish disappeared somewhere in one of the
neighborhoods of Paris,
and Jean M, out of a final instinct of friendship,
took Bloom to the train
station. Standing beside a murderer, every man
feels fear and pride.

143
Jean M. was standing beside a murderer named Bloom.
Why did you do that?, asked Jean M. And Bloom
didn't answer because he didn't know,
he shrugged his shoulders; and in his hand, which he had cleaned
in the meantime,
he held a train ticket.
I am returning to the place from which I departed, Lisbon. Jean
M. embraced
Bloom, Bloom entered the train car.
He didn't say goodbye, didn't thank him. The train pulled away.

144
So there goes a full man, sitting in
a train headed to Lisbon.
Beneath his perfect and clean right hand,
the small suitcase that had traveled the world:
inside it, rare books from the Occident
and the grand witness of his voyage to India:

an ancient edition of a mythical book called *The Mahabharata*,
stolen from a wicked master.

145
The train is rolling along; Bloom looks out the window.
He tries to remember popular proverbs,
lines of poetry, admonitions: nothing.
There isn't a single phrase that seems important to him.
He arrives in Lisbon.
No hatred is there to welcome him. No love either.

146
(November 2003.
I find myself in an enclosed
compartment.
Seen from here, the world is a feat of engineering
made from the alphabet; I'm crazy, clearly.
I write to educate my reasoning,
a habit that is practiced with a gun
pressed against your head.)

147
Bloom returned to Lisbon
through a dark door.
A friend immediately informed him:
the police are after you for two murders
—one here and another in Paris,
and your mother died months ago. She didn't leave behind any letters, nor an inheritance.
Bloom is thus alone—as when he left—
and is being chased, so he hides, flees.

148
But man resists, it is part
of his duty as an animal. Even when bored,
he still has instincts that don't abandon the organism.
The streets give out onto requests to the living:
an older man, for example, grabs his hat with both hands
because the wind had become indiscreet in late afternoon.
Príncipe Real, Bairro Alto, Alvalade, Areeiro,
Martim Moniz, Anjos, Terreiro do Paço,
Lisbon welcomes Bloom without making a commotion. Cities
have lost the ability to admire great voyages.
From a distance, Bloom looks at the house where he was once
happy; and feels nothing.

149
He sought the Spirit on his voyage to India and
encountered matter that he was already familiar with.
Now nothing makes him hesitate; well-behaved animals
chained to trees by their collars bark
when he passes by.
His shoes forge ahead, he smokes a cigarette,
goes into a café, and orders a glass of wine.

150
In the establishment, an old mechanical orchestra—
set up in less than one cubic meter of space—plays a
song that Bloom used to hear a lot when he was young
and Mary loved him.
He wants to weep, but he cannot find the right route within
his body.

He looks around: no one knows him.
He looks in the mirror: who is that?

151
Bloom heard stories,
read seven thousand books, studied, met men
and women, saw and touched more than two thousand
different objects; and now, as he walks,
he isn't thinking about anything.
He returned to Lisbon. And the end of the day
contains a walking cane and an old woman who
seem to recognize him: Good afternoon, they say. But Bloom
is afraid,
in a hurry, and a warm stomach; the blue of the sky is being
wiped away
by a nascent dark color.
The ceiling of the country has its habits: night is falling.

152
Bloom smiles, and the sound of his shoes as he walks
reminds him of the existence of his body:
"take counsel only from the experienced,"
he had overheard one day. And here is
a man who loved, suffered, and killed: who wants
to listen to him? No one. And the intense night carried on.

153
Footsteps behind Bloom's back. He is startled,
turns around: an old man, dignified and poor, Good
evening, Bloom says, Good evening, replies the old man. The
general
kindness of strangers, finally.
I would like to give you this suitcase,
Bloom suddenly says to the kind old man who is shivering from
the cold.

It contains a rare edition of an Indian book
called *The Mahabbharata*; it's worth money, a lot of it.

154
The old man accepted the suitcase, indeed, and Bloom bid him farewell.
No one hesitates when it's nighttime and cold out.
For the first time, he has nothing in his hands. The voyage
to India ended on a Lisbon street
in the hands of an old man who perhaps doesn't know how to read
and who maybe likes doodling
over the grandiose words. The city
has adequate signage so that a person who is returning home
doesn't get lost along the way. But it's growing colder
and Bloom doesn't know where to go.

155
Ingenuousness is irrecoverable.
Bloom is at the top of a tall bridge,
and the night conceals
his black shoes. No agitation
at all in the man who has returned to his point of departure.
There are various ways for a body to kill itself,
and falling from on high into water below is one of them.
A woman, however, is walking toward him.
Bloom turns his head; it's a pretty woman, she's smiling.

156
Do you want to talk?, she asks. Bloom shrugs his shoulders.
There is no one around, complete silence, the water
down below, at times a car.

He puts his hand in his pocket: not even the voyage could get
his father's old radio working again.
He walks toward the woman, and the world carries on,
but nothing that happens will be able to prevent the definitive
tedium
of Bloom, our hero.

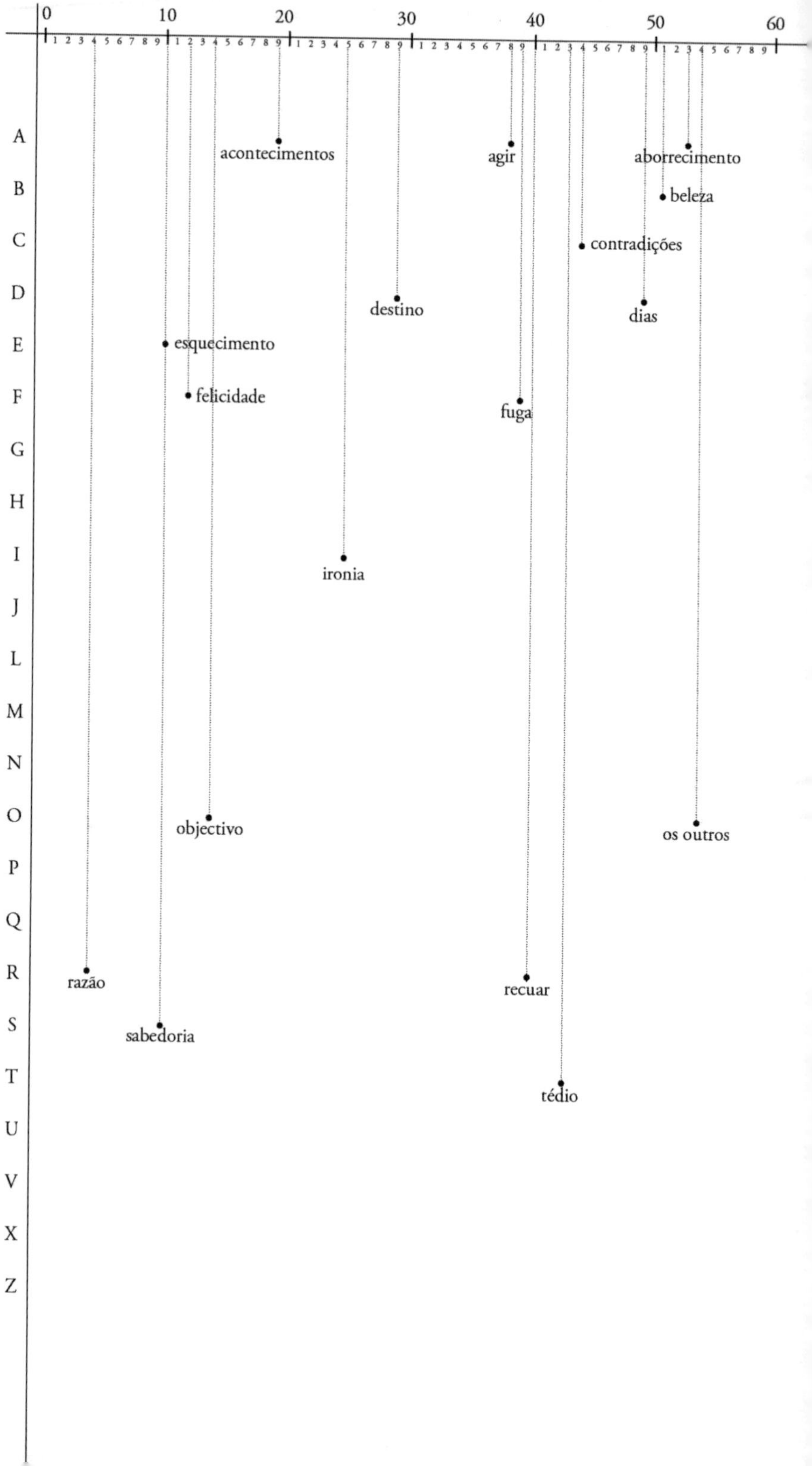
0
10
20
30
40
50
60
1 2 3 4 5 6 7 8 9
A
B
C
D
E
F
G
H
I
J
L
M
N
O
P
Q
R
S
T
U
V
X
Z
acontecimentos
agir
aborrecimento
beleza
contradições
destino
dias
esquecimento
felicidade
fuga
ironia
objectivo
os outros
razão
recuar
sabedoria
tédio

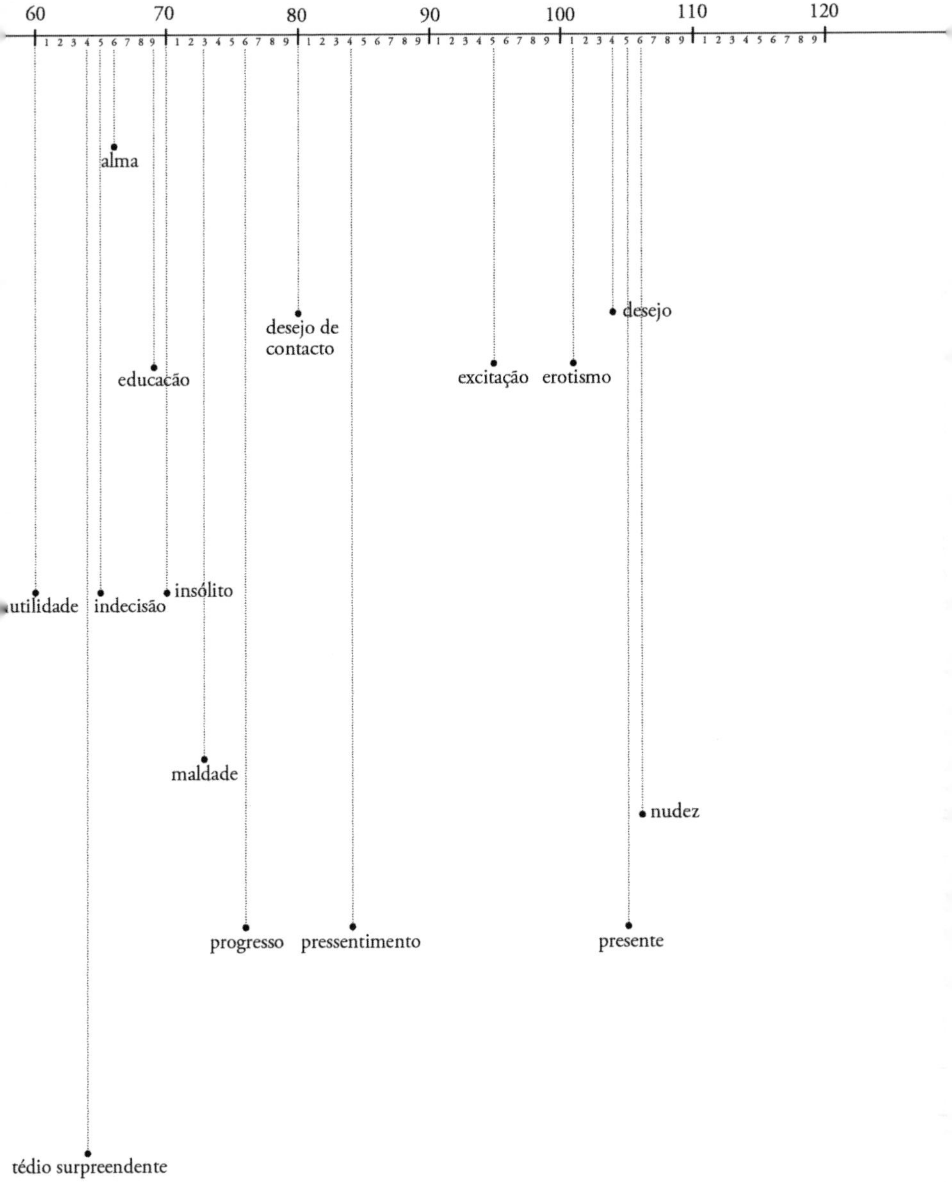
60
70
80
90
100
110
120
alma
desejo de contacto
desejo
educação
excitação
erotismo
utilidade
indecisão
insólito
maldade
nudez
progresso
pressentimento
presente
tédio surpreendente

canto I

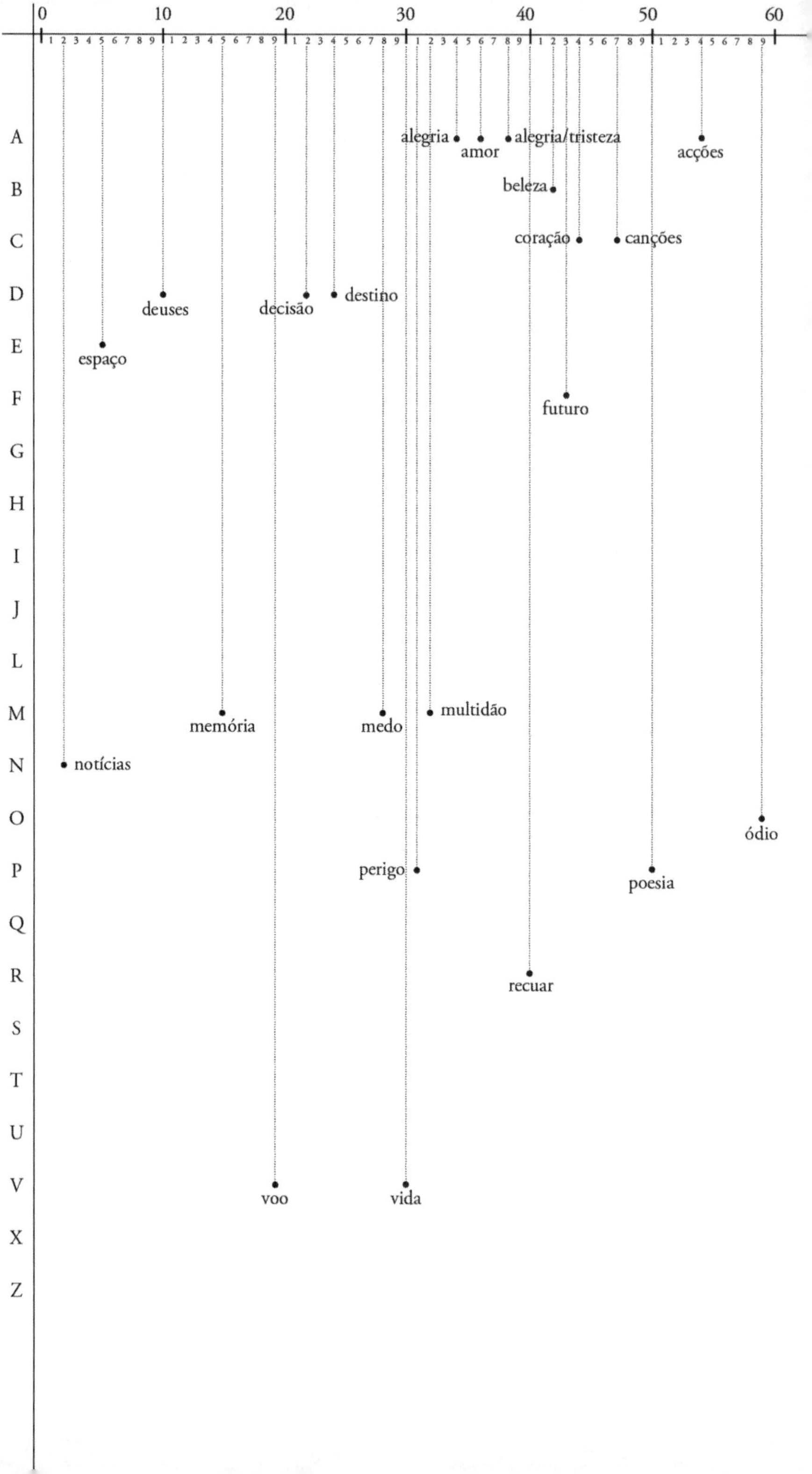
0
10
20
30
40
50
60
A
B
C
D
E
F
G
H
I
J
L
M
N
O
P
Q
R
S
T
U
V
X
Z
alegria
amor
alegria/tristeza
acções
beleza
coração
canções
deuses
decisão
destino
espaço
futuro
memória
medo
multidão
notícias
ódio
perigo
poesia
recuar
voo
vida

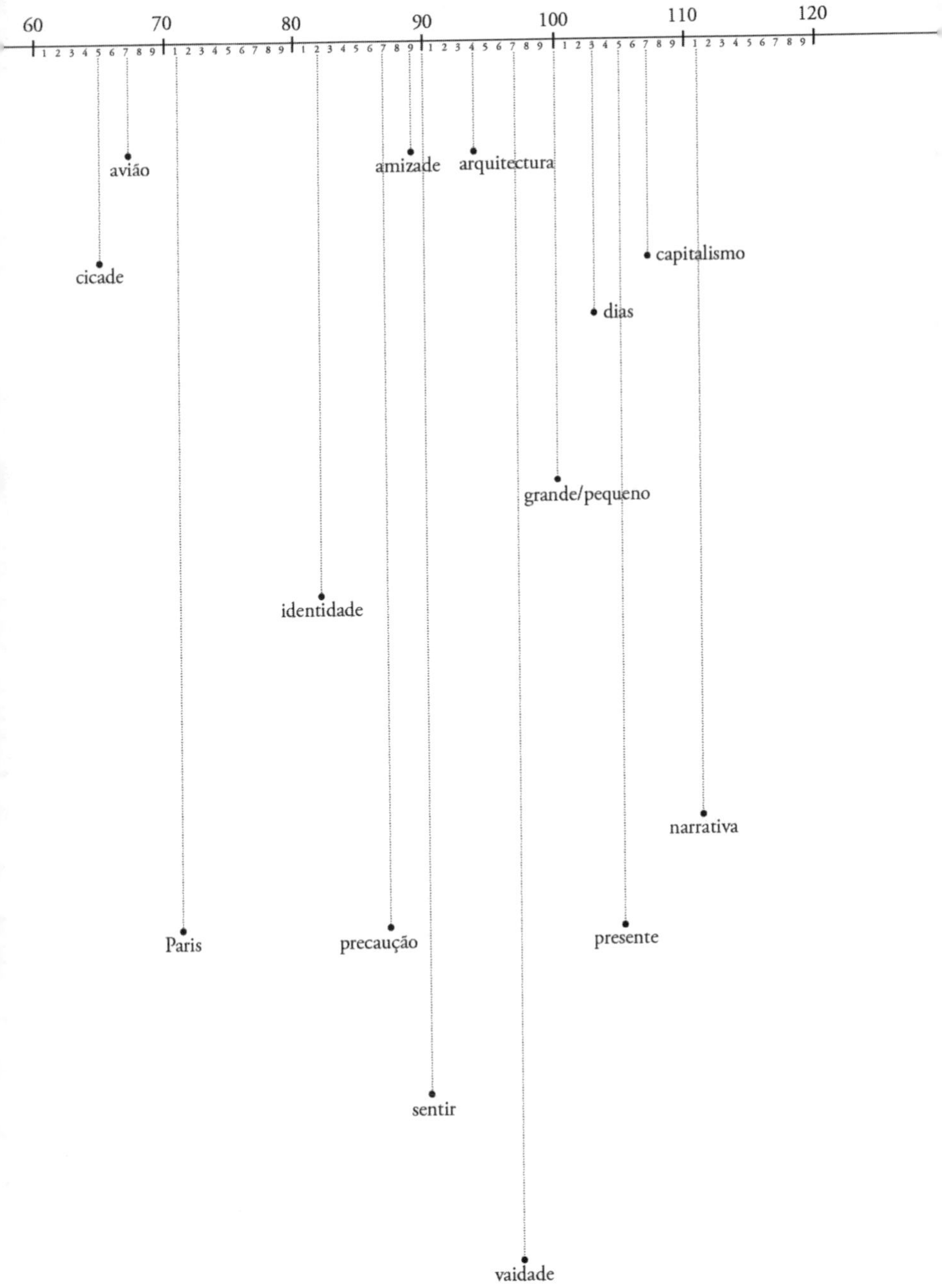
60
70
80
90
100
110
120
avião
amizade
arquitectura
cicade
capitalismo
dias
grande/pequeno
identidade
narrativa
Paris
precaução
presente
sentir
vaidade

canto II

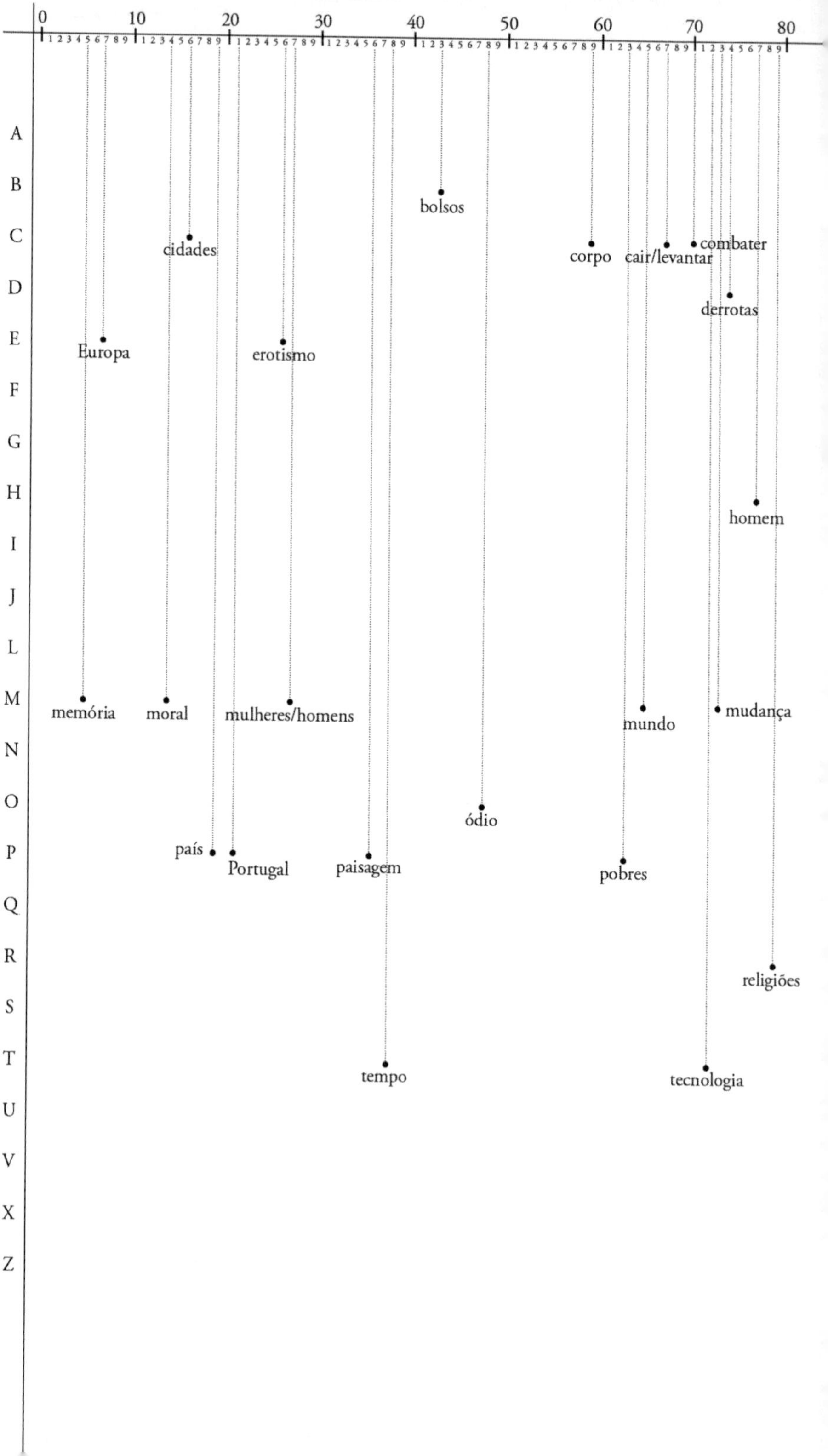

0
10
20
30
40
50
60
70
80
A
B
C
D
E
F
G
H
I
J
L
M
N
O
P
Q
R
S
T
U
V
X
Z
bolsos
cidades
corpo
cair/levantar
combater
derrotas
Europa
erotismo
homem
memória
moral
mulheres/homens
mundo
mudança
ódio
país
Portugal
paisagem
pobres
religiões
tempo
tecnologia

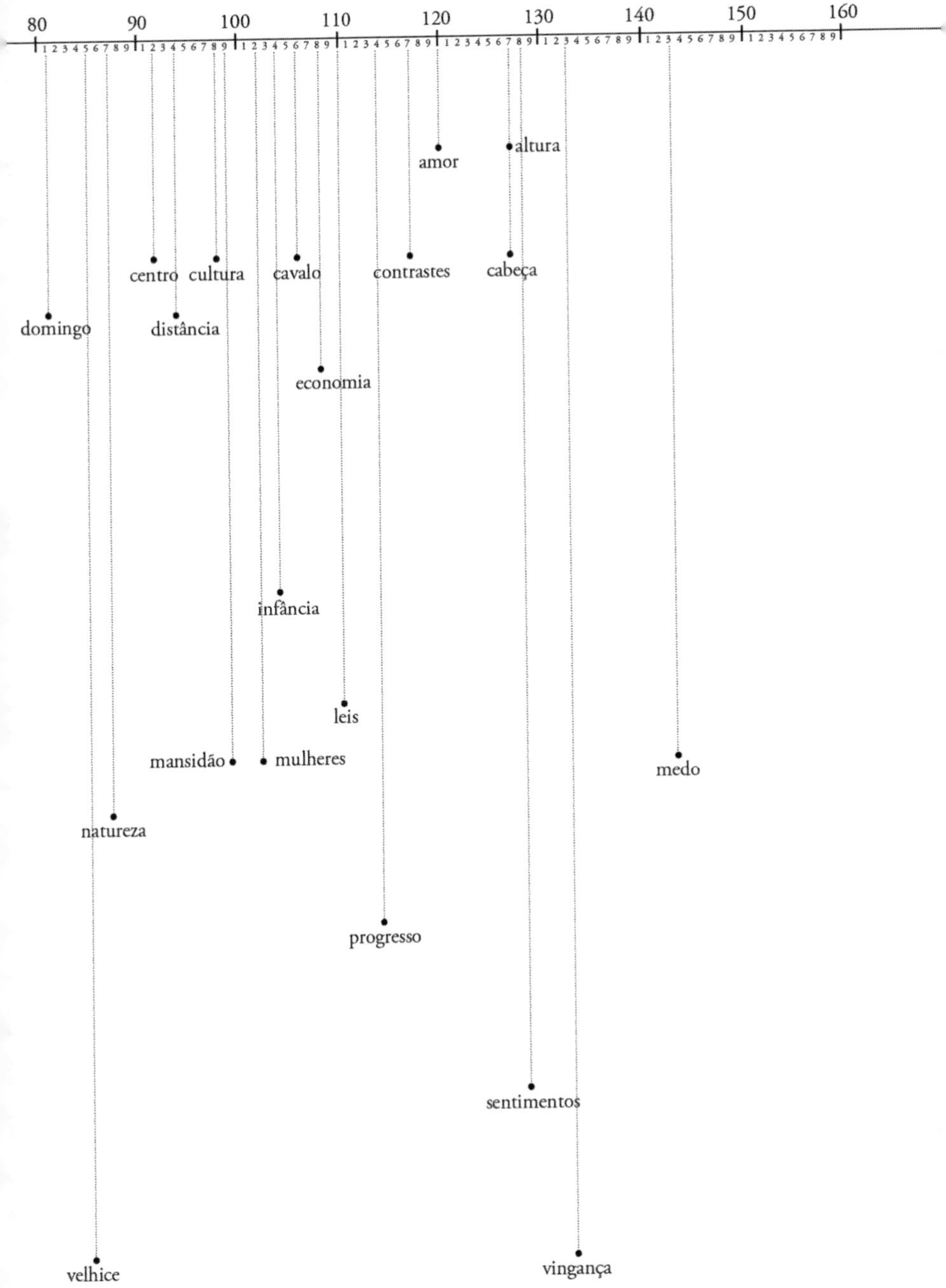
80
90
100
110
120
130
140
150
160
amor
altura
centro
cultura
cavalo
contrastes
cabeça
domingo
distância
economia
infância
leis
mansidão
mulheres
medo
natureza
progresso
sentimentos
velhice
vingança

canto III

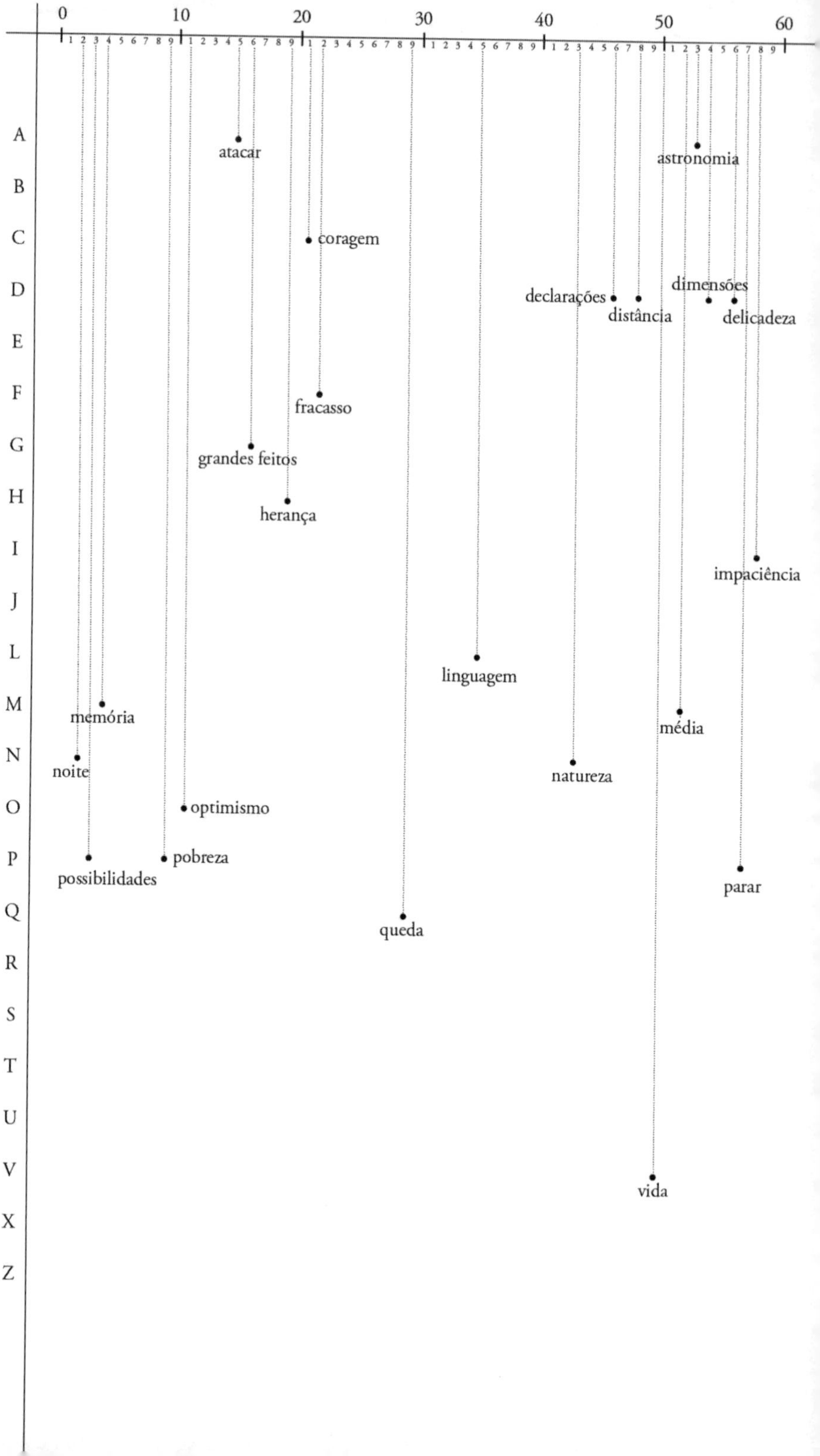
0
10
20
30
40
50
60
A
B
C
D
E
F
G
H
I
J
L
M
N
O
P
Q
R
S
T
U
V
X
Z
atacar
astronomia
coragem
declarações
distância
dimensões
delicadeza
fracasso
grandes feitos
herança
impaciência
linguagem
memória
média
noite
natureza
optimismo
possibilidades
pobreza
parar
queda
vida

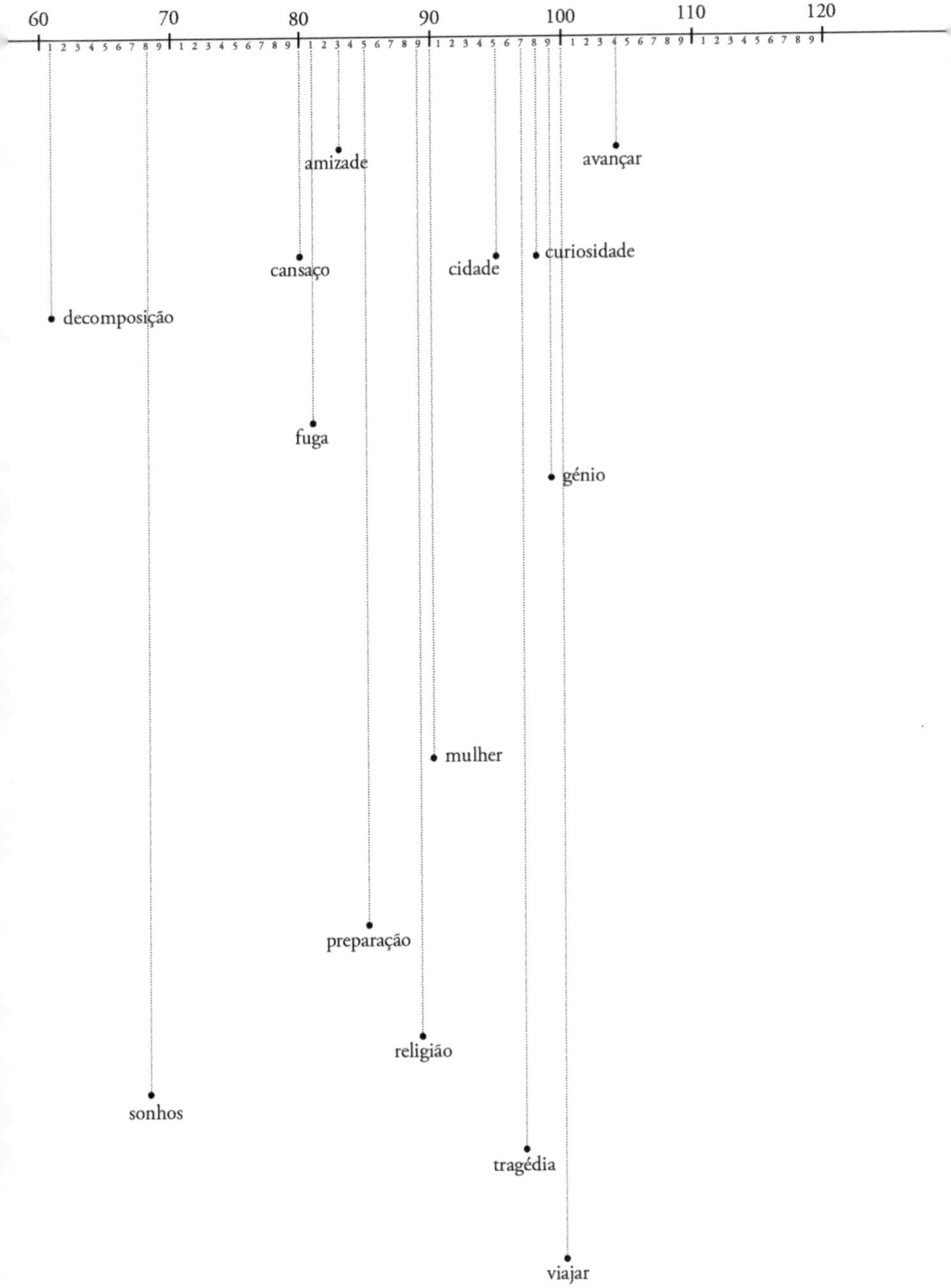
60
70
80
90
100
110
120
amizade
avançar
cansaço
cidade
curiosidade
decomposição
fuga
génio
mulher
preparação
religião
sonhos
tragédia
viajar

canto IV

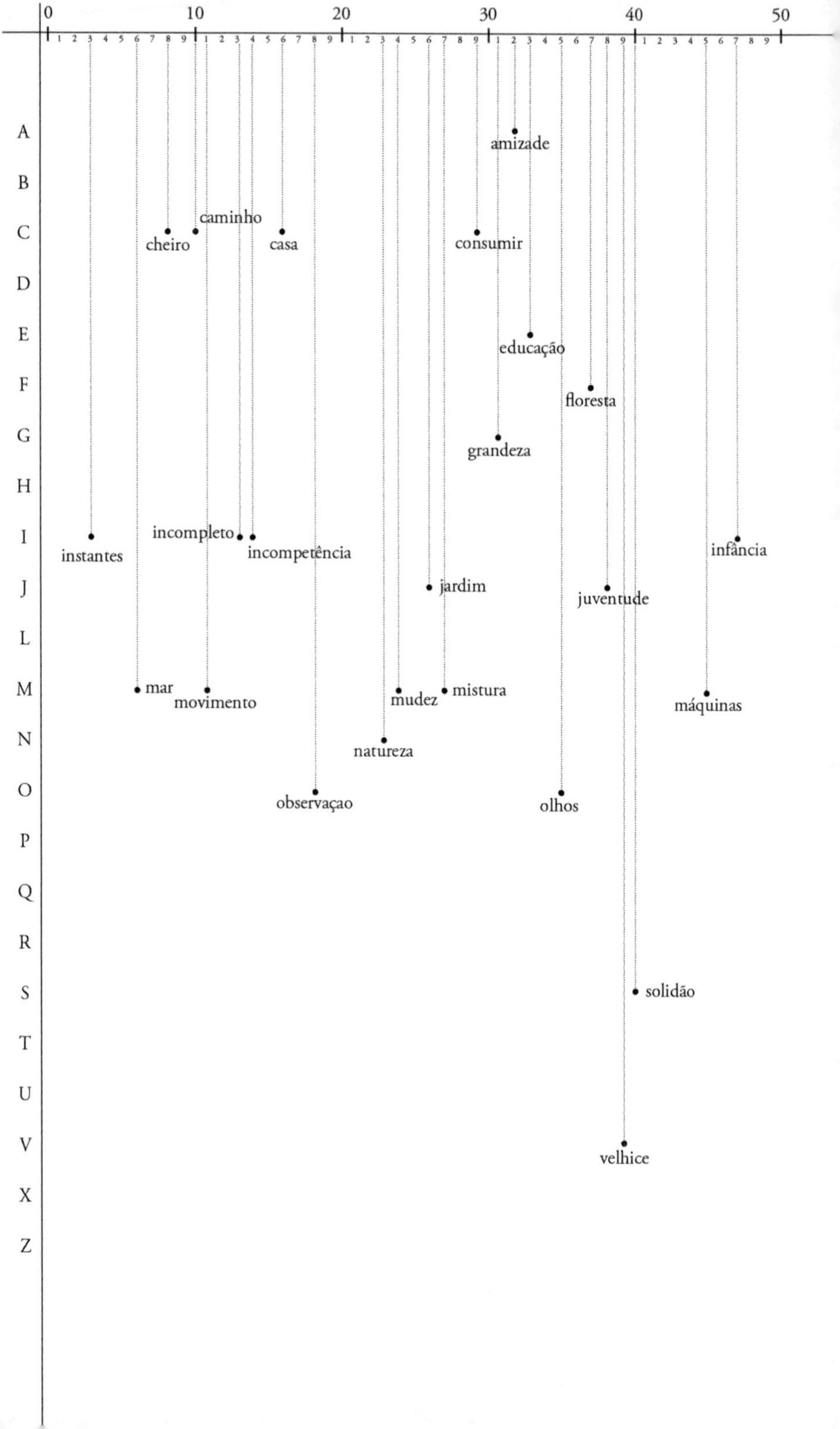
0
10
20
30
40
50
A
B
C
D
E
F
G
H
I
J
L
M
N
O
P
Q
R
S
T
U
V
X
Z
amizade
caminho
cheiro
casa
consumir
educação
floresta
grandeza
incompleto
instantes
incompetência
infância
jardim
juventude
mar
movimento
mudez
mistura
máquinas
natureza
observaçao
olhos
solidão
velhice

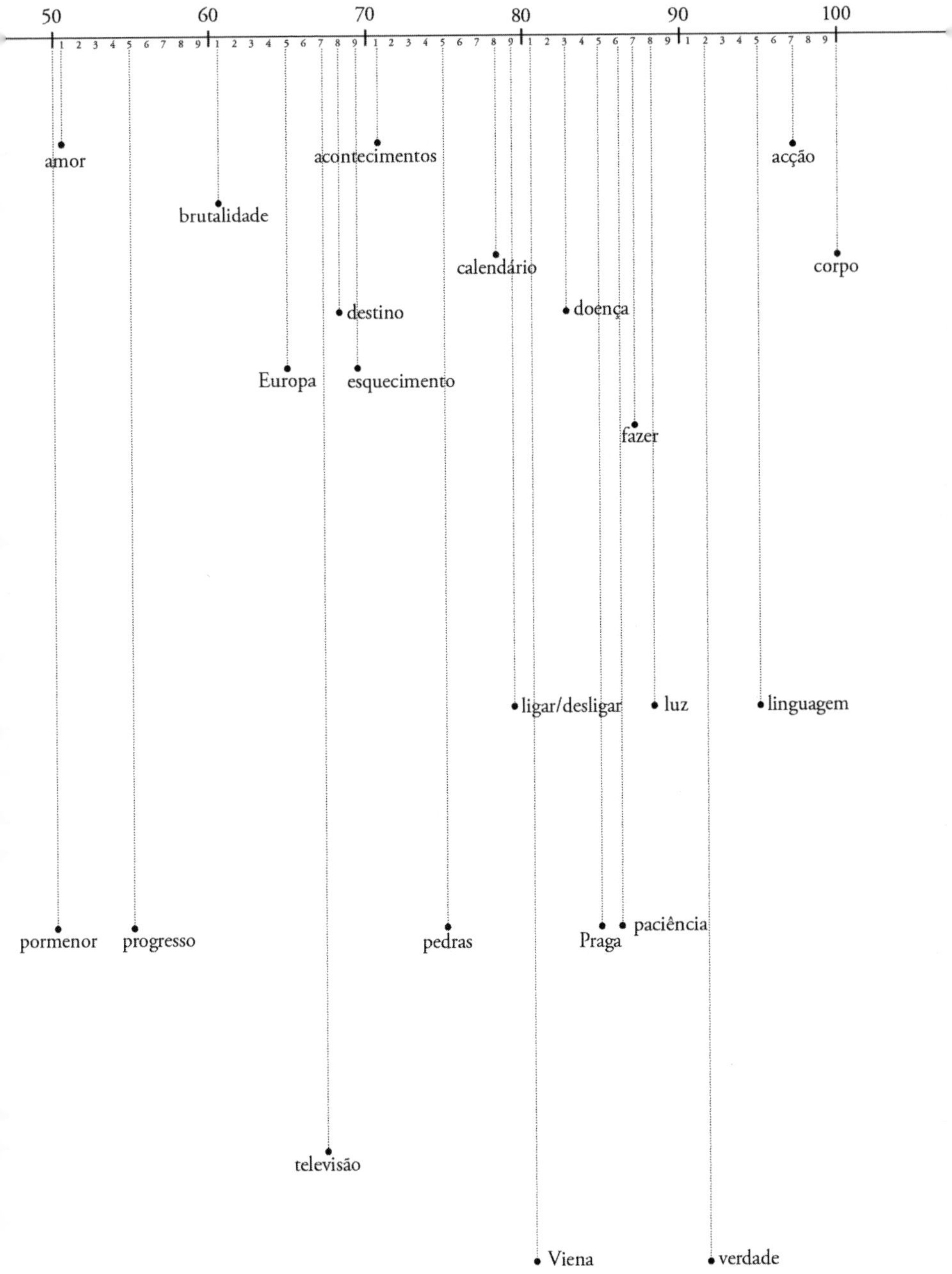
50
60
70
80
90
100
amor
acontecimentos
acção
brutalidade
calendário
corpo
destino
doença
Europa
esquecimento
fazer
ligar/desligar
luz
linguagem
pormenor
progresso
pedras
Praga
paciência
televisão
Viena
verdade

canto V

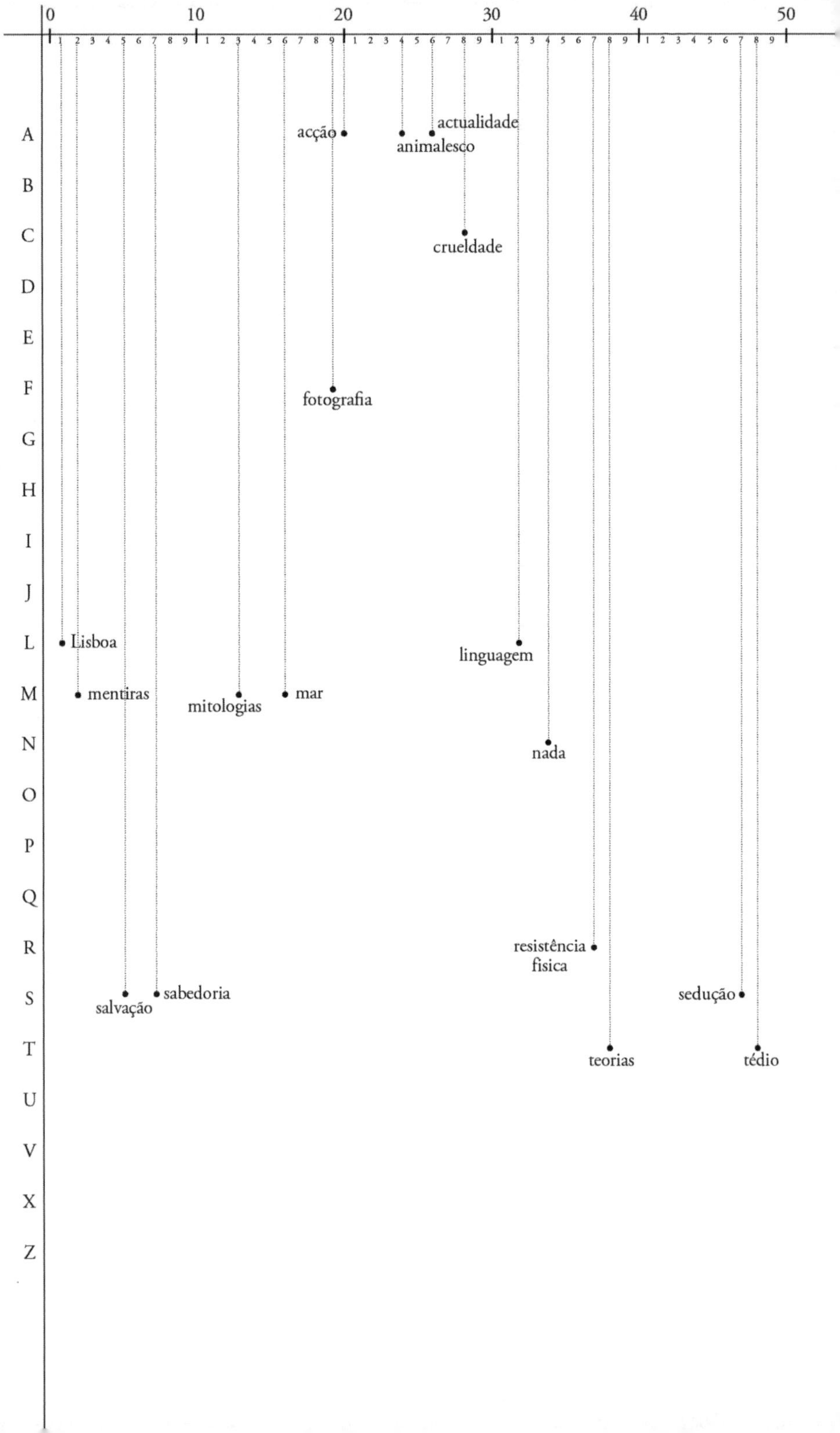

0
10
20
30
40
50
A
B
C
D
E
F
G
H
I
J
L
M
N
O
P
Q
R
S
T
U
V
X
Z
acção
actualidade
animalesco
crueldade
fotografia
Lisboa
linguagem
mentiras
mitologias
mar
nada
resistência física
salvação
sabedoria
sedução
teorias
tédio

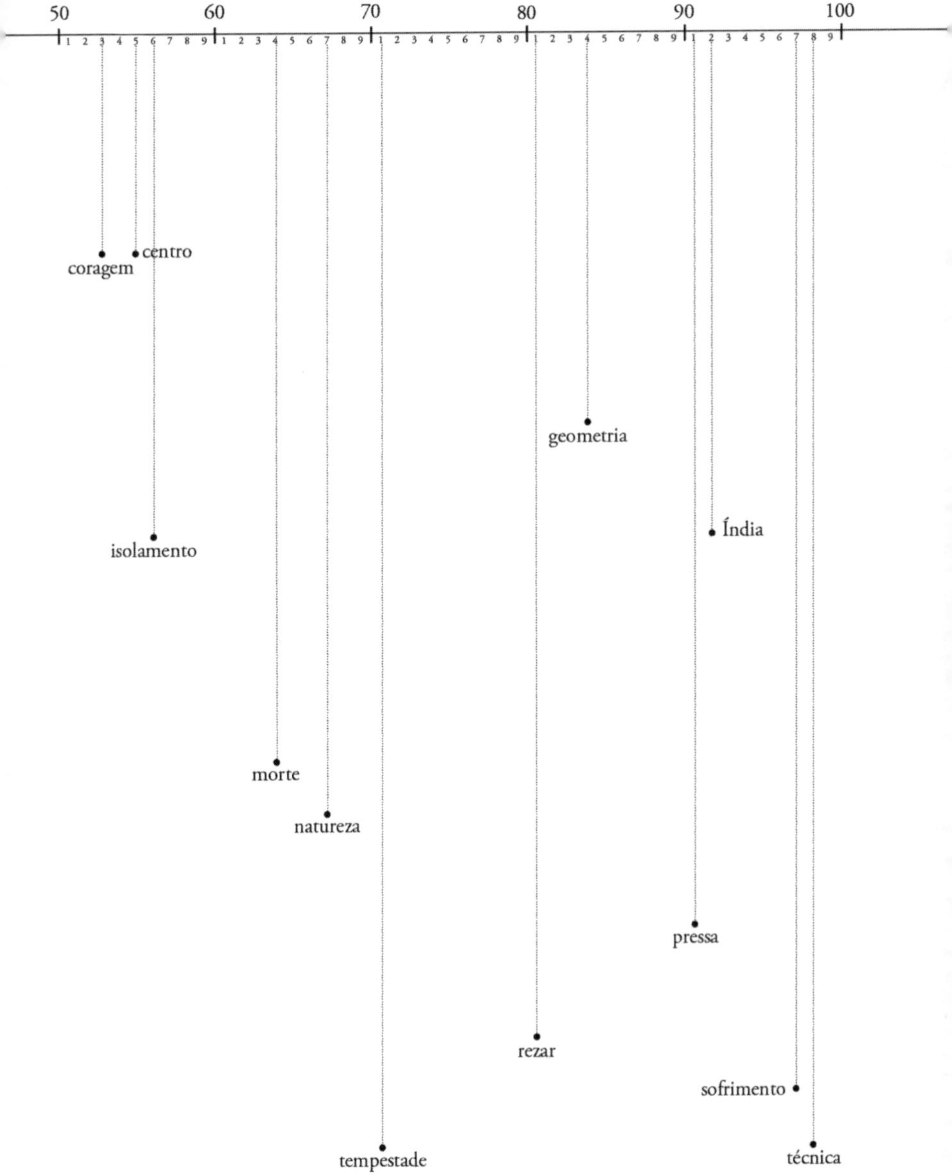

50
60
70
80
90
100
coragem
centro
isolamento
morte
natureza
tempestade
rezar
geometria
Índia
pressa
sofrimento
técnica

canto VI

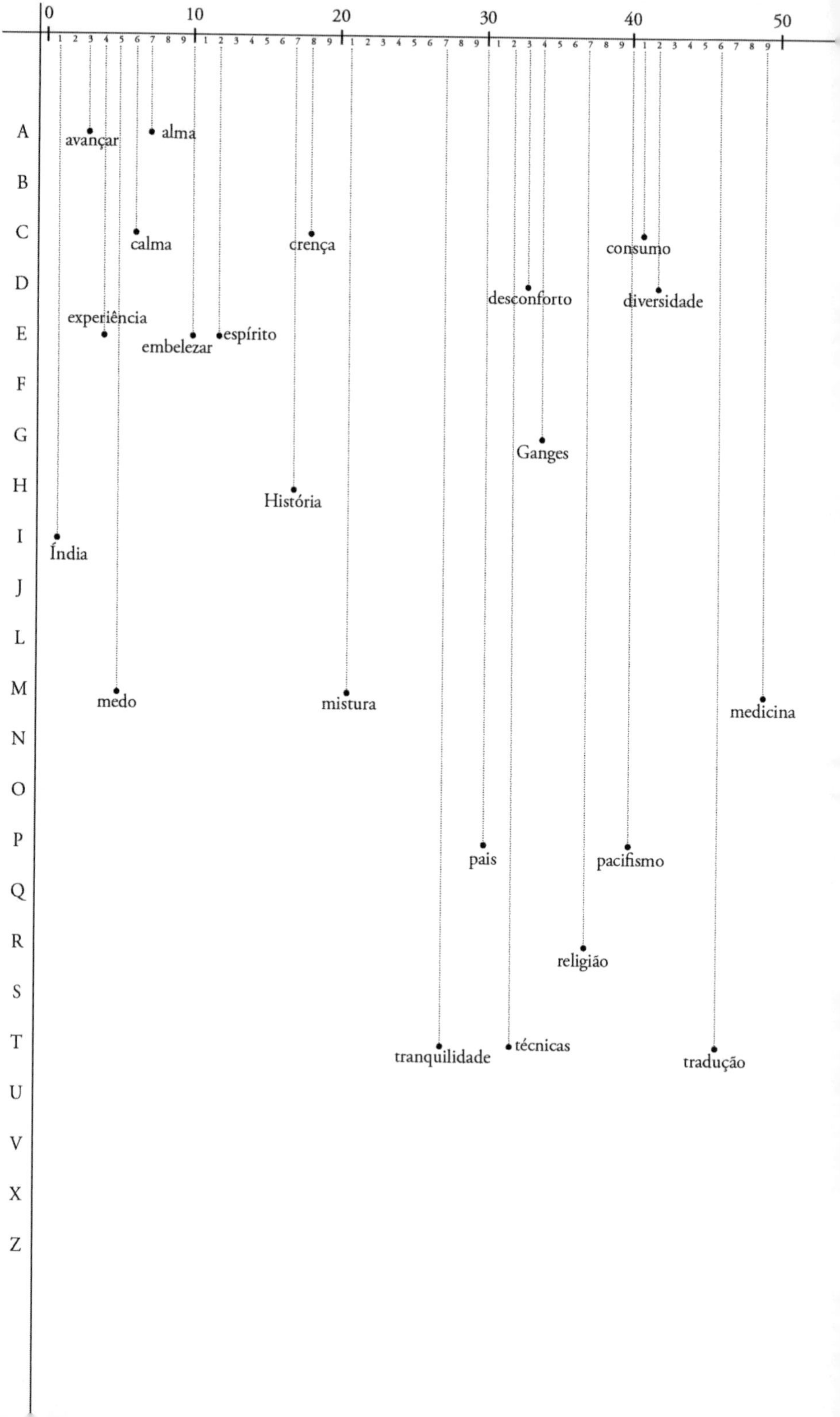
0
10
20
30
40
50
A
B
C
D
E
F
G
H
I
J
L
M
N
O
P
Q
R
S
T
U
V
X
Z
avançar
alma
calma
crença
consumo
desconforto
diversidade
experiência
embelezar
espírito
Ganges
História
Índia
medo
mistura
medicina
pais
pacifismo
religião
tranquilidade
técnicas
tradução

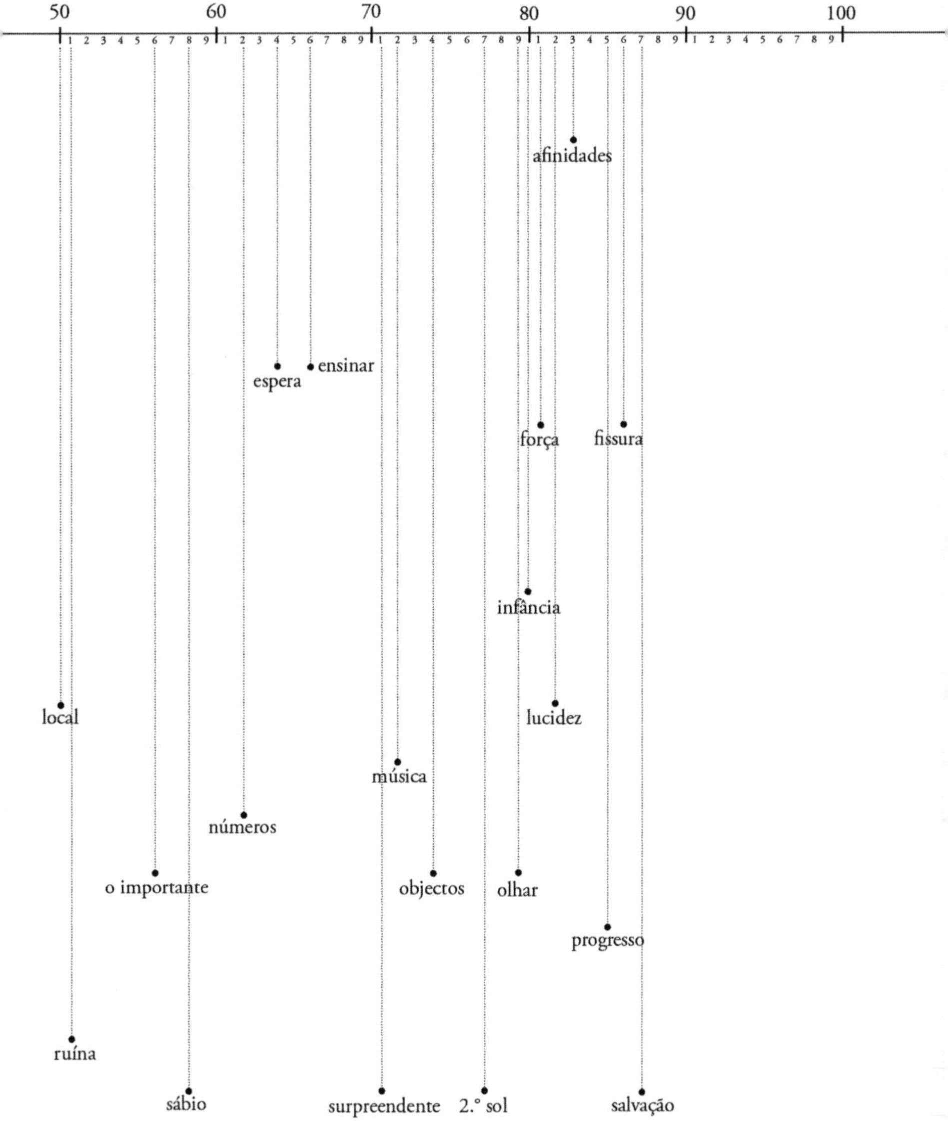

50
60
70
80
90
100
afinidades
espera
ensinar
força
fissura
infância
local
lucidez
música
números
o importante
objectos
olhar
progresso
ruína
sábio
surpreendente
2.° sol
salvação

canto VII

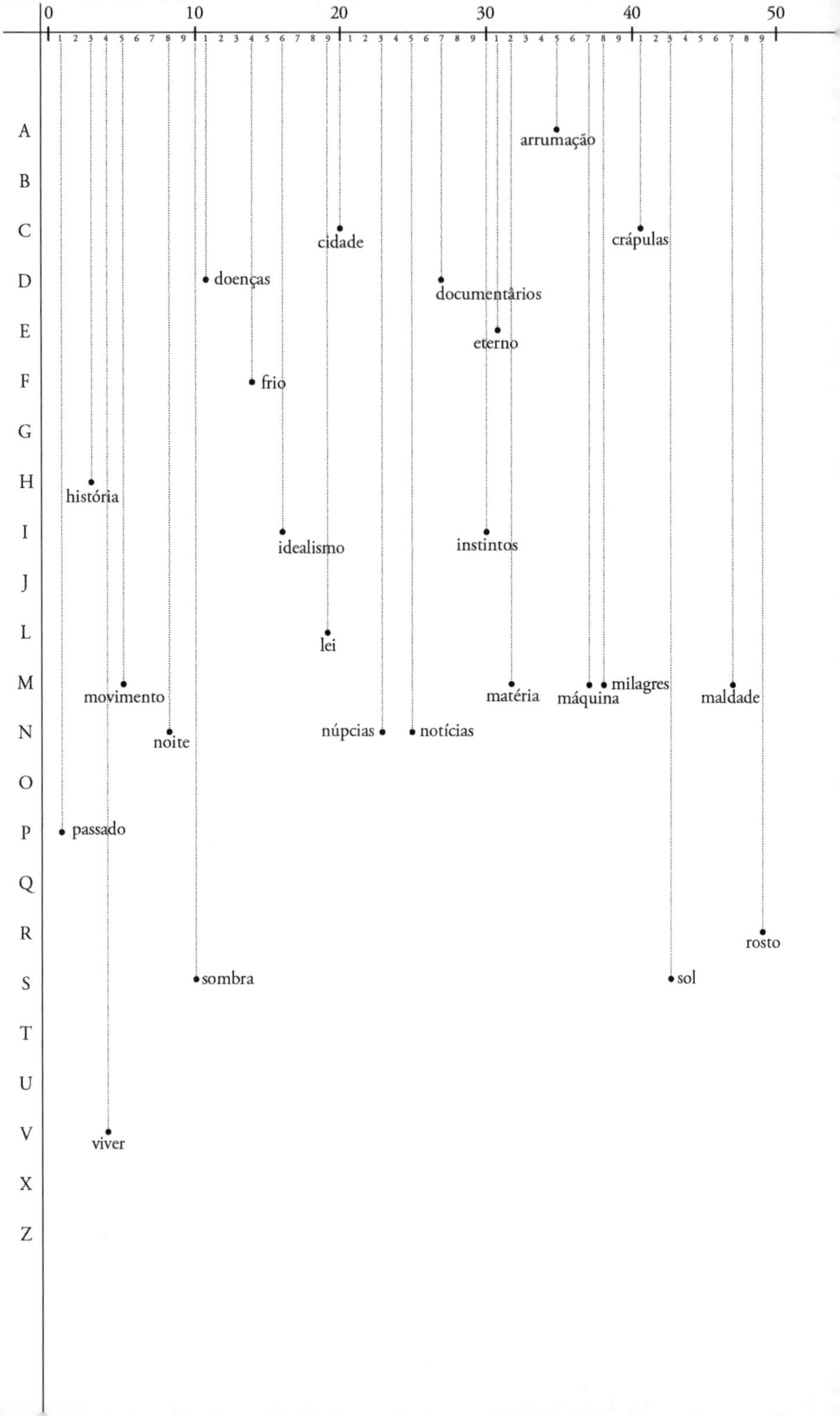
0
10
20
30
40
50
A
B
C
D
E
F
G
H
I
J
L
M
N
O
P
Q
R
S
T
U
V
X
Z
arrumação
cidade
crápulas
doenças
documentários
eterno
frio
história
idealismo
instintos
lei
movimento
matéria
máquina
milagres
maldade
noite
núpcias
notícias
passado
rosto
sombra
sol
viver

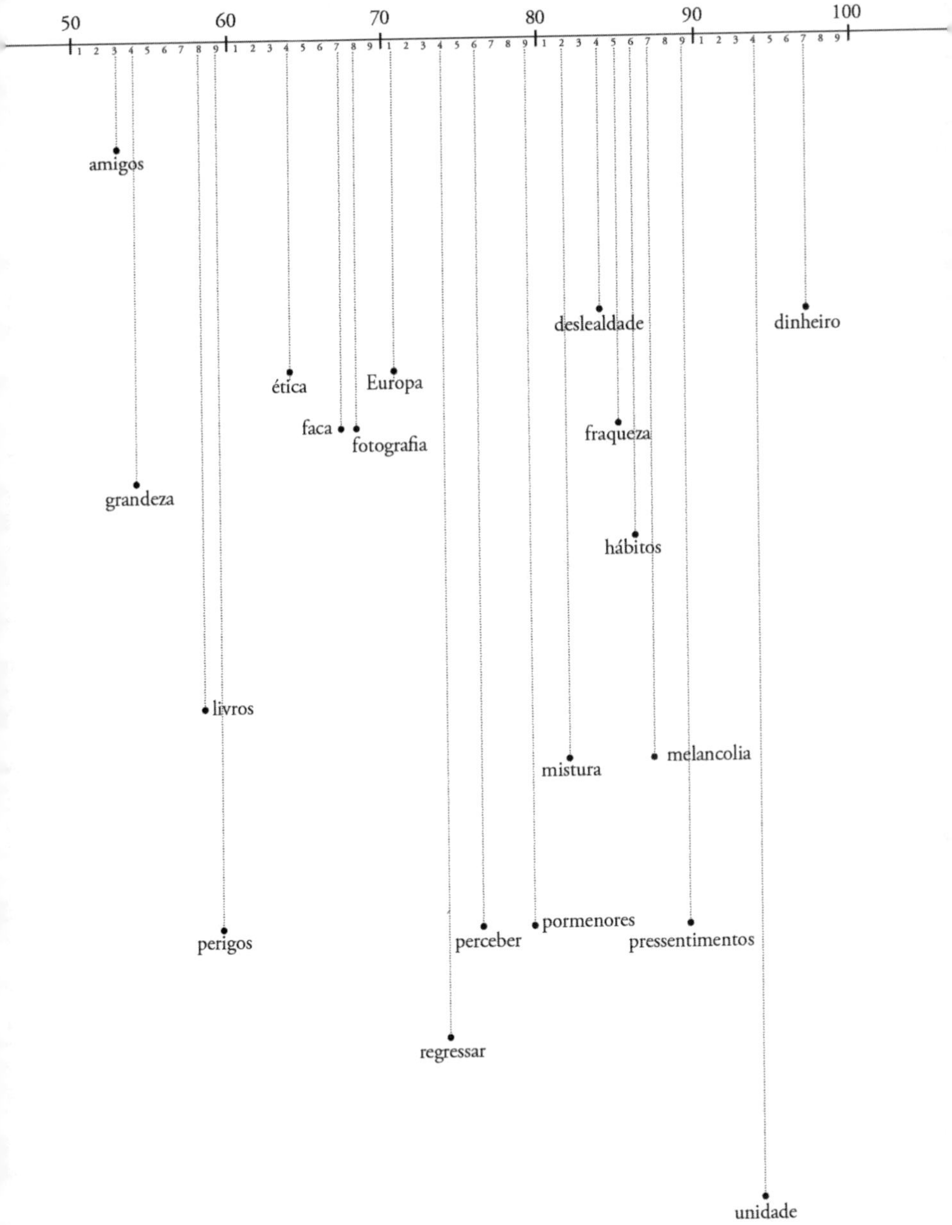
50
60
70
80
90
100
amigos
deslealdade
dinheiro
ética
Europa
faca
fotografia
fraqueza
grandeza
hábitos
livros
mistura
melancolia
perigos
perceber
pormenores
pressentimentos
regressar
unidade

canto VII

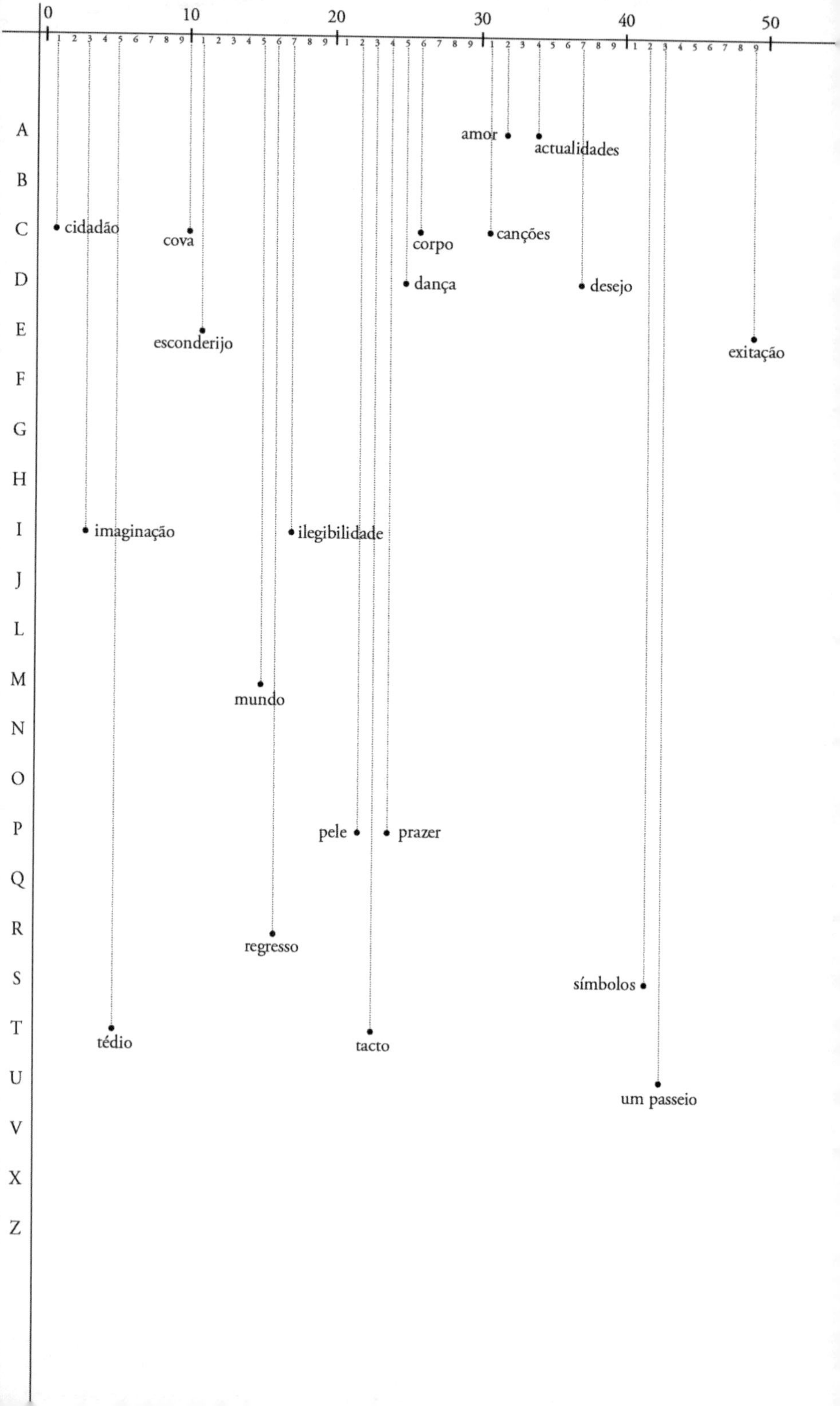
0
10
20
30
40
50
A
B
C
D
E
F
G
H
I
J
L
M
N
O
P
Q
R
S
T
U
V
X
Z
amor
actualidades
cidadão
cova
corpo
canções
dança
desejo
esconderijo
exitação
imaginação
ilegibilidade
mundo
pele
prazer
regresso
símbolos
tédio
tacto
um passeio

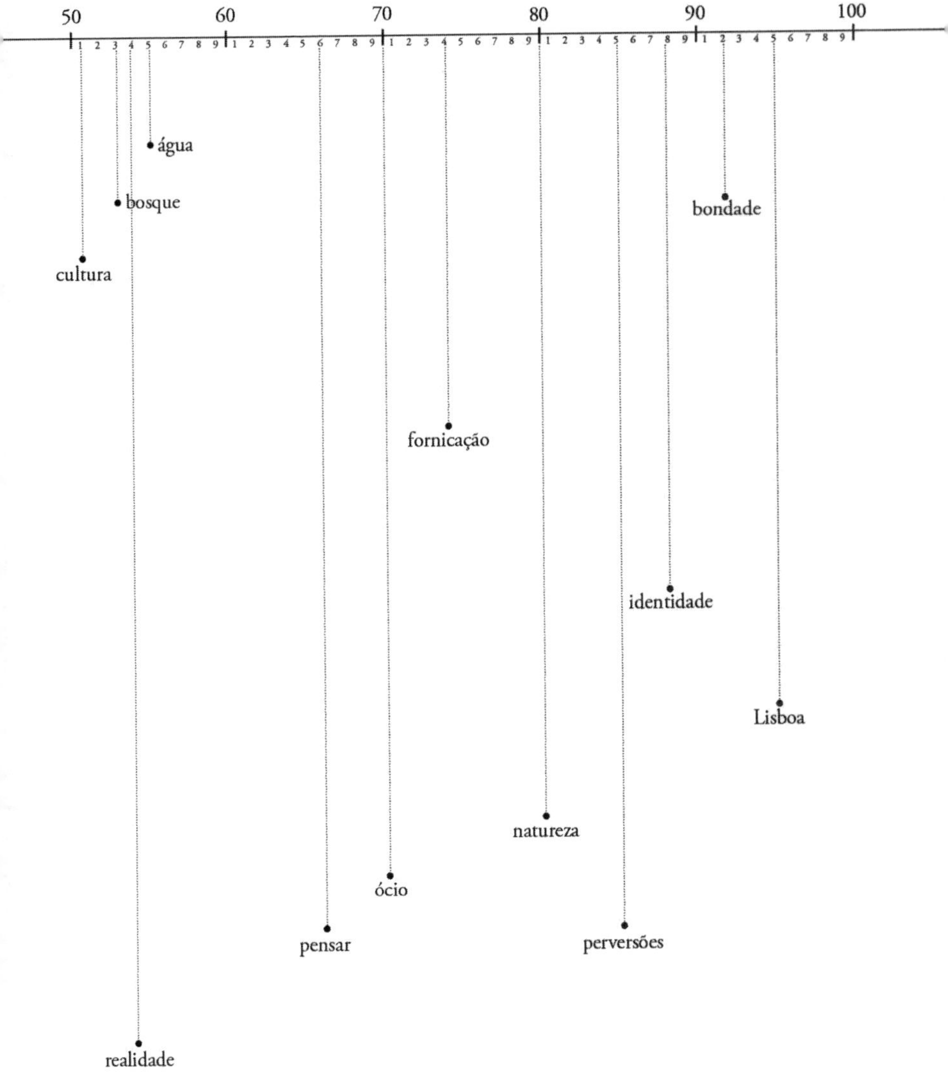
50
60
70
80
90
100
água
bosque
cultura
bondade
fornicação
identidade
Lisboa
natureza
ócio
pensar
perversões
realidade

canto IX

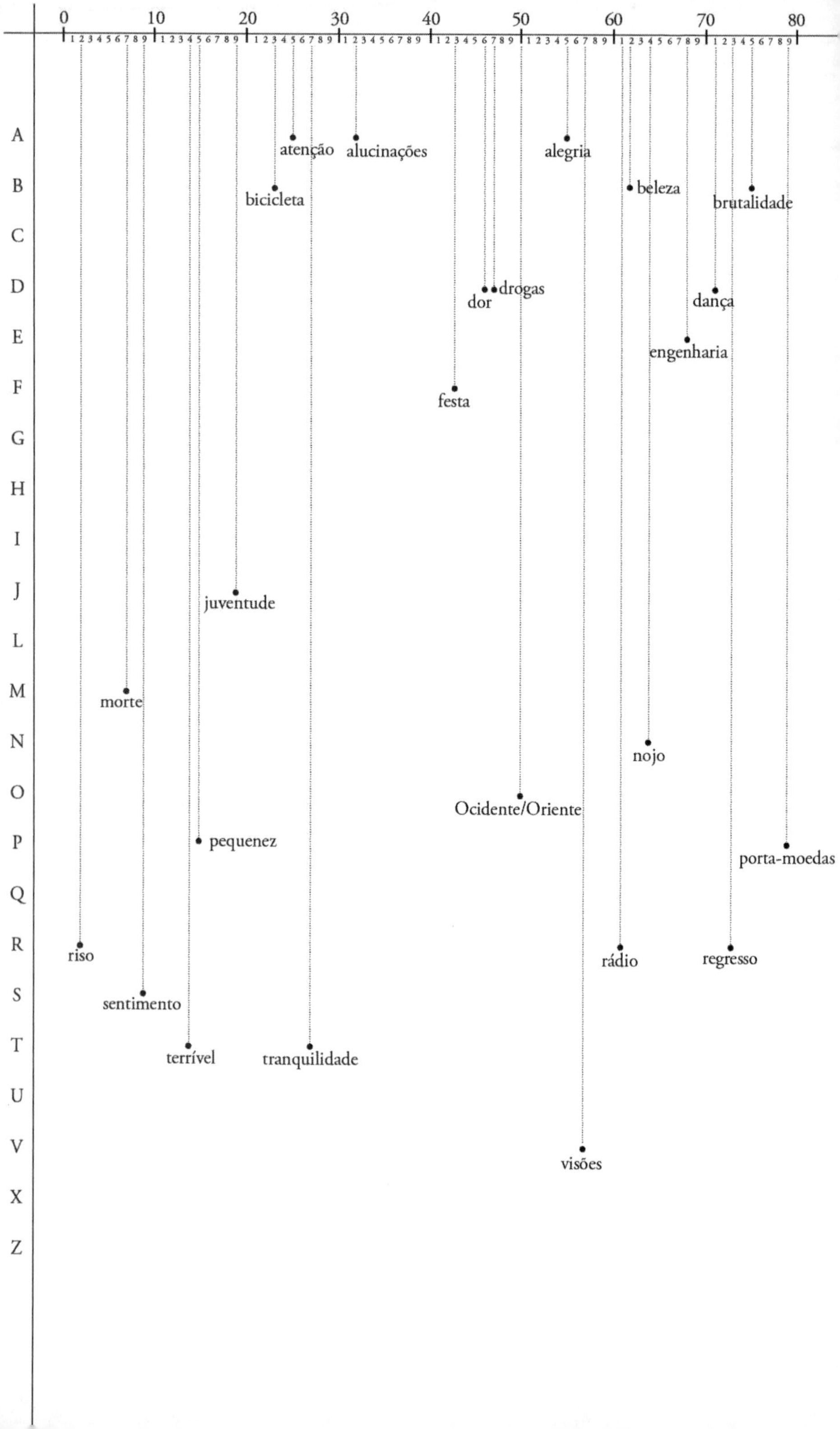
0
10
20
30
40
50
60
70
80
A
B
C
D
E
F
G
H
I
J
L
M
N
O
P
Q
R
S
T
U
V
X
Z
atenção
alucinações
alegria
bicicleta
beleza
brutalidade
dor
drogas
dança
engenharia
festa
juventude
morte
nojo
Ocidente/Oriente
pequenez
porta-moedas
riso
rádio
regresso
sentimento
terrível
tranquilidade
visões

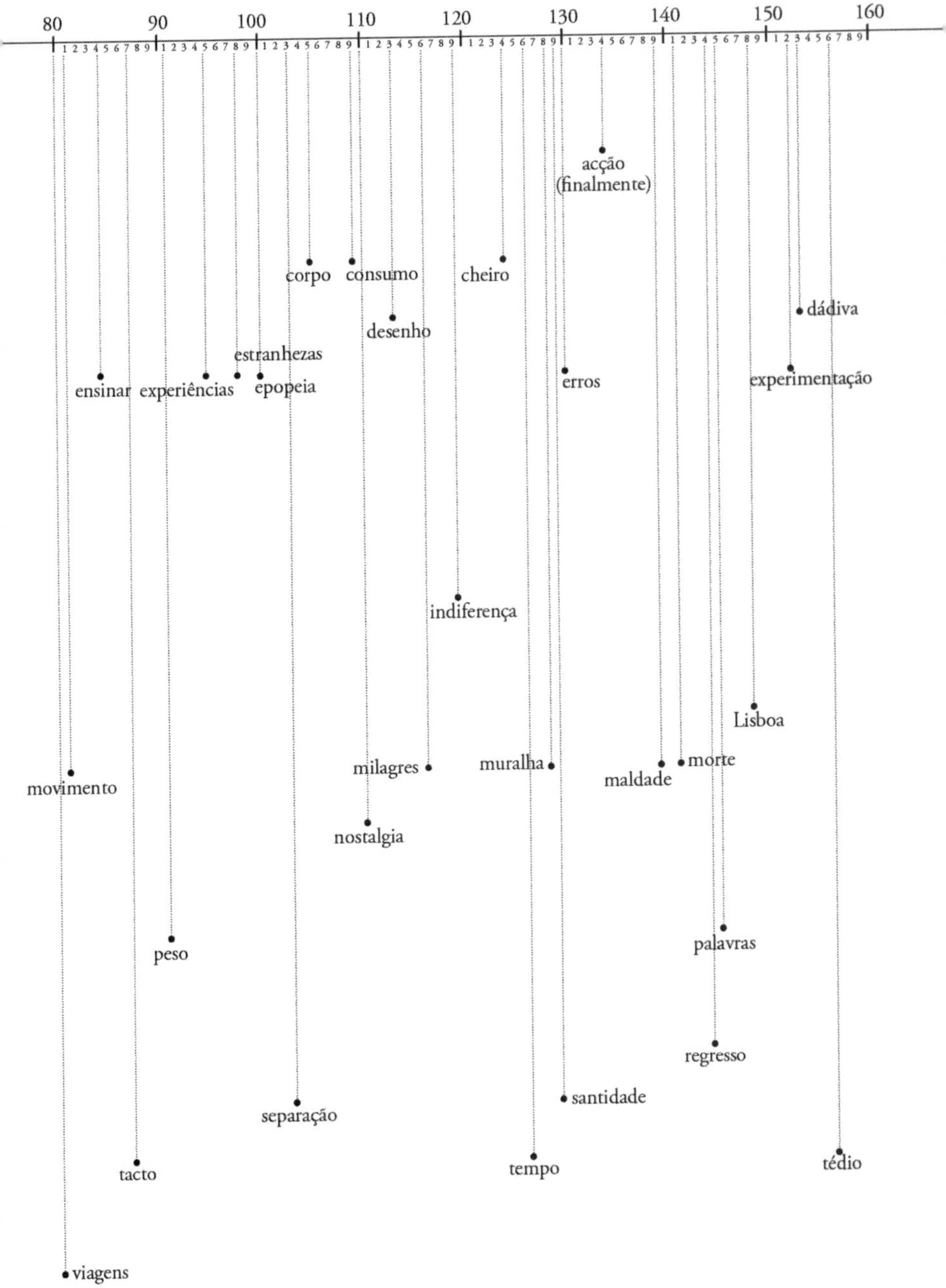
80
90
100
110
120
130
140
150
160
acção
(finalmente)
corpo
consumo
cheiro
dádiva
desenho
estranhezas
ensinar
experiências
epopeia
erros
experimentação
indiferença
Lisboa
movimento
milagres
muralha
maldade
morte
nostalgia
peso
palavras
regresso
separação
santidade
tacto
tempo
tédio
viagens

canto X

MICHAL AJVAZ, *The Golden Age.*
The Other City.

PIERRE ALBERT-BIROT, *Grabinoulor.*

YUZ ALESHKOVSKY, *Kangaroo.*

FELIPE ALFAU, *Chromos.*
Locos.

JOE AMATO, *Samuel Taylor's Last Night.*

IVAN ÂNGELO, *The Celebration.*
The Tower of Glass.

ANTÓNIO LOBO ANTUNES, *Knowledge of Hell.*
The Splendor of Portugal.

ALAIN ARIAS-MISSON, *Theatre of Incest.*

JOHN ASHBERY & JAMES SCHUYLER, *A Nest of Ninnies.*

ROBERT ASHLEY, *Perfect Lives.*

GABRIELA AVIGUR-ROTEM, *Heatwave and Crazy Birds.*

DJUNA BARNES, *Ladies Almanack.*
Ryder.

JOHN BARTH, *Letters.*
Sabbatical.

DONALD BARTHELME, *The King.*
Paradise.

SVETISLAV BASARA, *Chinese Letter.*

MIQUEL BAUÇÀ, *The Siege in the Room.*

RENÉ BELLETTO, *Dying.*

MAREK BIENCZYK, *Transparency.*

ANDREI BITOV, *Pushkin House.*

ANDREJ BLATNIK, *You Do Understand.*
Law of Desire.

LOUIS PAUL BOON, *Chapel Road.*
My Little War.
Summer in Termuren.

ROGER BOYLAN, *Killoyle.*

IGNÁCIO DE LOYOLA BRANDÃO, *Anonymous Celebrity.*
Zero.

BONNIE BREMSER, *Troia: Mexican Memoirs.*

CHRISTINE BROOKE-ROSE, *Amalgamemnon.*

BRIGID BROPHY, *In Transit.*
The Prancing Novelist.

GERALD L. BRUNS, *Modern Poetry and the Idea of Language.*

GABRIELLE BURTON, *Heartbreak Hotel.*

MICHEL BUTOR, *Degrees.*
Mobile.

G. CABRERA INFANTE, *Infante's Inferno.*
Three Trapped Tigers.

JULIETA CAMPOS, *The Fear of Losing Eurydice.*

ANNE CARSON, *Eros the Bittersweet.*

ORLY CASTEL-BLOOM, *Dolly City.*

LOUIS-FERDINAND CÉLINE, *North.*
Conversations with Professor Y.
London Bridge.

MARIE CHAIX, *The Laurels of Lake Constance.*

HUGO CHARTERIS, *The Tide Is Right.*

ERIC CHEVILLARD, *Demolishing Nisard.*
The Author and Me.

MARC CHOLODENKO, *Mordechai Schamz.*

JOSHUA COHEN, *Witz.*

EMILY HOLMES COLEMAN, *The Shutter of Snow.*

ERIC CHEVILLARD, *The Author and Me.*

ROBERT COOVER, *A Night at the Movies.*

STANLEY CRAWFORD, *Log of the S.S. The Mrs Unguentine.*
Some Instructions to My Wife.

RENÉ CREVEL, *Putting My Foot in It.*

RALPH CUSACK, *Cadenza.*

NICHOLAS DELBANCO, *Sherbrookes.*
The Count of Concord.

NIGEL DENNIS, *Cards of Identity.*

PETER DIMOCK, *A Short Rhetoric for Leaving the Family.*

ARIEL DORFMAN, *Konfidenz.*

COLEMAN DOWELL, *Island People.*
Too Much Flesh and Jabez.

ARKADII DRAGOMOSHCHENKO, *Dust.*

RIKKI DUCORNET, *Phosphor in Dreamland.*
The Complete Butcher's Tales.

RIKKI DUCORNET (cont.), *The Jade*

Cabinet.
The Fountains of Neptune.
WILLIAM EASTLAKE, *The Bamboo Bed.*
Castle Keep.
Lyric of the Circle Heart.
JEAN ECHENOZ, *Chopin's Move.*
STANLEY ELKIN, *A Bad Man.*
Criers and Kibitzers, Kibitzers and Criers.
The Dick Gibson Show.
The Franchiser.
The Living End.
Mrs. Ted Bliss.
FRANÇOIS EMMANUEL, *Invitation to a Voyage.*
PAUL EMOND, *The Dance of a Sham.*
SALVADOR ESPRIU, *Ariadne in the Grotesque Labyrinth.*
LESLIE A. FIEDLER, *Love and Death in the American Novel.*
JUAN FILLOY, *Op Oloop.*
ANDY FITCH, *Pop Poetics.*
GUSTAVE FLAUBERT, *Bouvard and Pécuchet.*
KASS FLEISHER, *Talking out of School.*
JON FOSSE, *Aliss at the Fire.*
Melancholy.
FORD MADOX FORD, *The March of Literature.*
MAX FRISCH, *I'm Not Stiller.*
Man in the Holocene.
CARLOS FUENTES, *Christopher Unborn.*
Distant Relations.
Terra Nostra.
Where the Air Is Clear.
TAKEHIKO FUKUNAGA, *Flowers of Grass.*
WILLIAM GADDIS, JR., *The Recognitions.*
JANICE GALLOWAY, *Foreign Parts.*
The Trick Is to Keep Breathing.
WILLIAM H. GASS, *Life Sentences.*
The Tunnel.
The World Within the Word.
Willie Masters' Lonesome Wife.
GÉRARD GAVARRY, *Hoppla! 1 2 3.*
ETIENNE GILSON, *The Arts of the Beautiful.*
Forms and Substances in the Arts.
C. S. GISCOMBE, *Giscome Road.*
Here.
DOUGLAS GLOVER, *Bad News of the Heart.*
WITOLD GOMBROWICZ, *A Kind of Testament.*
PAULO EMÍLIO SALES GOMES, *P's Three Women.*
GEORGI GOSPODINOV, *Natural Novel.*
JUAN GOYTISOLO, *Count Julian.*
Juan the Landless.
Makbara.
Marks of Identity.
HENRY GREEN, *Blindness.*
Concluding.
Doting.
Nothing.
JACK GREEN, *Fire the Bastards!*
JIŘÍ GRUŠA, *The Questionnaire.*
MELA HARTWIG, *Am I a Redundant Human Being?*
JOHN HAWKES, *The Passion Artist.*
Whistlejacket.
ELIZABETH HEIGHWAY, ED., *Contemporary Georgian Fiction.*
AIDAN HIGGINS, *Balcony of Europe.*
Blind Man's Bluff.
Bornholm Night-Ferry.
Langrishe, Go Down.
Scenes from a Receding Past.
KEIZO HINO, *Isle of Dreams.*
KAZUSHI HOSAKA, *Plainsong.*
ALDOUS HUXLEY, *Antic Hay.*
Point Counter Point.
Those Barren Leaves.
Time Must Have a Stop.
NAOYUKI II, *The Shadow of a Blue Cat.*
DRAGO JANČAR, *The Tree with No Name.*
MIKHEIL JAVAKHISHVILI, *Kvachi.*
GERT JONKE, *The Distant Sound.*
Homage to Czerny.
The System of Vienna.
JACQUES JOUET, *Mountain R.*
Savage.

Upstaged.
MIEKO KANAI, *The Word Book.*
YORAM KANIUK, *Life on Sandpaper.*
ZURAB KARUMIDZE, *Dagny.*
JOHN KELLY, *From Out of the City.*
HUGH KENNER, *Flaubert, Joyce and Beckett: The Stoic Comedians.*
Joyce's Voices.
DANILO KIŠ, *The Attic.*
The Lute and the Scars.
Psalm 44.
A Tomb for Boris Davidovich.
ANITA KONKKA, *A Fool's Paradise.*
GEORGE KONRÁD, *The City Builder.*
TADEUSZ KONWICKI, *A Minor Apocalypse.*
The Polish Complex.
ANNA KORDZAIA-SAMADASHVILI, *Me, Margarita.*
MENIS KOUMANDAREAS, *Koula.*
ELAINE KRAF, *The Princess of 72nd Street.*
JIM KRUSOE, *Iceland.*
AYSE KULIN, *Farewell: A Mansion in Occupied Istanbul.*
EMILIO LASCANO TEGUI, *On Elegance While Sleeping.*
ERIC LAURRENT, *Do Not Touch.*
VIOLETTE LEDUC, *La Bâtarde.*
EDOUARD LEVÉ, *Autoportrait.*
Newspaper.
Suicide.
Works.
MARIO LEVI, *Istanbul Was a Fairy Tale.*
DEBORAH LEVY, *Billy and Girl.*
JOSÉ LEZAMA LIMA, *Paradiso.*
ROSA LIKSOM, *Dark Paradise.*
OSMAN LINS, *Avalovara.*
The Queen of the Prisons of Greece.
FLORIAN LIPUŠ, *The Errors of Young Tjaž.*
GORDON LISH, *Peru.*
ALF MACLOCHLAINN, *Out of Focus.*
Past Habitual.
The Corpus in the Library.
RON LOEWINSOHN, *Magnetic Field(s).*
YURI LOTMAN, *Non-Memoirs.*
D. KEITH MANO, *Take Five.*
MINA LOY, *Stories and Essays of Mina Loy.*
MICHELINE AHARONIAN MARCOM, *A Brief History of Yes.*
The Mirror in the Well.
BEN MARCUS, *The Age of Wire and String.*
WALLACE MARKFIELD, *Teitlebaum's Window.*
DAVID MARKSON, *Reader's Block.*
Wittgenstein's Mistress.
CAROLE MASO, *AVA.*
HISAKI MATSUURA, *Triangle.*
LADISLAV MATEJKA & KRYSTYNA POMORSKA, EDS., *Readings in Russian Poetics: Formalist & Structuralist Views.*
HARRY MATHEWS, *Cigarettes.*
The Conversions.
The Human Country.
The Journalist.
My Life in CIA.
Singular Pleasures.
The Sinking of the Odradek.
Stadium.
Tlooth.
HISAKI MATSUURA, *Triangle.*
DONAL MCLAUGHLIN, *beheading the virgin mary, and other stories.*
JOSEPH MCELROY, *Night Soul and Other Stories.*
ABDELWAHAB MEDDEB, *Talismano.*
GERHARD MEIER, *Isle of the Dead.*
HERMAN MELVILLE, *The Confidence-Man.*
AMANDA MICHALOPOULOU, *I'd Like.*
STEVEN MILLHAUSER, *The Barnum Museum.*
In the Penny Arcade.
RALPH J. MILLS, JR., *Essays on Poetry.*
MOMUS, *The Book of Jokes.*
CHRISTINE MONTALBETTI, *The Origin of Man.*
Western.
NICHOLAS MOSLEY, *Accident.*
Assassins.
Catastrophe Practice.

A Garden of Trees.
Hopeful Monsters.
Imago Bird.
Inventing God.
Look at the Dark.
Metamorphosis.
Natalie Natalia.
Serpent.

WARREN MOTTE, *Fables of the Novel: French Fiction since 1990.*
Fiction Now: The French Novel in the 21st Century.
Mirror Gazing.
Oulipo: A Primer of Potential Literature.

GERALD MURNANE, *Barley Patch.*
Inland.

YVES NAVARRE, *Our Share of Time.*
Sweet Tooth.

DOROTHY NELSON, *In Night's City.*
Tar and Feathers.

ESHKOL NEVO, *Homesick.*

WILFRIDO D. NOLLEDO, *But for the Lovers.*

BORIS A. NOVAK, *The Master of Insomnia.*

FLANN O'BRIEN, *At Swim-Two-Birds.*
The Best of Myles.
The Dalkey Archive.
The Hard Life.
The Poor Mouth.
The Third Policeman.

CLAUDE OLLIER, *The Mise-en-Scène.*
Wert and the Life Without End.

PATRIK OUŘEDNÍK, *Europeana.*
The Opportune Moment, 1855.

BORIS PAHOR, *Necropolis.*

FERNANDO DEL PASO, *News from the Empire.*
Palinuro of Mexico.

ROBERT PINGET, *The Inquisitory.*
Mahu or The Material.
Trio.

MANUEL PUIG, *Betrayed by Rita Hayworth.*
The Buenos Aires Affair.
Heartbreak Tango.

RAYMOND QUENEAU, *The Last Days.*
Odile.
Pierrot Mon Ami.
Saint Glinglin.

ANN QUIN, *Berg.*
Passages.
Three.
Tripticks.

ISHMAEL REED, *The Free-Lance Pallbearers.*
The Last Days of Louisiana Red.
Ishmael Reed: The Plays.
Juice!
The Terrible Threes.
The Terrible Twos.
Yellow Back Radio Broke-Down.

JASIA REICHARDT, *15 Journeys Warsaw to London.*

JOÃO UBALDO RIBEIRO, *House of the Fortunate Buddhas.*

JEAN RICARDOU, *Place Names.*

RAINER MARIA RILKE, *The Notebooks of Malte Laurids Brigge.*

JULIÁN RÍOS, *The House of Ulysses.*
Larva: A Midsummer Night's Babel.
Poundemonium.

ALAIN ROBBE-GRILLET, *Project for a Revolution in New York.*
A Sentimental Novel.

AUGUSTO ROA BASTOS, *I the Supreme.*

DANIËL ROBBERECHTS, *Arriving in Avignon.*

JEAN ROLIN, *The Explosion of the Radiator Hose.*

OLIVIER ROLIN, *Hotel Crystal.*

ALIX CLEO ROUBAUD, *Alix's Journal.*

JACQUES ROUBAUD, *The Form of a City Changes Faster, Alas, Than the Human Heart.*
The Great Fire of London.
Hortense in Exile.
Hortense Is Abducted.
Mathematics: The Plurality of Worlds of Lewis.
Some Thing Black.

RAYMOND ROUSSEL, *Impressions of Africa.*

VEDRANA RUDAN, *Night.*

PABLO M. RUIZ, *Four Cold Chapters*

on the Possibility of Literature.
GERMAN SADULAEV, *The Maya Pill.*
TOMAŽ ŠALAMUN, *Soy Realidad.*
LYDIE SALVAYRE, *The Company of Ghosts.*
The Lecture.
The Power of Flies.
LUIS RAFAEL SÁNCHEZ, *Macho Camacho's Beat.*
SEVERO SARDUY, *Cobra & Maitreya.*
NATHALIE SARRAUTE, *Do You Hear Them?*
Martereau.
The Planetarium.
STIG SÆTERBAKKEN, *Siamese.*
Self-Control.
Through the Night.
ARNO SCHMIDT, *Collected Novellas.*
Collected Stories.
Nobodaddy's Children.
Two Novels.
ASAF SCHURR, *Motti.*
GAIL SCOTT, *My Paris.*
DAMION SEARLS, *What We Were Doing and Where We Were Going.*
JUNE AKERS SEESE, *Is This What Other Women Feel Too?*
BERNARD SHARE, *Inish.*
Transit.
VIKTOR SHKLOVSKY, *Bowstring.*
Literature and Cinematography.
Theory of Prose.
Third Factory.
Zoo, or Letters Not about Love.
PIERRE SINIAC, *The Collaborators.*
KJERSTI A. SKOMSVOLD, *The Faster I Walk, the Smaller I Am.*
JOSEF ŠKVORECKÝ, *The Engineer of Human Souls.*
GILBERT SORRENTINO, *Aberration of Starlight.*
Blue Pastoral.
Crystal Vision.
Imaginative Qualities of Actual Things.
Mulligan Stew. Red the Fiend.
Steelwork.
Under the Shadow.
MARKO SOSIČ, *Ballerina, Ballerina.*
ANDRZEJ STASIUK, *Dukla.*
Fado.
GERTRUDE STEIN, *The Making of Americans.*
A Novel of Thank You.
LARS SVENDSEN, *A Philosophy of Evil.*
PIOTR SZEWC, *Annihilation.*
GONÇALO M. TAVARES, *A Man: Klaus Klump.*
Jerusalem.
Learning to Pray in the Age of Technique.
LUCIAN DAN TEODOROVICI, *Our Circus Presents . . .*
NIKANOR TERATOLOGEN, *Assisted Living.*
STEFAN THEMERSON, *Hobson's Island.*
The Mystery of the Sardine.
Tom Harris.
TAEKO TOMIOKA, *Building Waves.*
JOHN TOOMEY, *Sleepwalker.*
DUMITRU TSEPENEAG, *Hotel Europa.*
The Necessary Marriage.
Pigeon Post.
Vain Art of the Fugue.
ESTHER TUSQUETS, *Stranded.*
DUBRAVKA UGRESIC, *Lend Me Your Character.*
Thank You for Not Reading.
TOR ULVEN, *Replacement.*
MATI UNT, *Brecht at Night.*
Diary of a Blood Donor.
Things in the Night.
ÁLVARO URIBE & OLIVIA SEARS, EDS., *Best of Contemporary Mexican Fiction.*
ELOY URROZ, *Friction.*
The Obstacles.
LUISA VALENZUELA, *Dark Desires and the Others.*
He Who Searches.
PAUL VERHAEGHEN, *Omega Minor.*
BORIS VIAN, *Heartsnatcher.*
LLORENÇ VILLALONGA, *The Dolls' Room.*
TOOMAS VINT, *An Unending Landscape.*

ORNELA VORPSI, *The Country Where No One Ever Dies.*

AUSTRYN WAINHOUSE, *Hedyphagetica.*

CURTIS WHITE, *America's Magic Mountain.*
The Idea of Home.
Memories of My Father Watching TV.
Requiem.

DIANE WILLIAMS,
Excitability: Selected Stories.
Romancer Erector.

DOUGLAS WOOLF, *Wall to Wall.*
Ya! & John-Juan.

JAY WRIGHT, *Polynomials and Pollen.*
The Presentable Art of Reading Absence.

PHILIP WYLIE, *Generation of Vipers.*

MARGUERITE YOUNG, *Angel in the Forest.*
Miss MacIntosh, My Darling.

REYOUNG, *Unbabbling.*

VLADO ŽABOT, *The Succubus.*

ZORAN ŽIVKOVIĆ , *Hidden Camera.*

LOUIS ZUKOFSKY, *Collected Fiction.*

VITOMIL ZUPAN, *Minuet for Guitar.*

SCOTT ZWIREN, *God Head.*

AND MORE . . .